MANNERS & MUTINY

MANNERS & MUTINY

FINISHING SCHOOL ✷ BOOK THE FOURTH

GAIL CARRIGER

Ⓛ Ⓑ

Little, Brown and Company

New York Boston

Copyright © 2015 by Tofa Borregaard
Schematic illustration copyright © 2015 Mike Schley
Excerpt from *Etiquette & Espionage* copyright © 2013 by Tofa Borregaard

Little, Brown and Company

Hachette Book Group
1290 Avenue of the Americas, New York, NY 10104
Visit us at lb-teens.com

Little, Brown and Company is a division of Hachette Book Group, Inc.
The Little, Brown name and logo are trademarks of Hachette Book Group, Inc.

The publisher is not responsible for websites (or their content) that are not owned by the publisher.

First Paperback Edition: October 2016
First published in hardcover in November 2015 by Little, Brown and Company

The Library of Congress has cataloged the hardcover edition as follows:

Carriger, Gail.
    Manners & mutiny / Gail Carriger. — First edition.
        pages cm. — (Finishing school ; book the fourth)
    Summary: In an alternate England of 1851, Sophronia Temminnick is the only hope for her friends, her school, and all of London when she must put her espionage training to the test to thwart an evil Picklemen plot.
    ISBN 978-0-316-19028-2 (hardback) — ISBN 978-0-316-29978-7 (ebook) — ISBN 978-0-316-29977-0 (library edition ebook)   [1. Boarding schools—Fiction.   2. Schools—Fiction.   3. Etiquette—Fiction.   4. Espionage—Fiction.   5. Great Britain—History—Victoria, 1837–1901—Fiction.   6. Science fiction.]
I. Title.   II. Title: Manners and mutiny.
    PZ7.C23455Man 2015
    [Fic]—dc23

                                                                    2015008685

Paperback ISBN 978-0-316-19029-9

10 9 8 7 6 5 4 3 2 1

RRD-C

Printed in the United States of America

Thanks to Kate for starting us all on this crazy float; to Kristin, who piloted the dirigible; and to Deirdre, who landed it. To Sophie, who was my sounding board. To all my lady sooties in the boiler room, making everything go, and to Mac, keeping everything sane. And to Staar Shmellow (and her friend Steve, who donated to Worldbuilders) for her invention of a Most Amazing Hat.

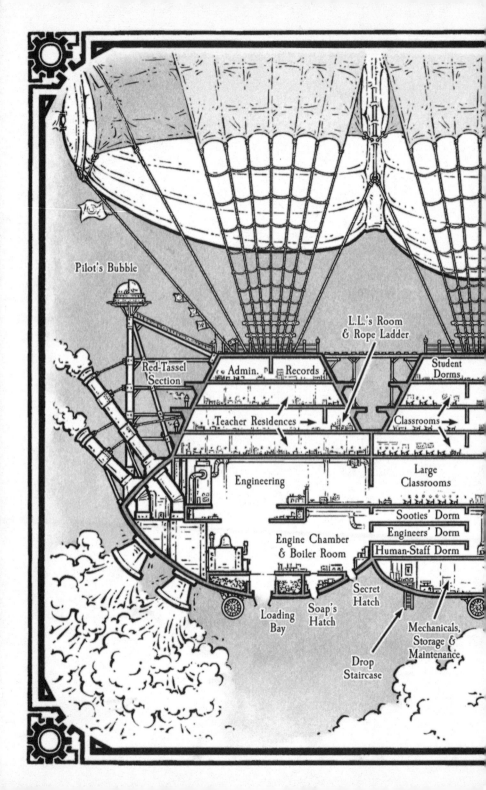

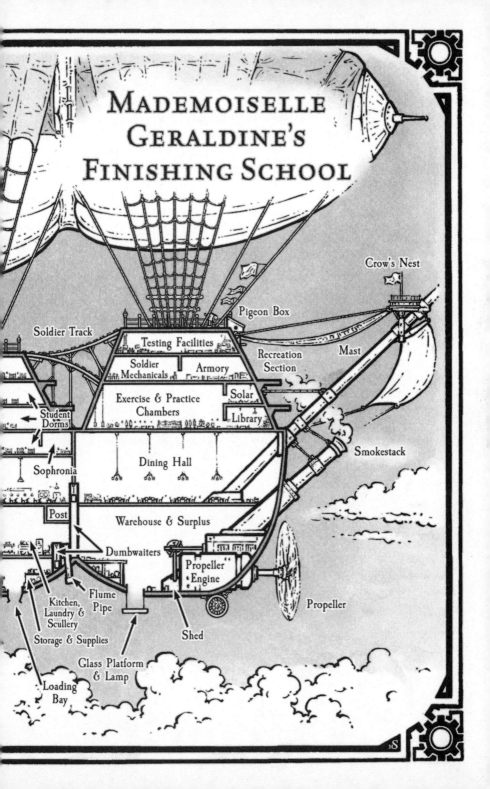

INCOGNITO IN CHARACTER

A ball, at last!" Dimity Plumleigh-Teignmott sank back into her chair in delight.

At the head table, Mademoiselle Geraldine finished her announcement with a similar collapse, stays heaving with repressed excitement. She would not be attending said ball, as she never left school grounds, but she appreciated that her young ladies of *quali-tay* were about to engage in a social event of *great import*. Lady Linette put a gentling hand to the headmistress's arm, wary of a full infection of flutterings.

It was too late. The school erupted into chatter.

"It's only Bunson's," Preshea Buss said to Dimity. "We know all the boys there, and most of the best prospects have gone on to university."

"Oh, buck up, Preshea, do. That means fresh meat. You should be thrilled, since you prefer your young men innocent and ripe for the plucking," shot back Sophronia.

Preshea couldn't refute that—in a way, it was quite the compliment. So she turned her back on Sophronia and her friends.

Sophronia sipped her tea, feeling victorious, green eyes assessing the reactions of those around her. Dimity's delight was to be expected. Agatha Woosmoss, their other close friend, was notably reticent when confronted with large gatherings involving the opposite sex. She had very flushed cheeks that suggested interest—or possibly paralytic fear. The debuts were in a tight huddle over the Scones of Iniquity and the Jam of Trepidation. Professor Braithwope was bouncing in his chair like a delighted baby, although he would not be attending. Professor Lefoux's lip was curled in disgust as she stood to make the supervisory rounds.

"What to wear?" murmured Dimity, rolling a Chelsea bun between thumb and forefinger.

Professor Lefoux pounced. "Miss Plumleigh-Teignmott, what are you doing to that bun? Your fingers are all over sticky. Only look at the crumbs. And you've misplaced currants. You should know better."

Dimity dropped the bun.

Sophronia jumped in. "We are working on a language for crumb and currant communication."

Professor Lefoux was not fooled. "Indeed? Pray continue."

"The number and location of the crumbs indicates intent."

"And the currants?"

"Instructions, of course."

"And how do you propose to control quantity when utilizing less adhesive bread items?"

"That requires further study." Sophronia was brazen to the end.

Professor Lefoux sniffed. "Perhaps you should stick to less messy forms of communication. But your inventiveness has merit."

It was, of course, impossible to tell whether this compliment was directed at the idea of a crumb communication system or whether Professor Lefoux was complimenting Sophronia on coming up with an excuse for Dimity's mishandling of buns. Whatever the case, Professor Lefoux caught sight of one of the debuts actually *tossing* her bun at another girl and dashed away without further comment.

Dimity ate her sticky treat before it could result in more unwanted attention. She shoved her empty crumb-covered plate in front of Sophronia. "Go on, then, read them."

Agatha giggled. "Like Madame Spetuna."

"What do the crumbs say of my future?" Dimity's round face was eager.

Sophronia bent over the carnage and muttered, "You shall marry well and live a long and happy life. So long as you avoid all contact with . . ." She drew out the suspense.

Dimity hung on her words. "Yes?"

"Sturgeon."

"What, the fish?"

"Sturgeon bodes you ill will. Beware, or all will be lost."

Dimity grinned. "Oh goodness me, how ominous. And how damp."

Agatha shoved her crumby plate across the table. "Do mine?"

Sophronia assumed a sepulchral tone. "You will cause a stir

in high society with your wit and charm." Agatha blushed. "So long as you allow yourself to speak on occasion. Beware..."

"Beware what?"

"Philosophy!"

"Oh, good, I'm already quite wary. Do your own fortune?"

"Everyone knows a girl can't predict her own future." Out of the corner of her eye, Sophronia watched Professor Lefoux return to her seat. Lady Linette stood and began to move from one tea table to the next. She was making an announcement, gesticulating at each student in turn, and moving on, leaving behind a much quieter and more thoughtful gaggle.

Dimity took Sophronia's plate. The Chelsea bun atop it was untouched.

Agatha looked bright eyed and inquisitive. "What does it say about our Sophronia, Dimity?"

"That she has terrible taste, and should know when to stop telling fibs and simply eat her bun."

Agatha and Sophronia were both startled into a laugh.

Dimity ate Sophronia's bun, since it was clear her friend wasn't going to accord it gastronomic respect. Then she turned the conversation onto her favorite topic, attire. "So, what will you wear to the ball, Agatha?"

The redhead looked doubtful. She had recently exchanged much of her tubbiness around the middle for endowments further up. Mademoiselle Geraldine was most impressed by what she referred to as Miss Woosmoss's *increased assets and aesthetic abilities*. Agatha was mortified. Fortunately, or unfortunately from Agatha's perspective, she had a father who took a keen interest in the latest fashions—more for what it said about his means than for what it might do for his daughter's standing. As a result, Agatha had many gowns to choose from.

No one asked Sophronia what she would wear. Her own figure was decent enough and had not shifted substantially during her time at Mademoiselle Geraldine's Finishing Academy for Young Ladies of Quality. Fortunate indeed, as she subsisted mainly on her sisters' castoffs. Those sisters having married away, castoffs were increasingly rare. Sophronia had only one ball gown, and it was a transformation dress that served double duty as her best visiting dress.

Despite her many options, Agatha was a problem. "I'd like to wear the mustard."

Sophronia suppressed a choke.

Dimity was gentle with their friend. "Oh, but the pale lemon is much more stylish."

Not to mention more becoming to her complexion, thought Sophronia.

"But the lemon is so very fluffy." Agatha did not understand that this was a good thing.

Sophronia and Dimity exchanged a look.

"It has a much nicer cut," Dimity pressed.

"It's too low!" Agatha fluttered her hands about her chest.

Dimity was wistful. "Exactly! What I wouldn't give to..." Dimity had tried every remedy for bust improvement that Mademoiselle Geraldine suggested, from massage with a tincture of myrrh, pimpernel, elder-flower, and rectified spirits, to preparations of nux vomica mixed with Madeira, to a diet composed mainly of comforting, breast-pampering foodstuffs. Dimity did not find the diet challenging, as it emphasized

pastry, milk, potatoes, and similarly farinaceous foods. However, she was also avoiding tea and refraining from indulging
in anger, grief, worry, and jealousy. Emotions, everyone knew,
affected the size and quality of one's endowments. But despite
her efforts, nothing had, so far, *improved.*

"I should give you my share if I could." Agatha was nothing
if not generous.

Dimity was exactly as perceptive as people never gave her
credit for. So she stopped pressuring Agatha and said to Sophronia, "You're very subdued this evening. Are you nervous?"

"About a ball?" Sophronia was mock offended.

"About Felix being at the ball."

Images flashed through Sophronia's mind. Felix's beautiful pale eyes lined in kohl. His dark hair. His leg bleeding. His
warning her, too late. And that fateful shot, and Soap falling.
It was all so complicated—and to think he was originally nothing more than a means for practicing flirtation. "I can handle
our dear Lord Mersey."

Dimity was unconvinced. "Oh, yes? Then explain the
melancholy."

"Perhaps I'm bored."

"With what?" asked Agatha.

"Oh, you know. Flirting, pretty dress, espionage...death."

Dimity huffed. "La you! I seem to remember someone enjoying Professor Braithwope's lesson on resourceful reticules this
afternoon. Even if he is all over dotty."

"True. Perhaps I'm restless."

"School not exciting enough after stealing trains?" Agatha
sounded sympathetic.

Dimity cocked her head. "Hogwash. Mention of the ball brought this on. If it's not Felix, then—" She paused. "Oh. You miss Mr. Soap. It's not like he could have actually escorted you, Sophronia."

"I know." Of its own accord, Sophronia's hand delved into a secret pocket where Soap's latest missive, months old, rested crumpled and well read. That she heard from him at all was a joy, but that someone else was teaching him to read and write was bittersweet. "He seems very far away."

"Poor little bean." Dimity was a good enough friend to sympathize with Sophronia's heartache, even though she felt that the object of that affection was inappropriate.

Sophronia appreciated this. And part of her sorrow was that, in the end, she agreed with Dimity. Soap *was* inappropriate. What future did they have outside of social ostracism? He was, in the eyes of society, the wrong class, the wrong skin color, and now, the wrong species. "Ugh, this is getting maudlin. There is nothing any of us can do about it."

Sophronia groped desperately for the one topic that would guarantee her best friend's distraction. "So, Dimity, what will *you* wear to the ball?"

Dimity charged forth to conquer the conversation, taking no prisoners. "I was thinking about the pink, but it is a few seasons old and I *have* worn it before. What do you think? It projects a certain happy innocence that might be exactly the *thing* when surrounded by evil geniuses. Then again, there's the jewelry to consider. I'd have to wear my pearls, and pearls may be too drab for a winter ball. But they are really the only thing that works with the pink. So then I thought perhaps the orange. It is such a bold statement. The level of maturity and consideration required to wear orange at my age might make the young men take me seriously. But do I *want* to be taken seriously? And then I thought the peach, but it never really recovered from the whole kidnapping and werewolf transport operation. So then I thought—"

Sophronia and Agatha were content to let her ramble. There was something comforting about the force of intellect Dimity brought to bear on her apparel. Manipulation through proper dress was by far her best subject. She could prattle on happily about exactly the amount of disregard engendered by eight ruffles, as opposed to six, and why one might, or might not, want to add a sash into the equation.

Then Lady Linette arrived at their table. "Your attention, please. Miss Buss, you as well. Now, I appreciate you are all excited about the winter ball, but we teachers are adding our own special twist to the occasion."

No one at the table was surprised. They were old hats at this kind of thing. Perhaps not *old hats*, but instead, they were *last season's gloves*, soiled but still suited to any occasion, including inclement weather and dead body disposal.

"You are all to attend. Yes, even you, Miss Woosmoss. But you are not attending as yourselves. Instead, in consideration of our recent schoolwide focus on identity shift, you are to attend this ball as *each other*, within your year group. As you four are established students, better acquainted with one another than the younger girls, I expect you to execute perfectly *and* set a good example. You will, of course, be evaluated on your performances. Miss Temminnick"—she pointed to Sophronia—"you are to go as Miss Woosmoss. Miss Woosmoss as Miss Plumleigh-

Teignmott. Miss Plumleigh-Teignmott as Miss Buss. And Miss Buss as Miss Temminnick."

Preshea gave Sophronia a horrified look.

Sophronia was thoughtful. There were dangerous avenues of mockery inherent in this assignment. They would all have to be careful not to insult the person they emulated, while doing a good enough job to convince the teachers. That was probably part of the test. No doubt they would each be asked how well they thought the other person enacted them.

Agatha looked terrified and Dimity nonplussed.

Preshea wanted the important particulars. "Do we have to borrow each other's clothing? Sophronia only has one ball gown. Could I use something of mine and make it look as old-fashioned and boring as her dress?" Preshea always spoke in a clipped tone. Sophronia thought she would have to work on her diction if she wanted to sound like Sophronia.

Lady Linette had been expecting that question. "You may. It's better if you can borrow, but I'm well aware not all of you have the means, or the ability, size-wise, to dress as one another. You are to obey the style, but not necessarily the stitching, of the assignment—as it were."

Sophronia was privately relieved. She'd hate to give her only ball gown to Preshea. The girl would spill cranberry cordial all over it out of pure spite.

Lady Linette drifted off, having thrown a veritable stoat among the woodcocks.

The heavy silence was broken by Preshea's loud "Well, at least I didn't get *Agatha*. Can you imagine? *Me* in olive drab." Her various cohorts at the next table tittered obligingly.

Agatha, accustomed to such barbs, didn't flinch. "I will have to wear so many sparkles."

"Can I dress you as me, Agatha?" Dimity fairly vibrated. "Oh, you will look stunning!"

Agatha was doubtful. "Will I fit your bodice?"

Dimity's smile was evil. "You'll have to cinch very tight."

Agatha blanched and said hurriedly to Sophronia, "You can borrow anything you like of mine, of course. The lemon ruffles, even, although we'll have to lengthen the skirt."

Sophronia thought yellow would make her look jaundiced. It suited Agatha well enough, but Sophronia had indifferent brown hair, skin prone to freckles, and the occasional spot. It would play hell with her complexion. "Perhaps the brown stripe?" she asked hesitantly.

Dimity was appalled. "Sophronia, you'll look like a gangly sparrow! No offense, Agatha."

"None taken."

"Yes, but it'll be easier to add a ruffle to the bottom."

Dimity had to agree with this assessment. She had it the easiest, for Preshea was always elegant. Well, perhaps that wasn't easy for *Dimity*. She'd have to leave off her customary jewelry, and the personality switch was going to be rough. Dimity would have to be cruel and calculating.

Sophronia figured Lady Linette had chosen specifically with such challenges in mind. Each of them had been assigned the girl most unlike her own personality. Although Sophronia bet Lady Linette was in for a surprise. She had a certain amount of Agatha in her. And she'd wager good money Dimity could be quite mean—she was plenty brutal to her brother given the slightest provocation. Sophronia also felt Agatha had untapped sparkling abilities. Even Preshea was more like Sophronia than she liked to admit. They certainly both had the same interest in calculated manipulation. It was only that Sophronia had a conscience and Preshea didn't. She was grateful Preshea had been assigned to act like her instead of one of the others. Preshea's goal would be to humiliate the object of her imitation, as well as obey the letter of the assignment. She would be good at both. Sophronia was able to withstand humiliation—her friends were not.

Thus the young ladies, outfitted in each other's finest—and each other's personalities—descended upon Bunson and Lacroix's Boys' Polytechnique for a winter ball a few weeks later. There existed no little animosity between the two schools. They disagreed on the subjects of politics, supernatural acceptance, techniques of instruction, and teatime provisions. But they were linked by necessity. Bunson's town, Swiffle-on-Exe, was the way station for Mademoiselle Geraldine's. And really, what other partners could girls trained in espionage find at short notice, except boys trained as evil geniuses?

The boys always expected something odd from Geraldine's girls, but they seemed unclear about what exactly was occurring. Nevertheless, they soldiered manfully in, requesting dances from out-of-character young ladies. Bunson's was not a particularly attractive school, but they'd done up the ballroom to an extreme. Evil genius-ness was like that—showy. There were automated lanterns high above filled with a yellow-colored noxious gas, suspended on small rails from the ceiling. Four mechanicals had been reconfigured as a string quartet in one corner, where they played a rotating series of five, yes, *five* whole songs, over and over. *Someone's final project*, Sophronia heard the whispers. *So good he'd been recruited directly out of school as a Cultivator-class Pickleman.* Other mechanicals circulated, carrying large brass trays loaded with nibbles and punch. Sophronia was suspicious of some of the nibbles (they could be explosive), so she stuck with recognizable foodstuffs. Someone managed to dump absinthe in the punch, and it took ten whole minutes for Professor Lefoux to discover it and order a new batch. Things were jolly indeed, for ten minutes.

The boys had cleaned up as much as could be expected from those inclined toward evil. Civilities were observed to even Lady Linette's standards. *Carnets de bal* were requested and filled in. Sophronia was proud of hers—it doubled as a garrote, among other things. She did not hold it up eagerly, as her compatriots did—that was not Agatha's way. She skulked to the back of the room, finding refuge in a small crook-legged chair hidden behind a razor-edged metal fern.

Sophronia watched interactions through its fanged fronds. There were a number of *understandings* between Geraldine's girls and Bunson's boys, despite a school policy that insisted these boys were for practice, not permanent liaison. There were certainly enough long-running courtships for the young men to know something was unusual. They approached customary objects of flirtation only to be confused when conversations deviated or did not occur at all. The face was the same, but the dress and interaction were at odds with all previous encounters.

Preshea—as Sophronia—was flirting outrageously. Yet Lady Linette did not object. *Am I that much of a flirt?* Sophronia wondered. Preshea was eyeing Felix Mersey and edging toward him. Sophronia hid a sneer. Preshea would have done that no matter what. But it showed she was unaware of recent history. It was true Sophronia might have showed him favor, a year ago. Not anymore. In this Preshea got her entirely wrong.

Felix hadn't seen Sophronia yet, and if she had her way, he never would. He looked older and tired. His hair was too long and his eyes slightly sunken, without their customary kohl liner. Had he been ill? Or was that guilt? He still looked better than any other man in the room, but her heart no longer fluttered at the sight. Instead she felt…what? A slight nausea at possible confrontation, mixed with minor disgust. Sophronia had cut off all correspondence with him last February. She'd returned his letters unopened.

"Crikey, Sophronia, what's the matter with your lot this evening?" Of all people, Pillover had found her hiding spot.

Dimity's little brother had a longstanding relationship of such casualness with Sophronia as to make him treat the boundaries set by polite society with brotherly disregard. Sophronia had learned to accept this treatment, although she found it uncalled for; after all, she already had more than her fair share of brothers. Sophronia and Pillover were also, so far as Sophronia's mother was concerned, engaged.

"Here you are, lurking like some reluctant hedgehog. Most out of character. Why, for goodness' sake?" Pillover must be ruffled. Usually he never said more than one sentence in a row.

Sophronia looked at her toes so as not to show interest in the dance. She dearly loved dancing, but Agatha hated it. Ordinarily she would have said, "Pillover, you're positively loquacious. Are you running a fever?" But Agatha wouldn't, so Sophronia didn't.

He looked her over, head to toe. "And I can't spot Bumbersnoot on you anywhere." He plopped down next to her without waiting for an invitation. He had shot up into gangliness over the course of their acquaintance, accidentally cultivating an air of dissolute idleness that most ladies found fascinating. They thought he had a broken heart in need of repairs. In actuality, he was conjugating Latin verse in his head. As there was nothing Pillover disliked more than being the object of feminine attention, he remained utterly unmoved by their interest. This, of course, only made him more desirable.

"Sophronia?" Pillover had left off calling her Miss Temminnick shortly after she forced him to dress in her petticoat in order to escape Bunson's. Such intimacy demanded use of given names.

"Good evening, Mr. Plumleigh-Teignmott." Sophronia was gravely formal. Several of her teachers were wending through the crowd. The Bunson's professors thought this was normal chaperoning, but the ladies knew better. Sophronia suspected Sister Mattie—or more properly Sister Mathilde—of being within eavesdropping distance at that very moment.

"Sophronia, for goodness' sake, snap out of it!"

"I assure you, Mr. Plumleigh-Teignmott, I am in perfect health."

"You are behaving like a wilted violet. No, strike that, a wilted olive tree." Even Pillover didn't like Sophronia in Agatha's dress. "My sister has nary a sparkle in sight. And Miss Woosmoss looks like a"—words failed him—"chandelier in slippers!" He seemed most offended by this last. Pillover had a soft spot for Agatha. He thought her restfully chatter free— the most desirable quality in a girl. Sophronia suspected him of being distressed by the degree of attention Agatha—as Dimity—was garnering. The pink ball gown suited her very well. Her hair was a glossy pile of russet curls, dotted with silk flowers. Draped about her neck was a string of pearls—her own and likely real. Her round cheeks were rosy from the attention, the dancing, and the embarrassment of both. Quite apart from everything else, they had, indeed, had to cinch the girl in *very* tight to fit her into Dimity's ball gown. The resulting décolle-tage could be seen from the aetherosphere.

Agatha had lamented this. "I look in imminent danger of spilling!"

"The gentlemen will be most intrigued," vowed Dimity. "And you can be certain if I had the assets I should do exactly that, so it isn't at all out of character. Simply beyond my ability."

"Oh, dear," wailed Agatha, nevertheless submitting to pink ruffles. She needed a high mark in this assignment. Agatha was in ever-great need of a high mark. So she cinched and took the consequences. Much to Pillover's disgust, his sister's predictions were correct. The gentlemen did seem most intrigued.

Dimity herself was milling around in a white dress with royal-blue trim. It was cut on elegant lines and not overly fluffy, making the most of her figure rather than trying to emphasize what she didn't have. She had ribbon rosettes of blue and white in her honey-colored hair, which was dressed fashionably but without fuss. She wore one expensive-looking diamond bangle and no other jewelry at all. The diamonds were fake, of course, but you'd never know without close inspection.

Preshea was wearing a lovely black gown with gray lace ruffles and wine trim. It was more modern and stylish than Sophronia could afford, but certainly to her taste. Preshea had fashioned a dog-shaped reticule, which she wore slung cross-wise across her body. She was chatting companionably with one of the teachers. *Am I really such a goody-goody, as well as a flirt?* wondered Sophronia. *Or is Preshea mocking me?*

Bumbersnoot, the real Bumbersnoot, was slouching about the cloakroom. Knowing her little dog mechanimal was a dead giveaway that she was not obeying the identity shift protocols, Sophronia had smuggled him in under Agatha's fur cape. She certainly wasn't going to loan him to Preshea, of all people!

Agatha twirled past in the arms of some handsome young buck.

Sophronia was pleased. "I think she's doing very well."

Pillover subsided into glumness, slouching forward and putting his elbows onto his knees and his chin into his hands. It was a shockingly lower-class way to sit, as though he were in a public park, or worse, the House of Commons.

"Go cut in," suggested Sophronia quietly. It was a non-Agatha suggestion, so she did her best to deliver it in an Agatha tone.

Pillover didn't move. "I never," he objected to the floor.

"You must act as if Agatha is your sister, or you won't get anywhere."

"*That* is a disgusting suggestion."

Sophronia sighed. "No, I mean, treat her as you would a young lady of your sister's type."

"Dimity is a type? You mean, there may be *others*?" Pillover was horrified out of his moroseness.

"Do shove off, Pillover. How can I be a proper shrinking olive tree with you here? Shrinking olives are solitary creatures. Oh, and don't forget," she hissed, "we have to throw each other over at some point. I can't afford to stay indefinitely engaged to you."

Pillover looked a mite less glum at the prospect of a broken engagement. Accordingly, he stood and mooched away. He could be a bit of a wet blanket, but one had to admire a boy who followed instructions.

Sophronia continued to sit, watching her classmates employ each other's personalities as weapons against the young men around them. It was almost pretty.

Dimity was twirled to a stop by a tall young man with unfortunate ears who looked most interested in further twirls. Dimity delivered what was clearly a barb about some other girl, and the young man laughed appreciatively. Dimity looked upset with herself, but soldiered gamely on into Preshea's sour temper.

The tall boy was not alone, for as soon as she sat, Dimity was surrounded by interested parties. Sophronia was willing to wager her friend's dance card was full. Dimity sent various admirers off in pursuit of nibbles and punch, much as Preshea would have, leaving herself accompanied by only the two most persistent. Through the cleared masses, Sophronia caught her eye.

Dimity gave the chin-tap fan signal of important information to impart.

Sophronia flicked open her own fan. It was her filigree bladed one, safely capped for the evening with a leather guard, and delicate enough to pass for a normal fan.

What? she fluttered at Dimity.

Dimity flicked hers open and gave the swirl and dip for *enemy among us*. Then she tilted her head, as if flirting with a pale-haired boy to her left, but really pointing Sophronia's attention to that side of the room.

A woman had entered the ballroom. Her hair was dressed in the high curls of maturity that Geraldine's girls were permitted to practice but not wear in public, so she was no student. She faced away from Sophronia, talking to Lady Linette. Even from the back, Sophronia's training told her many things. The woman's bearing marked her as an aristocrat, or at least trained to the correct posture to pass as one. Her hair was naturally blonde, and her dress was certainly Parisian—snow white with rose-pink ruffles, and silk roses sewn into the drapes of the overskirt and clustered at the puff of the daringly short sleeves. A coronet of roses, *real*, not silk, which meant hothouse, perched atop her hair, an amazing expense for a provincial school ball. Instead of a necklace, the stranger wore a lace ruff tied about her neck, likely to disguise the fact that she had vampire bite marks.

Sophronia knew who it was before she turned.

Monique de Pelouse.

INVASIONS AT A BALL

hy? Sophronia fluttered the question at Dimity. What on earth was Monique doing out of London during the holiday season? It was true much of the town shut down, but the vampires took that as an excuse to throw lavish parties.

Dimity couldn't answer even if she knew, for Monique left Lady Linette to stand in front of her instead. As Monique was a former student, fan fluttering communication was useless against her. She had left Mademoiselle Geraldine's to become a drone to Countess Nadasdy, vampire queen of the Westminster Hive, some years ago, but she would keep turning up, like grease at the top of the dishwater. At their last encounter, Sophronia had had the great pleasure of throwing her out of a train.

Dimity and Monique appeared to be exchanging pleasantries, of all things. Then Monique moved on about the room.

Sophronia sank into the shadows. She couldn't afford a

confrontation with her old nemesis, not if she wished to stay in character. Sophronia had to bite down her pert answers at the best of times, and Monique practically begged for them. Agatha was never pert and rarely had answers. Better to avoid all contact.

So far as Sophronia knew, Monique's main drone assignment was to keep an eye on the Picklemen. Their free enhancements to all mechanicals over the past six months must have driven her crazy. Despite vampire opposition, anyone who owned a mechanical was delighted to see it upgraded with a new crystalline valve frequensor, which reputedly fixed the spontaneous opera problem of last winter and improved performance.

Sophronia, her friends, Monique, the vampires, and a handful of others knew the real reason for the valves. The Picklemen wanted complete control over all the mechanicals in England. Yet since the upgrade, no attempt to seize that control had occurred. The vampires' fuss over the enhancements had been dismissed as supernatural hysteria by the government and passed unnoticed by the popular press. Everyone who knew there would be a problem was forced into waiting for that problem to occur. And they had no idea what the Picklemen intended to do with their army of mechanical domestic servants. Last time all they'd done was have them sing "Rule, Britannia!" What was next? A ruthless bout of ballet?

Still, if Monique is supposed to be monitoring the situation, static as it may be, what is she doing here?

Someone sat down in the chair recently vacated by Pillover.

"Ria, my dove, it has been too long."

Sophronia had actually relaxed her guard. *Debut move!* She

marshaled her irritation into a defensive mask of Agatha-like nervousness. "Why, Lord Mersey, how do you do?"

"Like that, are we?"

"Pardon, sir?"

Felix was no intelligencer. His training was in machinations and evil machinery. He cut directly to the point, with no attempt at subterfuge, "He's my father, Ria. I had no choice."

There is always a choice, or at least evasive tactics, would have said Sophronia. "Why, my lord, I'm afraid I fail to follow your meaning," she said as Agatha.

"Please don't be like that. He is working to save the country. Save the Empire. His ends are noble."

How unexpectedly revealing. How much, Sophronia wondered, *can Agatha get out of Felix where Sophronia failed?* She had underestimated how much he wanted her good opinion. Not to mention how much frustration brought about confession.

"My lord, please, that isn't necessary."

"Ria! What else was I to do? Surely you would have done the same in my position."

White-hot anger almost threw Agatha out of Sophronia's head. She might be a spy, and a relatively good one, but she was loyal to her friends. Felix had betrayed them all, not only Sophronia, when he revealed their disguises. And then...

"Your father killed Soap," she hissed, breaking character.

Felix was cheered by her return to form. "Ria, my dove, look on the bright side, at least he has stopped trying to kill *you.*"

Only because I've been safely at school for three-quarters of a year. If there was anywhere the Picklemen couldn't infiltrate, it was a mobile academy for female intelligencers.

She reached once more for Agatha's quiet spirit. "Oh, Lord Mersey, you are so droll. What makes you think I care two whits for your father's murderous opinion?" She tapped his arm with her fan in a self-conscious flirtation, as though she were awkwardly following instructions. On the pullback from the tap, she sent the wrist swirl signal with her closed fan, *Damsel in need of rescue*. She had no idea if Dimity would see, but she required an extraction.

Felix looked grim. "Back to that, are we? Very well, if you insist on playing games. Would you care to dance? You'd be afforded the opportunity to cut me in public by leaving me on the floor as per usual."

If Sophronia had any guilt over her shoddy behavior in the past, his ungentlemanly mention of it certainly cured her. She'd had good reason for abandoning him on the dance floor, every time. It was poor manners for him to discuss her indiscretions.

Then, of all people, Agatha came whirling up. Her partner, Lord Dingleproops, seemed taken with the pearl-drenched Agatha version of Dimity. Odd, as he had once rejected Dimity herself.

"My lord, might we rest a moment?" Agatha whipped out her fan, in evident need of cooling. *You requested rescue?* she signaled Sophronia.

Sophronia blew out her cheeks in a sigh of both exasperation and relief.

Agatha understood this silent commentary on social predicament. She turned her attention onto Felix. "Lord Mersey, how do you do this fine evening?"

Felix looked confused. Prior to that, Agatha had barely

strung three words together in his presence. "Miss, uh, Woos-moss, is it?"

Agatha curtsied. "I understand from Lord Dingleproops that you are something of a whiz with waistcoats? He claims you have three apparatus, a monocle, and a pack of cards stashed at all times. Is this true?"

Felix was no inferior gentlemen to resist a request from any lady when couched in such incontestable terms. He stood, bowing over Agatha's proffered hand. "Dear lady, indeed it is."

Agatha tittered. "La, my lord, how droll of you. Can you show me any of them without, ah-hem, unbuttoning?"

Sophronia was driven to gasp! To mention the act of undress, and to a young man of little acquaintance! That was flirting beyond even Dimity. Agatha was taking things too far.

Sophronia used her fan to disguise shock.

Felix and Lord Dingleproops found the mention of buttons enchanting.

"Oh, la, I'm positively parched." Agatha grabbed Felix's arm and sailed smoothly away, angling toward the punch.

Felix could do naught but follow.

It was, Sophronia had to admit, a perfect extraction. Agatha had hidden depths of shallowness. Or she was a better study than anyone thought, and merely needed a different personality to bring out her abilities. Or she had partaken too freely of the absinthe-spiked punch.

Sophronia turned her attention back to the gathering. Monique was making her way around the room. Whatever she was looking for, she hadn't found it. Sophronia harbored a brief, horrible thought that her old enemy was hunting for her. They were, after a fashion, allied against the Picklemen. Perhaps she had a message from the dewan, Sophronia's soon-to-be patron.

Then someone *else* invaded her corner. Clearly it was not so hidden as she'd hoped. This time, however, it was a welcome invasion.

Genevieve Lefoux, once known as Vieve and currently known as Gaspar Lefoux, appeared at Sophronia's elbow. Now twelve years old, Vieve had shot up and was almost as tall as Sophronia. She was looking likely to be as much a beanpole as her aunt. Since she intended a long career disguised as a man, Vieve was no doubt delighted to find the Lefoux genes running true to form, or more accurately, true to figure.

At Bunson's, Vieve purported to be Professor Lefoux's nephew, who exhibited such extraordinary engineering talent it had forced Bunson's to take on a French charity case. Although she had never officially been a finishing school student, preferring to spend her time in the boiler room, something had rubbed off. She had grasped enough espionage to be good at maintaining her ties to Mademoiselle Geraldine's, without exposing her connection or her gender.

Vieve bowed low over Sophronia's gloved hand.

Sophronia pretended nervousness at having been discovered by a stranger. "Oh. Um, how do you do, Mr. . . . ?" But her green eyes sparkled with delight. She could not deny a real affection for the funny creature, and had genuinely missed her company. Still, she did not break Agatha's character, nor did she pretend they had met before. She was, after all, a Geraldine's girl.

Thus it was for Vieve to open the conversation. "Good evening, miss. Please excuse me for approaching you without introduction." Vieve was in full impeccable evening dress from head to toe. Her dark hair was cropped short. She did not sport the mustache she once coveted, nor had she faked a deeper voice— as yet she had no need. Even with dimples and a feminine cast to her cheekbones and nose, she had the manners and movements of a young man. It was impressive.

"Mr. Lefoux, at your service, Miss…?"

"Temminnick," said Sophronia tremulously.

"Indeed, yes. Although I did think, for a moment, from certain descriptions prior to this greeting, that you might be Miss Woosmoss. Quite apart from the hair color, of course." In addition to a head for engineering, Vieve had an eye for fashion. Not to mention a familiarity with most of Sophronia's age group.

Sophronia allowed a hint of a smile. "I can see how you might make such an error."

Thus they understood one another. Vieve knew Sophronia was under an assignment to act like Agatha. Sophronia knew that Vieve had probably figured out who the others were as well.

"Would you care to dance, Miss Temminnick?" offered Vieve, gravely, as though to a wallflower cousin.

Sophronia knew such a dance could only lend Vieve's disguise credence. She also knew Agatha might dance with Professor Lefoux's nephew if pressed. So she agreed.

Vieve was an expert at the reel and a decent lead. She'd obviously been practicing, or been made to learn. They danced the first pass through in awkward silence, as befitted Agatha.

On the second, Vieve said, dimples flashing, "I understand we share an acquaintance?" Her eyes shifted to Monique.

Sophronia hesitated. She needed the information Vieve implied she had, but she also needed to stay in character. "Unusual, don't you feel, for an ex-student to return to a dance such as this?"

"Very," agreed Vieve. "And we have had other visitors, of late."

Here comes the important part. "Have you? How fascinating. Do tell?"

"Very well-dressed visitors. Except, they strangely insisted on green bands about their hats."

Picklemen! Sophronia's slight panic showed in a missed step. Fortunately, it lent credence to her Agatha. It was at about this point in any dance that Agatha became uncomfortable, stumbled, and found a way to end the prolonged contact with a member of the opposite sex.

"How recently, if I may ask?"

"Oh, you may." Vieve was gloriously mild in her delivery. "They could still be here, on school grounds."

Ah-ha! So Monique wasn't here for the ball, she was tracking Picklemen. But what business would they have with Bunson's? The crystalline valve was in their possession and under production. True, some of them had sons at the school. Where else would an evil secret society send its progeny? But to visit in person? Particularly as the boys were about to head home for the holidays.

Does Monique know why they're here? Or is she following them because she doesn't? Sophronia found herself, much to her disgust, contemplating arranging a conversation with the dratted blonde.

The reel was coming to an end. There was no way to stay Agatha and converse further with Vieve. Throwing caution briefly to the wind, but keeping her voice hesitant, Sophronia said, "Perhaps a consultation, later this evening, Mr. Lefoux?"

"I am at your disposal." Vieve guided her respectably off the floor.

Where to meet? Sophronia didn't know Bunson's well enough to get around after hours. Vieve would have to break curfew and leave the grounds. "Behind the Nib and Crinkle? An hour before dawn?"

Vieve gave her a grave look. Then a sharp nod.

"Mr. Lefoux, I shall have my Italian reticule with me."

Vieve was suddenly more interested. "Is it still stylish?" Code for whether Bumbersnoot was in working order.

"Indeed. But I should like you to perform some modifications, if possible."

"I shall bring my tools." With a perfunctory bow that suggested the dance had not been up to snuff, Vieve drifted off to approach one of the newly minted debuts for the next dance. A pretty little blonde with big violet eyes looked hugely flattered at the attention of such a handsome young man.

Sophronia was about to skulk back to her corner when a voice behind her said, "That was an unexpectedly lively conversation, Miss Temminnick."

Sophronia turned to find Professor Lefoux looming.

"Well"—she injected a tremor of fear into her voice—"we know each other, from before, you understand."

Professor Lefoux frowned, unsure as to whether Sophronia was hinting that she knew that the professor's niece was illegally pretending to be her nephew as a threat, or whether Sophronia was pretending to be Agatha to such an extent that she would blunder into mention of this delicate subject in public.

Nevertheless, Professor Lefoux was intent on reprimand, and Sophronia couldn't really fault her for it. "That dance, Miss Temminnick, was too much. I expected better from you. Are we understood?"

Sophronia said, as Agatha, "Yes, Professor. I do apologize, I am afraid I forgot myself. I—" She hesitated, wondering if she should risk telling Professor Lefoux about the Picklemen. The professor was drone to Professor Braithwope, and, as such, allied with the supernatural. By rights she should be against the Picklemen. Then again, becoming a drone to a rove vampire would be excellent cover. She had, after all, worked with Professor Shrimpdittle on the contraption that failed to protect her vampire when he was flown into the aether. She could be sabotaging her own master.

Best not to tell. "Would you, by any chance, have a spare lace tuck?" Sophronia asked, hunched and meek.

Professor Lefoux, who favored high-necked dresses, even for a ball, and thus never needed a tuck, gave her a dirty look. "Certainly not. Now, go rectify yours having slipped. The necessities room is that way."

Sophronia bobbed a perfectly executed slightly bad curtsy— which caused her teacher to snort and say something about this kind of assignment encouraging regressive behavior—and went in the direction indicated.

She spotted Dimity holding court near the punch bowl, surrounded by admiring young men. Dimity said something, no doubt cutting, and the boys around her laughed. They were mostly Pistons, a Bunson's club known for churning out new Picklemen. At a school for evil geniuses, these were the most evil and the least genius. Pillover waltzed by and gave his sister a disgusted glare. The Pistons had made his first year at Bunson's miserable. His attention returned to his partner. A lively Agatha looked up adoringly into his face. Pillover's expression went soft—still glum and morose, but certainly soft.

The dance ended and Sophronia sent a longing look at all the happy flirting, hoping Professor Lefoux saw. She paused to watch Pillover lead Agatha off the floor. He pressed a tiny parcel into her hands. Agatha colored, looking as self-conscious as normal. Then she faked a laugh and tucked the gift down her cleavage in a flirt so blatant Pillover looked as if he might faint.

Lady Linette caught the maneuver and moved purposefully in Agatha's direction. Whether intent on praise or reprimand, it was difficult to predict. Sophronia, mindful that Professor Lefoux's eyes were glaring, could not linger. She made her way out into the hallway.

Felix did not try to speak to her again. Vieve contented herself torturing the debuts. Monique didn't stay much longer, and Sophronia wasn't blessed with the opportunity to engage her in conversation. Pillover danced with Agatha twice, much to Agatha's pleasure. And possibly to Pillover's as well. Hard to tell with Pillover—he had an almost spylike ability to maintain a sulky expression.

Such a public preference for Agatha, however, afforded

Sophronia the ideal excuse to cry off her engagement with Pillover. Which she did, by letter to both him and her own mother, as soon as possible. The missive was prettily penned and very civil, stating only that she felt—given his two dances and provision of a bosom-worthy gift to another young lady—that they were no longer suited. He was young, she forgave him his transgressions, and hoped he would accord her the courtesy of never renewing his addresses. She could only suppose that Pillover's delight upon reading her note would balance out her mother's misery.

The gift he'd given Agatha turned out to be a Depraved Lens of Crispy Magnification. "Don't you think it kind of Mr. Pillover?" Agatha was disposed to be chatty after her euphoric all-conquering ball. "Did you know he's reached Nefarious Genius? He's developed the technique of having most everything he makes explode upon contact. The Pistons have stopped bothering him. Lord Dingleproops nearly lost an eye to Pill's exploding hair tonic applicator. Pillover is ever so proud."

"His hair did look nice," said Sophronia.

The girls were preparing for bed. If *preparing for bed* could be characterized by lounging about in nightgowns, caps, and robes, sipping tisanes and gossiping.

Even Preshea had joined them, in a rare moment of camaraderie. "Sophronia, I must say, being you was unexpectedly fun, for someone who never says what she actually thinks."

"Difficult to hold back on the barbs, was it?" asked Dimity, in an indisputably barblike manner. Her Preshea characteristics seemed to be taking a while to wear off.

Preshea noticed. "Clearly you enjoyed being me."

"Somewhat. It was frankly exhausting to insult everyone all the time. And hard never knowing one's real friends."

"Now, Dimity, don't be rude." Preshea's smile was glassy with contempt. "Who needs real friends?"

Sophronia was struck with a sudden pang. Was Preshea's nastiness a front? They had never given her a chance, as she'd allied with Monique from the start. After Monique left, Preshea had organically assumed the position of cruelest pretty girl. But there was something wistful in her tone. Perhaps it was only a lingering bit of Sophronia. No one ever doubted that Sophronia valued her friends above all things.

Lady Linette was prone to saying that if Sophronia had any major weakness, it was her unswerving loyalty. To which Sophronia always responded that she intended to prove that was a strength.

Preshea couldn't tolerate even a moment of sympathetic expressions. "Oh, stop it, all of you." She stood. "As if I should trade my status and standing for the likes of you."

Just like that, they were back on familiar ground.

"I, for one, do not want to be scolded into bed by Professor Lefoux. Good night." With which Preshea left. As older students, they had been moved into more luxurious accommodations, and each had her own private room. Sometimes Sophronia missed sharing with Dimity. As she'd grown up sharing with sisters, this was her first foray into the unparalleled privilege of a solitary bedchamber. But she did have Bumbersnoot to warm her toes.

The remaining three huddled in for whispered gossip, knowing Preshea was more likely to listen at her door than actually seek her bed.

Sophronia told the other two about the Picklemen and that Monique was likely there in pursuit. "I'm only waiting until lights-out before I go back down. I've arranged to meet Vieve for a quick consult on Bumbersnoot. And I have a letter to post."

Dimity worried easily. "Is he ill?"

Bumbersnoot was contentedly sitting in a corner of the parlor, nibbling a small bit of coal. Steam leaked out his carapace slowly, in a sleepy manner.

"No, but I have a theory about the crystalline valves that I want to discuss with Vieve. Also, it's an opportunity to see if she has anything more on the Picklemen. I must say, Agatha, it is difficult being you. I mean, it's easier to have clandestine meetings on the sidelines, but harder to exchange information during dances."

"Well," said Agatha, "I had a marvelous time being Dimity. Thank you." She turned bright eyes to the object of her impersonation.

Dimity grinned. "It was a pleasure to watch you butterfly about. My brother seemed suitably intimidated."

Agatha blushed. "Oh, do you think?"

"You like him, don't you?" teased Dimity.

"Younger man, careful there." Sophronia teased as well.

Agatha looked to Dimity, worried. "You don't mind?"

"Mind? 'Course I don't mind. You're a great deal better than those silly chits that keep hurling themselves at him. No offense meant, Sophronia."

Sophronia was quick to defend herself. "*That* was all Mumsy's idea."

Dimity continued, "Frankly, I don't understand it. It's not like he has much consequence. And he is a human gumboil."

Sophronia nibbled her lip. "For once I think the ladies don't notice his lack of consequence."

Agatha's hands clasped together in a maneuver they had been taught by Lady Linette, but which Sophronia suspected in Agatha's case was instinctual. "He's very fine to look at."

Dimity put her hands to her ears. "Oh, dear me no, none of that. I couldn't bear it, not after such a long evening."

Sophronia changed the subject. "And how did you find being Preshea for a night, Dim?"

"Horribly easy. I simply said any nasty thing that came to mind, so long as it wasn't indiscreet. Best if it cut some other girl down. I'm afraid I might have been very cruel about both of you."

Sophronia and Agatha shrugged. That was the assignment.

"It was an interesting place to visit, but I wouldn't want to live there," Dimity concluded. "Preshea's personality is quite putrid. Poor thing."

Sophronia wondered if that was part of the logic behind the assignment, that by dancing in each other's shoes, they might develop sympathy for their fellows, as well as further their subterfuge abilities.

"Well, I enjoyed the opportunity to spend most of my evening observing." Sophronia rested her head on Agatha's shoulder affectionately. "You were fun to be."

Agatha blushed in pleasure.

Any further praise she might have meted out for Agatha's self-worth was cut off prematurely as Professor Lefoux let herself into their parlor.

"Bedtime, ladies. You know the regulations."

The girls stood and bobbed curtsies. "Yes, Professor," they chorused. Under her austere glare, they traipsed off to their respective beds.

CRISIS 3

Enemies in the Roses

Vieve was waiting for Sophronia behind the Nib and Crinkle as arranged. She smelled as though she had managed to persuade the proprietor to serve her a pint—and then gone swimming in it.

"Really, Vieve, ale?"

"It's the kind of thing a boy would do. I spilled most of it intentionally, caused a fuss, and got myself booted out. Now if Bunson's discovers I'm out, they have a story about where I've been."

"All that for little old me?"

Vieve winked at her. "Never say I don't care, green eyes."

Sophronia laughed. Clearly Vieve was also working on how to flirt like a boy. Following in the footsteps of Pistons, was she? "Vieve, you're turning into a rake."

"Do you really think so? Topping."

Bumbersnoot chose that moment to shoot a bit of smoke out

his ears, flapping the leather in greeting. He didn't like being ignored. Sophronia had him flung over her neck and one arm for transport. He was still wearing the frilly lace reticule disguise they'd devised for the ball.

Vieve's attention was diverted. "There you are, my beautiful boy."

Much as she adored Bumbersnoot, Sophronia would never describe him as beautiful. Vieve, however, possessed an indescribable love for technology. She saw Bumbersnoot not for his dented and rusty carapace, his patchwork metal bits, or his mismatched leather ear flaps, but for the work of mechanical genius beneath all that. Inside, Bumbersnoot had a high-grade aether-tapping miniature boiler and a steam-processing mechanism so sophisticated the rest of Europe still hadn't discovered the technology. Vieve loved him for the cranks and valves that made him move with realistic smoothness and for the cyclical protocols and punch commands that told him how and where to go. She appreciated the two ways he could swallow—into storage or into his boiler. Vieve saw Bumbersnoot for what he really was—a technological masterpiece. She'd had the care of him ever since he came into Sophronia's possession. While they both knew mechanimals were a Picklemen product, Bumbersnoot had never yet led them astray.

Vieve set the mechanimal reverently on the ground and popped him open to check his internal workings.

Sophronia let her tinker in silence. They were secluded near the pub behind some large rosebushes. A good spot, for it afforded them a decent view of Mademoiselle Geraldine's, anchored outside of town. The massive dirigible bobbed quietly. It was low to the ground, fortunately for Sophronia. She'd be able to get back on board using the sooties' rope ladder.

"Everything looks in order." Vieve drew Sophronia's attention back to Bumbersnoot. "What was it you wanted adjusted?"

Sophronia tossed Vieve a small object. It was a faceted crystal valve, almost like cut glass with metal components embedded within. It was awfully familiar looking to those who knew the style.

Vieve knew it. "One of the newest crystalline valve frequensors. Where'd you get it?"

"You heard about my train misappropriation last winter?"

"I heard you eliminated a shipload of these pretties. Terrible waste."

"Let's say one of them came into my possession. Only, this one is special."

"How so?"

"It's the one the vampires were using to track the Picklemen. Bumbersnoot and Dimity smuggled it out."

"You think it's somehow tracing the other valves?"

"The vampires would have triggered this valve to react to the activation of the new ones. Could you hook this into Bumbersnoot? I know he's only a mechanimal, so he wouldn't be able to react exactly as ordered to whatever new protocol the Picklemen transmit. But if we could get him to do that steam whistle alarm he makes in times of crisis?"

Vieve followed her reasoning. "You want him to be the canary in the coal mine? Alert you when the Picklemen make their move?"

"I do."

Vieve grinned. "Brilliant idea. It's large for such a little beastie. I'll have to install it in his storage compartment. You'll lose half that capacity. Hooking it in so it activates his alarm, when I'm not sure..." She rubbed the side of her nose in thought, smearing it with grease. "Plus, not knowing precisely what the Picklemen intend the valve to trigger..." Vieve had a habit of leaving her sentences unfinished in times of contemplation. "Well, it's a unique idea, I'll give you that much."

She looked intrigued enough to take on the assignment. That was the thing with Vieve, she wouldn't do it if she didn't think it a challenge. Sophronia had once asked her to construct a bladed fan. Vieve had scoffed at the very idea. "It's already been done. Why would I bother?"

But this, this was something new and subversive.

"It's going to take time. I'll need to keep him with me." Vieve stood, decided.

"Of course. How long do you need?"

Vieve frowned. "A week. Will that work?"

"Perfect timing if you can make it. The school should be back at Swiffle for the holiday break. Meet you here the night we come in? Midnight? You'll have to keep an eye to the moor, for the airship."

"I always do. If I don't make the deadline, I'll send him to the sooties while the school is in port. They'll pass him along to you after Christmas."

Sophronia nodded. "You aren't going home?"

"Can't go to my aunt, since she stays on board with Professor Braithwope, and I've no other family. Honestly, I like having

Bunson's to myself. No one tries to stop me using the expensive equipment. I may visit the sooties if I have time."

"They send their regards, by the way."

Vieve smiled wistfully. "Of course they do." Her small face fell, dimples vanishing. "I miss Soap."

Sophronia could feel her own face shuttering closed. "Me, too." She quickly changed the subject. "Anything else you neglected to tell me about the Picklemen?"

Vieve considered the question, pocketing the valve and slinging Bumbersnoot over her shoulder by his reticule strap. "Four of them. Lower down the ranks—I'd suspect merely Spicers. Younger. Saw them leaving Bunson's, on foot, just before I did."

Sophronia frowned. "What did they want?"

"That's your business to find out, no? I'd best get back."

"Thank you, Vieve."

Vieve gave her a mocking little bow. "Pleasure is all mine, as always."

Sophronia watched her friend stride confidently back toward Bunson's. Then she left the seclusion of the rosebushes to shadow the goat path, rather than walk down the middle of it. Too visible from the air. As a result, she almost ran into Monique, who was standing in the dark under a holly tree, binoculars to her eyes, watching the front half of the school.

Sophronia froze, terrified that she would step on some loud twig and give herself away. She'd been intent on not being seen. She should also have been thinking about not being heard.

If Monique had heard her, she gave no sign.

Sophronia crouched down slowly, shifting so she was on the other side of the tree. She watched, trying to determine what the blonde was staring at. Sophronia never went anywhere without the standard Geraldine's armament: sewing scissors, handkerchief, perfume, lemon, hair ribbon, and red lace doily. She also carried her own special items: hurlie, obstructor, fake mustache, tea sachet, and chatelaine, from which hung her *carnet de bal*, a Depraved Lens of Crispy Magnification, and a velvet pouch containing a small pork pie. Unfortunately, this vast collection did not include binoculars. She pulled up her lens. It was better for examining details and setting things on fire, but could be peered through over distances if one had no other option.

Something was going on at the pilot's bubble.

Sophronia squinted, wishing the moon were fuller and the mists not quite so low. Shadows, three of them, climbed toward the base of the scaffolding that held the bubble up and away from the front decks of the dirigible. Shadows wearing top hats.

Picklemen were breaking into her school! They were scaling the outside by stages, using grappling hooks not unlike Sophronia's hurlie. They were positioned in such a way as to be entirely out of view from the teachers' balconies. *What in all aether do they want with the pilot's bubble?* Sophronia was one of the few students who'd been inside it. It was a mess of gears, coils, valves, and cables. It contained nothing particularly worth stealing. Certainly not for the Picklemen, who were generally wealthy in all that mattered: property, technology, and consequence.

Why take such a risk? Mademoiselle Geraldine's was the nest of the enemy. It was one of the few institutions that not only knew all about the Picklemen's secret society but opposed them, and had the spy network to do so properly. Yet this was obviously a well-planned penetration. They would have had to see schematics of the airship to know that an approach from down low and in small numbers was most likely to succeed. Sophronia could not help but admire the operation.

"No proximity alarm?" Monique muttered to herself.

Sophronia was wondering the same thing. The pilot's bubble had extra protections. How had the Picklemen disabled the school's soldier mechanicals? Did they have an obstructor? They made mechanicals. She wouldn't put it past them to have the means to turn them off. She wouldn't put it past Vieve to have sold the technology to the highest bidder, either. They must be doing something, for the school remained slumbering and silent.

Then Sophronia remembered—the alarms around the bubble had been disabled. Something to do with Professor Braithwope continually setting them off. He'd had a fascination with walking the top stabilizer beam out to the bubble—or dancing along it—ever since his fall and tether snap. It was one of his more consistent symptoms of separation insanity.

Nothing for it, thought Sophronia. *I must get on board and set off the alarms myself. And quickly, before they steal whatever it is they're after.*

She broke cover and sprinted toward the ship.

Monique gasped. "What?" But whatever Monique's orders, they didn't include stopping Sophronia.

The Pickleman guard, on the other hand, was a different story.

Stupid, Sophronia. Vieve *had* said four Picklemen. Only three were climbing.

He stepped into the path, facing her, pistol drawn and very deadly.

Sophronia froze. After what had happened to Soap and Felix, she was not particularly fond of guns. She thought them quite vulgar. However, she would wager this man didn't want to fire, as that would awaken the school.

Impasse.

"Running around the moors alone at night, little girl? That's not safe at all. That's how little girls get hurt." He wiggled his heavy gun around almost casually, although keeping it pointed at her.

Sophronia was not impressed by threats. "What are you after?"

"Currently? Stupid little girls." He moved closer.

Sophronia almost wanted him to get within striking distance. Except there was the gun to consider.

A shot fired. Loud in the silence of the late night, but it wasn't from him. Instead, the man looked startled and dropped his gun to clutch at his side with both hands. His legs buckled and he fell to his knees.

"Stupid little boys should learn to *use* guns and not wave them around." Monique walked past Sophronia to the man. She held her own small pistol steady. She put one pretty little kid boot on the man's chest and shoved him to lie back, coming to stand over him, pistol pointed at his head. She didn't even look at Sophronia.

Sophronia added, "And that stupid little girls travel in pairs." Then she sprinted past, heading for the ship. Things were changing there. The climbing Picklemen, instead of coming to their friend's rescue, were moving much faster and more frantically. A few lights were on in the front module of the ship, the red-tassel section, the area forbidden to students. That shot had woken teachers.

The hatch to the boiler room was open. A few dirty-faced imps, also known as ship's sooties, were dropping a rope ladder and gesturing at Sophronia to hurry.

She was up it in a trice.

"Miss, are you hurt?" A thin young man spoke first, offering her a hand through the hatch. Sophronia took it. No cause to be rude or churlish. She'd learned to value sooties to an extent entirely at odds with her upbringing and her training.

"Not me, Handle. But we've got another problem. Infiltration."

"I didn't hear no alarm."

"Exactly! What's the nearest well-patrolled hallway?"

Handle, so called for the size of his ears as well as the usefulness of his actions, knew better than to ask questions of Sophronia when gunshots had been fired. He'd inherited her from his predecessor, Soap. And while not as proactively accommodating to her needs, he appreciated a system of barter that served them both admirably. Sophronia brought the sooties tea cakes as often as possible, and the sooties honored her odd hours and odder requests—when they were a low risk to themselves.

Handle had been selected as their new leader by the sooties' cat, Smokey Bones, rather than by any democratic process. Smokey Bones liked Handle best, after Soap. So when Soap left, Handle was in charge. Simple as that.

He led Sophronia over to a door she'd never noticed before at the back end of the boiler room. Since engineering was vast, this shouldn't be a surprise, but Sophronia had thought she knew all the airship's secrets by now. The door was so small she had to crawl through it.

She emerged into the hallway that ran through the sooties' sleeping quarters and from there into the kitchen and serving rooms. These last were littered with tracks designed to carry and power the many household mechanicals that ran the day-to-day lives of the students and teachers. Even late at night, with most of the steam turned down, some were around tending to laundry and the morning meal. Sophronia hadn't frequented this area before, as she spent most of her time trying to *avoid* the most trundled hallways.

Where normally Sophronia would have whipped out her obstructor and stilled any clangermaid she encountered, this time she allowed herself to be noticed.

The maid took only a few seconds to realize it was an intruder. It was an odd-looking creature, as mechanicals went—faceless, with its head gears exposed, yet it wore a pinafore protecting the front portion of its conical carapace, as though an actual human maid. This particular clangermaid carried a basket full of dirty linens.

Upon sensing Sophronia, it paused and let out a whistle of inquiry. When Sophronia did not respond, it whistled again, imperiously. Then the whistle turned into a very loud shriek, like that of a teakettle. Soon this was picked up by other mechanicals nearby and then throughout the ship. Those that had been shut down whirred to life, screaming as if awoken from some nightmare of coal shortages.

Regulations required that all the students stay wherever they were when an alarm sounded. This meant the students were trapped in their quarters while the teachers hopefully investigated and found the infiltrating Picklemen.

With most of the mechanicals zipping to defend as protection protocols dictated, the maid who'd found Sophronia approached, menacing. Mechanicals were supposed to keep an intruder trapped, if possible.

Now Sophronia brought out her obstructor. She blasted the clangermaid into silent stillness—the alarm still sounded by dozens of others—and slipped past. She dashed through the kitchen, blasting those who seemed inclined to stop her and avoiding those who had other protocols in place. Afraid that if she ran into a teacher, she would be stopped, Sophronia took to the exterior of the dirigible. It was a less direct route, but it would be faster than having to explain herself.

Sophronia shot her hurlie and swung from one balcony to the next, moving at a dangerous pace. If it hadn't been so low to the ground, even she wouldn't have risked it. The hurlie was relatively new, with fancy modifications from Vieve—smaller and stealthier, faster to emit, and with an added winch to pull taut as needed. Excellent changes, all. Should be, as Vieve had made the design alterations based on Sophronia's experience. There was also a marked dexterity to the fancy India rubber soles of Sophronia's special walking boots that only a certain cobbler on Bond Street could attest to. Add to these tools the fact that Sophronia boasted muscles on her arms that no young lady ought to have, and the airship didn't stand a chance at containing her. She increased her speed through the red-tassel section, aware that inside, the shadows rushing through the hallways were those of teachers awake and hunting.

Sophronia made it to the very front of the dirigible, hung on a protrusion, and tilted her head way back. There it was, above her—the pilot's bubble. Sort of like a crow's nest, only enclosed, it looked like two large bathtubs, one overturned on top of the other. It was held, suspended above and in front of the prow, by a set of struts and one long beam from the forward squeak deck.

The three Picklemen were better equipped than she, for they had managed to climb up the scaffolding and were now crawling over the outside of the bubble. One of them appeared to be already inside. The ship's pilot was a mechanical comprised of a jumble of gears, levers, chains, and valves, many of which were probably valuable. Her only guess was that the Picklemen needed something for which they didn't hold the patent. Some nefarious part of their scheme to take over England.

There was nothing she could do to stop the invaders. She'd once been stuck inside the pilot's bubble precisely because of its precarious position jutting out on spindly supports into nothingness.

Where are the teachers? Distracted by something? Did the Picklemen plan for that, too?

The smallest of the three emerged, and they all began to climb down. Sophronia couldn't see if the man's satchel was bulging in any recognizable manner. She scuttled out of view, hiding behind a balcony support beam.

She peeked around in time to watch them rappel off the bubble, dropping rapidly, like spiders extending threads. She'd never done anything like this before, but someone had to do something. Not sure of her timing, she hooked her hurlie over a sturdy rail and with a deep breath kicked out off the side and swung out on an interception trajectory.

She was a little off. She didn't exactly knock into the littlest Pickleman. But she did knock off his hat, which tumbled sadly to the moor below. In their desperate grapple, she also managed to rip the satchel off his back, before swinging back toward the ship. It was all done in a weird silence, because even startled by a flying female, the three men did not yell, intent on getting away as quickly and quietly as possible. They landed on the ground below, unsnapped themselves from their ropes, and took off at breakneck speed down the goat path.

Sophronia was left, dangling, clutching a sack. At which moment, Lady Linette, Professor Lefoux, and Sister Mattie finally emerged onto the front squeak deck. Lady Linette stuck her head over the edge.

"Sophronia Temminnick? Is that you? I might have known. Get up here *this minute*, young lady."

Sophronia sighed. "It may take me more than a minute, Lady Linette."

Sophronia tried to explain what had happened, but they focused on the fact that she had been caught. They thought she was concocting a wild story to explain triggering the alarm. They refused to believe there had been an attack. "We have people in place to warn us of such things," dismissed Professor Lefoux. They thought she'd been off at Bunson's *trysting* with a boy! That was the downside of training intelligencers—it was impossible to tell when they were fibbing.

Of course Sophronia couldn't defend herself with, "I've been climbing around for years without triggering your infernal alarm!" That would only incriminate her further, and they'd likely confiscate her obstructor and her hurlie.

She showed them the satchel she'd managed to grab off the Pickleman.

Empty.

"How do we know it isn't yours, young lady?" asked Professor Lefoux.

"But it's so ugly!" objected Sophronia.

"Exactly, to throw us off."

"This is ridiculous. Would one of you at least check the pilot's bubble? See if anything is amiss."

Lady Linette was firm. "We have wasted enough time on your shenanigans this evening, young lady. To bed with all of us. Tomorrow we will come up with a suitable punishment."

Sophronia turned to a more sympathetic ear. "Sister Mattie?"

The friendliest of her teachers shook her head. "A ladybug cannot change her spots."

Lady Linette sighed heavily. "Tomorrow night I'll have Professor Braithwope run over and—"

"Professor Braithwope! What good could he possibly do?" Sophronia was so frustrated that she interrupted.

Lady Linette was equally frustrated. "That is *enough*, young lady. To your chambers this instant, and if I see you outside of proper hours or classrooms at all in the next week, you risk being sent down permanently! Am I understood?"

"Yes, Lady Linette," said Sophronia.

CHARTING AN UNSTEADY COURSE

Sophronia's punishment was a course of such rigorous training and scullery duties that she could not find the time, let alone the energy, to check the bubble. Every free moment was spent assisting Sister Mattie to repot her prize begonias, or cleaning out every vial in Professor Lefoux's lab, or decanting deadly perfumes for Lady Linette. She was constantly under such focused instruction that she was practically escorted by each teacher from one lesson to the next.

While she labored under the consequences of lack of evidence—*Oh, why was the satchel empty?*—her friends concentrated on their lessons. As older students, they were encouraged to focus on their strengths. Agatha was showing affinity for Encrypting with Flower Arrangements with Sister Mattie, which surprised everyone, including Agatha. She was doing a special study on tussie-mussies and airborne poisons, creating stunning—in all ways—nosegays. Dimity focused on Millinery and Machinations. She would never admit to decorating her own hats, but there was something to be said for the concealment possibilities inherent in a well-endowed bonnet.

The only lesson they had together anymore was weaponry with Professor Braithwope and Professor Lefoux. In the old days this would have been Captain Niall's purview, but since the werewolf teacher had left to clean up a pack mess in Scotland, the school hadn't replaced him.

Today the class was working with crossbows, much to Sophronia's relief.

After her near miss on the goat path, she had gone from indifference to guns to outright dislike. She could not shake the memory of Felix lying bleeding from a gunshot wound, and later, Soap dying of one. Not to mention the fact that guns were loud and terribly hard on one's gloves.

Strangely, it was Preshea who put it best. "If I am going to kill someone, I should be more elegant about it. Guns seem sadly crass."

Dimity was the only one who actually liked the French-issue ebony-stock percussion muff-pistols that the school provided for student training. "They are easy to use. And all the mess is some distance away."

By which Dimity meant blood. Occasionally, she still fainted at the sight of it, but she had mainly gotten over the response after Soap went down. Now her inclination to faint was only overwhelming when blood spattered on her clothing. A sensation that Sophronia could almost understand. Dimity was developing a style that involved shooting her target and then instantly looking in a different direction. Professor Lefoux despaired of her.

For some reason, Sophronia did not feel bad about the crossbow. Possibly because it was a weapon most often applied to vampires. And while she had made her peace with the hive temporarily, she didn't trust them as far as she could throw them—not after they'd kidnapped Dimity. Truth be told, even with Sophronia's arm muscles, vampires could hurl her a great deal farther than Sophronia could hurl vampires. A great tragedy of life, no doubt.

The others noticed Bumbersnoot's absence but accepted Sophronia's excuse that he was with Vieve getting a special holiday overhaul. With extra Professor Lefoux classes, this was a relief. Sophronia spent a great deal of time making certain Bumbersnoot and Professor Lefoux never encountered one another. Even when Bumbersnoot was disguised as an unbelievably frilly reticule, Professor Lefoux was too gadget-savvy to see the sausage dog as anything but a mechanimal. Unregistered mechanimals were illegal, even groundside in regular society. Professor Lefoux would not be understanding in this matter.

With Bumbersnoot off ship, Sophronia no longer had to be constantly worried about what he might be up to. It was a relief knowing there was currently no way he could get into trouble. She wondered if that was a bit of how the teachers felt about her sometimes.

Professor Lefoux was giving them crossbow lessons on one of the midship decks. They were shooting at handkerchief targets, held in the claws of soldier mechanicals arrayed on the inside of the deck. This allowed the bolts to go through the material and embed themselves in the pitted wall behind.

"You ladies are developing into passably good shots." Professor Lefoux indulged in a rare moment of praise.

"We should be," muttered Preshea. "We've been at it for ages."

Preshea could hit the handkerchief well enough to knock it out of the soldier mechanical's grip, but not to pin it against the wall. Agatha missed one out of every four shots. Dimity struggled to get the bolt loaded but after that did fine.

"Everyone, see how Miss Buss holds her bow?" Professor Lefoux instructed. "But her stance, too angled. Square up, Miss Buss."

Agatha was staring off into space, fingering her Depraved Lens of Crispy Magnification.

Sophronia caught her at it and couldn't resist. "I suppose that could be considered a courting gift, from an evil genius."

Agatha dropped the lens as if it burned.

Professor Lefoux focused on them. "Miss Temminnick, if you would be so kind as to demonstrate the draw?"

Sophronia hefted her crossbow, loading the bolt and pulling back on the string. Then, without much thought, she raised her arm, pointed, and fired—hitting a dead-on bull's-eye through the handkerchief. This was a surprise to Sophronia. If she had known she would be that good, she might have purposefully failed. It seemed to be a surprise to the soldier mechanical as well, for it puffed out smoke from beneath its neck attachment in a little stutter of shock.

"There she goes," sniffed Preshea under her breath.

Professor Lefoux approved, as much as her personality would allow. "Adequate, Miss Temminnick. But consistency is also vital. I want both accuracy and precision. Do it again."

Sophronia loaded, pointed, and shot, casually, hoping she would miss but not willing to do it on purpose now that the teacher was watching her closely.

"Another bull's-eye. Have you been practicing extra hours, Miss Temminnick?"

Sophronia shook her head.

Professor Lefoux grunted. "I suppose natural talent happens. I will move you up to a more weighty draw."

Agatha dropped her bow with a clatter while Professor Lefoux was talking to Sophronia, then bent over to pick it up, spilling cleavage everywhere willy-nilly.

"Miss Woosmoss, act like a lady!" remonstrated the professor.

Agatha modified her bend into a crouch, stays creaking.

Professor Lefoux rummaged about in an immense carpet-bag with six little wheels affixed to its bottom, producing a teakettle-like object, an embroidery roll of wrenches, and a few other tools. Eventually, she found another crossbow, larger and heavier than the others. She handed it to Sophronia.

"Now, class, note how much stiffer the string is on this one? That will yield a more forceful bolt. This is more deadly and more accurate at distances. Go ahead, Miss Temminnick."

Sophronia gave it her best effort, but it was impossible to pull back the string. It snapped forward several times, nearly taking her fingertip with it. She finally managed it by bracing against the wall with her foot and using both arms. Shooting the higher-impact crossbow was fun—the bolt flew with satisfying force and fairly tore the handkerchief in half before hitting the wall behind with a loud thunk.

"Miss Temminnick, keep with that one. Now, class, after

sunset prepare for a co-lesson with Professor Braithwope, at which point we will use a moving target."

"What target?" Preshea looked wary.

Professor Lefoux looked at her as if the answer should be self-evident. "Professor Braithwope himself, of course. He'll hold up a large wood trencher. We'll use metal bolts so as not to do any permanent harm should you actually hit him."

Dimity trembled in agitation. "We have to shoot directly at a living target?"

"Not exactly living, but yes." Professor Lefoux was remarkably unperturbed.

Sophronia felt bound to object. "I, for one, should prefer not to shoot at someone I like."

"Admirable scruples, Miss Temminnick. Get over them, for you will do it anyway."

"Yes, Professor." Sophronia wanted to object further. Professor Braithwope wasn't in his right mind. It didn't feel sporting to shoot at a crazy person, even if that person was a vampire who'd agreed to the job. Then again, mental fragility might make him unpredictable and harder to hit. Still, Sophronia would hate to add crossbow injury to her long list of transgressions against a teacher who, in the end, was nothing more offensive than undead with excellent taste in clothing and a curiously unstable mustache.

"I suppose she'd know if it weren't a good idea." Agatha was obliquely referring to the fact that Professor Lefoux, as the vampire's drone, was responsible for his well-being. She *was* his food source.

They continued the crossbow lesson until sunset, at which

point they were allowed a short rest. It was one of those rare clear nights on the moor—a midwinter rain had washed the mist away. Soon the fog would be back. It was like table settings. The skies of Dartmoor were perpetually set for visitors, rarely bare of decoration.

The girls, tired from their physical exertions, leaned against the rails and watched the sun sink over the upland heath, gossiping quietly. There was some argument over an article in last week's popular papers, retrieved for analysis by the teachers in Swiffle-on-Exe. Gossip columns were a vital part of training, as one had to read between the lines not only to understand the way society worked but also to puzzle out aristocratic machinations, determine the bias in the press, and look for encoded missives within the back promotionals. An advertisement for muffs was getting a great deal of attention. A few girls were contemplating essays on the subject. Sophronia thought it was simply an advertisement, but others believed there was an embedded message concerning Scandinavian infiltration into northern Scotland. Something about the muffs' looking more like the hats favored by the Danish guard. Add to that the fact that the Scandinavians had been keeping an awful lot to themselves recently, and many were left wondering if they could be trusted. Pickled herring was, in the end, a hugely suspicious food.

Professor Braithwope joined them after sunset. He was dressed quite somberly, his dark burgundy cravat tied neatly in the waterfall style, his waistcoat, jacket, and trousers all charcoal gray. His eccentricity of mind sometimes reverberated in his attire, causing him to wear odd items like a stovepipe beaver hat or a satin cape, but he never wore them badly. He might have lost his mind, but never his fashion sense. Tonight, however, he looked more undertaker than vampire.

The girls were tentative about the assignment, but it became clear that Professor Braithwope, while batty enough to insist on dancing an Irish fling the entire time, still had all his reflexes in working order. It was impossible to shoot him. He either dodged or intercepted the dart with his wooden trencher.

"Do you see? Not so easy to kill a vampire, is it?" Professor Lefoux sounded smug.

Sophronia wondered if the vampire had noticed anything different about the pilot's bubble recently. She decided to try to converse with him. She hoped Professor Lefoux would see this as an attempted diversion tactic for getting in a shot.

"Professor Braithwope, have you seen anything interesting dancing 'round the school recently?"

"Condiments are scarce in the skies, whot." The vampire was serious on this subject.

"Not so much as you would think," Sophronia contradicted, wondering if he was aware enough to actually be referring to the Pickleman break-in. "Lost your mustard powder, have you?" She loaded in a bolt, taking her time.

"No, relish." The vampire twirled away. Preshea's shot went wide.

"Thought as much," said Sophronia.

The vampire's eyes focused on her. "Why would I have lost anything? Not all wandering mechanicals are lost. Besides, often you're left with a hold full of pets, whot." He said this as though offering a special tidbit of information.

Sophronia took it as such. "I'll keep that in mind, Professor."

"Sooner your mind than mine, little miss. Mine seems to be full of holes, like a tea strainer."

Professor Lefoux interrupted. "I don't think your tactic is working, Miss Temminnick. Take your shot or try something else."

"How about a variation on the fan and sprinkle?"

"For a vampire?" Professor Lefoux was skeptical, for that was a werewolf manipulation.

Sophronia produced a cream puff from within the confines of her pagoda sleeve. She broke it open to reveal the white filling. With her left hand she tossed this at the professor's immaculate trouser leg. Occupied as he was, fending off crossbow bolts, he did not expect an attack of low-flying stickiness.

With a cry of distress, he registered the smear of cream on his shiny shoe.

When he bent to examine the carnage, Sophronia shot.

She was still not fast enough.

He got the trencher up and caught her bolt at its center with one hand while his other was occupied extracting a handkerchief to repair the damage.

It was Sophronia's last bolt. But she followed her shot with a charge, whipping out her bladed fan into an arc of deadly metal, the leather guard off and fallen to the deck.

She had it in and against the vampire's neck before he could straighten upright.

He let her, surprised.

Professor Lefoux tutted. "Did I say other weapons were allowable? Besides, what good is that fan? It's not wood."

Sophronia snapped the fan closed and backed off. "I wanted to see if I could get that close."

Professor Braithwope gave her a funny look. Well, funnier than usual. "You know, pretty little miss, you could have simply offered me your *carnet de bal*. I would be delighted to dance with you."

"Oh, really, Sophronia, now you're in the way of everyone else," Professor Lefoux reprimanded her.

Sophronia turned to return to the line, but the vampire caught her hard about the waist and dragged her close.

Sophronia swallowed suddenly, frightened. Professor Braithwope's eyes, absent of intelligence, followed the movement of the muscles in her throat.

Why didn't I wear a high-necked gown?

"Sophronia." Professor Lefoux's voice was soft but firm. "Cover your neck and back away slowly."

Sophronia could wriggle enough to bring her fan up and flick it open in front of her bare throat, but the vampire's arm about her waist was like iron. She could not shift it, and she certainly could not back away.

"Don't you want to dance, little one?" Professor Braithwope's voice was a seductive rumble. His funny little mustache, always one to lead the charge, looked menacingly fluffy. It was like a cat with its back arched and its fur bristling. Below the bristle, Sophronia could see the points of fangs sticking out of his mouth.

"Your neck is very white," complimented the vampire.

"Thank you." Sophronia was pleased her voice didn't shake. "I've worked hard over the years with lemon and buttermilk under Mademoiselle Geraldine's guidance. I started out with freckles, you know?"

"I've always been fond of freckles." Professor Braithwope leaned in. "Little spots of delicious seasoning, whot."

Then Professor Lefoux was there, crowding in on them. She stuck her arm right in front of the vampire's face. She had nicked her wrist slightly, probably on a crossbow bolt.

The arm around Sophronia's waist slackened.

She spun out and dashed away, shaken.

Dimity hugged her with one arm. "You all right?"

Sophronia nodded.

Agatha's eyes were huge with concern and she patted Sophronia's shoulder in awkward sympathy.

Preshea muttered, "They ought not let him stay on board. He's not safe. This is a *school*, for goodness' sake!"

Sophronia jumped to the vampire's defense, surprising everyone. "You think the outside world is so very safe?"

"You say that, after nearly being bitten?" Preshea was shocked.

"It's happened before and it will happen again." Sophronia reached for calm. Part of the training. Only Dimity could feel her shiver.

They watched—crossbows slack at their sides, resting among the folds of wide skirts—as Professor Braithwope sucked at Professor Lefoux's wrist. It was oddly intimate and embarrassing and disgusting.

Sophronia looked away, busying herself by holstering her fan.

Dimity allowed herself to be shrugged off. "Sophronia?"

"I'm perfectly spiffy, thank you." Sophronia's voice was

steady, though her brain kept reliving her brush with fang. She forced herself to analyze the encounter as Lady Linette instructed. *After every unladylike action, there must be an equal and opposite reaction. Consider the necessary, analyze the consequences, clean up the mess.*

Sophronia thought about the vampire's movements and the strength in that arm encircling her waist. Professor Braithwope's reflexes were good enough for the crossbow, but they weren't what they once were. And he seemed only able to focus on one task at a time.

She moved away from the others, pretending to hunt for new bolts but really trying to control a sudden pang. Fear. Guilt. Grief. The vampire's condition was deteriorating. It wasn't only his self-control—it was his supernatural abilities as well. She had hoped a vampire could recover from tether snap. That if he stayed within his home territory of the airship, his tether would reestablish, and he would find his full wits once more. It seemed, instead, that he was getting worse. *How did I miss that until now? How much have the other teachers been working to hide his condition?*

She stared at Professor Lefoux, who was bandaging her wrist and leading the vampire away from the students. She looked tired and older than before.

Will he become even more dangerous? After all, werewolves went mad at full moon. What might happen to a vampire who was losing his mind? Preshea was correct, for even Geraldine's girls weren't equipped to deal with *that*. The debuts, for example, were at risk. She hoped the teachers were locking the vampire down after the students went to bed.

After his snack and a brief rest to digest, the vampire seemed able to continue the lesson. By the end of two hours the girls had sore arms and fingertips and were eager for supper. The incident seemed to have been largely forgotten as simply another one of Sophronia's pranks—except by Sophronia.

They changed and then had a half hour for contemplation. Sophronia spent it staring glumly out the porthole window. Agatha spent it in indecision over jewelry. Dimity read a novel of some woefully romantic persuasion.

Finally Sophronia shook off her mood. "How's the book?"

As much as she was enjoying it, Dimity would always rather talk about reading than actually read. In fact, Sophronia suspected she only read enough to have something to discuss. "Oh, it's *very good*. I've just got to the bit where the vampire has taken the heroine to his town house and we don't know if his intentions are honorable or dastardly."

Agatha gasped. She'd been getting an annotated commentary on said novel for the past week. "Oh, really? Does he want to suck her blood?"

"Far worse. He wants to give her a makeover." Dimity fiddled with the mother-of-pearl buttons up the front of her peach brocade dinner dress. She didn't want Agatha to see how excited she was to relay more.

Agatha squeaked in titillated horror. "A *full* makeover?"

Sophronia snorted. She thought the novel very silly.

They arrived back in Swiffle-on-Exe mid-December. As usual, they came in over the river, took on water in the wee hours, and circled back to rest near the goat path. Parents would send carriages for their girls the next morning. The young ladies were happily occupied well past bedtime, packing and giggling and exchanging gifts with friends before parting ways.

Winter holidays were the longest offered by Mademoiselle Geraldine's. The young ladies were let out earlier than most because they had so little contact with the outside world the rest of the year. One could not order in Christmas gifts when one was drifting idly over the moors. Shopping must be accounted for. So Mademoiselle Geraldine's girls had an early pickup well before Christmas. They returned shortly after, as Geraldine's girls traditionally spent New Year's together. Something about making certain the New Year came in deadly and stylish.

Sophronia left her fellows to the tribulation of fitting everything into hatboxes and portmanteaus. Dimity was trying to decide which of her sparkles to pack and which she might reliably expect to be replaced by the *real thing* this Christmas. Poor girl. She was doomed to disappointment. Her parents had made some improvement to the family's circumstances by selling the crystalline valve, but not enough to afford sapphires. And Dimity adored sapphires. And rubies. And emeralds. And... not diamonds.

"But they sparkle," Sophronia protested.

"They aren't colorful enough," Dimity explained. "All that white is so flashy, don't you feel?"

"Until this very moment, I didn't think you found *anything* flashy."

"Really, Sophronia, credit me with some taste!"

Agatha was mooning, purposeless, not bothering to pack. Much as she disliked school, it was better than home.

Sophronia, for her part, never wasted too much time preparing for travel. As Preshea said, it wasn't as if she had much to take with her. Instead, she drifted out of the door and into the hallway, unnoticed. It was after curfew, but Sophronia so rarely kept to legitimate hours that even her enemies didn't bother to rat her out. For all they knew, she was under orders from one of the teachers. There were even a few, Preshea included, who accused Sophronia of taking over Monique's duties as Professor Braithwope's second drone.

"That's why he went for her during crossbow training," Preshea explained to her new friend Frenetta.

Sophronia allowed the rumors. It was as good a front as any, that she would entertain vampire patronage. No one need know she had already struck a deal with the werewolves. She had bargained her freedom to the dewan for Soap's survival, and she considered it a fair deal. At least, right now she did. She had no idea what the dewan would want once he got her under his command. But in the end, wolves were better than vampires—or she hoped they were.

In the interim, if her late-night peregrinations were perceived by her fellow students as part of some bloody agreement, she was not one to gainsay gossip that stood her reputation in good stead. Especially not gossip that stopped others from interfering.

Vieve was waiting at their prescribed location behind the rosebushes, once again smelling strongly of cheap ale.

"You're going to get a reputation as a swill tub tosspot."

"Good." Vieve also liked to be underestimated because of a perceived reputation. She handed over Bumbersnoot.

He looked the same as ever, if perhaps a bit shinier and free of rust. He tooted smoke at Sophronia, his little tail tick-tocking back and forth in cheery greeting.

"How did the installation go?"

"Difficult to tell, as there is no way to test ahead of time. We have to wait for the Picklemen to make their move, and only then will we know if the crystalline valve–linked alarm trigger works. If they activate their command for all the mechanicals to do something, Bumbersnoot should squeal like an abused hand brake. But I'm only saying *should*."

"Not the best situation to be in. My life could depend on this alarm going off."

Vieve raised an eyebrow. "Could it? Well, I suggest you arrange things so that particular scenario doesn't occur."

"You have an overabundance of faith in my abilities."

"As you have in mine."

They shared a smile.

"Will I see you at the New Year's tea?" Sophronia wondered.

"Are we engaging in more interschool fraternization so soon?" Vieve was good at acting the part of absentminded boffin. They both knew she was perfectly well aware of the party.

"That's the gossip." Sophronia played along.

"I thought the teachers were at odds."

"That seems to be reason enough for another gathering."

"It's so much more fun for everyone if a school rivalry is committed close up and in fancy dress?" suggested the younger girl.

"Exactly," agreed Sophronia.

"Well, at least the food will be better. I tell you, Sophronia, if there's anything rotten about being a boy, it's the food. They expect us not to have any kind of discerning palate. The swill they give us to eat ought to be considered unlawful child endangerment." Vieve sounded particularly French in her disgruntlement.

"I'm sure it's nourishing to the noggin."

"One wishes the tongue were also under consideration. I do miss tea at Geraldine's." Vieve sighed. "Will this party have crumpets? I'd kill for a proper crumpet."

"I don't think you'll have to kill anyone, although you never know." It was best not to use that particular figure of speech around Geraldine's girls, Sophronia always thought. "Can't you invent a crumpet emitter or something?"

"Cooking gadgets never work properly." Vieve looked sad. "Try to kill someone or take over the world and boffins are all for it, but baking a cake is a more serious business. Must be left up to proper pastry chefs, I'm afraid. Cooks are always human, never mechanical. And Bunson's cooks are several puffs short of the pastry."

Sophronia nodded, adjusting Bumbersnoot to lie crosswise over her back, the better to climb. He tooted at her and shed a bit of ash down the side of her dress. "Bumbersnoot!" she reprimanded.

"Oh, yes," Vieve was unperturbed by this rude behavior. "I'm afraid he'll be doing that more frequently. Diminished storage capacity. I had to make room for the new valve. I did warn you the results could get messy."

"No, you didn't."

"I didn't? Well, you should take that as fact with anything you ask me to modify. My own inventions, from design to execution, are intended to be compact and elegant, but messing about with other people's inevitably has untidy consequences."

"Noted. Very well. I forgive you, Bumbersnoot." The metal creature looked neither chastised by the reprimand nor excited by the reprieve. In the end, sometimes he was simply a mechanical sausage dog.

Vieve said, "Before you go, could I give you a present for my aunt? I don't think we can arrange time to see one another secretly over the holidays. It's best if we don't remind people we are related. Gaspar Lefoux is supposed to be an *estranged* nephew."

She produced a massive box from the shadows of the rosebush. It was quite wide enough for several Bumbersnoots to fit inside.

"Um?" Sophronia hesitated. *How am I supposed to get around the ship carrying that?*

"I put on straps, see, here and here? You can wear it across your back like a lute. Bumbersnoot will dangle below."

Sophronia took it, glad that at least it didn't weigh much. "What on earth is it?"

With a wide grin, Vieve unstrapped the gift, which proved to be some kind of hatbox, and popped off the lid. Inside was, not unexpectedly, a hat.

Now, it ought to be pointed out, at this juncture, that the lighting wasn't good behind the Nib and Crinkle, among the rosebushes, near the goat path. The moon was not full. The fog was low. And yet there was no doubt about its appearance.

"Vieve, that is an inordinately ugly hat." Sophronia would call Professor Lefoux many things, and not a one of them was *leader of fashion*, but her taste certainly wasn't *that* bad.

Vieve seemed to know her own aunt less well than Sophronia. "Isn't it hideous? Do you think she'll like it?"

Sophronia quirked an eyebrow.

"Oh. Of course. Only see what it does." Vieve carefully removed the hat from its box. It was a massive sunshade style made of deep midnight-blue satin, instead of straw. The wide brim was sprinkled with small bits of glass, in a simulation of stars. Upon closer inspection, the sparkling dots were in the formation of several popular constellations. The very top of the hat's crown was painted yellow, obviously indicating the sun, with rays extending down over the side toward the brim. This alone would have made it one of the most curious hats that Sophronia had ever seen, but that was merely the foundation. Vieve had constructed a miniature winch device, like those employed by music boxes, dangling near one ear, that when wound up and released caused seven planets to orbit about the hat. These were on long wires of different lengths, anchored to rails at the brim, sticking up to revolve about in patterns simulating the solar system. Each planet was colored according to the latest scientific evidence: Venus being pale blue because of all the turquoise deposits, the Earth green for the lush landscapes, Jupiter orange for its iron-rich sands, and so forth. There was a dangling feather ball off the back on a particularly long wire—a comet? Stuck to the midnight blue were a few sporadic small puffs of down.

"What are those?"

Vieve glowed. "Recent pamphlets suggest there's a kind of cosmic mist, no name as yet, but I thought my aunt would appreciate the homage to modern astronomical theory."

Sophronia was impressed with the artistry and the execution, if not with the resulting style statement. Since Vieve's shining eyes clearly indicated an expectation of some form of praise, Sophronia said the nicest thing she could think of without lying. "It's very well made."

"Do you think my aunt will like it?"

"Does she have anything to go with it?" Sophronia was cautious.

Vieve laughed. "Crikey, no. I do know something about fashionable headgear. No, no. I don't expect her to *wear* the wretched thing! It's a bit of a family joke."

Sophronia relaxed. "Oh, well, in that case, I think it's wonderful."

Vieve's dimples became more pronounced. She resettled the solar hat into its box and took great pains when strapping it to Sophronia's back.

"Well, my dear Vieve, amazing work as always. Someday you must allow me to repay you for all you've done."

"Sophronia, *ma mie*, I'm counting on it." The girl doffed her hat and strode back toward Bunson's, hands thrust deep into her pockets, whistling an off-key tune under her breath.

SISTERS AND THEIR CONSEQUENCES

W hat will I do if they've forgotten about me?" Sophronia, Dimity, and Agatha were inside the main
teahouse in Swiffle-on-Exe, waiting for retrieval over
pudding. Pickups took most of the day, and the school
had long since disappeared.

"Enjoy the blessed freedom of a Christmas without family?"
suggested Agatha.

"I don't know about that. Some of them aren't all *that* bad.
I quite like Ephraim's wife." Having not seen them in a while,
Sophronia was disposed to be magnanimous about her siblings.

"You could come back with me," suggested Dimity.

"Your parents wouldn't mind?" Sophronia brightened at
the idea. Someone else's family holiday traditions are always so
much more exciting than one's own.

"Hardly. They know a little about you rescuing Pill and me
from the hive. They're more likely to be embarrassingly gra-

cious. There might even have been some correspondence between our mothers on your brilliance and the excellent nature of our friendship."

"Goodness, your mother didn't say anything to mine about our *real* education, did she?"

"Certainly not. She'd never reveal Mademoiselle Geraldine's secrets. Mamma takes subterfuge seriously."

Sophronia relaxed. "Good. And they know to pick you up here?"

"Standard practice, since Geraldine's always has an early holiday let-out."

"What about your brother?" asked Agatha, trying to seem disinterested.

"Unspeakable worm. What about him?"

"Is he meeting here as well?"

"No. Bunson's isn't out for another week. Mummy always grumbles about having to arrange travel twice. Although not this time, thanks to you." Dimity flung a companionable arm around Agatha's shoulders. Agatha hid a grin at the affection by nibbling pudding.

Since her home was only slightly off the route to London, Dimity was to ride with Agatha. Agatha liked the companionship, and Dimity no longer enjoyed trains. Soap crashing a locomotive into a dirigible and subsequent events had given her train-related nightmares.

The girls were in the window seat of the teahouse, which had an excellent view of the meeting square. Agatha's near-limitless expense account was always good for the best seat at any watering hole. They watched their fellow students being retrieved and gossiped about each. Unfortunately, the pudding was alcoholic enough to appeal only to Bumbersnoot, who always showed interest in things that could catch on fire. The little dog sat on the bench next to Sophronia, under cover of the pouf of her traveling gown's teal skirts, and ate whatever she fed him with gusto.

All speculation proved moot at that point, for a carriage pulled up intended for Sophronia. Of course they did not know this until the owner of said carriage emerged.

Her sister looked slightly stouter, but otherwise unchanged. As Petunia stepped down, no one could doubt she was related to Sophronia—same oval face and muddy green eyes. Petunia's hair was a shade darker and her cheeks rounder, both tinted slightly red by art and science. Her curls were set by a French maid, while Sophronia's were the product of Dimity and madly wielded hair-rags. But the sisters shared the same straight nose and firm mouth, and were of a height.

Sophronia exchanged startled looks with her friends. "Well, I never!"

She immediately gathered up Bumbersnoot, for it would not do to keep *Petunia* waiting. She collected her luggage from the cloakroom, leaving Agatha and Dimity to see to the last of the tea.

Petunia stood looking around at the quaint town with ill-disguised hauteur. Her traveling dress, fur muff, well-trimmed bonnet, and velvet gloves screamed *London*.

"Petunia? I say, this is a surprise." Sophronia plopped down her carpetbag to give her sister a polite peck on the cheek.

"Sophronia, still carting around that horrid Italian dog reticule, I see." Petunia's hat had ostrich *and* peacock feathers—for travel! Even more shocking—her sister was actually smiling.

"It has sentimental value. But Petunia, what on earth are you doing here?"

"You may well ask. Middle of nowhere. I understand why Mumsy sent you to finishing school, really I do, but why not France or Switzerland? Why Devon?"

"Expense, I suppose."

Petunia shook her curls and tut-tutted at open mention of pecuniary matters, even among sisters. She had married well and after only one season. It was a match so advantageous, she herself could hardly believe it. True, Mr. Hisselpenny wasn't as blue-blooded as Petunia would have liked, but he was well set up in town. From what Sophronia could gather, Petunia had proceeded to spend most of her husband's fortune attempting to break into the upper crust, with limited success. Her doting husband catered to her every whim, including, evidently, a coach and four.

"It has done you good, I will say that." Petunia issued a rare compliment, looking Sophronia over with an eye to her appearance and posture, as if Petunia were decades her senior.

"Thank you very kindly." Sophronia resisted the urge to bristle. Petunia was one of those who responded better to cordial than to barley water. "I do value your good opinion, sister."

Petunia looked smug. "Is that all you have?"

Sophronia's baggage included only one valise and two hatboxes. And Bumbersnoot, of course. "Afraid so. Mumsy doesn't send me many dresses anymore. Since you married, there have been none to hand down. Everything I have is worn and not worth packing."

Petunia's eyes lit up. "Exactly what I suspected! This is why I volunteered to collect you. You are, after all, soon to come out, and as I am now residing in town, I decided to see you properly outfitted. And I know you would like to do your Christmas shopping in London, for once."

Ah-ha, thought Sophronia. *Having spent as much as she dared on herself, and becoming bored with society, Petunia wants me for her new entertainment.* Sophronia grimaced at being thought a doll, but she could not deny a thrill of excitement. Who didn't want to go to London for the shopping? Of course, her eagerness had nothing, whatsoever, to do with the fact that Soap was currently living in London. *Nothing at all.*

Petunia took Sophronia's thoughtful silence as dissent. "You don't want to? Oh, why must you be such a bore?"

Where, in the past, Sophronia would have snarled in response, instead she applied praise. "Of course not, sister dear. It's a delightful notion. And so kind of you to concoct it. I'm a little surprised, that is all. But I'm certainly not one to look a gift London in the mouth." *Even if it comes packaged with a meddling sister.* Sophronia and Petunia had never been close, but Petunia appreciated the airs and graces finishing school had given her, and Sophronia was willing to put those airs and graces to the test in tolerating Petunia.

Petunia grinned—actually grinned!—and even blushed a little. "Well, no need to babble on. There's more for you still to come."

"Indeed?"

Agatha and Dimity trotted up at that juncture.

Petunia turned to them. "Which one of you is Miss Woosmoss?"

Agatha curtsied politely. "Pleased to make your acquaintance, Mrs. Hisselpenny."

"Ah, yes. Well, my husband and your father are business associates, and as I was coming down to collect Sophronia, he suggested I bring you and your little companion—Dimity, is it?—along. We shall make a merry party of it all the way to London."

Agatha and Dimity made delighted noises, and Petunia glowed at being thought the magnanimous benefactress. *How is it I never knew that all she wanted was to be a gracious hostess?* Sophronia was curious as to whether these were changes in her sister, or in her own perception of her sister. But Petunia did seem to genuinely enjoy herself—ordering about the coachman and ensuring the safety of the luggage as it was lifted up top.

"Now, who prefers facing? Miss Woosmoss?" Petunia had obviously been instructed by her husband to be particularly *nice* to Agatha. However, none of Geraldine's girls were so foolish as to antagonize without purpose. If Petunia wanted to make a fuss over Agatha, they were happy to let her.

"Why, Mrs. Hisselpenny, what a lovely carriage. So well padded." It was only adults and boys who threw Agatha off. Petunia, Agatha could manage.

"Did you notice the foot warmers? My dear Mr. Hisselpenny is too good to me," gushed Petunia.

Dimity hopped in next. "Lovely."

"Thank you." Petunia had not yet grown so accustomed to luxury that it failed to improve her goodwill, particularly when seated in the lap of it.

It was an uneventful journey. Sophronia stuck to a policy of saying the third nice thing that came into her head, rather than the first snappish one. Agatha was pleasantly warmhearted, as only Agatha could be in the face of abject frivolity. And Dimity and Petunia filled up the space in between with chatter so unending as to make them fast friends by the end of an hour, and bosom companions in the most superficial way by the end of the first day's drive.

Petunia's new magnanimous nature saw them set up in the best suite of rooms at the inn and dining in rustic splendor on mock turtle soup, roast sirloin of beef with horseradish, Brussels sprouts, cabinet pudding, and Stilton cheese with celery and pulled bread.

Petunia seemed inclined to eat mainly her vegetables, turning quite green at the smell of the Stilton. This surprised Sophronia into asking if her husband belonged to a religious sect to which Petunia had converted. Why else give up cheese?

"Dear me, no." Petunia lowered her voice, even though they had a private dining room. "I am increasing."

That, of course, caused much squealing. For although unmarried ladies were not to know of such things, Geraldine's girls had some training from Sister Mattie on the subject of preventative measures. After all, children were very incommodious when practicing espionage. This, Sophronia realized, opened up the perfect topic of conversation for the remainder of their journey to London. Because, of course, it had been decided that both Agatha and Dimity must, simply *must*, also come to town. Well, Agatha lived there, but Dimity *must* stay with Sophronia and the Hisselpennys. For they *must* all shop together.

Dimity sent a letter to her parents from the inn, convinced that they would welcome the opportunity to punt her off to London. Sophronia made certain to confirm this in private.

"They're in the middle of a new invention. Plus, they never know what to do when only one of us is home. When it's me and Pillover, they insist we can entertain each other. Sometimes I think that's why they had two of us. Poor Pillover—as a baby it meant a lot of dress-up. Thank goodness I was older. Can you imagine what he might have done to me, if I were the younger? Doesn't bear contemplating."

"Capital. I really am looking forward to it. And Petunia doesn't realize we've been learning more than simply etiquette." Sophronia gave her best evil smile.

Dimity giggled. "Which speaks well of either your talent or her willingness to be deceived."

"Is that a compliment?"

Agatha shook her red curls. "You should take it as one, Sophronia. Remember what Lady Linette says about compliments?"

"They are better than jewelry when hung about a girl."

Dimity was suspicious. "Which I've never quite believed, but if it's what you've got, take it."

Petunia's house was lovely, if not as grand as Agatha's. It boasted two mechanicals, buttlinger and clangermaid, as well as a man-of-all-work and a cook. Dimity and Sophronia had to share a room, because the other was being converted to a nursery, but they had done so before and enjoyed the return to form.

Petunia was inconvenienced most mornings and occasionally of an evening, which was enough separation for Sophronia to find her society bearable. The rest of the time Petunia was vested in paying calls and shopping as much as possible before her condition became apparent and she was forced into confinement.

Sophronia left Bumbersnoot behind on most jaunts because of her sister's evident dislike of the unfashionable accessory. No doubt he spent his time hunting stray bits of string and the occasional dust bunny, depositing in his turn small piles of ash in one corner of the room. Luckily for Sophronia, who had to clean it up, he always chose the same corner.

Dimity was so enamored of the shops they visited that Petunia turned an increasingly fond eye to her. Sophronia would never have thought her friend and her sister could grow close, but already Dimity had a standing invitation to return for another visit, with or without Sophronia.

"Would you look at those gloves? Have you ever seen anything so pretty? And the leather, it's like butter." Dimity was in ecstasies.

"Oh my, yes, Miss Plumleigh-Teignmott, they are indeed *divine*. Do you think they could be made up to match Sophronia's new walking dress? Oh, Mr. Pilldorff? Mr. Pilldorff, these exquisite little gloves, in mauve, do you think?"

Sophronia nipped in to throw a spanner in the works simply

because she could. "Did you see the lace ones, sister dear? Did you ever imagine such a thing as *lace* gloves?"

Petunia's head snapped up, not unlike that of an excited squirrel. "Lace? Did you say *lace* gloves? Surely, you jest, sister."

Sophronia rarely jested without purpose. She pointed mutely.

Petunia and Dimity scuttled off to the other display, followed by the obsequious Mr. Pilldorff.

Agatha sidled up to Sophronia. "What are you up to?"

Sophronia wasn't interested in gloves. In her line of work, their detrimental effect on dexterity left her mainly engaged in constant removal of said accessory. Although the reinforced leather tradesman style were invaluable for climbing ropes. "Causing a ruckus for my own amusement."

"They hardly need your assistance."

"True. My poor brother-in-law. Although he doesn't seem to mind much."

Sophronia, after a few days' confined acquaintance, was growing to like Mr. Hisselpenny. He was a gentleman of middling years with an ungentlemanly interest in investment banking and an unreasonable urge to spend most of his capital on his silly wife. Petunia could not have designed herself a more amiable husband. One could easily overlook the bushy eyebrows. Theirs was a match made in consumerism and pecuniary advancement. He liked the pecuniary aspect, and Petunia liked to consume.

Sophronia and Agatha drifted to the back of the shop.

"You're doing well out of it." Agatha gestured to the stack of packages they'd acquired on this one trip alone.

"I do need new things." Petunia had decent taste, and they had the same coloring, so Sophronia was tolerably confident in her selections. Occasionally, she voiced a preference for extra pockets or a stronger belt, practical choices that Petunia took into account, thank goodness, because the rest of the time Sophronia let her decide. As a result, their sisterly relationship had only improved. "I'm not complaining, even if it is all in pursuit of an advantageously blue-blooded match."

Agatha smiled. "She married for money, so she thinks you should marry for rank?"

"She saw me with Lord Mersey. For herself she wanted a husband who dotes, but for me...? I think she believes her new money plus my training at a finishing school can advance us both socially. Which sets up her progeny for improvement by association. That is, if she does not spend all her husband's funds on gloves first."

Agatha was somewhat upset by this assessment. "I believe she actually enjoys spending time with you."

Sophronia was startled. "You think that likely?"

Agatha looked almost pitying. "Must everyone have an ulterior motive, even your family? What has Mademoiselle Geraldine's done to you?"

For the first time Sophronia worried that her training— the first thing she had ever really been good at—was turning her hard. Was it negatively coloring her view of the world? It was protecting her, of course, but at what cost? And here was Agatha—whose father pushed her and whose mother was absent in all ways but death—noticing.

Sophronia turned to her quiet little friend. "I don't mean to be harsh."

"No, you don't. That's what worries me."

A glad cry from Mr. Pilldorff at the front of the shop distracted everyone. Petunia and Dimity, plus the other shoppers, moved in his direction. He had a new delivery from Paris. Even Agatha was tempted. Or perhaps she wanted to give Sophronia time alone to think. Agatha could be thoughtful like that.

The distraction was, of course, something Sophronia found suspicious. Instead of gravitating toward the yelling, she looked around the shop—was someone trying to steal something? Perhaps Agatha was right and she saw conspiracies everywhere, but this was her training, and she couldn't shake it.

A tall young man materialized out of the workroom at the back of the shop. He brushed aside the curtain as if he had been there, milling hats, all this time. He was dressed elegantly in a cutaway jacket, buckskin breeches, and a modest top hat, with a single fall of emerald silk at his throat. Not quite a dandy, but certainly a man of fashion. He would have been nondescript, any one of a hundred gentlemen shopping on Bond Street, except that his skin was a dark mahogany color unheard of in society.

Sophronia almost didn't recognize him. Not because of time, for it had been only nine months, but because of the clothing and the way he moved. Before, he had been gangly, muscled and strong, but suffused with the awkwardness of nascent adulthood. Now his movements were liquid and his pace predatory, not all that surprising considering he was a werewolf.

"I didn't know the sun had set," said Sophronia.

"You've been here for ages. I was waiting for you to come out, but began to suspect you never would."

"Is that your doing?" Sophronia gestured to the chaos at the front of the shop.

"Of course."

"Beautiful work."

The pause was awkward, full of unsaid truths and impossible actions. Sophronia's brain swirled with options: apologies, confessions, caresses—so many possibilities that she froze with indecision. She had a wild desire to throw herself against him in a manner that would give her sister—and possibly Mr. Pilldorff—histrionics. Instead, her back snapped straight, inspired by thousands of lessons in posture. She held her hands stiff to her sides.

Finally he spoke. "You smell like lemon and roses."

Impressive. Her bottle of tincture was with her, of course, but tightly shut. "It's so good to see you again, Soap."

"I might better have believed that if you'd come to call when you first entered London."

"Be reasonable. I'm staying with my sister."

"*Reasonable* would remember you are trained in the art of subterfuge. How challenging is it for you, of all people, to sneak out of a town house?"

"Touché."

"So? It is Lord Mersey after all?"

"Felix? Don't speak gammon. His father is a Pickleman." Surprise shook Sophronia out of her stillness. She looked directly into Soap's eyes. His face hadn't changed much, though he clenched his jaw more.

"His father always *was* a Pickleman."

"Yes, but once I thought he might rise above that. Now I know he can't." *Why are we talking about Felix?*

"Because he betrayed you on the tracks?"

"Because he betrayed all of us, and you were killed because of it." Sophronia allowed a little of her frustration to leak into her words. *Why is he simply standing there?*

"Oh, I *remember* that part." Soap moved finally, so that they stood shoulder-to-shoulder, like spectators, watching Mr. Pilldorff and the ladies unpack and exclaim over the box of goodies. The ladies vied with one another to try on scarves, to compliment each other on such exquisite taste. Dimity and Agatha might have noticed Sophronia's visitor, for they seemed intent on keeping Petunia occupied.

"So, why haven't you come to see me, then?" Soap spoke in one breath.

He sounds . . . what? Frightened? "I didn't know if I would be welcome." Sophronia didn't care for artifice with Soap. She never had. He was the only one granted the privilege of complete honesty. *I wonder if he realizes that.*

"You bargained your freedom for my life. I can't"—Soap paused, almost choking on his words—"I can't *ever* repay that."

"You see? There it is. I don't want debts owed between us." She shifted infinitesimally closer to him and put two fingers very gently on his forearm where it curled at his waist.

He looked down at her touch, then quickly up again. "Then what do you want between us?"

"Friendship would be a start."

"No, miss, friendship would be a finish."

CRISIS 6

AN INVITATION TO DINE IN OR ON?

S oap's tone of voice was no longer servile, but colored with the attitude of an equal. He was now an immortal, and he had the superiority of time on his side. True, he would have to fight for that privilege against other werewolves. Much as he had to fight against madness for his soul every full moon. Sophronia supposed that would change anyone, even a former coal scuttler. With one bite, Soap had gone from sootie to supernatural. Where once skin and station had held him back, wolfskin and loner station had made him her equal in rank in the eyes of the law—if not society.

He wasn't going to dance to her whims anymore.

Perhaps that's really why I stayed away. So much has changed between us. Am I afraid that I am no longer the one in control? Bitter with herself, Sophronia lied. "I'm not afraid of you."

He moved then, supernaturally fast, one second the prescribed distance for renewing an old acquaintance, the next plastered up against her in an intimacy that would be permitted to no one in public—not husband, not brother, not child.

"Soap! What are you—?"

He slipped one hand about her waist and whirled them, as if in a waltz, behind the curtain and into the workroom. Sophronia's feet never touched the ground. Soap had always been strong, but now she was nothing to him—biscuit light.

Before she could get her bearings, his other hand reached up to touch the side of her face, a peculiarly Soap-ish gesture. She fixated on the fact that he hadn't lost the calluses on his fingers. They had come with him into eternity. He was marked forever by a menial upbringing.

She loved those calluses.

Unthinking, Sophronia turned her face into his hand. Then she remembered how off this all was. How impossible. She moved as Captain Niall had taught her, a dip and twist, using leverage rather than strength to break his grip. It worked, but only because he was surprised.

"It's not only lemon and rose. You smell delicious."

Werewolf ability. *Am I food?* Sophronia wondered.

She felt Soap lean in close enough for his breath to muss her curls, the ones skillfully arranged by Petunia's French maid to fall over one ear.

"No more friendship, Sophronia. That boiler is dry."

"What, then? We can't be more." Her voice almost hitched, and she forced it to steady. "There's no future for us." They could never marry, not even if the dewan blessed the match and permitted Soap to come out into supernatural society. Right now his metamorphosis was closeted. The dewan kept his cards close, and a new werewolf was an ace in the hole. *Or is that ace in the closet? I'm getting my metaphors mixed up.* She wasn't sure on his reasons.

Sophronia blamed her distracted thoughts on the persistent heart flutters that Soap's proximity caused. Or was it excitement from their verbal sparring? Must be that.

"I can hear them, you know."

"My thoughts?" Sophronia panicked, suspecting unreported werewolf abilities.

"No, silly, your heartbeats. Gives me hope."

"I didn't think they were that loud."

Soap tilted his head at her. "Supernatural hearing, remember? At first it was so strange. I had no idea there were so many small sounds all the time, everywhere. It took me months to function in the outside world and hear only what was important. And that's not the half of it. Now I understand why new pups need an Alpha to guide them."

His speech patterns were so refined. *Part of his werewolf training?* Sophronia wondered.

He drifted his hand over her cheek, sure but slow, as if gentling a horse. His old familiar grin lit up his face.

"Soap, this is most unseemly."

The hand dropped.

"And you could kill me in a thousand different ways if you wanted to."

"Not anymore."

"Lost your ability?" Soap could not believe that.

"Mostly trained for humans, remember? You're a werewolf.

I've only got about three ways to kill you in my repertoire. They're good ones, though, so take care."

He tugged her in so she was flush against him again. He was warm, which surprised her. She had thought an undead creature would be cold.

"So I can court you?"

"What did I *just* say?" Sophronia was terrified by the inevitable end of any romance between them. Her parents were not so progressive as to permit their daughter an alliance with a werewolf, even a landed Alpha, let alone one who was lowborn, newly made, and black. Safer not to start. Then she might get to keep a small part of him.

Soap was not so easy to put off. "Blast the future."

"So says he who has too much of one."

"And whose fault is that?"

Sophronia winced. Her shoulders sagged.

Soap clearly regretted this accusation. "I don't blame you."

Which was part of the problem. *You should. My plan put you in danger. Then I took all your choices away from you because I was too much of a coward to let you go. And now everything is confusing and messy and impossible.*

"I know." Sophronia turned to leave.

"I'm going to change your mind about us, Sophronia." Unusual statement, for Soap never said her name, and he now had twice. Things really had changed.

Sophronia shot back, tartly, "I'd like to see you try."

"Done."

Annoyed that her addlepated heart had allowed her mouth

to give him an opening, she snapped, "What do you want, Soap?"

"Now, why would you think I wanted something more than this?" He grabbed her hand and raised it to kiss. Even through her gloves, she swore she could feel the softness of his lips.

She gave him a long-suffering look.

Soap let her go, tipped off his top hat, and dug about in the inside band, producing an embossed card. He flourished it. "He would very much like to see you. Saturday evening."

It was an invitation to attend a dinner party and theatrical production. Sophronia glanced at it quickly before tucking it down the side of her décolletage. "I'm not out yet. It may be difficult to convince Petunia."

"I think she'll make an exception in this case. The invitation is directed at you and your chosen guests. If your sister wishes to attend, she cannot come without you."

"Will you be there?"

Soap's smile was somewhat sly, with a hint of canine to the sides. "I, too, am not yet *out*."

Sophronia nibbled her lower lip. Steeling herself. "Soap, I think we should establish a safe place to meet. If for any reason either of us goes missing. If our communication is compromised."

"Are you planning on disappearing?"

"No, but I like to keep my options open. You are the only real friend I have stationed in London."

"You are *such* an intelligencer." Soap sounded almost exasperated. "Very well. Regent Square, an hour before dawn." His dark eyes flicked once behind Sophronia's shoulder at the curtain, and then he was gone, out a window at the back. Supernatural speed put to secrecy was impressive.

Sophronia grimaced. He had asked to court her, but hadn't kissed her properly. She wasn't sure if she should be upset or grateful for the reprieve. She hated herself for the confusion.

She emerged from the back room just as Petunia went to stick her head inside.

Agatha and Dimity trailed behind, looking worried.

"Oomph! There you are, sister, what are you doing back here?"

Sophronia gestured at a table covered in trim. "I thought I saw a finished hat that wasn't on display."

"Did you? Where?"

"Turns out it wasn't finished. What was in the box from Paris?"

"Oh, the most divine shawls! Come see." Petunia swept toward the front of the shop.

Agatha and Dimity swirled alongside Sophronia, one to each arm, and hustled after. Three abreast was challenging given the displays, but necessary for private conversation.

"What is going on?" Dimity demanded.

"Soap," replied Sophronia.

"I was wondering when he'd turn up." Dimity's tone was cautious. "What did he want?"

"We have an invitation to dine and view a short play."

Dimity bounced, clapping her hands. "Oh, goody, who with?" Her face fell. "Not with Soap? That would be awkward." She brightened. "The dewan?"

"That would be boring and political." Agatha was thinking about the dewan's position in Queen Victoria's government.

"No, not the dewan." Sophronia did enjoy torturing her friends.

"Who, then? Don't keep us in suspense!" Dimity's eyes were wild.

"Lord Akeldama."

"The vampire? Oh, dear." Dimity was crestfallen. "You don't think he wants to eat *us*, do you?"

Sophronia managed to *discover* the invitation waiting for them in the hallway when they got home. She presented it to her sister. It was met with paroxysms of joy. This was the kind of event Petunia had craved since first entering society. This was the dinner party to end all dinner parties. The fact that there was a slim chance they might *be* the dinner at said party was a small price to pay for the honor of being invited.

"Oh, this is *too* exciting. This Saturday, it says. Hardly enough time. We must go out first thing tomorrow in pursuit of dresses. Oh, dear, we will have to settle for something ready-made."

Sophronia was feeling cheeky. "But sister dear, we aren't yet out. Do you think it wise to expose yourself to ridicule and us to social *faux pas*?"

"At a small private gathering with such an illustrious host? I think we can make an exception. You must trust in my judgment. After all, I have spent these last few days in your company. You are all well polished. That school of yours has much to recommend it."

"You don't know the half," muttered Sophronia.

Petunia talked over her. "Perhaps I shall send my daughters there." She patted her tummy smugly.

Dimity didn't even crack a smile. "How thoughtful. I shall tell Mademoiselle Geraldine. She will be charmed, I'm sure."

Petunia patted Dimity's hand in a condescending way. "Oh, but why did I think we would have more need of visiting gowns than evening wear? We have wasted two shopping days already. Miss Woosmoss, of course, I know you are well set up. And Miss Plumleigh-Teignmott?"

"I brought my best from last season. It'll do."

Petunia shook her head, forehead creased. "For anyone but Lord Akeldama. He is a *leader* of fashion. The Beau Brummel of our times, and many times in the past, before Mr. Brummel, for that matter. Oh, dear, I am all aflutter. Sophronia, do you have anything appropriate at all?"

Sophronia shook her head. "Could I borrow something of yours, perhaps?"

"Now, there *is* a notion. I might have something from my trousseau. How lucky that we are the same height and complexion."

Petunia sashayed off and returned with a pretty satin dress, simpler than expected given her taste. Sophronia liked it instantly. It was pale blue brocade with royal-blue flowers appliquéd on top and matching ribbon for trim. Copious quantities of some quality cream lace peeked out at the cuffs, enough to hide both obstructor and hurlie should she wear them. Her favorite part was the neckline, a deep but narrow V with lace collar. In a world peopled with scoop necklines, it was unique and flattering. It would make her appear tall and elegant.

"I adore it!"

Everyone stopped and stared at her. It wasn't like Sophronia to go into ecstasies over a dress.

"Are you feeling quite well?" Dimity hissed.

Sophronia was eager for distraction. *Perhaps a bit too eager.* It might have had something to do with Soap. She gave her friend the hand signal of *discretion*.

Dimity subsided.

"You're sure? We could try shopping tomorrow morning?" Petunia was not one to be waylaid where spending money was possible.

"I'd only want to find one exactly like this."

Petunia pinked with delight. "Very well, then. You may have it. By the time it fits me again, it will be sadly out of date."

"Oh, thank you." Sophronia actually hugged her sister.

Petunia allowed it and then brushed her away. "Really, Sophronia, I'm not accustomed to such emotional displays. It's quite exhausting. Now I must nap. Off with you three, go try things on. I know you want to more than anything. See about accessories."

The girls did as instructed. Although it must be admitted they spent some time also discussing how to hide deadly little knives in their hair, whether Sophronia's favorite *carnet de bal* garrote was too much at a dinner party, and if Bumbersnoot could be decorated to match the dress. They did not talk of Soap, although Sophronia could tell Dimity dearly wanted to.

The blue gown turned out to be exactly the correct choice. For while Lord Akeldama was a vampire who pursued excess in all things himself, he appreciated refinement in others. Although he appeared welcoming as he ushered them into his well-appointed home near Regent's Park, his eyes were critical. The vampire uttered not one negative word, but Dimity suddenly knew herself to be wearing too much jewelry. Petunia realized that her condition was no secret to the discerning eye. And Agatha, poor Agatha, was convinced she was a failure in all things fashionable, although her dress was *à la mode* and her hair had taken *three* hours.

Sophronia's subtle gown and understated pearls, however, met with approval. The ghost of a smile twitched at Lord Akeldama's perfectly pouty lips as he evaluated her attire.

"How lovely to see such beautiful *butterflies*. My, but I do adore groups of ladies. They always balance out my table so very *decorously*. I blush to admit it, but my assemblies are too often weighted in the gentlemanly direction. Speaking of which, drones! Oh, where are my drones? You butterflies simply must have *matched* escort flowers."

Lord Akeldama was dressed in emerald satin with a cream-and-gold striped waistcoat, and a cream silk cravat tied over with an emerald ribbon. He wore a gold-and-emerald tie pin that gave Dimity a small case of the vapors.

"Now, that," she whispered to Sophronia, "is most certainly *not* paste!"

At Lord Akeldama's summons, a group of stunning young men trooped down the stairs from their private chambers above. They were all dressed as impeccably as their master, if perhaps not quite so flash. Sophronia felt a pang of loss at having been forced to turn down Lord Akeldama's offer of patronage. *Only think, at one time I might have lived among all this beauty.* The drones stood, untroubled, as the vampire evaluated them carefully and then paired each with one of the young women—based on color, of course.

Sophronia privately suspected that character was also taken into account. Lord Akeldama was shallow—or he liked to be thought that way—but not so shallow as to sacrifice conversational flow on the altar of fashion. Not for an entire evening, at least.

"Mrs. Hisselpenny, such a lovely rose pink, you would go well with Peanut here." Peanut proved to be tall, with a shock of thick caramel-colored hair and a long, friendly face. He wore apple green, which paired with Petunia's pink to look very like a rosebush.

"Miss Plumleigh-Teignmott, such sparkles go well with Bolo. Good evening, Bolo, *my pearl*." Dimity was in a froth of layered cream muslin, demure except that the sleeves were transparent and the hem had a band of lavender embroidery. Of course, she was also wearing a great deal of—supposedly—amethyst jewelry. Bolo, a shorter, stouter individual with an angelic round face and the most stunning dark eyes, wore black velvet and gray and no jewelry at all, not even a pin.

"You are the *moon* to his night sky." Lord Akeldama ushered them off together.

Sophronia swallowed down a smile.

"Now, for Miss Woosmoss, perhaps Dingle?" Dingle stepped forward. If being matched with Agatha was an insult, his expression showed nothing but pleasure at her company. He was blond with blue eyes, his evening suit of chocolate brown.

Sophronia had to admit that if anything were to go with Agatha's unfortunate ruffled orange gown, that was it. Together they looked like a pumpkin patch.

While the others were led away, the vampire turned on Sophronia. "Which leaves you, my *dearest kitten*."

"Lord Akeldama, it is such a pleasure to see you again." Sophronia attempted to retain some of the conversational territory, which the vampire, in a remarkable imitation of a military invasion, had taken into his possession from the moment they pulled the bell rope.

He smiled, showing fang.

Sophronia took it like a girl who had been educated by a vampire. She gave him her best wolfish grin back, showing all her teeth and making certain it did not reach her eyes.

"Like that, is it? More *lioness* than kitten now." Lord Akeldama inclined his head.

He had given her an opening. "So unexpectedly kind of you to extend an invitation to three lowly schoolgirls."

"'Twas all for you, *my little posy* of teeth."

"You may find I also have claws."

The vampire laughed and extended her his arm to lead her in himself—quite the honor. "I shall take the risk, *my vicious pet.* I find you *terribly* intriguing." He waved away the rest of his drones and they vanished about other tasks.

"You find me intriguing? I should have thought that impulse passed by now, my lord."

"Now, now, no one, *kitten*, has ever called me *impulsive*. Many things, but *never* that. Time has so little meaning for me, I can afford to take it slowly. Carefully research any *subject of interest.*"

Sophronia wasn't certain how she felt about being a *subject of interest*, but she wished to make her situation clear—for everyone's safety. "My lord, you did receive my letter?"

Lord Akeldama allowed his face to fall. "Crushed, my *dearest moggie*. It's not often I offer for a female drone, you do realize?"

"I am aware of the honor. Circumstances, my lord, forced another choice upon me."

Lord Akeldama's perfect forehead crinkled. "*Coercion?* My dear, I do not like to hear that *at all*."

Sophronia hastened to prevent disaster. "It is not an unwelcome position. I am satisfied with my future and my bargain." With the Picklemen on the move, the last thing she wanted was Lord Akeldama, powerful vampire rove, and the dewan, powerful werewolf loner, at each other's proverbial throats.

Her letter had declined Lord Akeldama's offer of indenture without specifying who had won her instead. So far as she knew, the vampire remained ignorant of the fact that, when she left school, she would work for the werewolves. Sophronia was hoarding that story as ammunition. Lord Akeldama desired information above all things. There might come a time when she could use gossip about herself to bargain for his help. No sense in giving anything away. Lord Akeldama was no charity case. Even this dinner was no doubt in pursuit of some end to which her presence was a means. She was not so foolish as to believe it was actually an honor.

The vampire watched her closely. She hoped none of her thoughts showed on her face. Lady Linette had schooled them in impassive expressions, but she knew her eyes were hard to control. And Lord Akeldama was very good at perceiving without showing that he did. *I wonder if that is a product of his age or if he, too, once had training.*

Without further private communication, they followed the others into a large back parlor. The house was decorated in a baroque style, but what intrigued Sophronia was how many of the gilt frames, decorative lamps, and pretty vases were also deadly. They'd studied some of the makers. The gas lamp that detached and exploded on impact was from a Swiss clockmaker. The frames with the leaf corners that became knives were from a private dealer in Manchester. Lord Akeldama was a vampire after her own heart. Although, to be frank, her taste was less ornate. Dimity, however, was in raptures.

The back parlor was arranged like a music room, with couches and armchairs all facing a small performing area.

"This play, my lord, what is it called?" asked Sophronia, aware that they were now easily overheard by the others.

"It is a witty little invention of Bolo's. Currently, he is calling it *The Importance of Wearing Ermine*, but the title may change. Shall we sit?"

The play was indeed a witty little invention. Although clearly designed to appeal to ladies and poodle fakers, it was, nevertheless, replete with enough verbal skirmishing to delight even Sophronia, who customarily had more serious dramatic preferences. In Shakespearean fashion, all the roles were played by men. This only added comedic effect.

Dimity was heard to squeak with delight at more than one exchange of repartee. Petunia laughed several times. Even Agatha tittered. The result being that praise was heaped upon an ebullient Bolo as soon as the bowing commenced.

There was enough fodder in the play to engage them all in conversation over aperitifs until other guests, invited only for the meal, began to arrive.

At each announcement, Lord and Lady So-and-so, Mr. Such-and-such, Petunia became increasingly agitated. At one point, she dragged Sophronia into a corner to chatter about it before she exploded. "*Everyone* who is *anyone* is here tonight. And not only the known elements from the daylight society papers, but the real important types written of in the *Evening Cupboard*! Oh, Sophronia, please behave yourself. I know finishing school saw you turn over a new leaf, and you have been golden this past week, but don't hurl any food at anyone? Please?"

Sophronia, of course, knew everyone there. Before he went mad, Professor Braithwope drilled them on the *ton*—humans and supernaturals. Lord Akeldama was hosting a representative sample—four landed gentry, two active members of the Staking Constabulary, the chief field operative for the Bureau of Unnatural Registry, an overseer of the Vault of England, *and* a proper Ghost Wrangler. Sophronia even recognized those at whose import Petunia could only guess. The nondescript Mr. Thermopopple was, in fact, official inventor to the queen. And the mild-mannered sandy-haired professor was actually Beta to the local werewolf pack.

She was not surprised, therefore, when the dewan turned up. He sent a curt nod in her general direction. She understood that this meant their arrangement was to continue a secret and found it no challenge to ignore him. As expected, he had not brought Soap. She let out the puff of breath she hadn't known she was holding.

The other member of the Shadow Council, the potentate, was absent. Adviser to the queen, and the patron of Mademoiselle Geraldine's, he was no doubt *important*. But, with few exceptions, a vampire was not able to safely visit another's home. That said, Sophronia suspected at least one person come to dine was in the potentate's pay, possibly several.

They were called into dinner by a butler-type human. This was not so odd, as vampires refused to employ mechanicals. He was of middling years and so ordinary that Sophronia would have passed him by, except that he moved like he could kill someone and would be good at it. All three of Geraldine's girls looked at the butler with interest from under lowered lashes. He blinked impassively, holding the door. *He does not like to be noticed*, thought Sophronia. *And he doesn't like Lord Akeldama.*

There seemed to be no consideration of the order of precedence in seating. Instead, they were guided gently but firmly by the drones to sit in a pattern orchestrated by Lord Akeldama. The girls were seated as far apart from each other as possible. They would be unable to pass notes. Dimity was next to the funny little inventor, Mr. Thermopopple, to whom she paid rapt attention. Dimity would never misapply dinner conversation. She would take advantage of the man's expertise if it killed her. Given his flat voice and questionable subject matter—who cared about float capacity dynamics?—she risked at least being maimed by monotone. Agatha was next to the pack representative. The Beta was making an effort to put her at ease, but also trying to determine why three schoolgirls and their chaperone were in the midst of such august company. Petunia sat in a state of terror next to the dewan.

"Good evening," rumbled the dewan.

"Meep," said Petunia. Sophronia couldn't fault her—the dewan terrified her on occasion.

The dewan rolled his eyes and turned to his other dining companion.

The long table was decorated with statues of shepherds and shepherdesses, and Grecian urns full of fluffy ferns arranged in such a way as to make hand signals nearly impossible between Agatha, Dimity, and Sophronia. Sophronia, on Lord Akeldama's right, gave him a mock salute at the mastery of the arrangement. *Nicely done.* The known spies had been neutralized from communication. She felt isolated. But what the vampire had forgotten was that she had worked alone successfully before. Her friends were her strength, but not her *only* strength.

They were about to start eating when one final guest was ushered in—the type of guest who loved to make an entrance and had timed her lateness accordingly.

Monique de Pelouse was stunning in a dress of teal watered silk with black braid piping emphasizing her tiny waist. Her hair was a pile of gold, woven through with teal ribbon. Her sleeves were full enough to hide an armament, but not so full as to impede eating. Perhaps she wore a dash too much rouge, but only Sophronia suspected the rosy glow.

Lord Akeldama stood to greet her. He accorded her a distinction she did not deserve, gesturing her to the empty seat on his left, across from Sophronia.

"My dear Miss Pelouse, welcome. Does everyone here know Miss Pelouse? Lovely. Now that we have the countess's representative, perhaps we can begin?"

A parade of drones, not footmen—*Lord Akeldama wants only those he can trust working tonight*—began serving. There were beautiful dishes for the human guests, exquisitely arranged platters of raw meat for the werewolves, and champagne mixed with blood for Lord Akeldama.

Sophronia had predicted that Lord Akeldama's menu would be as frivolous as his dress. But in the matter of food, he either had simple tastes, or he farmed it out to someone who still ingested the stuff. The humans started with a pea soup made with ham broth, accompanied by bread sprinkled with powdered mint. The fish course was a John Dory in sage sauce, followed by a joint of beef with carrots, veal cutlets in curry gravy, and pheasant with truffles. They finished with a white pudding and stewed apples. It was delicious and perfectly prepared, but Sophronia could tell that others found it disappointingly familial.

Since Lord Akeldama was busy ensuring that the conversation flowed, Sophronia turned to her other dining partner. He had a laugh that sounded like he was chewing air and was already in deep conversation with his neighbor, unwilling to entertain the whims of a schoolgirl. She summarily dismissed him with equal disregard and greater contempt. Imagine discounting someone on the grounds of age and gender! Then again, she was trained to take advantage of exactly that kind of ignorance. However, it meant she was forced to look across the way, through the fern fronds, to Monique.

"Miss Pelouse, how are you this evening? I haven't seen you in ages." Sophronia dove in with a will.

"I suspect that is healthier for both of us, Miss Temminnick." Monique was as barbed as ever.

"Oh, my, you didn't suffer any adverse effect from your impromptu swim last winter, I hope?" Sophronia recalled Monique's offended squawking fondly.

"Certainly not. I have an exceptional constitution."

Sophronia nibbled her fish, pausing to phrase her next dart. "How are you finding the hive these days?"

"I consider myself quite pleasantly situated, thank you," replied Monique primly. "I understand you are in London for the holidays?"

"To visit my dear sister. Recently married." Sophronia gestured with her chin at Petunia, who was giggling desperately at the dewan.

Monique gave Petunia a disgusted look. "I suppose we all have our crosses to bear."

Sophronia said, with no little feeling, "Too true. So the hive is still comfortable despite your misfortunes?" She tried to play on a sympathetic angle.

Monique sidestepped her. "We acquired a rather nice dirigible recently."

"How excellent for the upcoming summer months. But surely, vampires cannot partake?"

"Sadly, no. But the rest of us are encouraged to learn the basics of floating. Drones must go where vampires cannot. It's our role."

"How nice for you. Is it a large craft?" Sophronia wasn't certain why Monique would intentionally pass on information about hive assets. *Is it a veiled threat of some kind?*

"Not very, but I understand it possesses not inconsiderable speed."

Now, that really was too much information. *What is Monique up to?* "Worried about flywaymen, are we?"

"No, not flywaymen."

Conversational flow being as it was, Monique's last phrase shot out into a lull and reverberated down the table.

Everyone looked at her.

Petunia broke the awkward silence. "Oh, *those* horrible miscreants."

Monique tossed her head. "Well, it's not them I'm worried about. Everyone knows who skulks behind the flywaymen these days. Is that not what we've been brought here to discuss? Or am I assuming too much, my lord?"

Sophronia looked through the fronds at her fellow diners for expressions of surprise. *Petunia, of course, and perhaps two or three others.*

Lord Akeldama leaned back, sipping his fizzy blood. "Has the countess told you something significant, Miss Pelouse?"

Monique stabbed at her fish. "Are you going to let them get away with it?" She looked down the table at the dewan. "Are you?" Then over at the werewolf Beta, gesturing at him with a fork loaded with John Dory. "Are you?"

"Come now, Miss Pelouse, no need to point fish. Let us allow the conversation to flow naturally, shall we?" As if by the vampire's command, the others turned back to their dining companions.

Sophronia tilted her head at her erstwhile nemesis. Monique looked annoyed.

"Have you any holiday plans, Miss Pelouse?" With her free hand she gave the signal, *What was that about?*

"I had thought to visit my family, touring in Paris. Beautiful city, have you ever been?" *You already know.* To Sophronia's surprise, Monique actually fluttered a reply. The problem with hand signals was that they were limited in specificity, being intended only for extractions from sticky social situations, or sticky physical situations, or, occasionally, both.

"Sadly, no. Someday I should very much like to. I hear the shopping is unparalleled." Why was Monique, of all people, trying to force the situation? Did she have insight into the Picklemen's immediate intentions? Was she was under orders from Countess Nadasdy to press the dewan's hand? The vampires fancied striking against the Picklemen first, asking questions second.

Monique chose to ignore Sophronia at that point, focusing on her food.

Sophronia did the same, listening closely to the conversations ebbing around her. The newspaperman with the piercing voice argued vociferously with the dewan about some *malfunction.* Whatever it was, Petunia was following, so it must be common knowledge. The newspaperman seemed the type to always argue, but Sophronia blessed his aggression because she could hear every word, even though they were halfway down the table.

"You cannot blame the government for a failure in private enterprise." The dewan defended the Crown.

"My dear sir, we blame no one. We're perfectly objective"—someone laughed coldly—"but public perception is that since everyone who is anyone has them, it is a society-wide situation, and the government is responsible. Like the water supply, or the gas, or even helium."

A hush met that statement. Imagine, mentioning *utilities* at the dinner table.

Dimity spoke up, compelled by her training to cover for his gaffe. Of course, she was also happy to appear driven to attend his mistake while actually seeking further insight. "Forgive me for asking, but I have been away at finishing school and am regrettably out of touch. Has there been another opera incident?" *Never underestimate Dimity.*

The newspaperman looked kindly upon ignorance packaged behind a lovely face with wide hazel eyes framed by honey-colored hair. "Yes, my dear. Only recently my paper—you know it, of course, the *Mooring Standard*?—reported that a wave of mechanical malfunctions has been sweeping the nation."

Sophronia was momentarily distracted by Bumbersnoot. He had been quietly slung over the back of her chair, but now was scrabbling to be set down.

Fortunately, no one seemed to notice except Lord Akeldama, who gave her a sideways look. Sophronia couldn't afford to hush Bumbersnoot with a protocol command, so she stuck him in her lap. He remained so restless, she set him on the floor. He scuttled out the door and down the hallway. Sophronia figured if anyone could cope with her mechanimal, it was Lord Akeldama's drones. They'd probably adopt him and dress him like a maiden aunt.

Dimity continued to coax. "Oh, but the opera, when sung by mechanicals, it is quite offensive. Can nothing be done to stop it?"

"My dear young lady, not *opera*. More a wave of small shut-downs, brief enough not to be noticed until one of my best investigators uncovered them. They have been happening in multiple households, in isolated pockets, all over the country."

Sophronia looked hard at the dewan.

Monique jumped on the opening. "You see? They *are* up to something. Perhaps intending to damage the core of the Empire itself."

The inventor chap, next to Dimity, joined the conversation. "We have seen no serious repercussions. Nothing but a spate of inconvenient shutdowns, and that first minor opera."

The newspaperman seemed to take this as criticism of his reporting. "But it *did* happen, and all over, and no one knew about the shutdowns until we exposed them."

Petunia moved gracefully back into the conversation. "I read your article on the subject with interest. We employ several mechanicals in our household, and I am concerned over their reliability. And the safety of my family, of course."

"Exactly my point." The newspaperman perceived this as support. "You are wise to be cautious, Mrs. Hunnelprissy."

"Hisselpenny."

Sophronia wished she could have a moment with the dewan. Had the government known about these shutdowns and covered them up, only to have the newspapers expose them? Or had they not known? The first meant they were evil. The second that they were incompetent and that the Picklemen were a step ahead.

"This is only a series of tests. They are planning something big." Monique spoke with utter conviction.

The newspaperman was interested. "Oh? And who is this

they of whom you speak? The government?" He looked ready to whip out his notebook.

The dewan was dismissive. "Nonsense, Gengulphus."

The newspaper man took offense.

So did Monique.

The dewan, Sophronia realized, had very little training in the matter of conversational manipulation. *I shall have to educate my own patron. How tiresome.*

The dinner table erupted into argument, political accusations flying. No one named the Picklemen, and it was clear the newspaperman—and others—didn't know of their existence. Some thought the conservatives might be trying to discredit the progressives. Some thought the vampires and werewolves, both always anti-mechanical, were somehow causing them to malfunction to prove a point.

Soon the entire table was involved. A gleeful Dimity egged everyone on. It was a good tactic, as high dudgeon often yielded information. Agatha paid rapt attention to the proceedings, inserting an occasional well-timed and seemingly innocent question that tossed more coal upon the fire.

Sophronia turned to stare, quite obviously, at Lord Akeldama. *What is he up to?*

The vampire's face was impassive, but the person holding most of his attention was the newspaperman. What was his name? *Ah, yes, Lemuel Gengulphus.*

Perhaps we are going about this wrong, Sophronia thought, watching both vampire and muckraker. Lord Akeldama wants to know what the Picklemen are up to. So does Monique. So do I. But perhaps this *is* what they are up to. *Perhaps their real plan is not death, destruction, or war but to make the government and the supernaturals running it look incompetent and unable to control technology. What if the Picklemen intend to force a major mechanical malfunction and then arrange for their political allies to heroically rescue everyone from the mechanicals? They could then overturn the supernatural stronghold on the government by arguing incompetence.*

The dewan seemed to think that greater controls should be in place over mechanical technology. His stance was that the government might have to step in and remove or destroy them all, by force if necessary.

Petunia practically fainted at the idea. "But what would we *do* without mechanized staff?"

The newspaperman and the other humans at the table, including the inventor, also found this idea scandalous.

"Knives are dangerous, my lord, but we do not regulate them!" objected the inventor.

"True," said the dewan. "But gas can explode, and we regulate *that.*"

The argument was becoming one of ideology rather than specifics, as these things do. Sophronia, however, wanted specifics. If she didn't know exactly what the Picklemen were up to, how could she stop them?

Lord Akeldama stood. He was not very physically imposing, but he was their host, and his rising caused the table to quiet.

"Most entertaining, my dears, but as the cheese is away, perhaps we should adjourn to the drawing room? I have *something* there that might interest everyone."

A murmur of excitement met that, and accordingly the gentlemen assisted the ladies to rise. The guests made their way out into the hallway. The dewan actually offered Petunia his arm. And Petunia took it!

Dimity, Agatha, and Sophronia lingered. Dimity pretended to have misplaced something. Agatha intentionally forgot her gloves. Sophronia found herself fascinated by the fern arrangements.

They clustered close.

"What do you think?" Sophronia asked.

Dimity's nose wrinkled. "The food was rather too similar to something we might get at school."

Agatha said, "Monique's dress is divine."

Sophronia glared at them.

Dimity giggled. "You are *so* predictable."

"Quickly, please."

"Now you sound like Lady Linette." Dimity still wouldn't play.

"So?" Sophronia was driven to put her hands on her hips.

Agatha crumbled. "The dewan doesn't like that the government might be accused of malfeasance, but he also doesn't want Parliament to attack the Picklemen openly. Not when, so far as they can prove, the Picklemen haven't done anything legally wrong."

"Agreed. Dimity?"

"Mr. Gengulphus is not as objective as his profession suggests. He would prefer to see the government humiliated, and if the vampires and werewolves share the sin, so much the better."

"Is he politically conservative or in the pay of the Picklemen?"

Dimity pursed her lips. "I don't think either. Simply one of those men who always suspects the people in power, whoever they may be."

Sophronia nodded. "I can understand that stance."

"Of course *you* can, you heathen." Dimity was slightly proud of her reprobate friend. "Except that we know that Picklemen in charge would be worse."

"Yes, we do." Sophronia bit her lip. "We'd better follow before we're missed. Plan of action?"

"I'll keep egging them on when I can." Dimity knew her strengths.

Sophronia grinned. "You do egg beautifully."

Dimity went all over sly. "It's all fun and information until the yolk breaks."

Agatha said, "I'll stick to the inventor. I don't know why he was invited. He doesn't seem to have a political stake in this situation, and while he works for the queen, he's not that powerful."

"Is it possible he's a Pickleman intelligencer?" suggested Sophronia.

"Would Lord Akeldama invite one into our midst?"

"I don't know. I haven't figured out why he's doing any of this." Sophronia was only mildly frustrated. She doubted anyone could fully understand their vampire host in the space of a human life-span, let alone during the course of a dinner party.

"A man of many motives," suggested Agatha darkly.

"Or, worse, none at all," replied Sophronia.

They made their way out into the hallway, precisely in time

to hear a shrill whining nose and then a *woof* sound, which ended in an impossibly loud boom.

The door to the drawing room exploded outward. Several top hats were carried with the blast, flying through the opening on a cloud of smoke, falling to roll sadly on the plush carpet.

Sophronia could only think of one thing.

"Bumbersnoot!"

A PROBLEM OF MOTIVATION

S ophronia, Agatha, and Dimity ran toward the door now hanging by its bottom hinge. Drones came dashing from all parts of the house.

Sophronia's mind was in a loop of worry. *Is Bumbersnoot in there? Is the explosion his fault? Or has he exploded himself, without permission?* And then, *Petunia!*

They clustered at the doorway, peering into chaos. The smoke cleared, exposing a remarkable tableau. Something large and mechanical had caused the blast. It had started out on a table in the center of the room, but now its parts were scattered everywhere and the table was cracked in half. It was hard to tell what it had been, but now it *wasn't* anymore. There were shards of glass or possibly crystal, as well as gears, valves, coal, chains, and springs everywhere. But what really drew the eye was the guests.

The supernatural creatures had leapt to shield the mortals.

Lord Akeldama had whisked Monique behind a couch. The sandy-haired werewolf had the inventor and the newspaperman down flat on their fronts with him partly on top. The dewan had taken Petunia under his wing. The deadly butler, who might or might not be supernatural, had two others shielded by an overturned table in the far corner. But they hadn't been able to get to everyone. There was a good deal of blood, mostly on arms and backs, as those without guardians had turned away to shield their heads. No one seemed dead, but several were certainly prone and writhing. Both active members of the Staking Constabulary, the chief field operative for the Bureau of Unnatural Registry, the overseer of the Vault of England, *and* the Ghost Wrangler were down.

Petunia looked sobered but showed no inclination to faint, scream, or cry. Sophronia felt oddly proud.

"Your sister has unexpected fortitude." Agatha voiced Sophronia's thoughts. "I suppose you must get it from somewhere." She sounded quite adult in her assessment of the Temminnick family character.

The rustle of a crinkling dinner dress and a small sigh next to them drew their attention.

Dimity had noticed not only the blood on the human victims but that the backs of many of the supernaturals had been torn to shreds by shrapnel and were leaking slow black blood in large dollops. She fainted into the willing arms of one of the drones.

Sophronia and Agatha left her to it.

Sophronia dutifully went to check on her sister, all the while covertly searching the room for Bumbersnoot. Agatha began to circulate with a dampened handkerchief and sympathetic expression. The drones ran to their master, and by proxy, Monique, helping them to stand, cooing and brushing them down. Lord Akeldama began issuing orders for hot water, bandages, dust removers, cleaning supplies, smelling salts, clothing, tea, and the like. The drones, having ascertained that he was both unhurt and unruffled, ran to do his bidding. He held a heavily perfumed handkerchief to his nose and passed the same on to the werewolves, so they would not be tempted by all the human blood.

Sophronia thought the vampire seemed more offended by the destruction of clothing than anything else. There was a hint of hauteur to his orders that was not ordinarily part of his public persona.

The victims began to slowly sit and take stock. The newspaperman, looking equal parts pleased and terrified, made hasty farewells. He retrieved his coat from the hallway, and throwing it over his now wrinkled evening suit, dashed off into the night. He had his headline for tomorrow's paper.

The supernaturals milled around, assessing the damage. The drones tended to the wounded.

"Petunia, are you unhurt?" Sophronia took her sister's hand in both of hers in a clasp she had read about in one of Dimity's horrible Gothic novels.

"It appears that way, sister. I am most grateful to the dewan for his protection. I believe I owe him my life. Too kind, too kind. Although I must say this was more excitement than I was anticipating from a dinner party. Even among such august company."

"What was it that exploded?"

"Some odd mechanical. Lord Akeldama was saying how it

had unexpectedly come into his possession and that he thought we might like to see such a unique specimen. Then there was this whistling teakettle noise, and it went *poof*."

Sophronia nibbled her lip. *Uh-oh. Whistling teakettle sounds like Bumbersnoot. I wonder if something in Vieve's adaptations conflicted with this mechanical?* Under the guise of helping her sister to her feet, she continued to check the room.

Still no Bumbersnoot.

Fortunately, none of the broken parts looked to belong to him. He was a particularly tiny mechanimal. All his bits were undersized, and the ones scattered around were too large for him. She noticed a large chunk of one of the new crystalline valves, distinctive in its bluish shade and multiple facets, which meant the Picklemen at one point had had their mitts on that exploding mechanical.

After helping Petunia to sit and serving her with a necessary cup of restorative tea—three sugars to cope with the drama—Sophronia joined Agatha in tending to the company. They helped where they could, all the while looking for important clues and evaluating the scattered parts.

There wasn't much to do. By the time Dimity had recovered from her faint, all the supernatural creatures were fully healed, and the drones had seen them dressed in fresh shirts and jackets. They no longer matched quite so well, but even Dimity's stylish sensibilities could not be ruffled so much by the new attire as to make her faint again. She joined the others in practicing the fine art of administrative small talk and ministrations after a crisis.

They were all obeying their training to the letter. *I don't mean to be crass, ladies, but keep your wits about you, for it is after a disaster that intelligence is most likely spilled,* Lady Linette always said. Thus they milled, and cooed, and soothed, and acted like little angels of mercy, and listened, and learned. So did Monique.

Sophronia was checking on the Ghost Wrangler, a crone shrouded in the long white veil and gray robes of her trade. Her upper arm and shoulder were badly scraped, and Sophronia tried to be gentle with the elderly lady, but she would keep twisting to try to say something. Finally, Sophronia got the bandage wrapped and helped the lady to sit on a nearby stool.

With a frantic glance around, the crone swiveled her face away from the company and parted her veil slightly. Sophronia thought she might be about to expectorate, but instead she hissed in a shaky voice, "Closer! I risked much to get this to you, and you missed the show."

Sophronia recognized the voice. Madame Spetuna! One of Geraldine's field agents, and their best Pickleman infiltrator.

"The explosion was intentional?" Sophronia could only see the intelligencer's mouth. It twisted in annoyance.

"No. But this gathering was at my request."

"You work for Lord Akeldama?"

"Sometimes. That is not important. What's important is that they are building war mechanicals. That's what this was. They used our pilot technology and intend to create mechanicals that can commandeer military dirigibles."

That's why the Picklemen snuck on board! Not to steal something, but to draw schematics so they can copy the school's pilot mechanical.

Madame Spetuna continued. "My communication threads

to the school have been eliminated, so it's up to you to relay the information."

"Lady Linette won't believe me."

"You must *make* her believe."

"How?"

"My file, the record room, there's a..." Madame Spetuna trailed off as Monique approached, looking quite interested in Sophronia's conversation. Then a drone appeared and ushered Madame Spetuna away, muttering something about visiting a surgeon. Sophronia had faith in Madame Spetuna's ability to extricate herself and return to the Picklemen. She was one of the best intelligencers Sophronia had ever met.

Things died down after that. Sophronia never did find Bumbersnoot anywhere. They delayed their departure as long as was seemly under the circumstances, in the guise of offering assistance. But Petunia would not be denied a graceful exit, and she certainly wasn't going to help clean. The restrictions of propriety must be honored. So Sophronia, not wanting to disturb Lord Akeldama with trivialities, left a note with one of the drones saying she had misplaced her reticule. It was dog-shaped and had great sentimental value. If he found it, would he please see it returned? She worried that someone from the party had stolen Bumbersnoot. But there was nothing more she could do given the recent crisis. Any fuss from her would look suspiciously selfish by comparison to injuries, destroyed evening wear, and a cracked table.

The dewan gave her a significant look before they parted ways. He probably expected a full report from her. *I don't work for you yet.* She glared at him.

They set off in Petunia's luxurious coach and arrived back at the Hisselpennys' town house feeling a little shattered. They were much earlier back than they had planned.

"Sister, may Agatha stay awhile longer? The night is still so young. For cards or something equally pedestrian? To calm us down?" Sophronia batted her eyes a little.

"Ah, I remember when I was young like you. Such energy." Sophronia hid a smile. Petunia was only eighteen. "Your father won't miss you, Miss Woosmoss?" Petunia made a token protest.

Agatha shook her head, red curls bouncing.

A small whirring heralded Petunia's mechanical butler proffering a red lacquered tray.

"Cards came while we were out?" Petunia tossed them over. Two invitations and a sweep-cleaning service. "Well, the invitations are not what they might be, but better than none, I suppose. And perhaps the chimneys do need cleaning."

The buttlinger buttled off.

"May I see them?" asked Sophronia politely.

Petunia arched a brow but passed over the tray. Sophronia pocketed the card for the chimney sweep, distracting her sister with, "How delightful that Agatha can stay! Shall we play loo? It's so very fortifying?"

Petunia pressed her temple with one hand. "I myself must rest. We shan't tell Mr. Hisselpenny of this evening's events, shall we, ladies? I'm afraid he is rather protective."

"Do not worry yourself on that account, sister. We shall be most discreet." *She's forgotten about the newspaperman. He, no doubt, will print a full report. Or perhaps Mr. Hisselpenny doesn't read the* Mooring Standard. "We will calm ourselves with loo and lemonade."

"Very good, ladies. Have the coach take Miss Woosmoss home when you're done. I'll bid you good night. And tomorrow..." Petunia brightened notably at a thought. "Tomorrow we shall go hat shopping." She left without further discussion.

The three girls curled up by a fire in the parlor, cards out, of course, in case someone came to check on them, but they played by rote. Sophronia told them of her conversation with Madame Spetuna, and they spent some time debating where her loyalties might lie and why she might be unable to transfer information any other way than via Lord Akeldama.

"Although we must admit it worked." Dimity was always one to give credit when due.

"The teachers won't believe us. It's such a crazy idea, war mechanicals. Too extreme."

"They won't *want* to believe us. Too scary." Agatha showed unexpected insight.

A pause while they all looked morose.

Sophronia added, "She said something about her records— maybe there is a code word there that commands trust?"

"What else did we learn?" Dimity moved them on to other speculations, as she didn't want to talk about the record room. It brought back bad—well, sticky—memories.

Agatha reported her observations. "The dewan used the explosion to push his agenda. He has something on the queen's desk called the Clandestine Information Act. It's designed to seize technological power for the Crown in the guise of patent control. I think he wants to persuade Lord Akeldama to this cause."

"Speaking of which, did any of you learn anything more about that suspicious butler?" Sophronia asked.

"Administering a damp handkerchief will only get a young lady so far." Agatha made a face.

"Me neither. But I think he had a vested interest in the politics of the situation." Dimity wound a hair ribbon around and through her fingertips.

"Why?"

"He moved toward the dewan anytime he mentioned controlling technology."

"Patent holder, perhaps?" Agatha had a brain under those red curls.

"A patent holder carrying at least two small guns, one up each sleeve?" Sophronia was suspicious.

"And a knife down his boot top." Dimity flicked the hair ribbon.

"Careful with that—you'll have an eye out." Sophronia put up a hand defensively.

Agatha remained focused on the butler. "I noticed that, too. Assassin in the employment of a patent holder?"

"Speaking of butlers." Sophronia drew out the calling card for the chimney sweep service. "If you will excuse me a moment? I believe there is someone waiting to speak with me outside."

Agatha and Dimity squinted suspiciously, but let her go with only an exchange of teasing smooching noises.

After creeping around a well-guarded floating school, the Hisselpennys' town house was ridiculously easy to escape, just as Soap
had told her it should be.

Soap was waiting for her in the back alley by the kitchen
delivery entrance.

Sophronia vibrated with awareness of him, but was careful
not to show it. "Good evening."

Soap was not so reticent. He moved in with supernatural
speed, and before she could protest, nuzzled into the side of her
neck in a wolfish manner. "Why do you always smell so tasty?"

In response, Sophronia sniffed him loudly, trying to lighten
the mood. He no longer carried the scent of coal and boilers.
He smelled of something raw and wild, a tiny bit like freshly
butchered beef and open fields. It wasn't unpleasant, but it
wasn't comforting, either. She had found coal dust and oil so
reassuring—once.

A throat cleared. "Touching as this is, youngsters, there's
work to be done."

Soap backed away and the dewan stepped out of the shadows.

Sophronia was mortified by the fact that she hadn't noticed
him there. Too much of her focus had been on Soap—how had
he done that? She curtsied exactly the right depth for the dewan's
social superiority. He was, after all, landed as the Earl of Upper
Slaughter, even if he couldn't boast an actual country seat.

"My lord, twice in one evening. To what do I owe the
honor?" She tilted her head—to the degree of inquiry, not the

degree of coquetry. It wasn't done to expose too much neck to werewolf or vampire.

"Now, now, little trickster, don't go throwing wiles in my direction." The dewan squinted at her.

Soap snaked an arm about Sophronia's waist and turned so that he stood shoulder-to-shoulder with her.

The dewan gave him a sharp look. "Like that, is it?"

Soap blinked at him. "I have always been hers. Although she is taking her time accepting it."

"I didn't realize you were so tame, pup," replied the dewan, then dismissed it as unimportant with a wave of one massive hand.

Sophronia tried to delicately shrug away from Soap, but his arm only tightened. His statement had held so much finality it made her uncomfortable. How could she possibly combat such a feeling?

The dewan proceeded to grill Sophronia about her observations from the dinner party. She told him some of them. After all, he would be her patron eventually, and she had the sinking suspicion she might need his help in the days to come. He gave her little reaction, even when she spoke of his own agenda of trying to garner support for the Clandestine Information Act. His expression only changed when she mentioned the butler.

"Noticed him, did you?"

"Two guns and a knife? Of course I noticed."

The dewan gave a funny half growl, half snort. "He's with me. At least, I think he is, for now. I wouldn't concern yourself overly. He was once a valet to an enemy of the Empire. But his master is dead, and the butler, as you call him, has great cause to play nicely with queen and country."

Sophronia looked to Soap for further information. Soap's expression said he was as mystified as she.

"What is your plan, my lord? Let the Picklemen expose and bury themselves, then slap a law on them? That's a very indirect approach, for a werewolf."

The dewan looked her up and down. "Should I take that as a compliment, coming from you, Miss Temminnick?"

"What if that's their plan, too? What if they are not intending an outright attack, but instead are trying to discredit you, the Shadow Council, and the entire supernatural set?"

"Queen Victoria would never allow it."

"And right now the general populace would never allow you to take their mechanicals away. But if the Picklemen cause one major nationwide malfunction, and blame it on a vampire vendetta, and then a Pickleman-backed manufacturer steps in and fixes everything? Then the supernatural are the villains and political power sways with popular opinion. So long as the papers spin it right."

"You think that is their game?" The dewan was intrigued.

"I think it's possible."

Soap said, "I told you her brain worked in mysterious ways."

Sophronia couldn't suppress a rush of pleasure. *He's been bragging about me to the dewan. How sweet.*

At least the dewan was considering her theory. Perhaps being indentured to him wouldn't be so bad, if he gave her opinions weight despite her age and sex.

Nevertheless, he disagreed. "I think it must be something

less subtle. They have gone to a great deal of expense installing the new valves, which allow them to control every mechanical in the nation. They only need the right command center."

Sophronia got excited. "So Lord Akeldama's exploding mechanical *was* a pilot designed to seize control of military dirigibles?"

The dewan continued as if she hadn't interrupted, "That's a lot of pawns in place for a supernatural character assassination, even if the end result would be a shift in political power. What you suggest requires delicate maneuvering and hinges on controlling popular opinion and the press, both notoriously difficult to influence. I think it more likely that their planned assault is more violent."

Sophronia saw his reasoning. Of course, she liked her theory even if it didn't explain the exploding pilot. She must remain open-minded enough not to ignore evidence that came up to discredit her. It was best not to have an agenda in espionage.

"I will keep my ears and eyes open, my lord. I have never been able to predict the duke's actions."

"The duke? You mean Golborne?"

Sophronia nodded.

"Ah, yes." The dewan looked at Soap, as if he had momentarily forgotten that the duke had been responsible for that fateful shot. "If I recall correctly, you had some doings with young Lord Mersey at one time."

Sophronia refused to blush. "Some, as you say, *doings*."

Soap tensed.

"Word is the duke's been elevated to Grand Gherkin. It is a significant position of power for such a disturbingly petty individual. There's only one Pickleman higher—the Chutney himself."

"As you say, my lord." Sophronia wanted to inquire further, but the dewan was speaking to her as if she should know all the details of Pickleman infrastructure. She didn't want to display ignorance when he was treating her so fairly.

"Perhaps young Mersey would be useful in this matter. Do you think he might be privy to his father's plans?"

Sophronia thought back to the recent ball. "I'm afraid that bridge may have been burned, my lord."

"Now, now. Pretty young thing like you? I highly doubt it."

Soap's arm left her waist. Sophronia felt the cold of its absence. She could see the dewan's reasoning. And, frankly, it would be a good test of her seduction ability. Could she win Felix back, on her own terms, knowing her affections lay elsewhere? A *challenge*. She did love a challenge. "I want it clear that I'm doing it because I'm curious—not because you've instructed me. You don't hold my indenture yet. But I will try Lord Mersey for information."

Soap growled. Actually growled!

Before Sophronia could get huffy about possessiveness, the dewan interceded. "Now, now, pup, remember what we discussed earlier. Controlling the wolf's emotions for civilized discourse is a requirement. Miss Temminnick here is planning on employing her intelligencer training in response to a specific target. It has no bearing on your"—his lip curled—"*relationship* with the chit. Whatever that may be."

Sophronia felt compelled to say something. "Really, my lord, why do you think we—?"

His snort cut her off. Strangely, Sophronia got the impression he was on Soap's side, that he, of all people, might support affection between a clandestine black werewolf and a young lady of quality.

She turned to Soap for understanding. Only to find that she'd momentarily forgotten how tall he was and how satiny his skin. She shifted in close against him. Employing affection was also part of her training.

Soap winced. "Don't."

Sophronia felt a pang of guilt, pulling away. *What kind of person have I become, that I chase information even though it may hurt those I adore? I've become so guarded, even with people I love.* She shook herself internally. "And while I do that, what exactly is your plan, my lord?"

"To stop them. Whatever it is they are going to do with those valves, I'm putting an end to it before it happens."

"And if you can't? What's your contingency plan?"

The dewan looked militant. "They will be stopped. That is all you need know."

Perhaps I have to be the one to develop a contingency plan. Sophronia wondered if Madame Spetuna was heading back to nest once more among the Picklemen and flywaymen.

"It's getting late." The dewan did not want to talk further. "I'd best get this one home before dawn. Make your good-byes, younglings."

Soap turned swiftly and kissed her, before she could protest.

His lips were soft and warm. He tasted different. Richer, like brown-butter sauce. More threatening, also. She probably liked that fact too much. Although she found herself grateful that it was the new moon—the safest time for a girl to be kissed by a werewolf.

Soap broke it off before she was ready, leaving her dissatisfied and annoyed with her own weakness. She had to remind herself again how impossible such a relationship would be—they'd be mocked and ostracized by everyone.

The look in Soap's eye said he, too, wanted more, but that was the point. If Sophronia were ever fully satisfied, she'd be bored, or dead. Soap was inclined to use that character trait to his advantage.

Because they both knew it, Sophronia headed back into the house without another word.

"Wait."

She turned at the door, and the dewan tossed something at her. Training kicked in and she suppressed the instinct to dive out of danger, catching it instead. It was a large velvet sack, well padded, and it thunked into her, heavy with the weight of something metal. She loosened the drawstring.

Tick-tock, tick-tock! went the sack.

"Bumbersnoot!"

"You shouldn't leave your mechanimal lying about all willy-nilly like that, young lady. Any werewolf could have tripped over him," said the dewan.

Soap chuckled.

And they were gone.

Sophronia envied them their speed and silence. The right werewolf, she thought, could make for a very accomplished spy.

CRISIS 8

RECORDS AND REGRETS

The remainder of their London visit was uneventful. There were other dinner parties and shopping trips but no explosions and no revelations, if one discounted Agatha's realizing, finally, that orange was not a good color for her. This, Dimity and Sophronia felt, was an epiphany of epic proportions but of little consequence to the fate of the Empire at large.

They made their good-byes with the utmost gravity. Dimity and Agatha thanked Petunia profusely for her hospitality. Dimity presented her with a bunch of hothouse blooms entirely to Petunia's taste. Agatha pressed Petunia's hand and assured her that Mr. Woosmoss would call upon Mr. Hisselpenny on a matter of business come the New Year. Everyone parted ways feeling the better for the visitation.

The young ladies repaired to their respective families for the holidays, declaring their London jaunt an unparalleled success.

They each had several new dresses, not to mention hats, gloves, shawls, and boots. Petunia was in raptures over their pleasant company, pleasing manners, and polite talk. A delusion which they considered a profound victory for espionage.

Sophronia enjoyed life back home with her family, grown only larger with married siblings now producing families of their own. But hers was a modest enjoyment. Conversation seemed provincial and limited in scope. Three days was more than enough mundanities. She was delighted when Agatha rolled up in her father's landau, having arranged to be their transport back to school.

Sophronia was permitted to give Agatha tea in the front parlor while the luggage was loaded. Presumably Petunia had told Mrs. Temminnick of Agatha's wealth and station. Such a privilege as being accorded privacy in the Temminnick household was unprecedented.

"Was your Christmas perfectly ghastly?" asked Sophronia, all sympathy after the niceties had been dispensed with and the first cups quaffed.

"Tolerably so. I envy you your massive family, Sophronia. I should dearly love to be out of the spotlight and forgotten on occasion."

"I don't know. My mother thinks more on her cats these days than me. When we were called in for Christmas dinner, she forgot to yell my name entirely. Not that I mind as such— before Mademoiselle Geraldine's my name was all too often yelled."

"Better to be forgotten than the focus of all your father's hopes and dreams."

"You have a point. It is a valuable thing for an intelligencer to be forgotten."

"Oh, I do wish I had a brother. Or had been born a man."

Sophronia reached across the sofa to squeeze her friend's hand. "Oh, Agatha, I'm sorry. Is he still making demands?"

"He wants to know why my marks aren't better. Why I don't speak fluent French. Why I can't kill a fully grown man with a nutcracker."

Their privacy was not to last, for the twins clattered in, yodeling excitedly and heralding the arrival of another coach.

Sophronia and Agatha finished the dregs of their tea, kidnapped the crumpets for the journey ahead, collected the last of their belongings, and rushed out to the courtyard.

It proved to be Dimity and Pillover in a hired hack. The Plumleigh-Teignmotts tumbled out with all appearances of having argued vociferously most of the way.

Since Mrs. Temminnick was otherwise occupied, Petunia saw them all situated and gave the coachman instructions to Swiffle-on-Exe with no little pride. She didn't object to Pillover's presence, although by rights he ought not to be left alone with the girls. They'd formed a wary friendship at Petunia's coming-out ball, and she still looked upon him with favor.

"Whoever knew I should grow myself a sensible sister, in the end?" Sophronia settled back against the plush cushions of the carriage. "Do you think it has something to do with the fact that she is increasing?"

Agatha gasped, gesturing to Pillover.

Dimity came to Sophronia's defense. "Oh, Agatha, he knows where children come from."

"Yes, but..." Agatha squeaked.

Dimity moved them on for Agatha's sake. "I should have preferred a sister like yours, Sophronia, rather than old Pill."

Sophronia protested, "He's not so bad. Petunia took a long time to grow a brain. Pillover has had one all along."

"Thank you for that," muttered Pillover from under his hat. He was slouched in the corner next to his sister. His chin was sunk into his cravat and his attention fixed on a small book of Latin verse. Occasionally, he popped a lemon fizzy sweet into his mouth.

"He's a dead codfish." Dimity wrinkled her nose at the fish in question.

At which Pillover gave every outward appearance of intending to ignore them all for the duration of the journey, although he did sneak a few glances in Agatha's direction.

Bumbersnoot, who had some minor appreciation for Latin verse, sat on one of Pillover's feet. Pillover fed him bits of brown paper from the sweets wrapper.

"The ladies seem to like him." Sophronia spoke simply to see whether Pillover would react.

Pillover flinched.

"One of the great mysteries of the universe. Like why anyone would eat cucumber." Dimity had firm opinions on cucumber, which she felt was nothing more than slimy, embarrassingly shaped water and should never, under any circumstances, be presented at table.

Sophronia moved the conversation on to young men of Dimity's acquaintance, and which of them might prove a suitable beau. Lord Dingleproops having been long since discarded, there were other prospects to discuss.

Pillover muttered translations down at Bumbersnoot. The mechanimal paid rapt attention.

Sophronia did not mention Soap. She kept silent about his kisses, even knowing the others might benefit from her experience, but she was both mortified and exhilarated by the memory. She did not want her friends to know, fearing their disgust or worse, pity. Her own feelings were conflicted enough—no need to add theirs to the mix. *I have a secret lover,* she thought. She experienced no little relish over the secrecy part, it must be admitted. It made her feel wise and bold, and better able to advise Dimity on her romantic choices.

Fortunately, Dimity could talk about her beaux, or lack thereof, for the entirety of a carriage ride. The Picklemen and the flywaymen and their valves were only briefly addressed. Pillover bestirred himself to participate in that part of the conversation. But even an insider from Bunson's couldn't add to their knowledge. Perhaps because it was Pillover—as insiders went, he never got very far in, as it were.

"We really must wait for the Picklemen to move first." Sophronia was not happy about this.

Dimity steered them quickly back to boys, for who could be bothered trying to save the nation from an amorphous threat when flirting was on the line?

A Christmas card addressed to Miss Temminnick, Miss Plumleigh-Teignmott, and Miss Woosmoss was waiting in their shared parlor at Mademoiselle Geraldine's. In and of itself that was rather charming, as so few people thought—or even knew—of them as a collective. However, this particular card was from Sidheag, which made it all the more delightful. Not that Sidheag was a great wit, or a particularly talented correspondent, but it was nice to hear from her. Once the staunch fourth member of their little band, Lady Kingair was home in Scotland, with her pack and her affianced, preparing to leave the country on what looked to be a protracted campaign in the Crimea. The card said nothing of consequence—mainly pleasant banalities. It also had little of import encoded. After all, Sidheag knew the teachers read their mail, the same teachers who had taught them how to code. But it was nice to know she was well, and her acerbic nature translated into an aggressive script, for all her prose stuck to the strictures of politeness. Sidheag hadn't stayed long at Mademoiselle Geraldine's, but she had taken some lessons to heart, in the arena of letter writing at least.

"She's happier there." Agatha's tone was sad. Sidheag had been her closest friend.

"How do you think things are with Captain Niall?" Dimity wondered.

"Difficult to tell. It's not as if she would write that down." Sophronia and Sidheag shared a dislike of discussing romance.

She gave Dimity a glance of inquiry over Agatha's bowed head.

Dimity inclined her chin in approval.

"Agatha, would you like to keep the letter?" said Sophronia.

"Oh, may I? You don't mind?"

"Of course not." Dimity's smile was warm. Then she glanced down at her necklace timepiece. "Oh, goodness, we have to be in the kitchens in five minutes!"

They had various new lessons, but by far the oddest was, of all things, cooking. Why a respectable female of good standing might need to *cook*, aside from the occasional poison, was a great mystery. But one did not question Professor Lefoux's orders. Chopping onions was the worst part, until Dimity discovered one could use floating goggles to good effect. Professor Lefoux was surprised out of her customary dour expression upon finding them attentive to the onions, garbed as if for a flywayman attack.

"Innovative" was her only comment.

With only a week before the New Year's tea party, the teachers were determined to get the girls back in form quickly. Parties were the best place to practice the art of espionage—holidays, shopping, and Christmas presents notwithstanding. Mademoiselle Geraldine's young ladies of quality were not allowed to be distracted by *anything*.

Sophronia tried to deliver Madame Spetuna's warning to Lady Linette, who was having none of it. "I fail to see why you would make up such a falsehood! How on earth would she be in London? Why reach out to you with such an outlandish story after cutting off contact for all this time? Why send proof to Lord Akeldama and not us? Absurd."

"But—"

"Silence. Nothing more on the subject!"

After that Lady Linette watched like a hunting hound, and Sophronia could do nothing but apply herself diligently to the routine of classes. She couldn't shake a feeling of suspension. It was as if she were hanging over an abyss. Any move she made might do more harm than good, and someone might come along at any moment and cut her safety line. She became convinced of, even obsessed with, the fact that Madame Spetuna was their only hope. She was their only contact on the inside.

"It's so frustrating!" she whinged over tea. "Why won't Lady Linette even entertain the idea?"

"Why is it you're good at so many aspects of espionage except the waiting?" Agatha nibbled a bit of orange pound cake.

Dimity answered that. "Because she likes to be in motion. Haven't you noticed? Our Sophronia is happiest when she is crawling over or swinging around something. Preferably a *something* that is large and in motion itself."

"But Lady Linette always says an intelligencer needs patience. And Sophronia is supposed to be one of the best."

"Maybe because I've managed to hide that flaw in my character?" suggested Sophronia. "No, I've left it long enough. She hinted at something in the record room that might make Lady Linette believe me. It's time to break into it."

"Again?" wailed Dimity. "It destroyed a perfectly lovely dress last time."

"Come on, it'll be diverting." Sophronia's green eyes lit up with excitement.

"Anyone ever taken you to task for a perfectly horrid idea of diversion?"

"Agatha, you in?" Sophronia turned to the redhead.

Agatha sighed. "I'd rather not. I do prefer sleeping."

"Dimity?"

"It's not worth the risk. The New Year's tea party is too close. You know if we're caught we'll be sent down and miss the event. You'll have to do this one on your own."

Sophronia grinned. "Tonight, I think, an hour before dawn."

Agatha was true to her word, but Dimity, of course, ended up coming along. It was too juicy a gossip prospect. While Sophronia was busy looking up Madame Spetuna's record, Dimity could look up the records of their classmates.

Last time they visited the record room, it had been protected by a soldier mechanical of a viciously viscous inclination. But when they approached the door this time, there was nothing more threatening waiting for them than a folding card table and three small chairs stacked haphazardly against the outside. The furniture looked to have been abandoned. The hallway was eerily empty and free of mechanicals.

The sign was still on the door saying RECORD ROOM— CONTAINING RECORDS OF IMPORT in big gold letters. Underneath, someone had pinned an embroidery sample that read DANGER, MISINTERPRETATION HAZARD. The two girls used every door exam in their repertoire, and there seemed to be no trap. Nevertheless, Sophronia picked the locks with a slow, steady caution that tried even Dimity's patience.

Sophronia could take her time under some circumstances, it appeared.

They swung the door open but did not enter immediately, peering inside from a body length away, to be safe.

The room was entirely unchanged. Machines and rotary belts ran along the walls and filled the corners. Thousands of records dangled above, clipped to conveyors mounted on the ceiling, like laundry hanging from a clothesline. The three desks, accompanied by leather seats, oil lamps, and writing pads, stood in exactly the same place they had last time. This was more disturbing than an army of soldier mechanical guards. It made no sense that after the room had been broken into, the teachers would respond by removing all security entirely.

Sophronia entered first. Dimity followed. They moved slowly, hands held cupped forward and down, in the position of modesty. Their backs were straight, their posture pristine. They were model examples of Geraldine's training—those hands were held in readiness, able to delve quickly into any one of a number of hidden pockets, to release wrist holsters, or to grab items dangling from chatelaines. The posture was one of anticipation, ready to move in any direction at the slightest provocation.

Sophronia's instinct was to fire the obstructor or draw her bladed fan.

Dimity had taken recently to a pearl-handled muff-pistol. Not precisely deadly but, as she put it, terribly cute. It was half out of its holster as she took one more dainty step into the room.

Nothing happened. All the machinery remained still and silent, the steam supply asleep along with the boilers down below. It would be loud to activate, but there was no other way to get at the right record. It had taken them some twenty minutes to get to the record room, using the quickest routes and the obstructor. Sophronia guessed the teachers would take about the same to catch them once the noise started.

"Dimity," she whispered. "I'm going to have to turn it on. Can you keep a twenty-minute time check? Warn me at five?"

"I don't do well with timing." Nevertheless, Dimity pulled up her necklace watch, getting ready to give the start signal.

Each desk boasted a brass knob with a lever sticking out the top, around the base of which was a large circular piece of parchment paper with writing on it. One could dial in a record using names at one desk, locations at another, and skill sets at the third.

Sophronia moved to the name desk. She did not know Madame Spetuna's real name. She had to hope that the file could also be found under her alias.

At Dimity's nod, she pushed the lever toward the letter S. The machinery of the record room came to life with an enormous clatter, made all the louder by the unnatural stillness that had preceded it. The whoosh of heat, the hiss of steam, and the great rattle of gears, pistons, and rotary mechanisms were enough to wake even Sister Mattie. They were sure to alert Professor Braithwope. Crazy he might be, but there was nothing wrong with his supernatural hearing. And he, at least, would still be up.

The records shifted from one part of the room to another, parting and regrouping. They whizzed around in a ballet of organization. A large cluster drifted in Sophronia's direction, stopping directly above her desk. She pressed down hard on the brass nodule and, with a loud clunk, the records dropped to eye level.

She flipped through them quickly, but none was labeled with the name Madame Spetuna. She swore and racked her brain for a clue, a memory, anything that might indicate more about the intelligencer whom she had known only by disguise. In their brief acquaintance, Madame Spetuna had gone from elderly fortune-teller to flywayman to Pickleman associate. She had appeared shipboard, borrowed Bumbersnoot, and reappeared in the heart of a vampire hive. Hers had been the assignment to read the pillows embroidered by an intelligencer in Westminster Hive, a girl who had been killed because Madame Spetuna had neglected her in favor of infiltrating the Pickleman operation.

I wonder, thought Sophronia, *what happens to those of us who disobey orders? I wonder what happens to young lady intelligencers who run away or join the enemy? There must be a record of sinners against the school. That would explain Lady Linette's anger, if she thought Madame Spetuna had stopped communicating because she was a traitor.*

She moved to the desk that dialed in locations. "Dimity, what would you label an intelligencer who turned bad? Or who went missing while under cover?"

Dimity ran to take her place and dialed in a name. While the records moved, she glanced at her necklace watch. "Ten minutes left. What would I label a traitor in code, you mean?"

"Yes, exactly. *Traitor* is for governments, *deserter* is for armies. What is it for us?"

"Carelessness." Dimity unclipped and read a record. She grinned over it and then returned it to its spot and dialed in another name.

Our head teacher would indeed think it careless to have misplaced an intelligencer. Sophronia dialed in the word *lost* to the location desk.

Records sped toward her. There were more than Sophronia had expected—a dozen at least. It made her nervous. *Lady Linette has indeed been careless.*

"Seven minutes!" Dimity was dialing in another name furiously. Sophronia didn't object—Dimity was entitled to her curiosity so long as she kept an eye to the time.

And then, there it was, the very last record, the most recent file.

Madame Spetuna was listed as an alias, and the intelligencer's real name was at the top: *Lavish Vivita.* Two decades she'd been in service, indentured to the school and farmed out, occasionally, to the potentate. Her record was one of consistent results through established identities, and Madame Spetuna was considered her most successful guise. There was an entry about becoming a flywayman. After that came mention of her using initiative, in the form of a mechanimal, to break into the Picklemen's inner circle.

There was a note at the bottom of her file, dated three months ago. *Miss Vivita is missing, presumed lost.* But there was no code, nothing that might help Sophronia persuade Lady Linette.

It was disappointing, and not only because it was of so little help. Something about it spoke to the disinterested nature of the use of intelligencers. *As if we are disposable.* Sophronia shuddered.

"Time!" Dimity ran over.

Sophronia flipped the file closed and pinned it back up. She dialed to a random location in the West Midlands, hoping Dimity had done the same with names. There was no way to disguise the fact that someone had broken in and activated the record room, but there was no need for anyone to know which files had been viewed.

"Scurry!" said Sophronia.

They ran out the door. Only to find Lady Linette, Professor Lefoux, and Professor Braithwope sitting in the hallway outside, playing cards.

"Ah, Miss Temminnick, Miss Plumleigh-Teignmott, what a surprise." Lady Linette put down her cards. "Do come over."

Professor Lefoux and Professor Braithwope continued playing, not glancing up. The vampire's mustache was in place and intact for once, waxed slightly at the tips into points of discipline. He appeared smugly pleased with his hand and not dangerous at all.

Sophronia and Dimity exchanged a look and then submissively walked to stand before Lady Linette. They both bowed their heads and crossed hands before them in the simulated meek—but actually ready for anything—position.

Lady Linette turned in her chair and showed them her hand. "Not bad, no?"

The girls looked at her and then at the others in the game. They said nothing. *Discuss someone's cards? Never.*

Lady Linette sighed. "Wait a moment, please, ladies, while we play through."

The girls waited.

Lady Linette was an odd sort of person. She was theatrically pretty, with a nice figure, modulated voice, and propensity for lavender scent. Her hair was blonde by artifice, not nature, and curled by iron, not heritage. She favored the pastel-colored gowns of a girl in her first season. Yet her face paint was applied to such excess she looked older than she actually was. Everything about her was a trick of expectation, making the truth impossible to wheedle out. Given that manipulation was one of Lady Linette's specialties, it was probably all by intelligent design in the end.

The game was some form of whist, except with three players. After another round, Lady Linette bowed out of the match. The other two continued.

Lady Linette piled her cards neatly, facedown. "You'll have to be punished, of course. Imagine, allowing yourselves to be caught."

Dimity's eyes began to well with tears.

Sophronia stood firm. There was no point in defending herself. Lady Linette hadn't believed her before and she wouldn't now, not if she thought Madame Spetuna a traitor. Then, horribly, Sophronia wondered if Madame Spetuna *was* a traitor. Was all this some kind of setup? Was the dinner party at Lord Akeldama's designed to lead them astray? Her mind whirred with the possibility.

"You'll be forbidden to attend the upcoming New Year's celebration."

"Sent down?" wailed Dimity.

"No, I think *not* sent down. We will put you in charge of Professor Braithwope for the evening. That way Professor Lefoux can attend the festivities, for a change. We will make certain he is well fed beforehand, of course. You'll be responsible for his entertainment and safety. You'd like that, wouldn't you, Professor?"

The vampire gave a glassy, disorientated fanged smile at the sound of his name.

Dimity looked scared.

Sophronia was resigned.

Professor Lefoux didn't flinch at all, although Sophronia was tolerably certain she didn't give two figs for attending the New Year's party. Professor Braithwope returned to his hand, giving little indication of following the conversation.

"Report to his private chambers one hour before the event begins. Bring cards and snacks. Oh, and carnations. Of late, Professor Braithwope has developed a love of green carnations."

Dimity and Sophronia flinched. Where would they find green carnations floating over Dartmoor?

However, they knew better than to question orders when being punished.

"Dismissed!" Lady Linette turned back to the game.

Sophronia and Dimity skittered away feeling foolish and disheartened.

Dimity cast herself dramatically on the couch in the parlor when they returned to their chambers. It was very late and they ought to be in bed, but such a calamity as this must be discussed immediately. "I told you we'd be tea party embargoed. Oh, the tragedy of it all!"

Sophronia said, "That was odd."

"No, it wasn't odd at all. It was exactly what I said would happen." Dimity's irritation presented itself as aggressively removing hairpins and then winding them together into a metallic nest. Her liberated curls developed wisps, making her look like a mad hermit—a sparkly mad hermit.

"No, not *that*. What's odd was when Lady Linette asked us what we were looking for in the record room."

"I missed that bit."

"Exactly! Sometimes the most important piece of information is the chunk left out of the conversation." Sophronia sing-songed the sentence in a fine imitation of Professor Lefoux's perfect elocution.

"Oh." Dimity put down her hairpin nest, interested despite her annoyance. "You think she knew what we were looking for?"

"Or the school has some kind of new technology that allows them to track what files we examined. Invisible powder? Feel anything on your fingertips?"

"No."

"Me neither. Then again..." Sophronia trailed off, biting her lip.

"Then again *what*?"

"It's possible they knew what we were after and planted false information for us to find."

"Could this be a lesson? Do they want us to figure that out?"

"Maybe. Or maybe it wasn't us they were expecting, not really."

"Lady Linette said she wasn't surprised."

"Lady Linette is the mistress of misdirection, remember?"

Dimity flopped back. "Sometimes I hate this place. Wouldn't you like it if just once everything was exactly as it seemed?"

"No, that's a horrible idea."

"You *would* say that. So what did you learn, misinformation or no?"

"Madame Spetuna's real name, and that she is missing, presumed lost to evil. That Lady Linette may think her a traitor, which is why she won't believe me. Or that she really is a traitor. In either case, I wager she is back with the Picklemen. And you? Whose files did you look at?"

Dimity sat up, gossip in the offing. "Yours, mine, Monique's, and Agatha's. You know Sidheag's is gone? Vanished. Wonder where they file those ones—you know, the students who got away."

"Possibly also with the lost. Anything juicy?"

"Not in mine, except they actually think I'm better than I think I am. Which is nice."

"But not a surprise, Dimity. Most of us think that."

Dimity blushed with pleasure. "Why, thank you. Monique's says a lot about her hive. When the school punished her by not allowing her to finish, they removed her from the viable intelligencer roster but kept her record in play. I guess she has enough training to remain in the game." Dimity knew Sophronia desperately wanted to hear about the Sophronia file. Of course, Dimity saved it purposefully for last.

Little drama-monger. Sophronia let her have her fun. After all, she felt guilty about getting them caught.

"Agatha's was interesting."

"How so?"

"Terribly fat. You know her father is in all sorts of pies?"

Sophronia had a vision of an older male version of Agatha with his head sticking out of a shepherd's pie, as if he were bathing in it. She snorted a laugh.

Dimity corrected herself without pause. "Well, his fingers are. And Agatha has met Lord Akeldama before, several times. They've had *dealings*."

"There was no indication of that at his dinner party."

"I know. And there's a note that says they think she's running a long-form field operation."

"Agatha? Really? On whom? Her family?"

"Didn't specify. Could be on the school. Could be on us, I suppose. But there you have it."

Sophronia frowned. She could hardly believe it. Agatha wasn't that good. Or was she? Sophronia shook her head. She didn't want to start mistrusting her dearest friends. Down that road lay a madness as horrible as Professor Braithwope's. She was already doubting Madame Spetuna.

"Could we ask her about it?" Dimity was cautious.

"We could. But at what risk? Would we lose her friendship through suspicion? Or truth?"

Dimity stood up. "I'm for bed. This has been an eventful evening."

"Dimity?"

"Yes, Sophronia?" Dimity's tone was very arch indeed.

Sophronia made herself sound as humble as possible. "I apologize for getting you into trouble this evening."

"Apology accepted. And?"

"You were right about the punishment being us missing the ball."

"Very good. And?"

"I shouldn't have been so impulsive as to plan this action without researching the target first."

"True. And?"

"Will you please tell me what was in *my* file?"

"Since you ask so nicely. It was pretty much what might be

expected. The fact that you are a covert recruit is at the top. There's a note that you'd make a good independent intelligencer and they recommend against marriage right away—unless you net yourself one of the princes or a high-up Pickleman. A prince of the blood, said the note, seems unlikely. They know Lord Akeldama offered for patronage. Your seduction marks are low. I guess they don't know about Soap, do they, Sophronia?"

Sophronia gasped. "Really, Dimity, I say."

Dimity was smug. "That would make you similar to Madame Spetuna, as an operative, I guess."

Sophronia was disappointed. She already knew all that— or at least suspected it. The recommendation for independent action in the field was nice. Most girls finished by coming out and being married into a position of power, the better to uncover information and manipulate society. Most would marry multiple times. It was an odd compliment to be thought capable of something different. It was also an insult to her seductive powers.

"That's it?" Sophronia pressed.

"That's about all." Dimity was holding something significant in reserve.

"Dimity, please?" It was like convincing a cow to lay eggs.

Dimity relented at last. "They know you made a promise to indenture to the dewan."

"What?"

"It says, right at the end of the file. No comment on how they know, who told them, or whether it's considered a positive. But they do know."

"I'm an idiot to think I have any secrets."

Dimity only looked more smug.

"Go to bed, do," ordered Sophronia.

Dimity laughed and went, but they both knew who had won that round.

Sophronia repaired to her room to find Bumbersnoot waiting for her.

Agatha had clearly been playing with him. He had one of her lace tucks tied about his head, like a jaunty tiara.

Sophronia picked him up for a cuddle. Not that a metal dog was the best cuddler, being hard, oily, ashy, and hot. But it made her feel better.

She put him on the foot of the bed, washed her face and hands, and slipped into her nightgown. She climbed under the covers, tucking her feet under her mechanimal for warmth, and tried to sleep. *If it's in my record that I promised the dewan, then Lady Linette has been told by someone.* She listed the possibilities: Dimity, Agatha, Soap, Captain Niall, or the dewan himself. Of the five, she was absolutely certain of only one person's loyalty—Soap.

She missed him so much it actually hurt.

CRISIS 9

TEA EMBARGO

New Year's Eve dawned damp and disgruntled, a soggy tea towel of a day. But by noon the rain had turned to mist, and by sunset it looked like there might be a clear sky over the evening festivities. The girls were delighted. Rain would keep them all inside the dining hall, but clear skies meant the squeak decks were open territory, and teachers could only chaperone so many couples at once. Mademoiselle Geraldine, proverbial apple cart almost overset by her heavy breathing, issued strict instructions that they were to avoid *tête-à-têtes*. But while the headmistress didn't know this was a school of espionage, the other teachers did, and were looking at a long night of tea-related canoodling. Professor Lefoux was positively dour at the prospect.

As the moon, almost full, popped up over the horizon in a cheery manner, Mademoiselle Geraldine's girls glided into Swiffle-on-Exe to find the Bunson's boys all standing, waiting, with flowers and other appropriate offerings at the edge of the goat path. Of course, Dimity and Sophronia weren't waiting with the other ladies on the midship reception deck. But they did have good box seats. They watched it all from the comfort—it must be admitted the deck chairs were quite posh—of Professor Braithwope's private balcony.

"And so we glide in on the wisps of receding fog, emerging out of the white with the rays of the dying sun highlighting all our puffy majesty." Dimity was moved by loss to muttering poetic twaddle.

"Don't be ridiculous." Sophronia would have none of it. "We are a chubby caterpillar with delusions of balloon grandeur."

Forbidden to attend, they were nevertheless dressed for the festivities. Even Professor Braithwope had rediscovered a measure of his old dapper nature in a suit of deep-purple velvet with a lavender brocade vest and purple cravat. He sat, docile, between the two young ladies, knitting what looked like a tea cozy in the shape of a hedgehog. Bumbersnoot, wearing a black cravat, lounged happily at their feet. Occasionally he wuffed at Professor Braithwope's yarn basket but so far showed no inclination to nibble it.

"Sophronia, hush. I'm enjoying wallowing in a maudlin humor."

"Apologies, Dimity. Do carry on."

They watched the sooties crank down the massive staircase. Billowing steam wafted up. The young ladies milled about in excited agitation.

"There they all are." Dimity was very good at wallowing. "Like colorful fruit being steamed for the pudding course. I should have so liked to be a piece of fruit on that table."

"What kind?"

"A peach, of course."

"Of course." Sophronia privately felt Dimity more of the gooseberry fool at the moment.

Dimity had optimistic plans to sneak off and visit the party, or at least one edge of it where Lady Linette and Professor Lefoux might not notice her. Dimity was never one to miss an event where tea cakes were on the line. Sophronia intended to try as well—after all, she was under orders to get information out of Felix. She couldn't very well do that while on vampire nanny duty. Thus both young ladies had dressed in their best gowns. It must be admitted that their attire pushed the edge between ball and dinner dress, but since they didn't have to pass any kind of inspection, they had both taken risks. Or, more to the point, Dimity had taken a risk and chivvied Sophronia into doing the same.

Sophronia self-consciously tucked her shawl around her shoulders. Perhaps she had taken *too much* of a risk.

Dimity caught her at it.

"Stop twitching."

"I'm cold," protested Sophronia, worried over the expanse of chest she was displaying.

"Rubbish." Dimity's dress was equally low cut, but, as she put it, she hadn't been blessed with Sophronia's turnips. Admittedly, when compared with Agatha or Mademoiselle Geraldine, even Sophronia was a mere radish, but the dress she had on exposed everything but the tips, so to speak.

Dimity's gown was peach silk with multiple pleats about the neckline ending in scalloped lace. There was a black bow at the waist, as well as one on each shoulder. It was actually quite elegant. She had accentuated the simplicity with jet jewelry, black gloves, and black slippers. Normally, jet was only for those in mourning, but it was an ingenious pairing. All that black against the peach of her dress and skin made Dimity looked pretty *and* wealthy.

Sophronia's dress was very sophisticated, possibly overly so. She could hardly believe Petunia had purchased it for her. Sophronia had objected at the time to its being too grown-up. But her sister, who might have been cautious had Sophronia liked it, had advocated heavily once she saw how afraid Sophronia was of the cut. It had no ruffles, no pleats, no lace—nothing but a fitted bodice and a full skirt. Nothing to hide any sins of the figure. The fabric was what made it shine, a vibrant red with black brocade flowers. The short sleeves did end in tiny puffs, but that was it, except, of course, for the extremely low neckline. It was better suited to a lady twice her age and firmly married. However, Dimity thought they might as well go all in, as they expected few would actually see them. And Sophronia felt that if she was to wheedle information out of Felix, this dress was the best help she could get.

They watched the young men board, picking out their particular acquaintances. Lord Dingleproops was there with Lord Mersey and the rest of the Pistons. Pillover trailed reluctantly at the back of the crowd. Both girls were delighted to find he was attending. It pleased Dimity, mostly because she knew he would be miserable. It pleased Sophronia because Agatha had been so unhappy at having to go to the party without them.

They did not see Vieve among the attendees. *Has she gotten*

into trouble? Worse, has she been exposed as female? Sophronia's scalp prickled in fear. There was great reassurance in knowing Vieve was their inside agent at Bunson's—not to mention her useful mechanical talent. If she had been compromised, they were all in trouble.

Professor Braithwope leaned forward as if only now noticing they had visitors, his knitting needles continuing to click.

"What's that, then? First course?"

"Fruit course." Dimity grinned.

Sophronia shook her head slightly. "It's a tea party, Professor. They are coming on board for the New Year's event, remember?"

"Whoever heard of such a thing? One never serves school-boys at a tea party. Too disruptive. Only the finest young ladies ought to be consumed, everyone knows that. Like yourselves. With a liver-and-egg butter sauce, of course." The vampire regarded them each in turn, out of the corner of his eye. There was such a focus on their necks that even Dimity pulled up her shawl to cover the exposed flesh, although it conflicted with the much-vaunted neckline of her lovely gown.

"Pity." The vampire returned focus to his knitting. "I'm not hungry for either, whot."

The boys looked a treat. There wasn't much leeway in the dress of a young man attending a tea party, so they were of a set. A few had gone to the pink, peaking up their collars and donning very tight and very loud plaid trousers and impossibly enormous cravats. These stood out among the rest like peacocks among the chickens. After all, Bunson's was a school for evil geniuses, and scientists weren't encouraged to experiment with fashion, only weaponry.

The boys having boarded and the staircase retracted, the school rose slightly. It wasn't going to drift off for an hour yet, in case there were stragglers. With nothing left to see and the night turning chilly, Sophronia and Dimity prepared to chivvy the vampire indoors. It had taken them an age to get him outside in the first place, so they were ready for a battle.

"Come along, Professor, do," wheedled Dimity.

The vampire jerked to his feet, head cocked. He sniffed. "Broiled monkey."

"Later, Professor." Sophronia opened the door for him.

A cough at their feet interrupted the coaxing.

Dimity squeaked as a small soot-covered face appeared by their toes. A sootie had climbed up to the bottom edge of the balcony and was peering at them through the rails.

Professor Braithwope looked down, his mustache quivering like a hound scenting the fox. "And this one comes to the table burned and dirty? I think not. Fire the cook! What terrible presentation. Send it away and demand another, whot." With which he drifted sedately into his chambers.

Dimity assumed—quite rightly—that any lowbrow visitor must be for Sophronia. So she merely gave her friend a telling look, snatched up the vampire's knitting, and followed him inside.

"Yes, Handle?" Bumbersnoot tottered over to join Sophronia in looking down at their visitor. The little mechanimal seemed thrilled—rarely was anyone at his level. Perils of being a sausage dog, mechanical or no.

The sootie grinned up at Sophronia. "You look mighty fine this evening, miss. Mighty fine, indeed."

Sophronia clutched her shawl to her bosom, realizing it was horribly visible when she bent forward to talk. "Thank you kindly."

"You got yourself a visitor groundside. Old friend. Says he made the trip special and you might want to hurry."

Sophronia nodded. "Drift-off is in an hour?"

"That's orders, miss, as they stand now. You know the Uptops—could change at any moment, and we can't hold the ship for you. Not even in that dress."

Sophronia nodded.

"You wearing your sproingy?"

Sophronia fished her hurlie out of Bumbersnoot. There was just enough room to stash it and the obstructor inside him, what with Vieve's modifications. She couldn't wear them outright, they clashed with her dress. She strapped her hurlie on and considered the obstructor.

"Will this take long, do you think?"

"That's rather up to you and the visitor, miss."

"It had better not. I'm not dressed for this. You'll have to provide an assist? Up for it?"

"Of course, miss. My pleasure." No doubt he was thrilled by the opportunity to look down her dress the entire time. *Why did I listen to Dimity?*

Sophronia hooked the hurlie grapple on the edge of the balcony, hiked up her skirts—much to the sootie's delight—and climbed over the railing to drop next to him. She looked down to the ground directly below, and there, indeed, was a familiar figure, waiting patiently.

Her skin prickled in a much less fear-driven manner.

She kicked herself off to swing down and then in to catch a lower balcony. Handle unstrapped her hurlie from Professor Braithwope's balcony and dropped it to her. It was always easier to go *up* the outside of an airship. Usually, for down, Sophronia utilized stairs and hallways inside, but with help, this method was fastest.

She hooked and dropped again. Then had to wait while Handle climbed down and unhooked her. He had no hurlie, so his descent was all skill. Sophronia though he ought to be teaching the young ladies of Mademoiselle Geraldine's lessons on climbing. Then again, climbing was part of his job. In addition to feeding the boilers, it was sooties who ran the rigging and repaired the outside of the balloons.

She dropped to the lowest balcony, the level above engineering, and tried to estimate the remaining distance to the ground. *Should be fine.*

One last unhook, reel in, and hook again, and she dropped the final length. She dangled about one story up, but considering who was waiting for her, she figured he could give her a lift back when she needed it.

"Catch!" Sophronia unstrapped the hurlie from her wrist and let go, falling the remainder of the distance.

She landed in his arms, easy for a supernatural creature to catch someone her size. The poufy skirts added cushioning.

Dimity's head poked out over the balcony edge far above.

"Oh, really!" her friend yelled. "I leave you for five minutes to have a conversation and this happens? You are certifiably impossible." Her eyes widened as she took in Sophronia's position, wrapped in a gentleman's arms. "And a *strumpet*!"

"You chose this dress," Sophronia objected.

"Bunter!" said Dimity.

"I'll be quick, I promise." Sophronia was not worried about being overheard, as everyone was now inside at tea.

"Yes, I understand that's part of the strumpet's profession." Even Dimity could be crass on occasion.

Sophronia tried not to laugh. "Just keep him knitting!"

"Thank you for your sage advice." Dimity snorted loudly enough for Sophronia to hear, even on the ground. Or perhaps she imagined it, because she knew Dimity would snort.

Sophronia turned in Soap's arms to look shyly up into his dark eyes. "You can put me down now."

"No." His smile was wide and his teeth were still startlingly white, but immortality had given them points where most humans had none.

Sophronia had always loved Soap's smile, but now it was more predatory than comforting. Fortunately, the twinkle in his eyes was the same.

"Please?"

Soap pretended to consider her request and finally set her gently on her feet.

Sophronia took a moment to put herself in order, touching her hair and untucking and smoothing down her skirts.

Soap's eyes widened into saucers at the cut of her gown. She swore she could hear his breath hitch. It was ridiculously satisfying. Then, annoyed with herself and the dress, she wrapped the shawl tightly 'round her chest. *I'm supposed to be putting a stop to Soap's romantic notions, not be charmed that he finds me attractive.*

Caught up in reprimanding herself, she gave a startled squeak as he snatched her up into his arms once more, unbalancing and kissing her. No hesitation, no tentative touches, a full deep hungry kiss. It left her breathless and discombobulated, and even angrier at the dress.

"Soap, we really shouldn't." Sophronia pushed herself away.

Soap was panting a little. She was secretly delighted to find that he was just as affected as she. It would be horrible to be the only one.

"I thought, after what happened when I died, that you loved me."

Sophronia winced and looked down at her hands. How to say anything to that without lies or heartbreak?

"Oh, I forgot. It makes you uncomfortable, doesn't it? To talk of feelings. Romance." Soap brightened.

Sophronia took the coward's way out and switched topics. "What are you doing here? Is the dewan with you? Are you all right? Is he all right? Has something happened with the Pickleman situation?"

Soap answered, ticking questions off with his fingers. "I came because I wanted to see you. The dewan is not with me. I'm well. He's well. The Pick—"

"Wait, he's not *here*? But *Soap*, tomorrow is full moon!"

"I know that."

"But you're newly made! You can't be parted from him at such a time, can you?"

"I'm tired of being attached to his apron strings." Soap looked more out of temper than he should over such a sensible comment. She was only thinking of his safety. He was almost growling.

"Oh, sweet heaven. You're not supposed to be here, are you? You came without permission. And you're not yet in control of shift. How could you be so *stupid*? Where were you sleeping all day? You must have traveled to get here last night. Who guarded you?"

A small figure materialized out of the shadows and put up his hand. *No*, her *hand*. "Um, that would be me." *Vieve*.

Sophronia turned her ire on the young inventor. "Do you *know* what an insane risk he's taking?"

"Don't get all grumpy with me, termagant. What was I to do? He turned up, it was dawn, I couldn't very well send him packing after sunup, now could I? Even I know a young werewolf can get seriously damaged under such circumstances. So I stuck him in the bathhouse."

"What?"

Vieve shrugged in that very French way of hers. "It's a boys' school. The bathhouse is rarely used. Then I figured you two could have your smooch, disgusting, by the way"—Sophronia supposed Vieve was too young to think of romance as anything but revolting—"and we could pack him off tonight none the worse for it."

"Oh, did you?"

"Yoo-hoo, don't I have a say in this conversation?" Soap had calmed while they bickered.

Sophronia turned on him. "Exactly why are you here *now*? And don't prattle on about not being able to stay away from me. If that's your real reason, you had better come up with an alternative or I shall box your ears, werewolf or no."

Soap took a breath. "The Picklemen have one or more intelligencers infiltrating your school tonight. Disguised as Bunson's students."

"Impossible. Surely the professors would spot new boys."

"They've been vouched for by a wealthy patron."

"But why would the Picklemen want to attend our New Year's party? It only a tea."

"The dewan thinks it's to gather information of some kind, that it's not very important."

Sophronia nodded. "You disagree with him?"

Soap went oddly flat. "A pup does not disagree with his Alpha. Not if he wants to escape discipline."

Sophronia looked from him to Vieve. "What do they hope to accomplish?"

Vieve said, "They could be after a piece of technology, something of my aunt's, perhaps. She's not always"—a pause while she considered word options—"*safe* in her inventions."

"They did visit once before."

"They did? You didn't tell us that," said Soap.

"I don't work for the dewan yet."

"And what am I, chopped liver?" Soap paused. "Oh, chopped liver sounds tasty right about now."

"Soap, you are his get. I'm not stupid."

Soap looked hurt. "Does that mean you don't trust me anymore?"

Sophronia paused—*did it?* "If I had told you of the first infiltration in confidence, would you have reported it to him?"

"Not if you asked me not to."

"Well, it's pointless to discuss now."

"And yet it is in your nature to be dishonest, even with me." He was angry.

Sophronia was hurt, especially given how hard she had been working not to have to lie to him about her feelings. By all rights she should simply tell Soap that she didn't love him, send him away with no hope of any kind of future together. In the long run, that would be better for both of them. And she could do it, too. She had the training. *But I'd lose him entirely. He said there was no possibility of friendship. I'm weak*, thought Sophronia. *It is not the thought of Soap's pain that keeps me silent, but of my own.*

So she said, "Why are you so upset? You are the one person whose loyalty I have never doubted."

"That is *not* the same thing," growled Soap.

Vieve was impatient. "Are you two having your first lovers' spat? Right now? You realize your school is drifting?"

The dirigible had moved some distance away. Yet there was something impossible to resist about their disagreement. Sophronia had never before wanted so much to be *right*. *How dare he expect me to simply tell him everything? It is my livelihood to be circumspect. Not to mention my nature. Does he want me to change? Does he want to limit me to his—or worse, the dewan's— expectations of a woman's place?* Those thoughts refused to be separated from her other worry. *How dangerous is it for him the night before full moon? And how much in danger is poor Vieve, forced into guarding him?* There was also guilt. He had risked everything to bring her this information, and yet she played close and tight with her own knowledge. She should have told him about the pilot's bubble. Shouldn't she?

"Trust is a lot to ask of someone," she said, finally.

"Exactly. I should think that I, at least, have earned your trust." Soap hunched his shoulders and lowered his voice. "Is that why you won't let me court you?"

Sophronia couldn't help her frustration. Why was he so willfully obtuse? "Oh, for goodness' sake, be reasonable. How could I? You are a newly made werewolf loner, secret pawn for a political player."

"And your soon-to-be patron."

"And so we marry and what happens? What world do you think we live in, Soap? What of my family, my friends, my position in society? Are you asking me to give them up?"

"Of course not!"

"So what courting do you propose?"

"I could be discreet."

"And you would be, what, my dirty little supernatural secret? I keep you boxed away and hidden along with my espionage activities?" Sophronia was moved to verbal indiscretion.

"Why not? You would be wonderful at it."

"Because you're better than that, Soap! We're better than that!" Sophronia didn't even know she felt it until she yelled it.

"So you *do* love me."

Sophronia lost her anger on a breath of air and crumpled into sadness. "It doesn't change the state of society."

He reached for her and she jerked back. "No."

Soap drew back. "I can wait."

"Don't."

This time it was Soap's turn to flinch.

There was something wrong about his mouth. As though he were trying to swallow his own teeth, or was that canines? Was he starting to shift? She'd read somewhere that excess of emotion could affect the control of young werewolves, and the moon was almost full.

Soap hunched forward a little more. He seemed to be shivering.

"Soap! Are you unwell?" Vieve lurched forward. Sophronia had almost forgotten she was there. How embarrassing.

Soap's teeth were beginning to extend. "I'm sorry. I'm so sorry. But I think you both should run." His hair was becoming very shaggy, as though it wanted to creep out of the tight curls and descend all over his body as fur. His ears looked like they were stretching slightly, and his eyes were turning from brown to gold.

Sophronia couldn't help but back away.

Vieve, with casual grace, reached over one shoulder, pulled a blunderbuss from a strap on her back, pointed it at Soap, and shot.

"Wait, Vieve, what are you . . . ?" Sophronia trailed off, for no massive silver bullet emerged. Instead the gun emitted a large mesh net, with weighted edges like a fisherman's, that flew out into a wide arc, completely surrounding Soap.

"Ouch, that stings." Soap looked like a disgruntled bride.

"Good." Vieve was unsympathetic. "Now get ahold of yourself."

"Yes, Captain." Soap came over all meek.

Everything about him seemed to shiver and tighten, pulling in on itself. His hair went back to the tight black coils Sophronia was so fond of petting. His ears returned to their roundness, his eyes to their liquid brown.

"How do you feel?" Sophronia moved back to stand near, wanting to touch him through the net.

"Ashamed. Trapped."

"Controlled, I hope." Sophronia hid her worry.

"I think you should kiss him." Vieve's small face was grave.

"Thank you for the advice. It shall be recorded for posterity that you once encouraged public courtship." Sophronia pretended outrage.

Vieve was offended. "No, silly. Wolves respond well to touch. His instinct for protection and preservation should kick in through concentrated affectionate exposure. This might limit his capacity for shift under constraints of emotional surety."

Sophronia looked at Soap through the mesh veil. "I think she's speaking English, but I'm not convinced."

Soap laughed. "She thinks if we kiss it will control my desire to shift, convince my wolf side to see you as family, not food."

Sophronia considered. "And what do you think?"

"Can't hurt to try."

"Opportunist." Sophronia bent forward and kissed him, mostly because she wanted to. The cool metal of the mesh between their skin seemed to burn Soap, yet his lips were eager under the barrier.

Sophronia drew back.

"Also, you two need to make up." Vieve began coiling in the net, moving toward them as she did so, but ostentatiously looking away from the region of their mouths.

"Is it working?" Sophronia asked.

Soap closed his eyes, as though running an inventory of his internal organs. "Feels like."

Vieve looked to Sophronia. "Ready?"

Sophronia nodded.

Vieve whipped away the silver net and Sophronia stepped into Soap's arms. She pressed her lips to his again—for medicinal purposes only, of course. They embraced, perhaps with more urgency than passion, but it was firm and good.

When they parted, the anger was gone—from both of them.

"See?" Vieve was unbearably smug.

Meanwhile, the massive dirigible had drifted farther, and there were shouting heads peeking out of the hatch of engineering.

Sophronia went red as a beet. They had been observed!

She grabbed Soap by the hand. "Come on."

With Vieve following, they dashed after the airship. It probably looked ridiculous, the three small figures madly chasing a low-flying dirigible. Luckily, there wasn't much breeze that evening, a rare thing indeed on the moor, so they caught up to it easily.

"Can you lift me up?" Sophronia asked Soap.

"I could as a wolf, but it's too dangerous to shift now." He shook his head regretfully. He whistled up three sharp toots and gave a birdlike caw and the sooties dropped down their old rope ladder.

"You coming too, old man?" Handle stuck his head out the hatch.

Soap smiled sadly. "Not anymore. I can't float, even if I wanted to."

"Gone on to bigger and fuzzier things, I hear."

"So they tell me."

"Don't you forget us when you get all over covered in high-and-mighty werewolf-type business, you hear?" ordered one of the other sooties.

"Never," replied Soap. "Ready?"

"Yes."

Before she could protest, Soap kissed her fiercely one last time and then tossed her upward.

Sophronia caught the end of the rope ladder and hoisted herself up, climbing easily, even with her massive skirts. Below, there came another pop as Vieve shot out her net. Once more it draped over Soap, like a veil in a Greek tragedy.

He didn't seem to be inclined to shift, but it was a sensible precaution.

"Come along," Sophronia heard Vieve say. "Let's get you to that bathhouse. This is getting ridiculous, you realize? What am I supposed to do with you tomorrow night? You'll be a full-on wolf whether you like it or not. Net or no. How do I hide a wolf in a bathhouse?" Sophronia was through the hatch at that point.

Vieve's lecture faded away.

Sophronia could only hope the dewan guessed Soap's location and came after. She was immensely grateful to Vieve—the small inventor had saved her and those she loved yet again.

The sooties were impressed by her dress. Sophronia put her humiliation aside to advocate for speedy travel to Professor Braithwope's quarters—with their assistance. They were only too pleased to help. Handle returned her abandoned hurlie.

Sophronia was up and over the vampire's balcony, brushing

down her gown and patting her curls, less than an hour after she left. She'd made excellent time.

Dimity didn't see it that way. She was playing backgammon with Professor Braithwope and sipping a small glass of some illicit beverage. "Where *have* you been?"

"Sorry, I was needed groundside. Is that *sherry?*"

"You were fraternizing," accused Dimity.

Sophronia was amazed at her powers of deduction. "How can you tell?"

Dimity looked smug. "Slightly bruised lips, spots of color on the cheeks, hair mussed. Who was it? Has Lord Mersey won himself back into your good graces?" Dimity was being purposefully obtuse. She wanted to squeeze a confession out of Sophronia.

"Hardly."

"Oh, no, you haven't found yourself another inappropriate sootie, have you?"

"No, it's the same one, as you very well know."

Dimity rolled her eyes. "Sophronia, I mean this quite kindly, but there is no possible future there. Quite apart from anything else, he has eternity and you do not. One way or another, you're going to break that boy's heart."

"I know, and I told him as much."

"Wars have been fought for less, whot." They had almost forgotten that Professor Braithwope was there.

Dimity waved a hand at the vampire. "Thank you. Exactly my point, Professor. You talk some sense into her."

The vampire leaned forward over the backgammon board, a serious expression on his pale face. His mustache drooped.

"Whatever you do, do not pickle gherkins. Onions, yes. Gherkins, never."

Sophronia nodded, lips twitching. "Certainly, Professor, very sage advice."

"So you have ended things?" Dimity knew from experience that Sophronia was attached to Soap in a manner Dimity could never comprehend.

"I tried." Strangely enough, saying that made Sophronia's eyes prick with tears. "Dimity, I am so afraid. I . . ." She took a shaky breath. "I find myself struggling to be sensible about matters of the heart."

Dimity instantly shifted to put a warm comforting arm about her. "Of course you do, my dear. We all have that struggle. I mean to say, look at me! I was driven to poetry by a Dingleproops! You haven't fallen that far, have you?"

Sophronia sniffed. "No."

"Well, then, that's something to be proud of, now, isn't it?"

Sophronia gave a watery nod.

Professor Braithwope passed her a large purple handkerchief, his mustache dropping sympathetically. Sophronia took it gratefully and dabbed at her eyes, concentrating on controlling her breathing.

Dimity, with perfect understanding, returned to the game so that Sophronia might gather herself together without further embarrassment.

The game ended when Dimity realized that she had already been beaten four moves earlier. The vampire picked up more knitting. This time it was some fine lace-weight work—an elegant lady's shawl.

"That's quite lovely, Professor." Sophronia was pleased to find that her voice did not wobble. "Does it say anything?" Knitted code was common parlance among Mademoiselle Geraldine's girls.

The vampire was confused at the question. "Say? No. I don't think so. The pattern is called dawn-light." He turned the pretty thing about in his hands. "Ironic, really." He focused on his task.

Dimity focused on Sophronia. "I think we could leave him for a bit, don't you?"

"Why, Dimity, are you suggesting we sneak down to the tea?"

"The perfect thing to cheer you up."

"How right you are. But we'd be in even more trouble if they discovered we abandoned our post. Then again, Soap came to tell me that we have Pickleman infiltrators among the guests. And I did say to the dewan I would try Felix."

"It would be a shame to waste our dresses on only the professor here."

The vampire looked up. "Whot, whot?"

"Nothing, Professor," singsonged the two girls in unison.

Sophronia cocked her head at Dimity. "Are you certain?"

Dimity's round face scrunched up as if she had eaten a sour lemon. "I hate missing everything. That's why I want to marry well and be a grand lady. Then I can host all the parties, all the time, and see everything that is going on *always*. How can you stand not knowing?"

"For you, it's gossip. For me, it's action."

Dimity blinked at this revelation. "I guess so."

"Shall we, then?"

Dimity grinned. "Professor, you don't mind if we step out for a few minutes, do you?"

"Certainly not. Bring some brandy, and some of those little cake thingies."

"But, Professor, you don't eat cake."

"Don't want to eat them. Want to toss them overboard at the wild ponies, whot."

"Oh."

"Man's gotta have some kind of entertainment on this floating barge."

"True, sir. Anything else?"

The vampire considered the question. "Well, if one of those young men is in the offing, I might like a snack in a half hour or so. Could hit the spot, if the stock is not too starched. Make sure to pick one of the sporty types. I loathe the taste of pasty dandies with delusions of intellectual grandeur and a propensity to lurk indoors. Spoils the flavor of the blood."

Dimity and Sophronia exchanged looks.

"Does it really?" Sophronia made a mental note. Pillover was safe.

Then, before he could think of anything else, they left.

IN A PICKLE AT A TEA PARTY

The tea party was in full vibration when they arrived. What probably started as mild talk and meek encounters around set tables had descended into a proper rout. The young persons were now circulating, seeking preferred partners or more engaging conversation. In some cases, this was out of custom; in others, it was the quest for adventure. A few young ladies had assignments. A small group danced at the back, accompanied by Miss Perriwonks on her lap harp with amplification dongle. There was even one table at cards.

Certainly, it was not done to have dancing and card play at a tea party, but the hour was late and it was New Year's Eve, so some laxness was permitted. Perhaps this had more to do with the fact that the professors had opted to break out the bubbly early. Professor Lefoux remained sober and glowering, but that was her lot in life. As yet she had not been driven to leave the head table and actually discipline anyone. Instead, she paid irritated attention to Mademoiselle Geraldine. Tea was the headmistress's favorite event, and though she objected to the presence of boys, she was disposed to enjoy herself.

The tea was very good—not to mention the champagne. Cook had truly excelled, for there were Scotch seedcake, grapes in brandy, glazed apples, orange biscuits with medlar jelly, almond torte—without cyanide, everyone hoped—and Charlotte pudding with Milanese cream. The boys gorged themselves, as was their wont, and even a few of the girls ate with more enthusiasm than delicacy.

Sophronia and Dimity glided through one of the staff entrances behind a clangermaid. Sophronia eyed a bowlful of glazed apples and plotted how to kidnap it for the sooties. The girls kept their fans up, covering most of their faces. They did not skulk, but instead acted as if they belonged, moving in behind the dancers as though observing the couples while engaged in a protracted private gossip.

"Do you see that?" Sophronia nudged Dimity to look at a table near the back corner, where Pillover and Agatha conversed. Pillover was almost animated as he relayed something to their friend.

"Do you think that is a declaration?" wondered Sophronia.

Dimity was disgusted. "My revolting brother has never *declared* anything, except perhaps an inexcusable love of Plutarch. This smooching of sooties has gone to your head."

"Smooching *werewolves*, please, Dimity." Sophronia took mock offense.

Dimity continued her affronted stance. "Pill is less firm in his commitments than calf's head jelly."

However, Pillover's face held a softness that Sophronia had never seen there before.

Agatha glanced up.

Sophronia flipped down her bladed fan for a brief moment, so Agatha could recognize her.

Agatha's eyes widened and she immediately raised her handkerchief to her face, drawing it across her lips. It was code, but not one Sophronia knew.

"What's she trying to say?" she asked Dimity.

Couples swirled between them. The debut blonde with the purple eyes was dancing with Lord Dingleproops. Dimity was entirely unruffled by this. So much for poetry.

"*I desire your acquaintance,*" interpreted Dimity. "It's not espionage, it's everyday ordinary flirtation."

Fancy that. Accessory manipulation for normal young ladies. "Why didn't Lady Linette teach us that?"

Dimity gave her a funny look. "You're supposed to arrive here knowing it, of course. Doesn't everyone? I was practically weaned on handkerchief manipulation. Not to mention the language of flowers. How on earth do you know if a man is interested without it?"

"Conversation?"

Dimity shook her head at Agatha to indicate they didn't understand what she wanted. "Why does she desire our acquaintance? She knows us already."

The two girls linked arms and huddled in, so that anyone observing would think they were undertaking serious rumor-mongering.

"She probably has important information to impart. Wants us to go over," suggested Sophronia.

"We can't," Dimity squeaked. "Sister Mattie is circulating."

Agatha began winding her handkerchief around her third finger.

"What does *that* mean?" Sophronia asked Dimity.

"*I am married.*"

That was even more confusing. Sophronia lowered her fan again and shook her head at Agatha in an accusing way.

Agatha gave an obvious sigh and then said something firm to Pillover.

Pillover grabbed up Agatha's handkerchief and began gesticulating at them with it.

"*I am a . . . new bride?*" Dimity tried.

Imagining Pillover dressed in white lace gave Sophronia a momentary attack of giggles.

Disgusted, Agatha and Pillover rose and moved through the tables. The settings were well conceived—tiered serving ware and low flower arrangements to encourage conversation. At the edge of the dance floor, Pillover took Agatha in his arms and began twirling her around, along with the other brave couples. Eventually, the set brought them close to Dimity and Sophronia. They swirled to a stop.

"Barred from attending, were you, Dim? How upsetting that must be. And how degrading to sneak into your own New Year's party." Pillover attacked his sister at her weakest point the moment they landed.

"Shut your cake hole, you revolting young blot," responded Dimity affably.

Pillover did not look at all put out, but he did clamp his mouth shut.

"Now is not the time to rankle, you two." Agatha sounded quite grown-up. "Mr. Plumleigh-Teignmott was recently telling me something terribly important. There are strangers among the boys attending our festivities."

They all turned to peruse the room, trying to spot enemies among them.

"Picklemen or their intelligencers." Sophronia saw no one notably out of place.

Pillover scrunched up his face, upset that they already knew.

Agatha rolled her eyes. "How did you know? Goodness' sake, you've been nannying a vampire. It's really too bad. I thought I had the leg up for once."

"*I* have been nannying a vampire." Dimity wanted this to be quite clear. "*Sophronia* has been sneaking off kissing sooties."

"Oh!" Pillover was almost cheerful. "Is Soap here? Bang-up chappy, that Soap."

"No, he jolly well isn't here. I sent him packing." Sophronia frowned.

"Not for good, I hope? I rather like the blighter." Pillover was remarkably egalitarian for a toff. This was possibly because he preferred Greek translations to evil inventions and had suffered under Piston recriminations as a result. Pillover, being disenfranchised, felt that the friendship of a dark-skinned member of the proletariat was solidarity, not stigma.

"Which ones are the infiltrators?" asked Sophronia before they could get distracted by her romantic entanglements.

Pillover turned to point to the far corner of the room, near the head table. "Over there, with Lord Mersey, of course. Oh, hold the horses. They've gone!"

"Of course they've gone." Sophronia whirled to find out where.

"Now, wait a moment, young lady." Dimity sounded like Mademoiselle Geraldine in her frustration. "We only *just* got here."

"You stay," said Sophronia magnanimously. "I'm going after."

"But you don't even know where they went!" objected Agatha.

"And you can't possibly leave without saying good evening to me." A new voice, warm as honey, joined the conversation.

"Gammon!" said Pillover, and then, "Come along, Miss Woosmoss. This is too rich for my blood."

Dimity also suddenly seemed to feel she was wanted elsewhere. Face still protected by her lace fan, she wandered into the crowd in a manner guaranteed to make her entirely unremarkable. She really *had* been paying attention in lessons of late.

"Ah, good evening, Lord Mersey." Sophronia's voice was equally honeyed.

"Miss Temminnick. I understood you would not be joining us this evening."

"Did you? How droll."

"Of course, silly me. You go wherever you want, don't you, Ria?" He seemed to be enjoying the fact that, this time, Sophronia was acting like Sophronia. Even if that meant she was sharp with him, or possibly because she was sharp with him.

"Not *everywhere*."

"They trained you too well, didn't they?"

Sophronia cocked her head. He was acting particularly combative. She shivered her fan slightly to expose something more of her neckline.

Felix paused, arrested, but it didn't seem to lighten his mood. If anything, it made him glower. "Seen any nice werewolves lately?"

"There was a lovely dinner party while I was in London last week. You should have been there."

"I probably should. But I was thinking, perhaps somewhat *more* recently."

Sudden dread hit the pit of Sophronia's stomach. *He knows Soap is here. Does that mean the Picklemen know? Is Soap in danger?* "What information do you think you have, Felix?" She lowered her voice.

Blow the dewan's seduction plan, she thought. *I'm going to strangle the little traitor right here. Where's my garrote?* Her free hand fisted around her *carnet de bal.* The long chains were strong enough to wrap around someone's neck—she'd made certain of it.

Felix looked down at his fingernails and pursed his beautiful mouth. "Nothing of any consequence. But then, neither is he."

Strangling is too good for him. Sophronia snapped the guard off her bladed fan with her thumb and stepped in a little closer. The razor edge gleamed.

"Now, now, Miss Temminnick, you wouldn't want to ruin that stunning—really, quite stunning, and so mature—dress with blood, would you?"

Sophronia gave a cold smile. "This dress is red, my dear viscount, with a pattern designed to hide stains."

Felix looked slightly uncomfortable. "Of course it is. And yet you can't help *him* by threatening me."

"Killing him once wasn't enough for you?"

Felix grimaced. "What, bitter you can't spawn tea-colored infants named Bubble and Suds?"

"Is that an attempt at humor? I wouldn't bother if I were you."

Felix spoke through gritted teeth. "You were mine and he stole you."

"Poor boy, is that what you thought?" Sophronia considered the root of his anger. *Was I some weird prize to him or did I actually break his heart? Terribly careless of me if I did. And either way, Soap suffers because of his bitterness?* "You never had me, silly. Even if you had, you would have driven me away, in the end. I don't like traitors."

Felix's beautiful blue eyes turned pleading. "I tried to warn you from the dirigible, remember? I tried to stop my father from shooting."

"And yet you told him we were Geraldine's girls, putting us all in danger in the first place."

"You've been safe all this time, no attempts on your life. Not from my people, anyway."

"Because we've been at school and you couldn't get to us!"

"And what about when you were in London recently?"

"You think I didn't know the werewolves had guards around my sister's house every night? Felix." Sophronia was frustrated. "Why are we always at dagger points?" Once, he had been a gentleman. She still remembered the prong incident fondly.

"Because you chose *wrong*."

Sophronia wasn't certain if he was talking about the Picklemen or Soap. "No, you did."

Something gleamed in his pale eyes. "You sure about that?

You don't know everything, Ria. You only think you do." There was something in his tone. Had his loyalties shifted?

"Actually, I know I don't. So you tell me. The Picklemen on board, what do they want?"

"Not you."

"Someone else, then? Someone who knows something. Lady Linette, perhaps?" She looked up at the head table over the sharp edge of her fan. Lady Linette sat chatting animatedly next to Mademoiselle Geraldine. There was no one lurking in the shadows to kidnap her. As if that were possible with Lady Linette.

"Something? Some device of Professor Lefoux's?" She pushed, teasing Felix with her ignorance. Pushing him to prove he knew more than she did, lord it over her.

"Poor Sophronia, you have no idea what is really going on, do you? No idea at all."

"Why don't you enlighten me, then?"

"Me? I'm only here for the tea." With which he turned and glided off—his well-tailored coat swishing. *Bother Felix for looking almost as pretty walking away as he does facing forward.*

Sophronia actually cursed. Then she returned to the real world. Felix's coyness was a hint that something more was afoot. Perhaps the Pickleman infiltrators included a key member of their infrastructure? The Chutney, even?

At which juncture, the school's proximity alarm sounded.

The proximity alarm was a series of very loud bells throughout the airship. Officially, it meant balcony access was restricted and all students were to remain stationary and *not involve themselves* in whatever was wrong. Unofficially, it meant that the school was under attack and the soldier mechanicals were marshaling on the squeak decks with cannons at the ready.

In the dining hall, the flirting and dancing and swilling of hot beverages ceased. The young ladies turned to look expectantly at the high table, awaiting orders. The nascent evil geniuses were less composed. One dropped his tea cake in alarm, a few dashed about in search of their hats—corralling one's hat is an instinctive response bred into all gentlemen. Eventually, they realized that they looked foolish, and settled into merely glancing nervously about. Verbal speculation, of course, was rife.

"Proximity alert, students. Remain calm and continue to enjoy your tea." Mademoiselle Geraldine's voice boomed out. "Geraldine's girls are not overset by a little ringing. Gentlemen of *quali-tay* do not seek their hats at the drop of a hat." She paused to grapple with her problematic metaphor, then soldiered on. "The teachers will investigate while I stay with you. Lady Linette, if you would be so kind?"

Lady Linette rose and nodded sharply to Professor Lefoux and Sister Mattie as well as a couple of the visiting Bunson's professors. They all marched from the room. Lady Linette paused at the doorway and issued a protocol order to the nearest serving mechanical. In response, the surrounding clangermaids and buttlingers rolled along their tracks to block the various doorways. There they clamped down hard to the rail, making it difficult for any student to leave the room.

Sophronia's mind was on the visiting infiltrators. Had the

Picklemen activated the alarm for some reason? Or could they be sabotaging the airship's defenses, making it easier for attackers?

There was no way she was staying trapped with tea at a time like this. Even knowing that watchful gazes were on the students, she inched toward the nearest door. She fished about inside Bumbersnoot for her obstructor. Throughout all of this, her little mechanimal remained quiet. At least she knew the Picklemen hadn't activated their valves. She thought to use her obstructor on the mechanical blocking the door and then climb out over its head.

"You there!" snapped Mademoiselle Geraldine. "Young lady in red, at the back. No leaving!"

Sophronia twitched at being noticed. She whirled to find the headmistress's eyes fixed on her.

Others turned to stare. Someone laughed, not nicely. Probably Felix Mersey. Or Preshea.

Sophronia kept her fan up, guarding her face, and made a neat curtsy of acknowledgment. Mademoiselle Geraldine looked like she might call her forward to reprimand her, but she was saved by a loud bang and a sad crunching noise.

The whole dirigible shuddered.

People screamed. Those still at tea rose from their seats. A few went for the doors. The mechanicals would not let them by. Sophronia's transgression was forgotten in the hubbub.

"Back to your seats, everyone!" ordered one of the remaining Bunson's teachers, rising to stand next to Mademoiselle Geraldine. Across the wide room, Sophronia could see he was pale and holding on to the head table in fear.

Dimity, Pillover, and Agatha used the panic to congregate around Sophronia.

Then the ship began to list to starboard.

Mademoiselle Geraldine looked less composed at this. "All will be well, young people of *quali-tay*. Stick to your tea."

"One of the balloons must be down." Agatha tried to console an unhappy-looking Pillover.

There was another boom and then a loud clanging sound. The ship shuddered again. The bells continued to peal.

Pillover said, "I hate adventure. Did I mention recently that I hate adventure? Well, I do. Sophronia, is this your fault? Have you arranged an unwarranted adventure for us?"

"I don't *think* so." Sophronia pretended to seriously consider the question. "Not this time."

"We are definitely under fire." Dimity ignored her brother.

Greatly daring, Agatha patted Pillover sympathetically on the arm.

The ship shook again.

Pillover turned green.

"Flywaymen or Picklemen?" wondered Agatha.

"Or both." Sophronia searched the room for Felix's dark head. She couldn't find him. He couldn't have gotten out—he hadn't near enough sneaking ability for that. He must be under a table or something.

Come to think on it, Sophronia couldn't see *any* of his ilk. "Where, oh where, have all the pretty Pistons gone?"

"Sophronia! You can't be thinking about flirting now," Dimity reprimanded.

"No." Sophronia lurched slightly as the airship vibrated like a dog shaking off water. "I'm thinking about taking cover."

The floor of the dining hall was now tilted to such an extreme, it was becoming impossible to hold one's footing in a dignified manner. The tables were all slipping toward the starboard wall, as only the head table was bolted down.

The students, some of them still seated and attempting to take tea, play cards, and engage in polite conversation, gripped the edges of their tables as they slid. The whole thing felt as if it were happening underwater. Apparently even a major battle was slow moving when floating.

"Hold fast, young persons of *quali-tay*. Hold fast!" sang out Mademoiselle Geraldine.

"We're sinking." Dimity's round face was pale and she clutched her tassel jet necklace as if it were a talisman she could wish upon.

"Come on." Sophronia led them to the starboard side of the room, which was now a steep downhill jaunt. The four of them backed up against the wall in the corner furthest from the head table. "Brace yourselves. We're going down."

"How do you know?" Pillover quivered in apprehension.

Sophronia tilted her head to where the Pistons had flipped a table on its edge, legs toward the starboard wall, and arranged themselves behind it, barricaded. If the ship continued to tilt, they would be effectively protected from tea party fallout. Except, perhaps, liquid damage.

Part of her wanted to stay with the Pistons, since they obviously knew what was going on. But the rest of her knew that the safest place from falling objects was actually the hallway, if they could only get past the mechanicals. Then again, with gas lines running throughout, if they did crash, the hallways might explode.

The floor was almost at a forty-five-degree angle. Everything that could slide, did. Things upended, and crashed and tumbled about. Several of the young ladies and—it must be admitted—the young gentlemen screamed. The young ladies were more properly padded for sliding, but it made for an undignified sight—ruffled skirts and petticoats, legs kicking about. In a few cases undergarments were visible!

Pillover fainted.

They all ended up bumped and bruised, piled together and leaning up against one another in an extremely intimate crush. As the proximity alarm bells continued to clang, any attempt at politely awkward conversation was impossible.

Mademoiselle Geraldine was looking quite worried.

Sophronia suspected that they were the only ones who realized they were sinking. One of the things about dirigibles, as with all balloon travel, was that without seeing the ground, it was difficult to know when one was falling out of the sky.

That is, of course, until one crashed.

Mademoiselle Geraldine's Finishing Academy for Young Ladies of Quality crashed into the moor with an impossibly loud thud. It shuddered in a way that put all previous shakes to shame. Then it rocked back and forth a few times, before ending up beached like a whale on its starboard side.

It was, after all, not designed to land.

No one screamed this time, but there were a number of gasps. A few of the young ladies who were nested near gentlemen of interest fainted delicately in said gentlemen's direction.

It was a very stately crash. Mademoiselle Geraldine had reason to be proud. True, tea was spilled, and cakes dropped, but general behavior could not be faulted. Even the debuts confined themselves to squeaks of alarm.

"Is anyone injured?" Mademoiselle Geraldine's voice rang out.

One of the young men had sprained his wrist and a debut had managed to scratch her cheek on a flower arrangement, but otherwise nothing serious. Everyone breathed sighs of relief and began to extract themselves from the pile.

Dimity slapped her brother awake.

They were still trapped in the dining hall. The mechanicals were unaffected by the tilting, since they were hooked into tracks. They could stay blocking the doors no matter what the angle of repose. However, Lady Linette's voice could be heard ordering them into movement.

Sophronia and her friends remained flattened against the wall, out of the way. Pillover, still pale and shaking, stuck close to Agatha, solicitous of her well-being, or more likely, she was solicitous of his.

Apart from Pillover, her little band was unperturbed by the fact that they had crashed. Except, of course, that they had no idea what exactly had caused the unexpected plummet. Falling out of the sky was one thing, but doing so for unknown reasons was quite unacceptable.

Having set the mechanicals back in motion, Lady Linette

skidded into the room, teetering on her heeled shoes to lean against the tilt.

"Oh, good, you're all still here. Mademoiselle Geraldine, is everyone well?"

Mademoiselle Geraldine had collapsed back into her seat at the high table. "It appears so. But, my dear, whatever has happened?"

"Flywaymen," reported Lady Linette. "We're grounded, I'm afraid. And we suspect a gas leak on the record-room level, so we must evacuate. Luckily, we drifted back toward Swiffle. We are only a few miles from Bunson's."

The teachers moved to inspect the refugees. Sophronia had no doubt there was more to the story, but this was what had been decided was worthy of headmistress and student ears.

Lady Linette began barking orders. "Ladies and visiting gentlemen, please congregate separately by year. Form orderly groups and follow me. We're going to climb out one of the nearest side balconies and drop to the ground from there. Ladies, grab your wraps and switch to practical shoes, if you have them. Dancing slippers over heels, walking boots over both. I will not have you catching cold or twisting ankles needlessly. Gentlemen, do not forget your hats. This is no lark—everyone is to stay respectable. We are safely landed, such as it is, so there is no cause to lose our sense of propriety."

Students scrambled about, searching for clothing and dropped objects. It took a few moments to get sorted, but they managed. Many of the more resourceful young ladies pocketed crumpets and other portable nibbles. Some even wrapped up whole cakes in their shawls. Everyone had heard stories about how bad the food was at the boys' school.

There was disappointment at the precipitous end to the celebration, not to mention the prospect of tromping across a damp moor in dinner slippers, but it was somewhat mitigated by excitement. There was an undercurrent of eagerness among some of the older girls. Preshea positively glowed. A late-night stroll across the moor might be utterly unpleasant, but it was an opportunity for liaison unprecedented by a mere tea party. After all, they were Geraldine's girls, always eager for a bit of peril. And this, it could not be denied, was shaping up to be a *most* perilous evening.

Sophronia's mind was calculating. She couldn't accept that flywaymen would attack for no other reason than to crash the airship. She would wager Dimity's jet necklace that they were being grounded for a specific purpose, and that the flywaymen—if indeed it was them—were under orders from the Picklemen. Sophronia had not forgotten that there were already Picklemen on board.

She had, however, forgotten Professor Braithwope.

EVACUATION SITUATION

P rofessor Braithwope came running in, mustache aquiver. He was still wearing full evening garb, but over it he had donned a yellow brocade banyan and sleeping cap. In one hand he clutched his knitting, and in the other a very special crossbow. He was quite absentminded about holding it, as though the crossbow were a stray profiterole that had caught on his sleeve. Sophronia had seen that miniature crossbow only once before, when she first arrived at the school. It shot a kind of targeting bolt, upon which the soldier mechanicals aimed their cannons. She had thought such an important weapon would be removed from the vampire's possession the moment his tether snapped. But for some reason he still had it, which meant the school had been unprotected during the previous battle.

He's been running around with that and the teachers didn't know where to find him because Dimity and I abandoned our post. Sophronia winced, guilt ridden. Was she responsible for the airship crashing, because she hadn't stayed to nanny a vampire?

Quick as the vampire had dashed in, he dashed out again.

Sophronia grabbed Dimity by the hand and nipped behind a tipped-over tea table. While the others obediently grouped by age, they made for the nearest door. Sophronia turned in the doorway and, pretending to breathe hard, dashed toward Professor Lefoux, dragging Dimity behind.

"Have you seen Professor Braithwope?" she gasped.

Professor Lefoux glared at them. "He was just here, but now he's gone again. Wasn't he your responsibility?"

Dimity fell in with the story easily. "There was all sorts of chaos, and then he grabbed up this tiny crossbow and ran off."

"We couldn't possibly hold him. He's too fast and strong." Sophronia padded the lie further.

"I hardly think that would stop you, Miss Temminnick." Professor Lefoux was not playing along.

"You didn't give us permission to use force. Certainly not on a teacher." Sophronia made her face as blank as possible.

Professor Lefoux shot them a suspicious look. "Why are you dressed like that?"

Dimity was ready. "My idea. Even if we were only going to see the professor, we wanted to look our best. It's New Year's Eve, after all."

Lady Linette came up, tutting. "We should never have put students in charge of a teacher. If we had known this would happen... Ah, well, can't worry over spilled tea. Where is the good vampire?"

"That's what I asked." Sophronia's tone implied that this was a most sensible question.

Professor Lefoux snorted. "He was here and then nipped off, with our sighting bolts, mind you. Could have used those half an hour ago. I had best go after him."

Lady Linette countermanded her. "No, he'll be fine. The ship is grounded and he can't very well stray. We are taking all possible victims with us. I need you to help with the students. Your drone duties will have to wait."

Professor Lefoux looked more annoyed at being told what to do than being denied the opportunity to check up on her master. Sophronia supposed being drone to an insane vampire was a bit different from being drone to a regular-type vampire.

"What about us?" she asked.

"You are absolved of your responsibility with regard to Professor Braithwope. Line up with the others to disembark. We're away until I'm certain all the leaks have been dealt with. Is that understood?"

Sophronia and Dimity curtsied.

A thought occurred to Sophronia. "Wait—Lady Linette?"

"What is it, Miss Temminnick? I have an evacuation to conduct."

"What about the sooties?"

Lady Linette arched one brow. "Concern for the lower orders? How terribly civic-minded of you, Miss Temminnick."

"Well?"

"Who do you think is responsible for fixing those gas leaks?"

Sophronia clamped down an immediate protest. Of course, sooties always got the dangerous tasks. The last time a cannon tore through one of the balloons, it had been sooties who climbed to repaired the damage. Gas leaks, by comparison, were easier dealt with—so long as they took care not to spark.

"And what about the danger to the sooties from Professor Braithwope?"

"You should have thought of that before you let him free, now, shouldn't you? I've no time to worry about the grubby necks of the working class. Do as you are instructed."

Despite Lady Linette's dismissive sneer, not to mention her own upbringing, Sophronia considered many of those grubby boys her friends. Soap adored them all. If they got hurt, he would never forgive her. That reminded her of Soap.

Suddenly, she wasn't so upset about being evacuated to Bunson's. She could warn Vieve that the Picklemen knew about Soap, perhaps even stop whatever evil they had planned for him. Although half of her still wanted to stay and protect the sooties.

"There isn't enough of me to go around," she muttered, climbing after the other students.

So it was that the tea party attendees—still in fancy dress—as well as the human staff and a handful of the off-shift greasers and engineers found themselves walking across a moor. The night was clear and the moon so near to full that, despite the cold, it looked to be a pleasant hike. One could easily pretend the lump of a tor off to the left was picturesque. Privately, Sophronia always thought tors looked like cow pats. Young men offered young ladies their arms. Bunson's teachers offered Geraldine's theirs. All was amicable.

Mademoiselle Geraldine stayed on board. She was still a

little tipsy. Sophronia hung back in hopes of catching a roving sootie. If she could get a message to Handle about the fact that there were loose Pickleman intelligencers—not to mention a loose vampire—on board she'd feel much better about the whole situation.

She overheard the headmistress's brief exchange with Sister Mattie.

"No, dear, no. You know I never leave the ship. I shall be perfectly topping here. I will avoid open flame, and roving fang, and finish the bubbly. Don't concern yourself on my account. I'll see you in the morning. Enjoy your midnight jaunt." She belched quietly.

"Oh, really," said Sister Mattie. "Just be careful?"

"Oh, my dear, what could possibly go wrong?"

Sophronia was never more sensitive to the headmistress's ignorance than at that juncture. It felt horrible, leaving the school without any protection. All the fallen dirigible had now was a headmistress who knew nothing, a crazy vampire who knew a whole lot but couldn't remember any of it, and a handful of sooties.

"Lady Linette." Sophronia wove her way through the long line of strolling couples to her teacher. Preshea had found herself a tall moon-faced lad who looking nothing short of stunned at his good fortune. Poor chap. She exchanged a brief glance with the deadly brunette, and then left her to her work.

"Permission to speak freely?" Sophronia had once heard a soldier use that phrase.

"At a school for spies, Miss Temminnick? Surely you jest."

Lady Linette stared at her, unblinking. They were of a height, for Lady Linette still wore her heeled slippers.

Sophronia was impressed—only Lady Linette would hike across the moor in Paris kid shoes with a military lift. She looked meaningfully at Lady Linette's escort, the oldest and most severe of the Bunson's teachers.

Lady Linette sighed. "Excuse me a moment, Professor Faldetta? I'm certain you understand. She's one of *those* students. You must have *those*?"

"Say no more, dear lady. Say no more."

Sophronia and Lady Linette moved away, out of everyone's hearing.

"Quickly, child."

"I wish to stay with the ship." Sophronia almost shocked herself with the statement. *My goodness,* she thought, *I am growing up. Either that or I'm learning the value of putting in the appearance of playing by the rules.*

"What did you just say?"

"I've no intention of actually going aboard, and I shall certainly stay away from any possible explosion. It's only that I don't feel right about leaving the professor unguarded."

"He has Mademoiselle Geraldine."

"She's partaken rather freely of the champagne." *Quite apart from her being a figurehead and incompetent.*

"Miss Temminnick! Imagine speaking of your betters in such a manner."

Sophronia gritted her teeth. Even when she wanted to be straight with Lady Linette, it was near on impossible to tell her the truth. At this point, both of them automatically twisted their words.

A new suspicion occurred—perhaps Lady Linette was behind it all? Perhaps this was her scheme—not to crash the airship—but to get them all inside Bunson's overnight, a mass infiltration. Sophronia switched tactics. "Whatever it is you want to find out at Bunson's, you can't possibly need me as well as everyone else."

Lady Linette cocked her head. "Is that what you think is going on?"

"I think it's a possibility. And if not, you are the type to seize on this as a serendipitous opportunity."

"But?"

"But I think the crash was arranged, and we both know who likely arranged it. I think the sooties are in danger and some-one has to stay with them. And I think there are Picklemen already on board. You didn't believe me before, and this is the result. You owe me."

"Do I really?" Lady Linette was a master at controlling voice and expression.

"Please, Lady Linette, I'm begging you."

"Are you indeed? A novel experience for us both. But it's hardly sporting of me to make an exception only for you, Miss Temminnick."

"Look at them. I'm the only one who even *wants* to stay." Sophronia gestured in frustration.

It could not be denied. The students ambling across the moor were clearly enjoying themselves.

"Point taken, Miss Temminnick. Very well, but do it quietly, and leave your *particular* friends out of it. All of them stay with me. If you get yourself killed, I'll deny everything and report it as a horseback riding accident to your family."

Sophronia arched an eyebrow, wondering how Lady Linette would finagle that, but not doubting her for a second. "Agreed."

Of course, Sophronia could have faded off into the shadows of the moor right then, but she had to talk to Dimity and Agatha first.

"So?" asked Dimity the moment she rejoined them.

"I'm going back."

"Very well." Dimity did not even flinch. "What are we waiting for?"

"No," Sophronia hated to say it. "This time, only me."

"That's not on. We're a team," protested Dimity, "like tea and milk, or cake and custard, or pork and apple."

"Yes, we get the point," interjected her brother.

"I agree. You can't do it alone." Agatha showed unexpected pluck.

This caused Pillover to emit an agonized grumble. He'd come along if Agatha insisted, but he knew Sophronia of old, and following her always got messy. Once, he'd ended up in a petticoat.

Sophronia explained. "It's not that I don't want you. It's that I was recently thinking: if only there were more of me. One to stay and another to go to Bunson's. Then I realized that there kind of is *more*. I have you lot. The Pistons know about Soap. They know he's hiding at Bunson's. He's vulnerable tonight, so close to full moon. He only has Vieve to protect him. You know she's not a fighter. You have to go take care of him for me.

Please. I'll find out what's happening with the airship. And I'll have Bumbersnoot with me."

"Oh, yes, Bumbersnoot, heaps of good he'll do." Dimity didn't like it at all. "One of us could still go with you."

"I'm sorry. I'd want to come in your shoes, but there's something bigger going on. Someone has to get word to the dewan as well. One of you should ride to London while the other stays with Soap. I won't ask Pillover. He hasn't the training, apart from his general…reticence." Pillover looked like he felt he ought to protest, as a gentleman, but preferred to be relieved.

"Sophronia sending to London for help? I never thought I'd see the day," mocked Dimity.

"I don't like it, but the dewan has to come for Soap. And he has to know that the flywaymen brought down the school. Although how to get him the message—"

Agatha interrupted, her voice cool with confidence. "I can get to him."

Sophronia turned to her in surprise. "You can?"

Agatha looked at all three of them. Her face was suffused with mixed guilt and pride. "You never guessed did you? Not even you, Sophronia?"

Sophronia's stomach sank. "Guessed what, exactly, Agatha?"

Dimity put her hand over her mouth, preparing to be shocked. Something awful was about to happen.

Agatha drew herself upright and took a deep breath.

Pillover ogled. Poor boy couldn't help himself. Dimity was too carried away by the drama to box his ears.

Agatha said, "I've been working for someone, all along."

"You mean the entire time you've been at the school you've

already had a patron?" Sophronia struggled to understand the specifics.

Agatha nodded. "My papa's not all *that* rich."

Dimity squeaked. "Oh, Agatha!"

Sophronia's brow wrinkled. She felt hurt and betrayed, but she was also impressed. "All along? Gosh. Were you assigned to infiltrate the school from the start, or were you sent here for training?"

Agatha tilted her head. "Bit of both." The redhead glanced at Pillover then, as if she'd been afraid to do so before. She was still the same person—there was her awkwardness leaking through. Still, Sophronia couldn't help but admit that Agatha was an excellent choice to infiltrate a school for spies.

"You don't seem surprised," Agatha said to Pillover, voice soft.

Pillover shrugged, dour as ever. "I always figured you were special. Lack of chatter."

Dimity was on the edge of tears. "Oh, Agatha, how could you? You aren't..." She trailed off, took a small breath, and then whispered, "You aren't working for *them*, are you?"

"Them who?"

"The flywaymen?"

"No."

"The Picklemen?"

"Certainly not!"

"The Westminster Hive? Alongside Monique?"

"Not quite."

Sophronia's mind whirled. She was calculating all the times Agatha had been in the right place at the right time, or absent when she might have been caught. She thought over all the strange glances she had interpreted as social awkwardness. All those gifts from Agatha's wealthy, but absent, father. All those dresses, so fine and fashionable, so exactly wrong for Agatha's coloring and figure. Almost too *exactly* wrong.

"Lord Akeldama," Sophronia stated rather than asked.

Agatha, looking miserable, nodded.

"Nicely done." Sophronia was impressed. "Are you set up to become his drone once you finish?"

Agatha shrugged. "He doesn't take females, as a rule. Although he once offered for you in a carriage about town." By which statement she proved she was telling the truth. Sophronia had told the others Lord Akeldama was courting her for indenture, but she had never detailed that private drive when the vampire first suggested he make her his drone.

Agatha continued her explanation. "But you're pretty. Plus, you'd stay in the field for work and in the background the rest of the time."

Sophronia opened her mouth to protest, as modesty demanded, but Agatha forged on, now looking more fierce than miserable. "I'm better at being invisible and dowdy. Being the wallflower. No, don't try to make me feel better. I know what I'm good at. But I also know I'm an object of pity. That's useful, too, but doesn't make a girl feel all that nice most of the time. He saw through it, you know? From the very first time we met. I was only ten. But he won't take me for a drone and he won't put me in the field where my talents aren't up to Sophronia's standards."

"So what are you getting out of this arrangement?"

"Enough money to set up my own household, if I want." Agatha was purposefully *not* looking at Pillover.

"No!" Dimity gasped. An unmarried woman setting up house was the mark of a mistress.

Agatha looked at Sophronia, but she was talking to Pillover. "I would be an independent woman of means. I could love as I willed without consulting my family. He even promised me an allowance, if I continued to pass on information."

Pillover looked at his feet.

As riveting as this all was, Sophronia finally recovered from her shock enough to bring them back to the point. They hadn't time to process Agatha's revelation further now. The string of students was ambling away, and Sophronia had a ship to save.

"So you can get a message to Lord Akeldama, and he'll alert the dewan."

Agatha nodded.

"You'd do that for me?"

Agatha nodded again.

"And Dimity, you'll check on Soap?"

Dimity nodded, although she was still staring at Agatha, eyes wide.

Pillover seemed genuinely afraid. "You aren't going to give me an assignment, are you, Sophronia?"

"I wouldn't insult your personality."

"Aw, Sophronia, you care." Pillover looked almost happy.

Sophronia nodded. "I'll follow when I can. If you haven't heard from me by morning, send help or come back yourselves?"

They didn't discuss what or how, but the two girls nodded.

"Good luck," said Sophronia.

Dimity rushed over and hugged her hard. It was most unlady-like. Bumbersnoot was crushed between them, the side of his carapace digging into Sophronia's hip bone.

It was wonderful.

"I trust you, Dimity." For Sophronia, this was as near as she got to an admission of affection.

Dimity sniffled. "Don't do anything too drastic, please?"

Then Dimity let her go and trotted after the other students, back set against Agatha.

Sophronia looked at Agatha. She felt a change in the order of things, a new respect between them. "She'll come around."

"But you aren't angry with me?"

Pillover, perturbed by the prospect of sentimentality, made a hasty bow and drifted after his sister.

Sophronia examined her feelings. She hated talking about them, but she intended to hit Agatha with the honesty that Agatha hadn't afford her. "I feel betrayed, but I would have done the same thing, in your position."

Agatha paled but took it like the intelligencer she was. "That's fair."

"You really will send to London for help? I can trust you in this at least?"

Agatha was in grave earnest. "Absolutely." Perhaps she would be a good match for Pillover. If they married, they'd have a wedding as near to a wake as might be. For some reason this thought cheered Sophronia.

"Take care of them?" Sophronia's hand gesture took in not only Dimity and Pillover but also Vieve and Soap in town.

Agatha smiled and turned to catch up to the others.

Pillover paused to offer her his arm.

They followed Dimity into the night.

Sophronia returned to the school in a roundabout way. If she were the infiltrating Picklemen, she'd have guards posted at the wreck. Taking into consideration that fact, plus their previous interest in the pilot's bubble, she angled to come around the stern of the airship.

The moon was bright enough for her to assess the damage as she crept through the underbrush. It wasn't pretty, but it also didn't look fatal. Some splintered wood, a balloon or two damaged, rigging dangling free.

She kept getting distracted by the fact that her chest area was freezing. Her stupid dress was too full and too low for clandestine activities not involving seduction. She fervently wished for a nice set of breeches and a man's shirt. In the end she settled for shedding her top petticoat and constantly tugging up on the neckline. The liberated petticoat she tucked under a gorse bush, where it sat like some sad forgotten fluffy creature. In one respect, she was grateful for the dress—dark red with black brocade was perfect for fading into the heath.

She shifted Bumbersnoot to lie across her back. The little mechanimal stayed silent but for the faint tick-tock of his tail. As she inched closer, she checked to make certain her *carnet de bal* and bladed fan still hung securely from her waist. She was as equipped as a ball gown allowed. She stripped out all the pretty frills and fripperies from her hair and used a ribbon to tie it tightly back and out of her eyes.

No Picklemen were in sight, but there were sooties everywhere, busy making repairs. Two greasers yelled instructions, one from the midship squeak deck and another from the balcony above boiler room level.

Two of the balloons had lost a great deal of helium. Despite the resulting limpness, they were solid enough to withstand the weight of sooties crawling over them, applying slap patches. That was causing the airship to straighten, like a student caught slouching and chided into proper posture. Still, the school wasn't floating anywhere without a refill, and that was going to be a challenge so far from the train tracks.

If anything, the whole operation was going suspiciously well. *The attackers never intended to cause permanent damage, but instead to force a grounding. Did they want an evacuation also?*

Sophronia almost slapped her forehead with her hand, she felt so stupid. *They are after the airship itself! They want the school, and they've wanted the school all along. That's what the pilot's bubble infiltration was all about. They were surveying the darned thing, learning how it worked, determining whether it would fill their needs. They weren't after war airships—they were after our school. It's the biggest dirigible in the country.*

Sophronia scanned the surrounding landscape. She gasped— quietly, of course. For riding low and coming in fast toward them were three flywayman airships...big ones.

ABANDONED SHIP

One of the sooties noticed the incoming ships and shouted, pointing. There was nothing they could do. They were sitting ducks. Or more precisely, one great big huge sitting duck.

At that moment, three large men appeared, one on each squeak deck. They held fierce-looking guns, which they swung around, pointing from one sootie to the next.

The sooties reacted instantly. They were not fighters and had no cards in this game. They were merely laborers, and the lowest of those. Grunts in the boiler room. They, quite rightly, thought only in terms of saving their own skins. Most of them froze where they climbed, then turned to face this new threat.

One sootie panicked and jumped off the lower deck. He ran off across the moor, fortunately away from Sophronia's hiding spot.

The forward deck Pickleman took aim and fired.

The sootie cried out and fell dead.

The man who had shot him raised a speaking tube to his mouth and shouted through it, loud enough for Sophronia to hear. Even though the leaking helium caused his voice to squeak, there was no mistaking the menace in his words. He sounded like a very angry mouse.

"And the same to any others who run. Now, you six, finish the repairs. The rest of you, prepare the fizz tube. We're bringing in helium. Greasers, you're with the boiler contingent. Don't even think about plotting to countermand my orders. You work for us now, or you die, simple as that. Prepare the boilers to burn up. I'm with you to keep you on track. Do as ordered and you may even be rewarded for your troubles. Now *move!*"

The sooties—street-smart and blood-wary—did as instructed.

The man with the speaking tube vanished below. The two others stood firm, weapons at the ready to ensure no others broke for freedom. No other sootie tried.

The six chosen sooties dutifully finished up repairs and assembled amidships, shoulders hunched and movements cautious.

Sophronia wanted to go to the fallen boy on the moor, but she did not doubt the Pickleman's aim. The boy's path had no cover under the moonlight. That poor lad was likely beyond what little aid she could offer. The living needed her now.

She continued toward the ship. The men with the guns were focused inward, concerned with holding prisoners, not checking for possible infiltration.

Sophronia ended up directly below the aft section with the

propeller and its lone smokestack above her. It was odd to see the airship so near the ground. The bottom part of the propeller almost touched the heather. Above her was the hold storage area, with the glass platform she'd ridden up the first time she came to Mademoiselle Geraldine's. That platform was locked into place, and there was no other point of entry.

She turned her attention to the middle section, the lowest level of which was where mechanicals were stored and serviced. The kitchens were above that. This section had a loading bay with massive doors that opened like a cellar's. Manned by mechanicals, these were too heavy for one person to push open. However, along the side between this and the hold, servicing the kitchen and dining hall above, ran a tube of dumbwaiters. There were rungs on the outside of the tubes, because the waiters often required maintenance. Sophronia shot out her hurlie at the lowest rung. She pulled back to get a grip and then climbed up. The incoming flywaymen were out of sight, and she was shielded from view by the bulk of the ship.

If the sooties had been ordered to prep the boilers, then her assessment of the situation was correct—the Picklemen wanted to kidnap the school. The incoming ships must be intending to provide cargo and crew. She would also lay very good odds that they intended to cannibalize the helium they needed from those balloons to reinflate the school's.

She didn't need to watch it happen. Soon as she could, she pulled out a hairpin and picked the lock of a maintenance hatch at the top of the dumbwaiter tube. It was relatively easy to climb down the inside. It was the right size for a girl bracing herself back and forth, although her wide skirts—even tucked up—gave the tube a thorough cleaning. Her climb was more an undignified waddle, but no one was watching. She felt that the kitchen was the best access point, since it was likely abandoned. Picklemen would think it beneath them to congregate in such a menial area.

The kitchen was indeed empty.

Sophronia found a small knife and, cursing her lack of pockets, fed it to Bumbersnoot. She filched a few apples, some bread, and a wedge of hard cheese, which she wrapped in her handkerchief, attaching it to her chatelaine. Lady Linette was very firm on the matter of nicking food. "A lady must always be prepared. Snacks are an essential part of espionage."

Sophronia used the stairs out of the kitchen, emerging into the middle-level hallway. This was the section with the assembly deck and drop-down staircase, as well as some of the bigger classrooms.

It was quiet enough to be unnerving. This area was normally crowded with students, teachers, human staff, and mechanicals. People rushed from tumbling class, or stage-to-street performance lessons, or flowerpot transplanting and tossing practice. Now there was nothing but empty stillness. Even the mechanicals were missing. Her obstructor was entirely unnecessary.

She heard the boilers start up—the airship was once again fully upright.

Sophronia sniffed the air and caught no lingering smell of gas. She kept out her obstructor just in case, and moved through the school on silent feet. There was a faint lifting sensation, and a quick glance out a porthole showed the moor retreating. It also showed three grounded flywayman ships with flaccid balloons. All of their helium had been transferred to Mademoiselle Geraldine's.

Should I check on the sooties or go see what is happening in the pilot's bubble? Do I try to find Mademoiselle Geraldine, or should I assume she's been taken hostage? And what about Professor Braithwope? Sophronia was overwhelmed with options. Lady Linette's voice rang through her head.

Never enter a situation, social or strategic, without understanding the personnel and protocols in place. In other words, it is always better to know the state, color, and number of handkerchiefs in a room before you blow anyone's nose.

Sophronia took that to heart, partly because it gave her an objective. First she would search the airship, count the number of Picklemen and flywaymen on board, and note their positions. She'd already seen the three with guns, and two of those were still up on the squeak decks. If she were in charge, she'd keep them as lookouts. The third was down in the boiler room. There had to be someone in charge of the infiltration, and he'd want a command chair. Would he station himself near the pilot's bubble or on a squeak deck? No, safer somewhere inside the ship. He'd need at least three runners to carry orders to the others. Then there were probably two in the pilot's bubble. Plus an assorted number of heavy lifters—bully boys. They'd have to spread out, with one to keep an eye on the headmistress and another to track Professor Braithwope. That was a lot of men to account for. Sophronia estimated a total—she wouldn't take on a ship of this size without at *least* a dozen men.

Now let's find out if I'm right.

She felt the propeller crank up. That meant they had one

Pickleman and half a dozen sooties working the auxiliary propulsion boilers. It also meant they were now high enough up to start the guidance system.

Sophronia dove into a classroom and out onto a balcony to see. Somehow she wasn't surprised to find they were heading toward London. And they weren't doing so under steam cover. The Picklemen didn't care that they would be seen by every small town they floated over. The secret of Mademoiselle Geraldine's airship school wasn't going to be a secret much longer.

If the Picklemen had any major cargo, it would be stashed in the hold with the glass elevator. Sophronia decided to check that first. She nipped around the dumbwaiters and down the access stairs. At the door, she put her ear to the jamb and heard minor thudding. She pushed it open a crack.

The hold was full of mechanimals. Bumbersnoot, passive until that moment, began upticking his tail in interest. His alarm did not sound, and he showed no particular eagerness to be put down to go to his compatriots. But he certainly was aware of them.

Sophronia's stomach sank and her cheeks tingled. These were no small dachshund-shaped creatures. These were huge monsters, similar to the massive mechanimal she had encountered in her mother's gazebo the night of Petunia's ball. They bore little resemblance to any specific creature, looking more like wingless gargoyles. The hold was crammed with them. One squatted, as though waiting, on the glass lift. They did not move, but they looked like they could at any moment.

There was something terrifying about a mechanical construct that did not need a track. Sophronia had not realized that until she saw them all assembled before her. With the most prevalent mechanimal in her life being Bumbersnoot, she hadn't thought the law making them illegal at all sensible. Now she understood. In that hold squatted a small but mighty army.

Shaken, Sophronia closed the door and continued with her assessment of the school.

She moved toward engineering, which, combined with the boiler room, took up the two lower levels of the front of the airship. She couldn't easily sneak in there, because the main entrance was at the top, and no doubt the Picklemen would station themselves there to oversee operations. With a resigned sigh, she made her way out onto a balcony and began climbing down and around the outside of the airship toward her standard entrance—the sooties' hatch.

There were no sooties waiting to help her inside this time. The massive room was suffused with the flickering orange of flames and a general smoky cloudiness Sophronia had grown to expect and find rather comforting. She made for her favorite coal pile, the one upon which she and Soap had spent many happy hours practicing reading and occasionally practicing smooching. Ordinarily, this part of the boiler room was humming, off-duty sooties mingled with those sent to tap the coal reserves. With only a kidnapped skeleton crew, there were no breaks, and the area was abandoned. Occasionally, Sophronia could pick out a strange new sound—a loud crack.

She peeked out from behind the coal pile to where the sooties were working the fireboxes. Or, to be more precise, where the sooties were slaving. They were running their normal patterns—feeding, stoking, checking the smooth motions of the main boilers—but they were doing so under ready punishment. The speaking-tube Pickleman was not on the supervisor's platform, but down among the workers. He stood armed with a bullwhip in one hand and his gun in the other. If any sootie slackened his pace or did anything the Pickleman considered amiss, the whip flashed out, striking the unfortunate boy across the back.

The sooties were grim-faced and sweating, working as hard as they could. When the whip flashed, the poor unfortunate would wince and grit his teeth but not cry out. They were tough boys who'd started on docks or up chimneys. Sootie to a floating school was a cushy job by comparison, but that didn't mean the lads had never before felt the kiss of a whip. They simply hadn't expected to do so again.

Sophronia, on the other hand, had never witnessed such a thing. Her parents weren't ones for harsh punishment, and she'd never visited the plantations of the West Indies, where, rumor had it, caning was commonplace. Every time the bullwhip struck, she winced and swallowed down a cry of sympathetic distress.

She watched as one small sootie got a second lick, right near the first. His shirt went ragged under the blows. He stumbled forward, and Handle jumped to his aid. She caught Handle's expression. It wasn't one of meek servitude. He was absolutely livid.

Whatever else her plans entailed, she had to determine a way to get them out.

Sophronia assessed the security. Apart from the Pickleman

with the whip, she counted two others overseeing the carnage from above. Without a projectile weapon, she couldn't do anything right away—plus, she had to obey her training and assess the shipwide situation first. But she made the sooties a silent promise to return and free them as soon as possible.

She wondered if she could find a gun in one of the teachers' rooms. The school had an armory, of course, and Sophronia even knew where it was, but she couldn't get into it. There was no entrance without activating a special drawbridge, and only Professor Lefoux and Lady Linette knew how to do that.

She withdrew, unhappy, from the boiler room. She stuffed a few pieces of coal down her cleavage for Bumbersnoot. The stupid ball gown had no pockets, and she was running out of means to attach stuff to herself. The little mechanimal was fine at the moment, but she wanted to make certain he stayed running. Back out the hatch, she skirted up past the second level so she could continue her sweep of the ship, starting with the teachers' rooms in the red-tassel section.

It was easier to get inside the teachers' private chambers via their balconies, so she stuck to the outside of the ship. At the very front, in the best suite, Mademoiselle Geraldine's display of fake tea cakes stood solitary vigil. The headmistress was not there. Sophronia didn't bother breaking in, as Mademoiselle Geraldine would have nothing of use.

Sister Mattie's balcony was crowded with vegetation, and her door was unlocked. The most easygoing of their teachers, Sister Mattie always felt that if she had done her job properly the students should have access to any poison they wished, not to mention good nutrition. She was also quite absentminded.

Professor Lefoux's balcony was full of gadgetry, with her door triple-locked and booby-trapped. Fortunately, both locks and trap were ones Sophronia had dealt with before. She picked and disabled them. She filched a few smaller deadlier items from each teacher, poison from the one, hooks and a timepiece from the other, ribbons from both. She upended both bedrooms searching for a gun or a crossbow. No luck.

Professor Braithwope's rooms were empty of both the vampire and useful items. She searched thoroughly, but the tiny special crossbow was nowhere to be found. Probably everything else had been removed after his tether snap, to keep him from injuring himself.

Lady Linette's rooms were bolted with a Devugge system so sophisticated it presented a real challenge. Sophronia spent a futile few minutes trying to pick the lock, only to have the mechanism slide out of her way every time she felt she was getting somewhere. *Excellent design*, she thought. She might have kept at it longer, except she realized her normal training—to get in and out without being seen—was irrelevant under these particular circumstances. She used her hearing trumpet to determine that there was no one inside, and then used Bumbersnoot's bottom to shatter the stained glass of the balcony door. She then upended the chamber. *No guns at all? What kind of spymasters are these? The best kind*, she supposed, *to leave no evidence of their true nature in their private quarters.*

In one corner of Lady Linette's room, in pride of place and quite incongruously surrounded by boudoir-style velvets, sat a large wicker chicken. It was heavy, and something inside was mechanized. It smelled faintly of brimstone and chalk. Sophronia remembered a conversation her debut year about Monique being gifted with an exploding wicker chicken from a Bunson's admirer. It would appear that Lady Linette had confiscated it—young ladies weren't allowed gifts of such magnitude. The chicken was bulky, but it was also a kind of projectile, and Sophronia was getting desperate. So, shifting Bumbersnoot around to a better angle, she used several lengths of curtain cord to strap the deadly bird to her back.

Of course, she was now nowhere near as sneaky looking. Nor, for that matter, as dignified. *Here I am, infiltrating a stolen dirigible, wearing a wicker chicken.* But she moved on, climbing to the scaffolding that supported the pilot's bubble. She knew from personal experience that it could only fit two men. So she simply took it as fact that there were two Picklemen inside and added them to her mental tally.

She moved back through the ship. The classrooms were all empty. She did find a water-projecting device filled with acid in Professor Lefoux's laboratory, which she liberated. She also put on the leather pinafore Professor Lefoux used when she was mixing chemicals. It was durable and protective, and, most important, it had pockets and a high neckline.

Sophronia didn't bother with the student residences. The enemy wouldn't be hiding there, and it would take too long to search through them all for anything useful. She contemplated returning to her own room and changing into breeches, but a certain sense of urgency convinced her she hadn't the time. Besides, the ball gown was less annoying now that she had covered it with leather. Leather, she reflected, was good like that.

The front section of the third level housed the exertion and tumbling classroom, the library, and the solar. She gave them a cursory look-through, unsurprised to find all empty. The Picklemen did not strike her as the type to enjoy physical discipline nor literary pursuits or sun exposure on a regular basis. Above her were the testing rooms and the compartments where the weapons and soldier mechanicals were stored. Assuming those were as inaccessible to the Picklemen as they were to her, Sophronia had only two zones left to explore: below her, the massive dining hall where they had been hosting the New Year's tea, and the very front forward top of the ship, back in the red-tassel section, where the administrative and record rooms stood, forgotten and unused.

It was when Sophronia reached the dining hall that everything became clear. It was impossible to sneak into the dining hall without the cover of a crowded tea party. So she took to the outer hull and peeked through one of the portholes that lined the top of the cavernous room under the crown molding. It was a great vantage point, but did not permit her to eavesdrop, only to observe. Her lip-reading ability was good, but most of the men wore beards, which made it nigh impossible. Perhaps this was on purpose? Dimity always said beards were suspicious. Now Sophronia was inclined to agree with her.

The bulk of the enemy had assembled there. Most of the tables were still up against the starboard side, but the head table was in place. It was set with salvaged food, and four Picklemen and three Cultivator-status younger men congregated around it, partaking. The younger men were acting the role of footmen, running errands, leaving the room for long periods before returning, likely being used as messengers to cohorts in the propeller room, in the boiler room, in the pilot's bubble, and on the squeak decks. These must have been the ones who had infiltrated the tea party—they looked young, and two were beardless.

A half dozen flywaymen also lurked about. Distinguished from the Picklemen by crass mannerisms and poor dress, each looked like a cross between a country squire out for the hunt and an old-fashioned pirate. By contrast, the Picklemen and their minions sported evening dress with green ribbons about their hats. Even though they were at a meal, they still wore their hats. Perhaps because it wasn't a formal engagement?

Sophronia scrutinized each man for any clue or relevant tidbit of information. Of the four Picklemen, the one in charge was distinguished by a wider ribbon around a stovepipe topper that was both taller and shiner than any other hat there. He was on the corpulent end of the spectrum, with a bushy beard and a large flat face that looked as if it had been sat on regularly. But when he stood, he moved so lightly on his feet that Sophronia knew to be wary. There was such an air of arrogance about him, and the others treated him with such respect, that he could only be the Chutney. His closest confidant was a gangly man with black hair, probably dyed, large gold spectacles, and terrible posture. He slouched over a note pad, jotting things down. The two others were heavy muscled bully boys.

Sophronia turned her attention to the flywaymen, determining which was in charge, which might be the most dangerous, and which was the weakest. It took her a moment, but eventually she realized that one of the flywaymen wasn't a man at all. It was Madame Spetuna, dressed as a man, but making no attempt to hide her femininity. She was conducting business as if she had always worked among the enemy.

She seemed to be liaised with the flywayman commander, either as a lover or as a lieutenant, or both. Sophronia wasn't sure what this meant. Had the record room been correct? Had she betrayed them? Or was she so deep in her infiltration that any move she made to extract herself was too dangerous?

It would be very useful, thought Sophronia, *if I had someone on the inside. But do I risk trying to contact her or will that expose us both?*

It occurred to Sophronia to worry about the record room. If the flywaymen got hold of the information stored there, all active intelligencers would be in danger. *I have to destroy it before they find it.*

Sophronia withdrew from her vantage point and began climbing up. As she got closer to the squeak decks, she was scared of being seen by the lookouts, so she made her way inside as soon as she could, heading at speed for the record room. This, however, proved more challenging than expected. As vacant as the lower levels had been, the uppermost hallway was patrolled by multiple mechanicals. She recognized them as belonging to the school but suspected they had been fitted with the new crystalline valves. There was no knowing what their new protocols might command them to do if they caught her. Fortunately, there were no soldier mechanicals in the mix, but clangermaid and buttlinger models could be dangerous enough with the right instructions.

Sophronia had to employ her obstructor the entire way to the record room. It was with some relief that she finally reached the door.

She barely inched it open. A quick glance inside had her twirling away and flattening herself against the hallway wall. At one of the desks sat a Pickleman, one of intellect rather than muscle. He was hard at work dialing in the records and making copious scribbles in a small notebook.

At the far end of the hallway, 'round a bend where the tiny administrative room occupied the very front of the ship, a door banged.

"And stay there, you imbecile!" a deep voice ordered.

Footsteps came along the corridor toward Sophronia, the voice now yelling, "Bawkin! Spice Administrator Bawkin? He wants your report immediately."

Sophronia turned and sprinted around the next bend in the hallway. Just the other side of the corner, she flattened herself against the wall, straining to hear what was said. The door to the record room crashed open—Deep Voice was inexcusably brutal to doors—and she heard him say, "You've had enough time poking about. You're wanted in the dining hall for the *next stage.*"

"But there is so much more to learn." The answering voice was higher and tinged with Yorkshire.

"Stuff it, Spicer. Gather your things. And come back to me before you head down. I've a few items of interest for the Gherkin"—*That means Duke Golborne is on board! How did I miss him?*—"and some notes from my interrogation for that idiotic book of yours. The blasted runner scampered off without pause, idiot boy. Where do we get our recruits these days? Honestly, I don't know why we bother." From the fading volume, Deep Voice was already walking back the way he'd come.

Sophronia stuck her head around the corner.

A large wall-shaped sort of chap was striding away. He'd left the door to the record room wide open.

I could go in, wicker chicken blazing, and take Note-taker out right now. Or I can target his notebook, and steal it after he's gotten the next bit of information from Deep Voice. Sophronia liked the second option best. Once Note-taker was on his own, headed to the Gherkin, he'd be vulnerable. Then again, if he had encountered Madame Spetuna's record and knew who she was, the man himself must also be eliminated. Sophronia nibbled her bottom lip. *How do I sabotage a Pickleman without giving my own presence away? Right now my only real advantage is surprise. No one knows I'm on board. But I don't want to kill the blighter.* She was capable, of course, but always found murder the least appealing part of espionage. She wasn't squeamish, like Dimity, but she wasn't as bloodthirsty as Preshea, either.

For now Sophronia elected to follow him until he collected more information. The intellectual chappy appeared in the record-room doorway, pulling on his coat and hat, and, notebook clutched under his arm, he headed after the other man.

Once he disappeared around a bend in the hall, Sophronia followed.

A CLASSICAL EDUCATION

The administrative room was Deep Voice's only possible location. Of course, Sophronia had explored the room before. She'd investigated most of the school by now. It was rarely used, for Mademoiselle Geraldine kept no proper administrators on staff. It was a cramped, dusty place, filled with piles of forms, bootlaces, defused mechanicals, old lesson plans, and irrelevant embroidery samplers. It was an odd place to station a Pickleman, its only advantage being a front-facing location and, perhaps, the fact that by comparison to other rooms, it was unused.

It was possible, Sophronia supposed, for an infiltrator to have been living there unnoticed for weeks. Or possibly to have stashed something important there, with no one the wiser.

She watched as Note-taker let himself inside. She then ran down the hallway after. The sign on this door read ADMINIS-TRATOR ACCESS ONLY, NO PEONS. Under it someone had pinned a scrap of paper that read NEEDS DUSTING. Under which someone else had penned another note scrawled with a prosaic WHY BOTHER?

Sophronia ignored the notes and took out her hearing trumpet, pressing it to the crack.

"Here, take this as well," Deep Voice was saying.

"Why on earth would I want that? You know I prefer reading to sportsmanship."

"It's not for you, idiot. It's for the Gherkin. The creature seems to think it's vital. I had a devil of a time getting it out of his claws."

"You do realize he's insane? What's vital to him is likely useless to the rest of us."

"Do as you are told, Spicer. Here, take the bolts, too."

There was a rustling noise and a funny kind of a moan.

"Shut your mouth, fang boy," barked Deep Voice.

Ah, thought Sophronia, *I appear to have found Professor Braithwope. Unfortunately, I wasn't the first.*

"Couldn't you be a little kinder to the poor fellow?" said another voice, this one rich and female. "He may be lost about the mind, but I assure you he is a gentleman and *quali-tay.*"

And Mademoiselle Geraldine is here, too.

Even realizing that her teachers were in trouble, Sophronia was relieved that at least she knew they were still alive. It made her feel less isolated. By her calculations, there were fourteen Picklemen, plus three younger runners, and half a dozen flywaymen, one of whom was Madame Spetuna. Against them Sophronia had about two dozen sooties, enslaved in the boiler and propeller rooms, and now, Mademoiselle Geraldine and Professor Braithwope.

I now know all the players and their locations. At last I can start to plan.

It was unfortunate that the enemy was spread all over the ship, making them harder to eliminate *en masse.* But it had one great advantage—it slowed communication. While she had been surveying the situation, the airship had kicked up speed, and they were heading to London at the fastest float possible. Admittedly, it wasn't very fast. Last time, the float to London took four days, but they had taken layovers and been under steam cloud cover. Pressing the issue, she thought it would be two and a half to three days.

Well, she thought, *if London is the target, at least I know I have some time.*

Not at the moment, however, for footsteps were heading toward the door. Once more she raced away. That was the one good thing about dancing slippers—at least she was soft-footed.

She heard Spice Administrator Note-taker shut the door, and she could guess what path he would take. The end of this hallway was a staircase down to the middle level. It was impossible to go directly the length of the ship on the upper level, unless one had a hurlie and the will to climb. So Sophronia ran ahead of him, heading for the classrooms.

She chose the first classroom after the stairs, Lady Linette's. It was open, as she'd left it during her search, dark and quiet. Sophronia dropped Bumbersnoot outside the door, in the hall, with a command to stay. She could only hope he would obey.

She and Vieve had never determined all of Bumbersnoot's protocols—as a result, he pretty much did as he pleased. Leaving the door ajar, Sophronia arranged herself inside the room. She opened the curtains so the moonlight would kiss her face. Then she sat down at Lady Linette's large harp, fortunately undamaged. *Staging, in seduction, is almost as vital as the seduction itself.* She dabbed a bit of lemon tincture on the floor so the scent permeated the air, and began playing softly.

Sophronia was perfectly well aware that she made the most absurd picture. She was still wearing the pinafore over her ball gown. Not to mention the fact that there was a wicker chicken strapped to her back. She angled so the chicken wasn't entirely visible, determined to make the best of the situation. She imagined its little wicker head peering over her shoulder suspiciously at the harp.

Sophronia was an abysmal harpist. She'd only had a few lessons in tinkling for torture and diversion and had done badly at those.

Nevertheless, when Note-taker came down the stairs to find the door open and a loose mechanical, how could he help but investigate? It was pure temptation.

And there he was, as predicted, peering myopically into Lady Linette's classroom.

The room alone was a shock to anyone, being a combination of conservatory, boudoir, and house of ill repute. It featured a good deal of red fringe, highly questionable artwork, and long velvet fainting couches shoved to one side by the crash. Lady Linette appeared to have evacuated her three fluffy cats, so at least they weren't in residence giving Sophronia's harping the yowls it deserved.

Sophronia looked up, arrested, as if caught on canvas by a master painter. She used the moonlight and the angle to her advantage, targeting an ethereal effect. She stopped playing as though interrupted in deep reverie. She floated one white hand gracefully up to push back a stray lock of hair, still maintaining its curl despite the trials of the evening. This exposed her neck, which Lady Linette said was a sign of vulnerability.

"Oh, dear." Sophronia gave a tremulous smile. "Did my playing disturb you, sir? I do apologize." Tremulous smiles were very effective when applied to the right victim.

Nothing could be more confusing to the poor man than Sophronia at that moment. He fell back on etiquette. What else was an Englishman to do when confronted with a wicker-chicken-wearing leather-clad tremulous smile? He drew the only ready weapon he had—manners. "Good evening, miss..." He trailed off.

Sophronia rose, sweetly innocent, and moved toward him as if she were a ballerina.

He, in turn, stepped into the room, as politeness demanded. Bumbersnoot scuttled in after, looking pleased with himself. He went to snuffle about the fringed carpet to see if it might be susceptible to singeing.

"Miss Pelouse. How do you do? Are you visiting for the party?" Sophronia's voice was breathy—due to the euphoria of her own transformative harp playing, of course.

The young man had a largish nose and floppy hair and the appealing gawkish posture of the literary-minded. He might also, Sophronia realized, have a gun. Difficult for him to reach for it, however, as he was carrying his notebook in one hand

and Professor Braithwope's miniature crossbow and three bolts in the other.

He clearly did not know what to do when approached by a pretty young lady wearing a wicker chicken who ought—by all standards of decency—to be long abandoned on the moor... chickenless.

Sophronia held out her hand, as if she were a bishop and wished it to be kissed.

The young Pickleman fumbled, his arms full, to finagle an appropriate response. He managed a truncated sort of bow over the offering. "Spice Administrator Bawkin, miss, how do you do? Is that your mechanimal?"

Sophronia gave him a perfect curtsy and then cocked her head, inquisitive. "Mechanimal? Where?" Bumbersnoot had conveniently rejected the fringe and was poking about the back side of the coal scuttle, out of view.

The young man abandoned that line of questioning for one of greater import. "Um, miss, how did you get here?"

Sophronia floated her fingers about in a dancer's confusion. "I walked. You would suggest some other method?"

"No, I mean, miss, the ship was *evacuated*."

"Dear me, was it? I hadn't noticed. I do get lost in my music. It is my one true passion. Do you have a *one true passion*, Mr. Spice-Bawkin?" Sophronia prattled in an airy-fairy manner. She did not let him answer. "Mine is music. I simply adore music. *Je l'adore, je l'adore!* It's so *transporting*, don't you find? Of course you do. Everyone does. When I sit at my harp, the world simply melts away. Like, you know, that creamy icy thing that melts. What am I thinking of? Oh, yes, Nesselrode pudding.

I'm afraid it may have melted too far just now, and I missed something important. An evacuation, you say? Are you the authorities? Have we been evacuated for political reasons? Oh, I always knew they would go too far."

"Who?" interjected the young Pickleman, almost desperately, overwhelmed by her blathering.

Sophronia was breezy and dismissive, "Oh, you know, *they*." All the while she chattered, she pressed the young man around and back, moving him into position by slightly crowding his social space. So vested was he in keeping the correct distance for conversation with a lady that he didn't even realize he had been moved until he came up against Lady Linette's mantelpiece, where her prized stuffed badger in a lace mobcap stared austerely down at him.

"Miss," he interrupted again, "why are you wearing a chicken?"

"Oh, this old thing? It's the very latest fashion accessory. Don't you like it? Mine is a bit big, I grant you. I was going to put it into my hair, but it was too heavy. You don't like it? I'm so foolish." She widened her green eyes as though she might burst into tears.

"Of course. I mean, I do like it. It's very, um, bendy."

Sophronia's lips trembled and her eyes welled.

The young man leaned in, solicitous.

She said, "I really am very sorry about this. You seem like such a *nice* man."

"You are? I do? Well, they should have found you after the evacuation. We sent a sweep around."

"My fault entirely, I assure you. I've never trusted chimney sweeps." Sophronia allowed one perfect tear to trickle over her cheek, staring up into his confused face with an expression of mild adoration mixed with shame.

The poor young Pickleman. He'd had no chance from the moment he entered the room. If there were a book on befuddlement with evil intent, Sophronia had just thrown it at him.

At which point she hauled off and hit him with it.

Or, to be more precise, she hit him with Lady Linette's copy of Mrs. Blessingbacon's *Hot Cross Buns for the Bunless*. It was a heavy tome that Lady Linette had left sitting atop her mantelpiece and that had managed not to fall off during the crash.

Sophronia whacked the Pickleman on the temple, precisely where she had been taught.

Spice Administrator Bawkin fell to the ground in a pleasingly floppy manner.

"That'll teach you to question a lady's wicker chicken!"

It was hard to know how much time she had while he was incapacitated—only a few seconds if she'd done her job right. She hadn't wanted to cause permanent damage. He might work for the Picklemen, but he didn't seem *that* bad.

Luckily, Lady Linette had a passion for lace drapes, gold cord, and velvet runners. Sophronia converted one of the runners into a gag. She tied the Pickleman's hands over his head and to the leg of the grand piano. She had always thought it odd, not to mention a waste of weight, that Lady Linette insisted on a grand piano in her classroom. But in this instance it proved useful. With Bawkin's wrists tied to one leg, and his feet to the leg kitty corner, he was efficiently immobilized. Sophronia found a large shawl and draped it over the piano, anchoring it with vases. Now, should anyone look into the room, it would appear empty, the young man well hidden behind the shawl.

Sophronia now suspected that Lady Linette had a piano on board for exactly this purpose. Feeling safe for the moment, and wanting to make certain he would wake up, Sophronia shut the door. Bumbersnoot reappeared from behind the coal scuttle, looking smug, as if he had found some loose coal. She scooped up the young man's notebook and held it in the moonlight to examine it.

The first section was filled with notes in cypher, some mathematical equations, sketches of mechanical functions, and a rough map of something mysterious. In the middle there were newer notes—messy and smudged from a hasty closing of the book. Still in cypher, the style of the text suggested names and dates combined with other pertinent information. This must be from the record room, probably an account of active intelligencers. Sophronia tore those pages out of the book.

"Bumbersnoot, come here, please."

The little mechanimal tick-tocked over to her.

Sophronia fed him the sheets of paper, one at a time, making certain they went into his boiler and were incinerated.

There was one page of additional notes after that, even more hastily written, in a different hand. The results of Deep Voice's interrogation, Sophronia supposed.

The rest of the book was blank. She extracted her own stick of graphite and drew a hasty schematic of the ship, marking off the locations of Picklemen and flywaymen with dots. She took great satisfaction in then putting an X through the dot representing Spice Administrator Bawkin. One down, thirteen

Picklemen, three runners, and five flywaymen to go. She tore out this map, folded it up, and put it in a pocket with her stick of graphite. Then she ripped out the rest of the notes, rolled them up tight, and secured them with a bit of ribbon. She removed Bumbersnoot's coal reserves from her cleavage to a pocket of the leather smock, and stuffed the notes there instead. Most secure place for them.

Even though the remainder of the notebook was empty, she tucked it under some couch cushions for safety. One never knew with Picklemen.

She then examined the crossbow, delighted to have it in her possession. If she could activate the soldier mechanicals, she would have a real weapon on her side. But she'd probably need Professor Braithwope for that, and who knew what mental state he was in at this point. Sophronia cannibalized a length of curtain cord to be a belt and tied the tiny crossbow to it, using more hair ribbons. Geraldine's girls carried extra hair ribbons at all times for exactly this kind of eventuality. She shoved the bolts into the biggest of the pinafore pockets. She practically jangled like a tinker with all the items she had hanging off her, but she felt much better about life in general. She took a moment to rearrange and redistribute so she wouldn't make noise as she snuck about.

She ducked under the piano and checked on the Spice Administrator. He was awake and his pupils looked fine. He lay perfectly still as she loomed over him.

She grinned, unaware of the maniacal expression in her green eyes. "Love of music—it can drive a girl to distraction. Or do I mean destruction?"

She patted his cheek in what she hoped was a reassuring way and left him. Poor thing hadn't even squirmed or groaned around the gag. She was certain he thought her quite mad. And should he somehow get free—and he would have to be a circus contortionist with supernatural strength to do so— he would have such a strange story to tell, it would make the other Picklemen think him drunk at best. "A girl wearing a wicker chicken and playing the harp bopped me with a book about buns and then stuffed me under a piano." It sounded like a funny dream.

Sophronia chuckled to herself but quickly sobered. Professor Braithwope and Mademoiselle Geraldine needed rescuing, and she still had sooties to save. She headed back up the stairs for her next victim. Deep Voice, she felt, was going to be much harder to disable.

This time Sophronia did not wear the chicken. She took it off and left it in the hallway outside the administrative room with the crossbow and Bumbersnoot and orders to guard. She armed herself with the water-projecting device filled with acid from Professor Lefoux's laboratory. Then she took out her small hoard of nibbles from the kitchen and knocked on the door.

"Come!" called Deep Voice.

Sophronia entered, eyes down, looking at the Pickleman through her lashes, pleased to find he had not been joined by any others.

"Who the devil are you?" He was a rough-looking fellow, his jaw dark with a nascent beard.

Sophronia had never seen such a thing as a seedling beard before, no gardener having tended it to greatness nor pruned it into submission. It was positively oafish in its incivility. She actually felt unwell at the sight.

"Only the maid, sir. I've brought you food." She proffered her own cheese, bread, and apple.

The man looked suspicious but also off balance—unable to decide whether to leave off what he was doing and approach or allow her to enter farther into the room.

Sophronia took his hesitation as an opportunity to assess the situation.

Mademoiselle Geraldine was sitting in a big chair in the far left corner, near the forward window, several large storage baskets pushed aside to make room. Before her was a low table set for tea. There was an empty seat across from her, shoved out of the way as if in haste. The headmistress looked so relaxed, Sophronia had the horrified thought that she was working with the Picklemen.

I have two enemies to disable, and only one ally to rescue, when I was prepared for the other way around! Sophronia cursed herself. It was a debut's mistake.

Deep Voice was in the other corner of the room next to a cage shaped like a bird's, only bigger. It hung from a hook in the ceiling and looked to be steel, woven through with a glass tubing filled with gas. This heated the metal red hot at multiple contact points.

Professor Braithwope was locked inside this cage, naked.

Sophronia quickly slid her eyes away, but not before she noticed welts on the vampire's arms, burns on his hands, and open cuts across his face. His mustache looked to have fainted. He was silent, half curled, half crouched—trying to make himself as small as possible so as not to touch the burning bars. Vampires, of course, could survive most things, but they still felt pain. The cuts, no doubt, were made with sharpened wooden blades and would be slower to heal as a result.

Deep Voice, orchestrator of this torture, left off prodding the professor and walked over to Mademoiselle Geraldine and the tea table.

When Sophronia moved to take the food to that table, he snapped, "Halt! You stay there."

Sophronia froze.

With a studied casualness, the Pickleman poured tea. Which made Sophronia realize that everything wasn't right with the headmistress. Mademoiselle Geraldine would never let a *visitor* pour, even if that man was her superior. It was *always* the hostess's responsibility to serve tea, evacuations and hijackings notwithstanding.

Sophronia lifted her lashes slightly to take in details she had missed earlier.

Mademoiselle Geraldine was strapped into her chair at the elbows and legs. She could raise up her hands to feed herself from a plate in her lap but was otherwise immobilized. The headmistress was behaving in a civilized manner, but she was not assisting the invaders. She was a hostage.

The headmistress looked at Sophronia with an expression of sublime indifference, showing absolutely no indication that they had ever met before.

Bravo, thought Sophronia.

All this time the students thought Mademoiselle Geraldine ignorant of the fact that her own school was an espionage academy. They had always acted to keep her immersed in that ignorance. In fact, it was a vital part of their training. Sophronia had wondered... but now she outright knew that Mademoiselle Geraldine had been in on it all along. She was too calm to be an ordinary headmistress tied to a chair. By rights, she ought to be in hysterics.

The Pickleman finished pouring the tea and handed a cup to Mademoiselle Geraldine, taking away her empty plate. Then he served himself and sat down, turning to face Sophronia. "I do not recall any maids being brought aboard, except mechanical ones. Who are you really, girl?"

"A forgotten student." Sophronia dropped the act and pocketed the food. She was grateful that she didn't have to use it. It was all she had to eat. At the same time, she palmed the acid emitter and let her other hand rest on her bladed fan, ready with either. She minimized any appearance of threat by hunching and keeping her eyes down timidly.

"Come in then, and have some tea. Pull up a stool. You realize, of course, that I must take you prisoner." The Pickleman was confident in his own superiority.

Sophronia could hardly believe it. Surely he knew what this school did? Surely he didn't see her as weak? But, then again, this was part of her education, to play on the perceptions, particularly of men. Girls were not dangerous.

She grabbed a pouf from a pile of rejected furniture and pulled up between him and Mademoiselle Geraldine at the table.

"You're a pretty little thing, aren't you?" He extracted an extra cup and saucer from a nearby tea trolley.

Sophronia considered herself only passing fair, but if he liked his ladies lean and muddy of hair and eyes, she wasn't going to gainsay him. "Very kind of you to say so, sir."

The man picked up the teapot, and Sophronia, with an apology to the tea gods for the waste, sprang at the man, animallike. She had the acid spray pointed at him in one hand, and her trusty fan was open, leather guard flicked off, in the other.

The acid hit him first. It took the Pickleman a split second to react to her attack. That was often the problem with big thuggish men—they were slow.

Then he yelled, both hands flying to scrape at his face, dropping the teapot in his distress. This spilled hot liquid in his lap, which caused him to scream again. He fell backward in the chair, getting tangled up in its arms and legs. By which time Sophronia was on top of him. This was not a womanly maneuver, and he was certainly strong enough to toss her off, except that she had her fan pressed to his jugular. She made certain to prick his skin so there was no doubt as to the danger.

He was crying openly and wiping his eyes, but he stopped the moment he felt the sharp metal against his throat.

"May I suggest that you stay quite still, sir?" Sophronia was careful not to forget her manners. After all, the headmistress was right there. Her voice was deadly confident. "You, I do not feel so kindly toward as I did my last victim."

"What? Who?" He shuddered, wanting desperately to toss her off.

Sophronia pocketed the acid without looking away. She

brought her free hand to his neck, above where her fan pricked. She pressed down firm and steady, cutting into his air intake, listening for the wheeze.

"Don't you worry about him, sir. He's all taken care of. And now I'll be taking care of you, too." Without turning, Sophronia asked, "Mademoiselle Geraldine, do you think you can scoot your chair over here? I have a knife somewhere, for your bonds."

Mademoiselle Geraldine's voice replied, "No need, my dear. I've had them undone for some time."

Sophronia was unsurprised, but she did not look up. "I suggest you unlock Professor Braithwope, then. We are, after all, enjoying tea. I should think he'd be grateful for a drop or two of the warm stuff himself, what with Professor Lefoux gone these many hours."

"My dear girl, what a cracking idea." There was a rustle of skirts as the headmistress moved around the prone Pickleman, feeling about his waistcoat for the keys. The man twitched. Sophronia pressed down with both her hands. A trickle of blood appeared from under the edge of her fan. Good. That would draw Professor Braithwope's attention.

Deep Voice fell still.

The click and clang of the cage being unlocked followed, and then a faint hiss and the smell of escaping gas.

"He tapped this contraption into our own gas lighting lines—quite ingenious, actually." Mademoiselle Geraldine seemed most impressed. "Best way to hold a vampire at short notice. Ah, there we are, my dear Professor. Right this way. We've prepared a light repast for you to enjoy after such a trying evening. I shall find your robe, shall I?"

A force slammed into Sophronia, pushing her violently aside. She rolled with it, away from the tea table, coming up to her feet, still holding the fan at the ready.

While Professor Braithwope might be insane by most standards, his feeding instincts functioned fine. They would be the last to go in any creature, Sophronia supposed. Although his table manners did leave something to be desired. This was only a casual tea, yet he was positively animalistic in his slurping.

The prone Pickleman writhed and gurgled but could do nothing to stop the vampire. Even weakened from torture, and having been confined without sustenance, Professor Braithwope was more than a match for a mere human. Not to mention the fact that after losing blood himself to the wooden knife of this captor, his urge to feed must be overwhelming. Really, the Pickleman had brought this on himself.

Mademoiselle Geraldine joined Sophronia, carrying Professor Braithwope's yellow banyan robe and looking on with complete indifference.

"It is troubling when a civilized creature becomes so gutfoundered he forgets technique. I had a fancy man like that once."

"Oh?" Sophronia was wildly curious, but the headmistress left it there.

The two ladies watched silently until Mademoiselle Geraldine added, "One ought to look away in disgust, I suppose."

"Agreed," said Sophronia. "But the one is our enemy and the other mad—we must think to our own skins."

"Well put, young lady." Mademoiselle Geraldine spoke to her as if she were almost an equal. It was charming. "You have a plan?"

"Of a kind." Sophronia handed the headmistress her spare knife, filched from the kitchen, and the remaining acid. "Keep an eye on things here for a moment, would you, please?"

Mademoiselle Geraldine nodded.

Sophronia nipped out, retrieved Bumbersnoot and his two charges, and returned, shutting and locking the door behind her.

"Do we let him feed the man dry?" The headmistress's tone was conversational.

Sophronia frowned. "I trust to your judgment in this. I will say, however, that if we did so, a man would be dead, and you likely know better than I how many legal issues always arise from that."

The headmistress sniffed. "He wasn't very nice to poor Professor Braithwope."

"Perhaps we should ask him, then."

"Excellent notion." Mademoiselle Geraldine shook the vampire by the shoulder. "Oh, Professor?"

No response. The Pickleman was extremely pale under that seedling beard and looking husklike from lack of blood.

"Please, Headmistress. Allow me." Sophronia snapped open the lid of her flask of lemon-infused tincture and dabbed a generous amount onto the vampire's nose.

Nothing happened for a moment.

Then Professor Braithwope sneezed violently, which forced him to unhook his fangs from the Pickleman's neck.

"Professor, dear," said Mademoiselle Geraldine, "I have your robe. Do put it on."

The vampire straightened, dazed but now free of any evidence of torture. All his wounds were healed. One could see this, of course, because he was still without clothing. He turned to face them.

Sophronia and the headmistress got a good view of all matters at that juncture.

Sophronia couldn't entirely hold back a squeak. It was so surprising. "Goodness. Well, I always told my mother this school provided a comprehensive lesson plan. It is a good thing she did not realize how comprehensive." She did not turn away, however. A lady of good breeding wasn't afforded many in-person anatomy lessons, not even at Mademoiselle Geraldine's.

Professor Braithwope struck an Adonis pose. "I was sculpted in marble. Did you know? I was once thought quite the fashion."

The headmistress smiled and draped the yellow robe about the vampire's shoulders. "Unfortunately, my dear man, this is England in the modern age, and you really must wear clothing. How would we otherwise get any work done? Such a distraction. And what will I tell this young lady's mother?" Even though the Pickleman was barely conscious, Mademoiselle Geraldine was careful not to use Sophronia's name.

If Sophronia had lingering doubts about the headmistress being a trained intelligencer, they were now put to rest.

"You tell her that her daughter got a bang-up classical education," replied the vampire.

Sophronia didn't entirely understand the subtext, but Mademoiselle Geraldine found this hilarious.

The vampire shrugged into his banyan, tying its fringed sash tight about his waist. Sophronia breathed a sigh of relief. It had been a bit much.

Mademoiselle Geraldine moved the conversation on. "Forgive me, Professor, but your meal? What should we do about him?"

The vampire looked at the prostrate man. "I'm full now." His tone was childlike.

Sophronia considered the problem. "We can't leave him. He will eventually tell what he knows."

"And what is that?" wondered Mademoiselle Geraldine.

"That I am here, that you two are free, that I've already eliminated one other man, and that I intend to eliminate more."

"Ah. I see. Your thoughts, Professor?"

"Every man should fly once in his lifetime." The vampire's mustache had recovered from its faint and was puffy with malcontent.

"Out the window, you think? Well, if you would do the honors." In an aside, Mademoiselle Geraldine said to Sophronia, "We have a good excuse, that way. He could have simply fallen off."

The vampire lifted the prostrate Pickleman. The headmistress opened a large porthole on one side, behind a pile of leaflets, and without ceremony, the vampire stuffed him through it.

Sophronia preferred not to think about the man falling to the countryside below. Even had he survived the bite, he would not survive that. *Death*, she thought, *laid at my door.* Absurdly, her brain fixated on the man's appalling grooming habits. At least she wouldn't have to look at that beardlet ever again.

She then found she wanted rather badly to cast up her accounts. But her stomach was empty. She could only hide the fact that she was retching by turning away and covering her mouth with her fan. That only caused her to notice the blood on the blade. She cleaned it hastily with her red doily, the one they were always supposed to carry with them but were never told why.

"My dear girl, was that...? Surely not. Your first finishing?" The headmistress took her arm, solicitously. "Come, I believe there is a little tea left in the pot. You look as though you could use a drop."

The teapot, on its side where the Pickleman had dropped it, did indeed still contain a splash of tea. It was enough for a much-needed, and very fortifying, tiny cupful.

Sophronia sipped it gratefully.

"There, that's the color back in your cheeks." Mademoiselle Geraldine patted her shoulder.

Professor Braithwope joined them, drawing up Sophronia's former pouf and perching on it like an odd buttercup-colored walrus. He seemed utterly harmless in his yellow quilted robe, his mustache bristling with satisfaction.

Sophronia had a difficult time looking at him.

"So, my dear, what's the occupation situation?" asked Mademoiselle Geraldine.

Sophronia felt better at the question. This was something she was prepared for, that she was equipped to handle with skill and training.

"I have a map for that." She reached into her pocket.

CRISIS 14

NOT WITH A BANG BUT A WICKER

They had to study the map at length in order to formulate a satisfactory plan of action.

It was Mademoiselle Geraldine who called a halt to the proceedings. "We should move. They may send a runner up here to find out what's happened to our airborne friend."

Sophronia nodded. "They are less likely to search student quarters, although with two men missing, they ought to begin a room-by-room sweep. That's what I would do."

"Do they have the manpower for that?" asked the headmistress.

Sophronia grinned, looking feral. "Not if we keep hounding them."

"I see why you were recruited, my dear."

No sooner had she spoken than one of the young fresh-faced Pickleman runners appeared, banging on the door to the administrative room, demanding entrance.

Professor Braithwope made quick work of him, not with his fangs this time, thank goodness. Instead, he merely whipped open the door and bopped him on the chin with a fist.

"We can't keep throwing them overboard," objected Sophronia when the vampire lifted the boy to carry him to the porthole.

"Can't keep them, either. Someone might find and release them." Mademoiselle Geraldine was more bloodthirsty than anyone might have imagined.

"I'm not all that hungry." The professor looked with mild interest at the young man's white neck, exposed by his lolling head and poorly tied cravat. "But I'd be willing to try. Only you, dear ladies, could turn me to gluttony." He sounded almost sane—his mustache looked disciplined.

"I have an idea." Sophronia grabbed the length of rope previously used to tie Mademoiselle Geraldine to her chair. "Bring him along, please, Professor, and I'll show you."

They left the administrative room. Mademoiselle Geraldine carefully locked it behind them. She had recovered her keys from Deep Voice.

On their way to student quarters, Sophronia demonstrated how to bind, gag, and tie the young man outside, under the balcony of one of the classrooms. He was effectively invisible from all sides, except where the rope showed at the bottom of the rails. Unless someone stepped out onto a lower balcony and looked up, he'd be impossible to spot. He resembled nothing so much as a suckling pig trussed for roasting, dangling from under the eaves of a porch.

"That should do, don't you think?"

"Indubitably," agreed Mademoiselle Geraldine. "It's a capital solution for the future, as well. If we can disable and truss every Pickleman, we won't have to kill any more. What do you think, Professor?"

"All of them? Can't I have a little nibble now and again, whot?"

"Of course you can, dear." Mademoiselle Geraldine patted him on the shoulder sympathetically.

He brightened. "Jolly good." Professor Braithwope was proving unexpectedly helpful. They could only hope his lucidity lasted.

"We're going to need a lot of rope." Sophronia led the way out toward the stern and the student residential area. She had her obstructor at the ready, in case they encountered malicious mechanicals, and her bladed fan open, in case they encountered malicious Picklemen. Mademoiselle Geraldine brought up the rear. The vampire walked between them so they could keep an eye on him.

Suddenly the vampire lurched at Sophronia.

"My bow!" he cried, fixated on the small crossbow dangling from Sophronia's improvised belt.

"Now, Professor." Sophronia scrabbled for some kind of logic he would understand. "Don't you think it goes so much better with my outfit than yours?"

The vampire blinked, looking down at his own yellow sleeve. The bow, which was a dark mahogany color, did indeed go well with her leather-covered red-and-black dinner gown.

"Oh, very well," said the vampire petulantly.

They continued down the hallway, finally reaching the suite of rooms set aside for Sophronia's year group. She opened the door and gestured to the others to enter.

Sophronia hissed in an aside to the headmistress as she passed, "Do you have the codes as well as the keys?"

"Codes?"

"To activate the soldier mechanicals."

"You think that's wise? After all, the soldier mechanicals are still mechanicals, and the Picklemen are in control of *them*."

"I don't think Lady Linette would be so foolish as to install new valves in the school's only major defense system. After all, it's the valve that is the true danger."

"That could be perceived as naïve, my dear. The valve is only their latest endeavor. They could have been planning this for a very long time, in which case even the most primitive models are suspect."

The headmistress moved into the parlor and collapsed onto a small chaise longue while Sophronia locked and bolted the door. She also set up a noise trap, using a propped chair and Dimity's hair receiver. When they roomed together, the ugly little pot used to drive Sophronia crazy. If it got broken when someone opened the door, so much the better.

"Should we go into my private sleeping chamber? Even safer there."

Mademoiselle Geraldine extracted herself from the chaise with a groan and followed Sophronia into her tiny bedroom. Professor Braithwope trotted behind like an eager puppy.

That door safely locked as well, Sophronia relaxed a little.

She pulled out the map, pointing to the locations of the enemy and explaining her dots. She crossed out the dot that represented Deep Voice and one of the dots for the runners.

"Now, if Professor Braithwope could handle whatever is

going on in the pilot's bubble? I'm remembering how well he dances the support beam."

The vampire was hopping after Bumbersnoot, wiggling his nose and making bunny noises. Bumbersnoot was not amused.

The headmistress said, "He will require supervision."

Sophronia nodded and pointed to the squeak decks. "I was thinking you could take out the two up top. They have guns, so they are a bigger risk. Are you prepared for that?"

The headmistress nodded. "I think so. Physical attacks were never my strong point, and I'm afraid of heights—that's why I stay inside all the time. But I'm willing to try."

Sophronia couldn't help being a little admiring. It was as if Mademoiselle Geraldine were an entirely different person. "Headmistress, you really are a remarkable actress."

Mademoiselle Geraldine blushed. "Thank you, my dear. I might have been great, you know, quite great. But there's more money and less risk in espionage work."

Sophronia was startled. "Than the theater?"

"Oh my, yes, dear. Horribly dangerous, the West End. Have you ever spent any length of time in the company of dramatic artistic types?"

"Not unless you count Lord Akeldama."

"Well, then, there you go." Much to Sophronia's disappointment, she didn't elaborate.

So Sophronia returned to the plan. "I thought I would go after the dining hall contingent. We need to cut off the head— then chaos should result. That should make freeing the sooties much easier."

The headmistress looked at the map. "But the dining hall is

where most of the enemy is! I can't let you do that. You're only a student."

"Ah, but I have the chicken." Sophronia gestured at the exploding poultry, which was currently reclining on her bed in the wicker chicken version of a seductive pose. Sophronia grinned at her own thoughts—she was beginning to give it a personality.

Mademoiselle Geraldine was uncomfortable with the risk. She might be treating Sophronia as an equal, but she still harbored remnants of teacherly concern. "You should take Professor Braithwope with you. How about you supervise the professor and the bubble while I handle the squeak deck?"

Sophronia considered. "Then we all hit the propeller room and free up some sooties? Recruit them to our cause."

The headmistress contemplated the numbers. "No, that leaves the bulk of the enemy with time to regroup. I think you were right with the first plan—the dining room and squeak decks must be first."

The discussion continued on toward dawn, at which juncture two of the three conspirators felt like they had a plan. What Professor Braithwope thought was anyone's guess. He had given up on Bumbersnoot hours ago and was humming to himself while looking through Sophronia's dresses.

Sophronia's eyes were heavy lidded.

Mademoiselle Geraldine yawned behind her hand.

Nevertheless, they persisted until the headmistress pointed out that Professor Braithwope had curled up inside the bottom of Sophronia's wardrobe, on top of her shoes, and fallen asleep. He looked, as was the custom, mostly dead. The sun must be properly up.

With a shrug, Sophronia shut the wardrobe door. Best to keep out as much light as possible.

"Whatever else, we must be coordinated." The headmistress gave a small sigh. "And we need the vampire."

Sophronia nodded. "Agreed."

"So we must hide out here for the day."

Sophronia didn't like that, for it left the sooties enslaved for that much longer. Not to mention that Madame Spetuna was in danger.

"You think they'll search the ship again, with three gone and us missing?" Mademoiselle Geraldine moved the wicker chicken off the bed. "Make room there, handsome."

"It's possible." Sophronia tugged up the low neckline of her bodice in a now ubiquitous adjustment. "Then again, it's likely making them nervous, which means they'll make mistakes."

"We can only hope so. And now, you look dead on your feet, dear. Get out of that dress and get some sleep. I'll take first watch."

Sophronia wasn't certain if she was happier to be out of the blasted ball gown or to be in bed. Both were accomplished rather more rapidly than delicacy dictated, but if Mademoiselle Geraldine chastised her for it, she didn't hear.

Sophronia slept until well past noon.

Then she sat watch while the headmistress slept, waking her before sunset.

Mademoiselle Geraldine got out of bed with her red hair wildly tousled and her face paint smeared. She made some desultory repairs, using Sophronia's small vanity and meager stores of rouge, but emerged looking somewhat like Lady Macbeth after the speech with the spoon. Or was it a knife?

Luckily, Sophronia still had the food she'd filched from the kitchen. Also, Dimity had a mound of tea nibbles set aside to take to the sooties. It was mostly cake, but better than nothing. They ate all of it, hoping they'd have an opportunity to steal more when they were out that evening.

Sophronia would have given a great deal for a decent cup of tea. She even contemplated sneaking down to the kitchen to brew herself a pot. She thought she could teach herself how. But even tea wasn't worth the risk—dire straits indeed.

She fed a lump of coal to Bumbersnoot while they waited for the vampire to rise.

This time Sophronia wore her boy's garb. Mademoiselle Geraldine made no comment at seeing one of her students in rolled-up trousers and a man's shirt and vest. Sophronia put the leather pinafore back on, liking the protection and all the pockets. She then checked over her devices and weapons. Everything was sharp and in good working order. She went about finding what kit she could for Mademoiselle Geraldine as well, filching stuff from Dimity, Agatha, and Preshea with a silent apology for entering their private chambers. She thought her two friends probably wouldn't mind. Preshea's room yielded up a wide variety of potions, poultices, and poisons, all neatly labeled, a selection of which Sophronia intended to put to good use.

She consulted with Mademoiselle Geraldine about the soldier mechanical codes, her best guess on how to activate the wicker chicken, and if there were any guns available. Then they fell silent. Plans already made and espionage in order, they had little in common and no other conversation. It seemed silly to fall back on the weather at a time like this. Sophronia might have asked the headmistress about her past or how she had managed to keep up the charade of ignorance so long, but she thought Mademoiselle Geraldine would resort to absurdities about the theater again. Sophronia couldn't take theatrical talk on only five hours' sleep.

The vampire emerged from the wardrobe looking mercurial and refreshed.

"Ladies." His tone was one of surprise. "To what do I owe the pleasure of your company first thing in the morning?"

"Evening, good sir," corrected Mademoiselle Geraldine.

"Is it? How droll. I have slept the day away?" He looked thoughtful. "I'm starving. Any tea?"

"Don't you mean blood, Professor?" Sophronia was gentle with him.

"Blood, whot? No. Or. Yes. Ah, vampire. Right. Why did I do that?"

"You wanted to live forever?" It was the only reason Sophronia could conceive.

"Did I? How curious of me. Yes, drop of blood would be nice right about now. You offering, pretty lady? Or, um, is it lad?"

"No." Sophronia's tone was flat, and she tilted her head at Mademoiselle Geraldine.

"Oh, me, neither, Professor, but we do have some gentlemen in mind for your breakfast. If you'd like to follow me. There may be a bit of tightrope walking involved, but I'm sure you aren't averse."

"Whot? Tightrope, you say? How lovely. Used to be quite the carnival artist in my day, did you know that?"

"Yes indeed, Professor. That's why you came on board my school, remember? The only vampire to tether the skies. Said you liked heights too much to stick to the ground and you'd take the risk."

"Did I? Well, there you have it." He trotted after Mademoiselle Geraldine.

Sophronia left the room with no little reluctance. It had felt like sanctuary for that one day. Even if the safe feeling was false, she had enjoyed it. She could not deny her love of adventure, not after the last few years, but right now she almost understood Pillover's reluctance. Nevertheless, she had a ship to save and possibly a nation. She shifted the wicker chicken on her back and checked that Bumbersnoot was dangling over her shoulder. He wagged his tail at her.

They were off.

Over halfway to London, thought Sophronia. The small town far below had gas streetlamps. She couldn't tell exactly where they were—possibly near Salisbury—but they were definitely making good time. They were now floating over increasingly populated areas.

Sophronia imagined reports in the local papers concerning a massive chubby dirigible spotted in the skies. Was the government spying on them? Or was it an invading enemy? The papers could get hysterical about such a thing.

She was surprised that they hadn't yet come under investigation by local authorities. Surely some of the wealthier districts kept their own investigative dirigibles for use by the constabulary? Or perhaps they had approached and the Picklemen had eliminated them.

Mademoiselle Geraldine and Professor Braithwope had disappeared to see about the pilot's bubble. After that, they would take out the two gunmen on the squeak decks. Sophronia had suggested Mademoiselle Geraldine get herself a gun first. The headmistress had muttered something mysterious about visiting her chambers and not needing a gun after that. Sophronia let her be mysterious—she had a dining hall to liberate.

She approached it with caution, heading for one of the side entrances. As hoped, the Picklemen inside were nervously running about, wondering why their men were missing. Accusations were being hurled back and forth in loud voices.

Sophronia let the door open wide enough for her observe as much as possible. This allowed her to learn something of the Pickleman plot. They did intend to use the pilot's bubble to control all the mechanicals in London. There was something about the way Mademoiselle Geraldine's pilot mechanical was designed that allowed it to transmit to multiple mechanicals at once. Or more precisely, transmit to all those fitted with the new valve. *That makes sense,* thought Sophronia. *After all, the school boasts a huge number of mechanized staff that always work in consort without crashing.* There was some feeling that if the ship were high enough, near the aether, the Picklemen might even be able to extend the reach to the whole of Southern England. The Chutney found this idea very exciting.

When the flow of men became concentrated around the high table, bent over some kind of chart, the flywaymen nearby craning their necks to see, Sophronia took a breath and entered the room. She clutched the wicker chicken to her chest, one hand on the trigger.

No one noticed her for what felt like a long time, although it could only have been a minute or two. Then again, she did look like a boy, so she didn't stand out as much as she might have ordinarily. She'd used some of Bumbersnoot's coal reserves to smudge up her face. They might think, at first, she was an escaped sootie.

Madame Spetuna was the first to notice Sophronia. In that first flash of recognition Sophronia realized she had maligned the woman in thinking she would betray the school. Madame Spetuna looked horrified to see her and made a frantic hand motion for Sophronia to *get out*.

Sophronia pointed at the chicken and mouthed *explodes*, making a bursting gesture with her free hand.

Madame Spetuna's eyebrows rose up, and she made a quick toss motion and pointed to herself. She clearly wanted to be in charge of the chicken.

Sophronia was frozen by indecision. It was awfully tempting to give up the responsibility to an experienced intelligencer. Then again, the chicken was her burden. But Madame Spetuna would know better how it should be deployed.

While she tried to decide what to do, Madame Spetuna turned and said something that drew everyone's attention. It was a bold move, designed to protect Sophronia and keep her unnoticed that much longer.

Sophronia was charmed, but wished she hadn't bothered. Because in that moment she saw suspicion suffuse the Chutney's face.

"I always thought it silly to have a female on board with us. After all, any woman could be working for the enemy."

"Now, now," said the head flywayman, "I vouched for her."

"And your cooperation was predicated on us allowing her aboard. And yet my men have been going missing. The prisoners have not been recovered. We have a traitor in our midst."

Oh, no, thought Sophronia. *They are blaming her for my actions.*

Madame Spetuna spat in disgust. "And you pick me because I am a woman? I've hardly left this room. How would I accomplish this miraculous interference?"

"But you *have* left the room a few times, to use the facilities, you claim. I find it interesting that Spice Administrator Bawkin disappeared after we sent him to the record room. As if someone on board had something to hide that school records might reveal. The only possible person . . . is you."

Madame Spetuna turned to her lover for aid, but even the head flywayman was looking at her distrustfully now.

"It would be exactly like this place to put their best agent in our midst. And you would have to be one of their best."

Madame Spetuna made no further protestations.

Sophronia realized that she was *trying* to take the blame, so that she, Sophronia, would remain safe. She wished they'd had time to consult, but decided she would honor the woman's wishes. In the end, Madame Spetuna knew more of what was going on than she did. Clearly, this inside intelligencer thought it more important for Sophronia to remain an unknown element and to destroy the center of the Pickleman operation herself. Sophronia put the wicker chicken down, tucked it against the wall with her foot, and slipped back out the door before anyone could see her. Then, fast as she could, she climbed outside to one of the upper portholes so she could see what transpired next.

The Chutney was saying something curt, issuing an order. Then he signaled his two bully boys and a runner to follow and strode from the room. This left Madame Spetuna with the gangly Pickleman, one runner, and five flywaymen. Several of the flywaymen closed in on her.

Madame Spetuna leapt away, managing to evade capture long enough to scoop up the wicker chicken.

With a manic look in her eye, she waited, clutching it to her chest, while the men closed in on her. Sophronia, horrified, realized that the intelligencer intended to sacrifice herself!

The chicken exploded.

Sophronia saw blood splatter everywhere. Top hats and flywayman scarves went flying. Madame Spetuna flew into the air, like a child tossed by an enthusiastic uncle.

And the window through which Sophronia was looking shattered outward into her face.

Sophronia jerked back, so shocked by the blast she let go of her perch and fell off the side of the dirigible.

Instinct had her shooting her hurlie at the side of the ship, grabbing on to the rope. Good thing, too, as she couldn't see anything. There was something in her eyes—she could only hope it was mostly her own blood and not glass. Thankfully, the hooks of the hurlie found purchase on some protrusion stable enough to support her weight. Then her arms were jerked almost out of their sockets and she crashed into the side of the ship, face-first.

The dark red of pain shredded through her brain, and then, blessedly, a bleak vacant black.

FALLING DOWN ON THE JOB

Sophronia had no idea how long she dangled, but it must have been a very long time.

When she awoke, the arm from which she hung— upon which she wore the hurlie—was entirely numb. Her face hurt like nothing she'd ever experienced before. A tender touch with her working hand suggested her nose was likely broken and much of her skin sliced by glass. She tried not to think about the consequences of scarring. Any future as an *agent provocateur* would definitely be impossible. She was thirsty and hungry, yet stomach-sick from the scene before she fell: Madame Spetuna exploding. All that blood. It was almost as painful as her shoulder out of its socket.

Mademoiselle Geraldine must have taken out the two guns on the squeak decks, or surely they would have seen her. At least Sophronia hadn't become a target while she dangled.

Every part of her hurt—belly, head, face, back, arms—but

what could she do? No one was going to rescue her. She had to ignore the pain and get herself to Sister Mattie's classroom to rendezvous with the headmistress and the vampire. And she had to do it by climbing, for she'd given Mademoiselle Geraldine her obstructor. Sophronia and climbing, under normal circumstances, were old chums. But now? The very idea made her want to scream.

When asked afterward, Sophronia never could articulate how she made that nightmare of a climb. Somehow she traversed two-thirds of the ship with eyes partly closed from the hit to her face—thank goodness the glass hadn't blinded her—and only one working arm. It made her rethink all previous hardships in her life. *I'll never complain of cold tea again.*

Eventually, she made it to Sister Mattie's balcony, collapsing in a heap among the potted plants. She was grateful for the leaves canopied over her, an odd kind of protection. The sky was turning gray beyond them, the sun soon to rise. Never in her life had it taken so long to climb anywhere. She hoped fervently that there was a vampire in residence to carry her to safety, because as she crawled with one arm toward the balcony door, she was convinced she would never walk again.

The door was locked and bolted. She knocked, but no one answered. She fumbled in her pocket for lockpicks, but the world seemed to be turning fuzzy as well as gray. Now her good hand wasn't working, either. And then she found, to her surprise and embarrassment, that she was lying flat on her stomach, shaking. She wondered, around an odd buzzing in her brain, if she was the first to arrive. Shouldn't the others have completed their tasks hours ago? Was it possible that they were in worse trouble than she?

And then she wasn't wondering anything at all. She was sliding down a long soft peaceful tunnel into a numb sleep.

A loud shriek, like an upset teakettle, woke Sophronia. Disorientated, she jerked, only then registering the pain shooting through her body.

Ouch. Wait, is that me *shrieking?*

No, it was coming from her stomach.

All right, not her stomach but the hard warm body tucked up against her ribs.

Bumbersnoot!

Sophronia extracted the screaming mechanimal with her working arm, flopping like a fish because she was lying on his strap. Every movement was agony. She tried to concentrate on which parts hurt most, where the serious damage might be. Her face seemed particularly bad.

I'm sunburned was her first thought. *That's why my face is throbbing.* The sun was beating down, although the potted plants were doing their best to protect her. They must be floating high enough to be above the clouds. *Oh, no, I'll get freckles and Lady Linette will be so disappointed.*

Automatically, she fumbled with Bumbersnoot, trying to stop his noise.

Only one working arm? Did I misplace my shoulder? How careless.

Vieve had never shown her how to shut Bumbersnoot's alarm off. Finally, Sophronia resorted to popping open the casing to his miniature boilers and dumping all the steaming water unceremoniously out onto the deck. With a smoky sigh, the mechanimal went silent. His tail tick-tocked ever more slowly until he was perfectly still.

Sophronia collapsed next to him. *I know how you feel.*

One small part of her brain realized that if any enemy was outside within hearing distance, they would come looking for the source of that noise. But she no longer cared. There wasn't any part of her that didn't hurt, including, now, her ears, which were ringing with the aftereffects of Bumbersnoot's alarm.

The Picklemen have activated the valves. Apparently the espionage side of her brain refused to stop functioning. Perhaps it was like Bumbersnoot's tail, the last to stop. *We must be up as high as they need.*

The door to the balcony banged open. Sophronia hadn't enough energy to lift her head. Depression hit her. *What matter if they find me now?*

"Oh, it's only you," said a jocular boy's voice. A shadow fell over her and his tone became high-pitched with concern. "Miss, what on earth happened to you?"

Sophronia groaned, finally remembering the events of the previous night. Fortunately, her jaw seemed to be working. "Exploded wicker chicken. Fell."

Handle's worried face appeared in her blurry field of view. "Was that you, making that squawk?"

"Not exactly. Help me inside, please?" She might have wondered what he was doing there, but her brain was only able to cope with one thing at a time. Right now it was busy remembering.

The sootie tutted and began to drag her inside—by her shoulders.

Sophronia suppressed a scream. It came out as a hoarse moaning cough. For the first time in her life, fainting genuinely appealed.

Handle let go of her.

Sophronia rolled onto her side and began to retch against the cool dirty wood of the deck. She hadn't eaten in a long time, so nothing came out. *Saved from one humiliation.*

"Oh, miss. Himself will never forgive me for this."

"What could you do?" Sophronia was weighed down with her own guilt. "You were under the whip. I'm sorry I couldn't come for you first. Had to be stealthy. Best possible plan."

"'Course you couldn't, miss. Don't talk waffle—sooties have been through worse. Now, how to get you in?"

"It's not at all dignified, but you'd best drag me by my feet."

Handle did so, and thus managed to get her inside Sister Mattie's chamber.

Sophronia pulled the partly disassembled Bumbersnoot carcass in her wake. She half expected to find other sooties waiting for her, sitting around in the student chairs wearing bonnets and acting the farce of lessons. *I must be delirious.*

There was only Handle.

"What's happening?" she whispered around the pain.

Handle attempted to prop her up against a pouf. She was still on the floor, mind you, but he was aiming for a more refined position. Sophronia managed it. Once modestly upright, she noticed a prone body on an improvised couch made of two chairs and a hassock wedged together.

"Who's that?"

"The headmistress was also hurt pretty bad. Took a bullet to the calf. I brought her in. The vampire's been sleeping in the potting shed, over there." Handle gestured to Sister Mattie's large wardrobe, which had been converted to a potting shed long before Sophronia's time.

"Oh, dear," said Sophronia. "I suppose *you* will have to pop my shoulder back in, then."

"What's that, miss?"

"It's out of the socket. We learned about it in a lesson on basic field medicinals and mock injuries. You have to put it back in for me. My nose, too, if possible. I'm pretty enough, but a crooked nose won't ever be fashionable. That's assuming none of my face cuts need stitches. If I'm scarring, we won't bother. Might as well have a crooked nose."

Handle looked sick as she explained, but he'd have to get over it, if the headmistress wasn't available.

On the other hand, instructing him made Sophronia feel better. She was injured, but she had a plan.

Mademoiselle Geraldine woke up at that moment. She looked hale enough, except her skirts were hiked up in a manner no gentlewoman ought to hike, and there was a large bandage around one calf.

"Miss Temminnick, what *do* you look like?" was quickly followed by "We gave you up for lost. Now I see we were nearly correct."

Sophronia was relieved, for Mademoiselle Geraldine could

guide poor Handle through the steps of a surgeon's dance. Fortunately, the headmistress did not flinch away from this duty. Even more fortunately, for Handle's sake, Sophronia did faint during the shoulder adjustment and stayed fainted for the rest.

She awoke some time later to find her arm braced and bound against her side and her head wrapped. The bandages probably started life as a petticoat and were a bright lavender color with cream lace.

"Ah, good, you're awake." Mademoiselle Geraldine was sitting up and drinking...

"Tea?" Sophronia whimpered pathetically. *Oh, glorious thing!*

Handle, that scruffy angel of mercy, immediately handed her a cup. Sophronia sipped in a reverent manner. She didn't complain that he'd put in a vast amount of sugar. Being a sootie, he rarely got sugar, and he likely thought he was spoiling her.

The headmistress reported in. "We put the shoulder back in and checked the nose, which wasn't broken, thank goodness, just askew. You'll have two black eyes, I'm afraid, and us with no raw meat to apply. None of the cuts were deep, so we dressed them with vinegar and one of Mathilde's best poultices. They should heal fine. So your career is safe. The sootie boy here did very well."

Handle was grinning, ear to juglike ear. "I never thought I had the healing touch."

Mademoiselle Geraldine nodded. "Real skill there. You help get us out of this safe and sound, young man, and I'll set you on a path to study medicine. You see if I don't."

Handle glowed with pleasure at the praise and the thought of a soot-free future.

Sophronia sipped her sweet tea and, much to her surprise, began to cry. Well, sob, really.

"Stop that!" ordered the headmistress. "Your bandages will get damp."

Sophronia wasn't certain if it was relief that her face wasn't worse—she'd never thought herself a particularly vain person—or grief over poor Madame Spetuna. Perhaps it was simply residual emotion from a very trying evening. Or something like joy, at the prospect of one of her sootie friends making himself a good life out of this awful situation. More chance than poor Soap had before the bite.

The thought of Soap seemed to cause her shoulder to ache even worse, which made her cry harder. Which made her hurt more.

"I'm a wreck," she blubbered. "Oh, this is so embarrassing."

Handle sidled over and handed her a smudged handkerchief, his face scrunched in sympathy.

Sophronia controlled her emotions by turning on her observational eye. She noticed that Mademoiselle Geraldine had returned the obstructor. Handle had strapped it onto Sophronia's good wrist. He'd moved the hurlie to that side as well, so both devices were on the same arm. Her sleeve had to be rolled up to compensate. It made her feel lopsided and unfashionable. Then again, what did she care for an exposed wrist? She was bloodied and bound and dressed as a boy anyway.

"What happened?" demanded Mademoiselle Geraldine.

Sophronia told her everything. Including Madame Spetuna's voluntary spectacular demise. "Why would she do that? I might have been able to rescue her. Instead, I handed her a deadly wicker chicken." She felt the sickening broiling acid of guilt, familiar since Professor Braithwope's fall.

Handle gave her a soft bread roll.

Sophronia gummed it gratefully, eating slowly, in tiny bites, sipping the tea in between. It settled her tummy.

Mademoiselle Geraldine looked infinitely sad. "She was a fine intelligencer and a good friend, but she knew the risks. And she knew her duty. You can't fault her for doing something you would have done in her place. She would have taken as many key agents with her as possible. And it's likely she saw no possible extraction for herself. Death and glory rather than torture and ignominy. Much alike, you and she. You know, *wicker chicken* would be a good code name. Suitably innocuous and an ode to her."

"You can't rescue them all, miss," added Handle.

Sophronia recovered enough to say, "Speaking of which, how did *you* get here, Handle?"

The sootie looked to the headmistress.

Mademoiselle Geraldine explained that Professor Braithwope had ejected two Picklemen out of the pilot's bubble. Then she had taken a bullet to the leg during their squeak deck liberation. All four were now gone, thrown overboard with guns and ill intentions in tow.

Professor Braithwope had brought the injured headmistress to the rendezvous point and then left to find food, driven to hunger by her bleeding leg. He'd returned with Handle, whom he'd managed to rescue during a chaotic moment in the boiler room and fuzzily determined was necessary to their cause, although he mistakenly identified him as Lady Linette's stuffed badger. Professor Braithwope safely asleep, Handle had fetched tea. They'd stayed holed up all day, waiting for Sophronia. Also, they needed the vampire's help to do anything further.

Handle reported that the sooties were fine and in reasonably good spirits, having seen him rescued by the vampire. "None of us have much interaction with old fangs, but if we have anyone on our side, we're grateful it's him. After that first attack, we all assumed he'd been killed."

"Handle," ordered Mademoiselle Geraldine, "give Sophronia my grenadines. Keep some for yourself, of course, but I won't be going anywhere soon and she's got working legs and one good arm."

Sophronia took a fortifying breath. The tea and food were helping, and Mademoiselle Geraldine was correct. There was work to do as soon as the sun set. Those attack mechanimals hadn't yet been used. The Picklemen weren't done. She had to gather her strength. She couldn't stop now.

Handle handed over a stuffed reticule. Inside it were several of Mademoiselle Geraldine's infamous fake pastries.

"What, what?" stuttered Sophronia, sounding not unlike Professor Braithwope.

"Small explosives," replied the headmistress. "All of them. I used up several last night. These are the last. Handle has a few. He'll show you how they deploy."

"I don't know about explosives, Headmistress. I haven't had much luck with them, so far." Sophronia was skeptical.

"Nonsense, young lady. You'll do as you are instructed. Use these pastries as needed and do not be scared or ashamed of the necessity."

"Yes, Headmistress."

Handle showed her how they were activated, by depressing the decorative element on the top, be it cherry or icing twirl. Simple devices, in the end. *And I always thought them merely beautiful representations of a very odd hobby. I should have known they were deadly as well as decorative. Everything at this school is both.* It was practically the school's unofficial motto. The official one being *Ut acerbus terminus*: To the bitter end. Madame Spetuna had taken that motto to heart.

"Tell me truthfully, Handle, how are the sooties, really?"

"Not bad, miss. We all know how to turn and shield the delicate bits. And, frankly, the whip-hand is not so good as he thinks he is."

Sophronia searched his face, hoping he wasn't making light of a bad situation.

Handle continued. "They need us to keep this boat afloat, so they feed us well enough. Won't lie, it hasn't been easy. We're running her faster and harder than ever, *and* with a skeleton crew. Plus, we didn't take on stores beforehand. They are pushing her. And us. But there are mechanicals to help with the heavy lifting—good ones, complex protocols."

"Tonight," promised Sophronia rashly. "I'll get them all out tonight."

"Even Smokey Bones?"

"Of course."

"Who is *Smokey Bones?*" demanded Mademoiselle Geraldine.

"Our cat, my lady." Handle poured more tea.

Mademoiselle Geraldine didn't seem to know what to say to that.

Sophronia took another deep breath. "I can only think of

one option at this point. We are too close to London. We have to crash the school and use the soldier mechanicals to do it."

Handle and Mademoiselle Geraldine both gaped.

The headmistress breathed out, "No!"

Sophronia explained. "The Picklemen have already used this airship to activate their updated mechanicals. That screaming noise you heard was my alarm to that effect. They needed our pilot's bubble, and they needed to be high enough to send the signal through the aether. You ask me, they took out every major key-point mechanical within aetheric transmission distance. Staff mechanicals would have gone bonkers, too, but were mainly side consequence. Now they only need to pacify the capital, and the whole country is theirs. I think they intend to drop down and offload the attack mechanimals from our hold into the city streets. If I were them, I'd do it after dark, right when people start to feel safe from further attack from the domestic mechanicals."

"Attack?" gasped Mademoiselle Geraldine.

"Or whatever the first part of the plan caused to happen. Domestics weren't the target. They're collateral. Infrastructure mechanicals were the target—train switches, station houses, government clangerclerks, record-room processing centers—that kind of thing. I overheard the Chutney himself before the chicken went off. It's almost sunset, and I wager we're sinking." Words piled up, one upon the other, as if through the act of talking Sophronia was understanding it all. If she didn't hurt so much, she would have paced the room.

Mademoiselle Geraldine and Handle were a gratifyingly riveted audience.

Sophronia continued, "Two stages of chaos—both requiring *this* airship to execute. No wonder they wanted the school so badly. They can't be allowed to complete their plan. They simply can't. There's only one way to stop them, and that is to crash with their mechanimal army still on board. Preferably destroying the belly of the airship. The trouble is, how to do this without killing everyone else?"

Mademoiselle Geraldine was thoughtful. "I knew that pilot's bubble would be a problem. Such advanced technology was always going to tempt thieves. Professor Lefoux often gets ahead of herself. And poor Professor Braithwope—what's left of his tether is to *this* ship." She added, "You'll have to aim the soldier mechanicals carefully or *everything* will explode."

Sophronia nodded. "Tell me how."

The rest of sunset was spent drinking tea and strategizing on how one young woman could sabotage an entire dirigible.

Handle, who had a sootie's affection for his ship, didn't like the idea one jot.

Sophronia tried to make her case. "The Chutney is on board, alive, and in an unknown location. He has two men with him. There is also his right-hand man, a record keeper with dyed black hair, and some of the five flywaymen who may have survived the wicker chicken incident. And there are two runners still at large."

"One runner," corrected Mademoiselle Geraldine. "Professor Braithwope got peckish during our peregrinations."

"He got one of the supervisors in the boiler room as well." Handle looked rather sick at the memory. He'd probably never witnessed a necking before.

Sophronia wondered at the ethics of utilizing the primitive feeding instincts of an insane vampire in their cause. *Is it justified? Are we harming Professor Braithwope further by allowing him to run amok or is this simply the way he is now?*

"So that's two still in engineering and one in the propeller room?" Sophronia crossed the appropriate dots off her map. "Approximately seven Picklemen and five flywaymen left. Some of them injured. I could maybe eliminate them in the space of a night—if I weren't injured myself. But as things stand, I'm sorry. It's better to destroy the ship."

Mademoiselle Geraldine and Handle, odd allies, exchanged apprehensive looks.

"So long as you do it carefully. Let's go over the plan again." Mademoiselle Geraldine's agreement was reluctant.

The sun set.

Professor Braithwope awoke and instantly tried to eat both ladies. They smelled of blood and weakness—Sophronia supposed he couldn't be faulted. Poor Handle had no alternative but to give over his own wrist to quiet the beast. Fortunately, Professor Braithwope was in an amiable mood and retracted his fangs after only a snack. He had eaten his fill the night before.

This left Handle disgusted, upset, and weak from loss of blood.

"Stupid vampire!" shouted the sootie, wrapping his own wrist in bandages this time.

"Sorry, little man," apologized Professor Braithwope. "You do have a pleasant char flavor to your skin, whot, with the added spice of smoke. Reminds me of the good old days of toast. I miss toast."

Handle sniffed at him. "Go find yourself a Pickleman next time."

"Pickled? I don't think I should like that. Fresh is best, even toasted."

"Never you mind," interrupted Mademoiselle Geraldine when Handle looked like he intended to argue further. "Our apologies, Handle. You did not sign up for mealtimes."

"No, I did not!" agreed the aggrieved Handle.

"Think of it as valuable experience for your prospective switch in professions."

Handle was thoughtful. "Bloodletting?"

"Exactly."

He was somewhat mollified.

Sophronia stood and tried to stretch. She ought to feel better after resting covered in Sister Mattie's poultices, but every part of her still ached. Now all the little muscles, strained from hanging and climbing and falling, also hurt. She hobbled like an old lady.

"I'm going to check the lay of the land." She headed onto the balcony.

They were flying quite low now, rooftops clearly visible although the moon was not yet up. *At least with the moon no longer full, some werewolves are available this evening if Agatha manages to get ahold of them.*

Ahead twinkled a vast number of lights. *London.*

Sophronia suppressed a shiver of apprehension. *Tonight I crash an airship. On purpose.*

She squinted into the lights. *Was that . . . ?* Yes, a small dirigible was approaching them at speed, under cover of darkness, flying stealthily, a dark shape against the twinkling background.

Somehow, Sophronia knew that this was her friends. There was something about the way the ship weaved through the air—intent, stylish, almost a waltz. It stank of Geraldine's training.

Sophronia unhitched the miniature crossbow from her belt. She took one of the valuable targeting bolts and created a satchel for it by weaving it through the lace edge of her red doily. Into this she stuffed a hastily scribbled note, torn off the corner of her map.

"Meet at soapy entrance. Bring this bolt back."

Only her particular friends would know what that meant. Even if she was entirely wrong and that ship was full of enemy reinforcements, nothing bad would come of her message.

The crossbow was so small she only needed one hand to fire. But still, everything took twice as long as it ought. She'd have to remember that in her calculations. She took careful aim and fired the bolt at the side of the gondola section of the approaching dirigible, now clearly visible.

There was a distant shout, and then a pause, and then the ship dropped down and altered its approach. *Success!*

Sophronia limped back inside. "Change of plans! Handle, you are with me. We take out the propeller room and free the sooties there first. Headmistress, if you and the good professor would meet us outside engineering? He'll help you get there."

"What good could I possibly do?" protested Mademoiselle Geraldine.

"I believe we have a rescue incoming. If all works out as I hope, they will be meeting us just outside the boiler room hull."

"Capital. How did you manage that, my dear girl?"

"I have capable friends," replied Sophronia.

Handle said, "That our tea cake angel?"

"Dimity? Yes, I believe so. Or someone sent by her."

"Good." Handle went all cheerful. "She's prime at pinching a tasty pastry."

"Not quite certain how that skill set has any bearing on this situation," objected Mademoiselle Geraldine.

"And yet how do we know it doesn't?" reasoned Sophronia.

Handle only tossed one of the explosive fake pastries up into the air suggestively.

There was no one in the hallway outside their room. In all probability, the Picklemen were occupied with their invasion, in the storage room readying their attack mechanimals.

With no time to waste, Sophronia saw Mademoiselle Geraldine off, carried by a docile vampire in the direction of engineering. She and Handle headed toward the rear as fast as she could hobble.

Eerie and empty as the school had been before, it was more so now. All the mechanicals were gone, their tracks abandoned. Her obstructor remained unused. It was a worry, but also a relief, for it allowed them to move quickly. With the excitement of the hunt back on, Sophronia's aches faded somewhat to the background. Or perhaps Sister Mattie's poultices were finally taking effect.

They found the propeller room, which was much smaller than engineering, manned by six sooties with one Pickleman supervisor. The man in question sported a nasty expression and held a crop, rather than a whip, and a smallish gun.

Sophronia's good arm was sound. Handle was enough of a boy to have hurled stones at random things in order to break them—as boys do. So when two fake pastries went flying, the world around that Pickleman exploded.

He collapsed, unconscious.

The sooties cheered, weakly but with real joy.

Sophronia trussed the Pickleman up with a strip of her shirt—she was running out of hair ribbons and curtain cords—and nabbed his gun. She gave his crop to a sootie with an equally nasty expression. He seemed delighted.

Handle explained the situation to his compatriots. They instantly shut down all boiler activity. Propeller work didn't keep the ship afloat, just headed it in the right direction, but this would stall the approach to London. The great whump-whump vibrations of the propeller slowed. It would take a while for the heat to work out completely, but it was a start.

The group of eight then dashed back through the ship, avoiding the area around the hold.

Mademoiselle Geraldine and Professor Braithwope were waiting for them, thank goodness. Near them was a limp body—the final runner. There were puncture wounds on his neck, and Professor Braithwope looked like a man who had overindulged in the cook's claret. He sat motionless on the hallway carpet, slumped back against one wall, hand over his belly.

"Is he dead?" Sophronia asked Mademoiselle Geraldine, who was hopping about on one leg, looking annoyed.

The headmistress made a disgusted nose. "No, gone to the cats."

"Not Professor Braithwope. The runner."

"Oh, him? Not yet." Even though it was said in an offhand manner, the headmistress sounded dangerous.

The sooties gave both Mademoiselle Geraldine and the vampire a wide berth.

That's two more off my list. Sophronia mentally crossed them off her map.

Professor Braithwope let out a belch. He was useless for the moment.

Sophronia gave Handle the gun. He passed it off to a tall muscled boy who looked like he'd grown up in dark places where guns were common. She and Handle armed themselves with exploding pastries. The other sooties were ready to grab whatever tools they could once in the room.

"Ready to reclaim your territory, troops?" Sophronia asked.

They nodded, grim-faced, eager.

The two Picklemen in the main boiler room were taken entirely by surprise by a coordinated attack from above. With one charge, Handle and the four unarmed sooties eliminated the supervisor on the platform overlooking the activity below. He tumbled over the edge with a shout, landing with a sickening crunch and sizzle on top of the biggest boiler.

Meanwhile, Sophronia and the sootie with the gun ran to the edge of the platform, knelt, and took aim. He fired and she threw. The man below was concentrating on his whip, fearing rebellion from within. Either fake food or bullet must have hit, because he folded into a heap. The sooties around him seized the moment, removing both his gun and his whip and administering a few well-earned kicks.

Just like that, the night was theirs and the remaining sooties were free. Sophronia's tiny invading army climbed down the stairs to greet them.

Sophronia assisted Mademoiselle Geraldine with her uninjured shoulder. By the time they arrived, Handle had all the sooties abreast of the situation and bustling about shutting down the boilers.

Mademoiselle Geraldine looked over the dirty triumphant group in awe. "These boys are quite wonderful, aren't they?"

"I've always thought so." Sophronia kept the annoyance out of her voice.

Handle explained. "As the boilers cool, she'll eventually sink to the ground. But it'll take days. The balloons are filled up tight, and very little helium escapes. You'll need to outgas to really get her down. I'll stay with you, miss, show you how."

Sophronia shook her head. "No, Handle, you've done enough. Professor Braithwope and I can take it from here."

Handle was not convinced. The vampire was still sagged in the hallway above in a drunken stupor. But it took a stronger man than Handle to disobey Sophronia. It took Soap.

"If you say so, miss." He turned to his fellows. "Let's find Smokey Bones, boys, and abandon ship."

A brief flurry of activity ensued while they looked for their cat, who, of course, when desperately wanted, had vanished entirely. Finally, they unearthed it beneath a particulate illuminator and picked the creature up, yowling.

Sophronia hid a smile. "Come on, everyone. Over behind

that coal pile in the corner. We should have a rescue waiting at that hatch I'm so fond of."

Handle popped open said hatch and there, nested up alongside the school in a display of real air ability, was the gondola of a second, smaller airship. Its balloon was crowded in alongside their own dirigible, somehow neither tangled in rigging nor popped by a balcony. *Very impressive piloting.*

Sophronia stuck her head out the hatch, her last piece of fake food at the ready, just in case. "My, but that's some pretty floating."

"Thank you. I've been in training these seven months," said a sharp cool voice in response. "Never thought it'd be for you, but we can't always pick our battles."

There, standing before her, looking well dressed and as stunning as ever, was Monique de Pelouse.

CRISIS 16

Out of the Flywaymen into the Fire

I got your note." Monique was almost smiling.

"Or rather, we got your note." Dimity appeared from behind the taller girl with a mercurial grin. She was wiggling Sophronia's doily-wrapped crossbow bolt gaily in one hand.

"As requested, we kept the bolt for you." Agatha ducked into view from the other side of the baffle.

"What *are* you all doing here?" Sophronia could hardly believe it.

"Agatha and I utilized Soap," explained Dimity. "Last night. You know, as a"—she struggled for delicacy under the circumstances—"lupine mount. Werewolves are really quite fast, and he was in enough control of himself not to eat us, as it wasn't full moon anymore. That said, I shouldn't recommended it as a long-distance mode of transport, not for three people."

"Three! Is Vieve with you?"

"Nope."

"Can't be Pillover."

"Never that rusty-gutted whiffin." Dimity was not about to give her brother any quarter.

"Who, then?"

"Felix Mersey."

Sophronia couldn't stop asking questions. This was all so amazing. "Felix?" She shook her head, which was a bad idea as it made her nose hurt.

Monique interrupted what looked to be a long inquisition. "Someone had to man the boiler on this airship, after all." Of course Soap would have been a better choice, but he could no longer float.

"You're using a peer of the realm for *manual labor*?"

"You can think of a better use?" Monique was getting quite vampiric in her old age.

"You trust him not to sabotage your ship?" Sophronia stared at Monique and Dimity. Both should know better, for different reasons, but still!

"Yes, with good reason, but never mind that now." Monique was impatient.

Dimity craned her head back and squinted up. "Sophronia, you look awful. What have you done to your face? Is that paint? Are you in disguise? And look at your slippers! They're filthy."

"Fell. No. No. And sorry about the slippers." Sophronia was grateful she wasn't actively bleeding anymore. The last thing they needed was Dimity fainting.

Agatha continued the assessment. "And your arm, did you break your arm?"

"Dislocated shoulder."

"Could we get on?" snapped Monique. "I can't hold this thing here forever."

It was then that Sophronia realized *Monique* was at the helm of the dirigible. It was one of the little ones with only two decks—one open on top under the balloon and the other below, housing the boilers. Rather startlingly, the airship appeared to actually belong to her.

"How many can you hold?" Sophronia accepted this fact reluctantly and moved on.

"How many do you have?" The blonde was as annoying as ever, even as she made expert adjustments to the balloon's height and propeller speed, to keep pace with the school.

"Two dozen sooties and one headmistress."

"Twenty-six." Monique calculated out loud.

"Twenty-five," Sophronia corrected. "I'm staying here."

"What? Why?" objected Dimity.

"I must crash the school."

"No!" Dimity and Agatha gasped in shock.

"Has to be done—trust me. Monique? Can I start loading?"

"Yes, yes." Monique was dismissive. "I'll adjust the air ballasts. We should be fine. Sooties aren't heavy."

Agatha ran to the opposite edge of the gondola to help stabilize.

Sophronia realized, without too much surprise, that Dimity and Agatha were acting as Monique's crew. With Felix Mersey down below. The dirigible must belong to the Westminster Hive.

"Handle, you first," Sophronia said.

"Right you are, miss." Handle slithered out the hatch and down the rope ladder. Smokey Bones was a fluff of disgruntlement, riding his shoulder like a small angry figurehead.

"Is that a cat?" wondered Monique. "Oh, *really*." But despite this verbal disgust, she looked on her furry passenger with unexpected affection. Sophronia would never have supposed Monique a cat lover, but when Handle marched over to get instructions, she made chirrup noises and scratched Smokey Bones under the chin. The cat narrowed yellow eyes but showed good sense and did not swipe at her.

The other sooties followed. A few collapsed against the gondola baffle. Most automatically headed below. It might be a smaller boiler room, but it was still a boiler room and they could make themselves useful.

Unfortunately, that meant Felix Mersey came up. He looked the same, perhaps more smudged than normal. Something was missing. Oh, yes, his waistcoat was plain with no gears sewn on. He lacked a brass ribbon about his top hat. In fact, he—shockingly—wore no hat at all. Fortunately for the state of the universe, he still wore a bit of kohl around his eyes.

"Ria, you're hurt." He looked up at her.

"Yes, but it's not important. Dimity, is that everyone?"

"Only me left." Mademoiselle Geraldine clasped Sophronia's good hand as a man might shake his fellow's after a night of carousing. "You are convinced that this is the only way?"

Sophronia was resolved. "I am."

The headmistress handed over her ring of keys, gripping one small gold one. "This is the key you want. Open the box and toggle the switch." She swung herself around and

began laboriously to hop, one rung at a time, down the swaying ladder. She stopped with her head still in the hold. "Miss
Temminnick?"

"Yes?"

"Congratulations. I pronounce you properly finished. Try to
survive the next few hours."

"Yes, Headmistress. Thank you, Headmistress."

Felix and Dimity helped Mademoiselle Geraldine down the
rest of the way.

"Now you, Ria." Felix's beautiful face was turned up to her.
She had a tiny pang over what might have been. Such a pity
about that whole betrayal thing. *Too pretty. Too late.*

Before Sophronia could disabuse him, Dimity climbed up
the ladder.

Sophronia let her get all the way to the top.

"If you're staying, I'm staying," insisted the best of all possible
friends.

"No." Sophronia smiled despite the fact that it hurt.

"I'm trained, too, remember? You don't need to protect me."

"I know that. Look at you! Allied with Monique, come to
my rescue. Of course you don't require protection. That's not it.
I have something important, and I can only entrust it to you."

Sophronia unbuttoned her man's shirt, ignoring the gasps,
and dug about in her cleavage, eventually producing her roll
of torn notes from the Pickleman's book. "Here. These are
in code, but I'm convinced someone we know can crack it.
I believe they are very important. They probably expose the
whole of the Pickleman plot, or at least the worst bits."

Dimity still hesitated.

"Take them." Sophronia pressed them on her friend. "Make copies. Deliver them to anyone you think might listen. Take them to the popular press if need be. Try that new head of the Bureau of Unnatural Registry, Sidheag's relation. I know she hates him, but he seems pretty upstanding—for a werewolf. I take it the dewan didn't believe you when you asked for aid and Lord Akeldama wouldn't interfere. So you went to the hive, and that's why it's Monique to the rescue?"

Dimity took the notes. "Couldn't Agatha . . . ?"

"No. Agatha works for Lord Akeldama, and Lord Akeldama likes to collect information, not share it. Monique works for the hive. The sooties don't have any useful contacts. You're the only one I trust. You have to stay safe. If I fail, you're the only hope to get the truth out. Now, quickly, please tell me what happened with the mechanicals."

"You know they were activated?"

"Bumbersnoot told me."

"Domestics everywhere went crazy. Started tearing apart their houses. Not the walls and furniture, but anything steam powered or automated. Often each other. It was bizarre. People were terrified. Oh! And all the major mechanicals failed. Trains aren't running. Ports are shut down. No one but us is floating. It's chaos down there. Rumor is someone was killed. By a mechanical."

Sophronia nibbled her bottom lip. "I figured it was something like. They've got a hold full of large angry mechanimals up here to finish the job."

Dimity's face went still. "Objective?"

"Probably toppling the government. It's too much effort for

anything less. How many steps removed do you think Felix's father is from the throne of England?"

Dimity blanched. "He's a duke...not enough." She tucked the notes down her own cleavage, then rearranged her lace tuck to disguise the bulge. "I understand fully."

And Sophronia knew, without having to explain further, that Dimity did, indeed, understand fully.

Face drawn and pale, her friend climbed back down.

"Will you come on?" yelled Monique.

"Dimity!" Sophronia shouted after her. "How's Soap?"

Dimity smiled. "Bony boy. Tough transport, but he's fine."

"Catch." Laboriously, Sophronia unhooked Bumbersnoot from where he dangled over her bad arm and tossed him down. She felt instantly lonely. It was as if he'd been hanging there most of her life—although it had only been three days.

Dimity caught him.

"I had to disassemble him a bit. Vieve can fix him. If I don't make it, give him to Soap."

Dimity's big hazel eyes went wide at the very idea, but she nodded mutely. She looked like she wanted to cry but didn't.

Monique and Agatha were engaged in a protracted conversation over the helm.

Next, Felix Mersey tried to climb up the ladder to Sophronia. She felt like an odd kind of Juliet, cursed with an overabundance of Romeos.

"I'm coming with you." His tone was dramatically romantic.

"No, you most certainly are not." Sophronia brandished her last piece of exploding fake food at him threateningly.

"But you're badly hurt. You need help."

"Not your help. You cannot be trusted."

Obstinately, he continued to climb.

"Dimity, a little assistance, if you would be so kind?" Sophronia summoned reinforcements.

Dimity reached up and grabbed Felix by the foot with both hands, twisting it sharply.

"Ow!" the boy objected. "What'd you do that for?"

"Get down here this minute, young man." Dimity sounded remarkably like Sophronia's mother in a temper. A glimpse into Dimity's future, should she find that nice innocuous parliamentarian and settle down.

Felix looked like he might try to continue up, although Dimity's grip had to hurt.

Sophronia decide the food didn't appear threatening enough. She put it away and whipped out her bladed fan. She'd lost the leather guard at some point. It looked quite deadly.

Felix climbed back down. "You're a hardhearted female."

"What are you even doing here?" Sophronia did not hide her exasperation.

He gave a little involuntary glance at Monique. There seemed to be some kind of arrangement between them. An odd and horrible thought occurred to Sophronia. Could he, all along, have been Westminster Hive's inside agent at Bunson's and within the Picklemen? Was his loyalty to his father faked? Rich, titled, beautiful—if he survived, he'd make for a good vampire. He had everything he wanted in life except immortality. And if he'd kept this hidden from her all along, he was also a very good actor.

Monique passed the helm over to Agatha, picked up and

strapped to her back a large carpetbag, and then started to climb the ladder.

Sophronia was getting tired of arguing. And, of all people, she'd be happiest with Monique. Never would she admit it out loud, but at least she knew Monique's motives and in what ways she couldn't be trusted. And, quite frankly, if they went down with the ship, she wouldn't feel guilty on Monique's behalf.

"Very well," Sophronia said.

The beautiful blonde hoisted herself nimbly in through the hatch, tugging up the rope ladder behind her.

"You think Agatha can handle your precious ship without you?"

"No, but she'll get the thing down in one piece, and that's all that matters. You look awful, Miss Temminnick."

"Thank you, Miss Pelouse." *Ah, familiar ground.*

"*Two* black eyes? You always were an overachiever."

Sophronia grinned and then stopped. It hurt too much. "It's a gift."

"So, what's the plan?"

Sophronia grunted. "Activate the soldier mechanicals and fire on the ship."

"Not a very complicated plan. How about we turn on all the gas in the hallways as we go up? More explosive that way."

"I like the way you think," said Sophronia before she realized what she'd said.

"I always hated this school." Monique wrinkled her perfect little nose. "Spent a lot of time imagining ways to destroy it."

"Now I see why you wanted to come aboard."

"Pure joy of it," finished the blonde with a sneer. "Let's get to it, then."

"What's in the carpetbag?"

"Options." Monique was annoyingly mysterious.

Sophronia didn't know what to think about that. Was Monique to be trusted? Probably not. But some things must be taken on faith. She probably did want to destroy the airship. Monique was simply a hard guardian angel to swallow.

The two girls made their way swiftly through the halls of the dirigible. They worked unfortunately well together—settling into a pattern. Sophronia would take one knee, and Monique, who was taller and uninjured, would stand on Sophronia's bent leg with a hand to her head for balance, knocking out the gas valves and fixtures in the hallways with a closed fan. They got good at it, like some weird acrobatic dance. They left behind them the redolent smell of gas and the fallen remains of knifelike chandeliers and parasol-shaped light covers. Dangerous indeed.

Professor Braithwope was nowhere to be found. They had no time to figure out where he had gone. Sophronia was, as a result, unexpectedly grateful for Monique's company, even though the older girl rarely said more than two words in a row. At least Sophronia had someone with her at the end.

She tried once to start up a conversation. "How long has Felix Mersey been working for your hive?"

"Long enough."

"Did you recruit him?"

Monique became all enigmatic, but she didn't outright deny it. That was confirmation enough.

"What are you after, Monique? What have you been instructed to collect?" The carpetbag wasn't empty, but it was suspiciously floppy. Even so, Sophronia was careful not to let the girl out of her sight, and, because she was no fool, not to let Monique get within fifty paces of the record room. Perhaps it was her imagination, but Sophronia was certain that frustrated the blonde.

Together they attained the forward squeak deck. Sophronia ran to the small brass box affixed to a railing on one side. She opened it with the gold key from Mademoiselle Geraldine, reached inside, and toggled the switch exactly as the head-mistress had instructed.

A loud bell began clanging—a bell with hundreds of sister bells throughout the airship. Now, if the Picklemen knew anything about the workings of the ship, they would know Sophronia's location. This squeak deck was the only place that particular alarm could be activated.

Sophronia turned to watch. The soldier mechanicals were stored in the rear upper deck, but she'd never seen them emerge before. Tracks telescoped out from the side of that deck. The soldiers made their way not through the ship, as she had always thought they would, but out onto the rear squeak deck and onto these bridges as if into nothingness, the tracks forming under the first mechanical's wheels as it moved. They rolled across the middle squeak deck and then over a second set of telescoping tracks that arched in over the railings and split into the multiple tracks inset in the wood under Sophronia's feet.

At each stage, a set of mechanicals stayed behind, so that the tops of all three decks were ringed with soldiers by the end.

In a synchronized movement, the mechanicals all settled back onto their rear wheels, locking down to each deck with a clunk. Hatches opened in the chest area of their carapaces, the whole upper torso sliding back. Each ejected the barrel of a small cannon. Then, in one smooth motion, they all swiveled and pointed their little cannons at...her.

Sophronia had been expecting it. After all, she held the tiny crossbow, and the bolts to go with it, but it was still unnerving.

Monique stared at her with mouth open.

"Never witnessed this, did you?"

"I was always inside as ordered. I knew the school had protections in place, but these are remarkable."

Sophronia took a deep breath. "Here we go." She slipped out of her arm sling. Her shoulder screamed in protest, but she did have some dexterity and mobility on that side. She would need both hands from here on out. Besides, her shoulder could always be fixed later, if there was a later. She pointed the small crossbow at the back balloon. *Do three bolts mean that each mechanical has three cannonballs? Or that only one-third of the mechanicals fire at a time?* Either way, she had to aim carefully.

Sophronia fired. The bolt whistled and thunked. A half dozen cannonballs all shot out at the same time. *Right, that's one-third for each bolt, two shooting from each deck.* Still, even with only a few shooting, Sophronia and Monique were surrounded by smoke and the smell of powder. The noise was deafening. If that didn't get the remaining Picklemen's attention, nothing would.

The six balls tore through the back balloon of the airship, leaving it in tatters, outgassing both its air and its helium. That end began to sag downward, the school now dangling from only the two front balloons. There was no explosion, but there were hot-air compartments, and the fueling mechanisms for these fell to the deck and caught fire. Not a very big fire, but it was a start.

Now Sophronia knew why the soldier mechanicals clamped down, because the deck on which she stood was tilting. She and Monique slid toward the rear side until they each came to rest behind one of the soldier mechanicals.

The deck wasn't overly steep. They could still brace themselves and stand.

"Now what?" wondered Monique.

Sophronia pointed her second bolt at the inside lowest visible part of the back section. It wasn't an easy shot. The bolt had to fly between rigging, but it hit where she hoped, about a third of the way down the gondola of the school proper.

As one, the soldiers swiveled, cannons pointing downward. Six of them fired again.

They obviously had no protocols against self-destruction. The two on the rear deck fired at their own feet. It was a good thing the airship was tilted, or the one on the far side of the deck from Sophronia might have hit her. As it was, the ball zipped directly over her head. Monique watched in delighted awe as the wood of the back section splintered while catch lines and belay ropes flapped free. The flames licked higher, provided with scraps of aged, lightweight, oiled wood to consume.

Because Sophronia wanted to keep Monique away from the

record room, they hadn't liberated the hallway gases in that section, so this was nothing more than basic destruction. But as the gondola there crumbled—shedding weight as mechanisms, furniture, rigging, and other items fell—the whole ship began to bob about.

"Look." Monique pointed up. "Shearing wind."

The ship was no longer floating safely within a breeze. Instead, the surviving balloons had caught in one wind, while the broken section and gondola were in another. Under normal circumstances, there were mechanisms, balance devices, ballast, and sooties to keep this from happening. Now these were failing or gone. As a result, the surviving balloons were caving in on one side and the whole ship was beginning to spin.

"Stop where you are!" The Chutney, his two bully boys, and the Pickleman recorder from the dining hall appeared on the squeak deck. All of them had guns, and all of them were pointed at Monique and Sophronia.

Now that Sophronia was facing him and not looking down from above, there was something awfully familiar about that dark-haired gangly recorder. What was under that trimmed beard and mustache?

Sophronia was pleased to see there were no flywaymen with them. Either they were needed elsewhere or they had given up this lark after the exploding wicker chicken and abandoned the cause.

The recorder with his too-black hair looked hard at Sophronia. His posture changed. He seemed to get taller. Sophronia shook her head, staring at him. His hair had been longer and silver last time she saw him. Also, he'd been clean-shaven and in a very nice suit.

"Miss Temminnick, I should have known," said the Grand Gherkin, otherwise known as Duke Golborne.

"Why, Duke Golborne, I only recently spoke with your son."

"Little traitor. What about him?"

"Oh, nothing, I'm certain he sends his regards."

"Have you been on board all along?"

Sophronia tilted her head at him in acknowledgment.

"Those disappearances. The sabotage!" He glared at his companion. "I told you our little flywayman infiltrator didn't have enough time. And for an intelligencer of that caliber to take herself out of the game like that, she'd have to have been protecting someone. That someone is Miss Temminnick here. I don't know the blonde."

Monique looked upset at that but wasn't suckered into revealing anything. She stood, having produced a little gun from somewhere. She was holding it with a remarkably steady hand, pointed at the Picklemen.

Sophronia felt introductions were in order. "Miss Pelouse, may I present the Duke of Golborne, also known as the Grand Gherkin, and—I believe—this is the Chutney. Forgive me, sir, I do not know your real name. Gentlemen, Monique de Pelouse, Westminster Hive."

Monique gave her a sideways glance that suggested she felt Sophronia needn't have included her affiliation, but she didn't comment. She swiveled a bit to make certain she had the Chutney covered.

Does everyone always have a gun but me? wondered Sophronia. Lacking any other projectile, she hoisted the crossbow, already loaded with the final bolt, and pointed it at the duke. She palmed her last exploding fake pastry in her injured hand.

The duke was not impressed. "I am not a vampire, Miss Temminnick, to be threatened by a flying wooden stick."

Sophronia didn't say anything.

Behind the Picklemen, one-third of the dirigible continued to fall apart rather spectacularly, and something exploded. Then a few more somethings.

"Propeller boilers?" Sophronia suggested this conversationally to Monique.

Monique inclined her head. "Most likely."

"There's no way out of this, ladies." Duke Golborne was forcing himself to be casual, but he wasn't as good as Geraldine's girls. "You are outgunned and outmanned."

"Nonsense, Mr. Gherkin, we aren't *manned* at all." Although Sophronia had thought there would only be three facing them. A slight miscalculation. Still, there was no time like the present.

"Now!" She dropped to the deck.

Monique was a split second behind her.

The Picklemen fired at where they *had* been standing, but Monique was already shooting from a prone position, and Sophronia was throwing food.

Before the Picklemen could reload, the fake pastry—a delectable-looking strawberry shortbread—exploded at their feet. The duke cried out in pain, falling over. One of the bully boys lay facedown, not moving.

The Chutney stumbled back. Monique had shot him in

the upper right shoulder. A bloom of wetness appeared on his immaculate black coat.

Before the Picklemen could regroup, Sophronia shot at their side of the deck with her crossbow.

What happened next was so fast and yet, at the time, it felt like everything moved through pudding.

The Chutney had some inkling of what that bolt meant, for he grabbed the duke and slid with him down the deck to where Sophronia and Monique crouched. The surviving bully boy followed.

The soldier mechanicals directed their cannons and fired.

Meanwhile, the three Picklemen engaged the two young ladies in fisticuffs. Monique was fighting the Chutney with teeth, nails, and elbows, like a vicious caged cat. He didn't seem to know quite what to do with her and certainly couldn't get a grip.

Sophronia struck out at the duke and the remaining bully boy with her fan. She dropped the now useless crossbow to the deck. It slid out under the railing and over the edge. While the duke was no fighter, the bully boy was good. He came in on her injured side and managed to wrap both his arms around her in a bear hug from behind. He began squeezing as tight as he could.

Sophronia couldn't get in a decent slice with her fan with her arms locked against her waist. The pressure against her shoulder was agony. Nevertheless, she kicked and struggled.

Then the upper portion of the deck exploded, wood showering down on them.

Sophronia was shielded by the man holding her. He took

the brunt of the flying splinters to his back. He screamed and stumbled to the side.

The duke dove and flattened himself against the rails, protected in part by the very mechanical that had just fired.

One of the cannonballs had gone wide—since the ship was bobbing and swaying so much—and hit the pilot's bubble. It exploded into a gout of blue flame and orange sparks a few seconds later.

One of the soldier mechanicals across the deck had been hit by friendly fire. It, too, exploded into flames.

Below them, the hallways were flooded with gas. With the massive cannonball holes, it was only a matter of time before a spark set everything off.

The bully boy let go of Sophronia. Too injured from the blast, he fell back.

The duke was occupied trying not to fall off the ship. The Chutney had collapsed to his knees and was bleeding profusely from a shredded side. The other bully boy—Sophronia swallowed bile—had been lying right about where one of the cannons landed.

Monique twirled out of the Chutney's reach and in a graceful movement crouched down. Unslinging the carpetbag from her back, she pulled out two square packs. They looked like wrapped foot warmers, only with reticule tops, and each had two straps.

She tossed one to Sophronia, who caught it with both hands, dropping her fan in the process.

"Parachute." Monique's smile was feral. "Latest design out of Paris. Put it on like so." She donned hers with the two straps around her arms and the boxy part over her back, reticule mouth up. "Jump over, and when you're well clear of the ship, pull the ribbon there. Should deploy like a great big parasol."

"It *should?*"

"They haven't been tested yet."

"Wonderful."

"You have a better idea? I know you want to be all noble and go down with the school, but Sophronia, who will be left in the world for me to dislike as much as you?"

"Why, Monique, I didn't know you cared." Sophronia tried hard to get the parachute on over her bad shoulder.

Monique gave her a look. Then she climbed over the bleeding Chutney, kicking him in the face hard with her burgundy leather boot, leapt over the railing, and with a tremendous heave, shot herself forward into the air. She'd need to clear the other decks as she fell.

Sophronia scrambled to see if she made it.

But the duke was on her, his hands around her throat. "Give me that parachute, young lady."

The Chutney struggled to his feet, nose bloodied by Monique's heel. He heard those words and then he, too, closed in, eyes desperately fixed on Sophronia's back.

One thing at a time, thought Sophronia. She heaved hard, trying to shake the duke from her throat. She'd dropped her fan. She hadn't any more explosives. Her nails scored at the duke's wrist.

He was yelling and punctuating each word with a shake. "You. Are. Not. Permitted. To. Marry. My. Son!"

If Sophronia hadn't been struggling to breathe, she would have disabused him of the notion. *The very idea!*

Then the Chutney was on her as well.

The men were fighting her but also fighting each other.

"It's *my* parachute," yelled the duke.

"Come now, Golborne." The Chutney sounded cool and reasonable. "I outrank you. Think of the good of the Pickle-men. By rights the chute belongs to me." He shoved at the duke's face with one hand while with his other he tried to rip the pack from Sophronia's back.

The ship lurched.

Any moment now, thought Sophronia, *the gas below us will ignite.* She had no idea how fierce an explosion that would be, or how it might affect the decks above and below. But now that Monique had provided her a means to escape, she actually wanted to live.

Her original plan had been to run to the midship and ride out the crash there, it being the least damaged part of the school. The whole point was that they crash down on the belly of that section, on top of the hold full of mechanimals, destroying their ability to function, but keeping them in one place for the authorities to find as proof of the Pickleman plot.

But right now, the parachute felt like a much better idea.

Sophronia twisted around and got a look up into the sky, or rather down toward the ground. It was hard to tell in the dark, but it certainly looked like the lights were getting closer. They were falling faster than they had been.

Then there came an animal scream. Like nothing Sophronia had ever heard before, human but not. Not werewolf, either.

Something hit the Chutney full force and landed atop him, carrying him backward.

Professor Braithwope's lips were stretched wide, his fangs impossibly long. His mouth seemed to split his head in two—a black maw slashed with sharp pointed death. Above it the mustache was all spiky menace.

The Chutney screamed, "You can't! You can't! We haven't been introduced!" But the vampire was beyond introductions. He bit down on the man's fat neck and began to suck.

Sophronia had only a brief moment to take this in, as the duke was still on her, trying to get one arm around her neck while the other tore at the pack on her back.

Not that I want you up against a strangler, ladies, Lady Linette's voice said in her head, *but remember one thing—if they are very earnest in their concentration, they forget to protect elsewhere.*

Sophronia wasn't wearing skirts. She kicked back, not at his gentleman's area, but hard to the inside of the man's knee. An unexpected strike toward a questionable choice of leg wear— yellow hose indeed!

He cried out in pain and his hold loosened.

Sophronia turned in his grasp so they were face-to-face. She scraped with her good hand, trying to claw out his eyes, but she couldn't get her arm up far enough. The most she got was an ear, which she yanked as hard as she could. Desperately, her bad hand searched her pockets for something, anything, a weapon, a...small bottle.

Almost of its own accord, her hand remembered what her brain did not, the execution of the fan and sprinkle maneuver. With her thumb she popped open the lid of her perfume container, specially designed by Vieve to be opened one-handed.

She dashed the contents into the duke's face. The world smelled briefly of grain alcohol and lemon. The duke squealed, piglike, and let her go, more, she thought, in surprise than in pain.

Sophronia took several quick steps away, leapt over the railing of the squeak deck, and launched herself, as if she were diving into a lake, out into the star-studded night. Well, to be less poetic and strictly truthful, it was a damp, misty night, full of smoke and the sparks of a dying dirigible.

She cleared the widest point of the airship, barely. She had jumped overboard at a point between balconies. A little to either side, and she would have landed with a splat instead of free-falling. It was not a graceful dive, more a frantic tumble. Thus, she was facing up when the whole forward section of the school exploded into flames—billowing orange gas and fire. The brightness of it lit up the sky, illuminating the carnage that had once been a friendly caterpillar-like dirigible.

Two balloons gamely tried to hold up the wreckage. In fact, as half the ship dropped away, the lighter burden caused what remained to bob upward. Until one of the balloons caught fire, flames licking at the oiled material.

Sophronia became occupied with her own problems, grabbing desperately for the deployment ribbon for the parachute. *I probably should have held it when I jumped, like Monique.*

The lights of the city below her were getting dangerously close. Sophronia finally found the ribbon and pulled. Something whuffed out behind her, and a moment later she jerked. Her bad shoulder screamed in pain, but she caught wind and was drifting instead of falling, like dandelion fluff upon a breeze.

She landed in someone's backyard in the outskirts of London.

Sophronia was not ashamed to admit that she positively *flopped*. She sprawled back onto a damp patch of earth, among what once had been, before she landed on it, a vegetable box full of Brussels sprouts. She lay on her back watching the carnage she had wrought flash in the sky above her and smelled the cabbage-fart scent of fresh Brussels sprouts. All her brain could contemplate was the fact that, of all vegetables, she was rather fond of sprouts.

IN WHICH WE ARE ALL FINALLY FINISHED

When the school exploded above London that night in early January of 1854, there were fewer witnesses than there might ordinarily have been. Many were occupied with a mass mechanical shutdown. Those who did see, dismissed it as one more eccentricity in a *very* eccentric night. Few knew what it was that died. Those who did, set out to find where the school landed when it fell from the sky.

The werewolves got there first. By the time the others arrived, they'd snuffled through the wreckage and extracted Picklemen and flywaymen—some already tied up, some bloodied, some bashed, some burned. All were annoyed with life, except, of course, those who were dead. The werewolves stacked them neatly in three piles—dead, not dead, and snack-sized.

Conveniently, one of the dead Picklemen had turned ghost and proved willing to cooperate. After all, he had nothing left to lose. After the werewolves found a vast number of illegal mechanimals, the ghost explained the whole invasion plan. The werewolves sent off for the Bureau of Unnatural Registry, various government representatives, the Staking Constabulary, and all manner of other authorities who might be spared from one mechanical crisis to see about another.

Soap was there. A wolf none of the others knew, a loner unwilling to fraternize with a pack. He hunted long after the others had stopped. His nose, although miraculous in its abilities, couldn't find the one scent it was looking for. The scent that lingered with him even when she wasn't near. So his hope turned to fear.

The hive's rescue dirigible arrived, full of sooties and Mademoiselle Geraldine. The headmistress explained everything she knew, or at least pretended to, under the solicitous attention of various large gruff men. She made for an excellent front, in more ways than one, while her students and sooties quietly avoided questioning.

Even Monique showed up, a great deal later, after she had reported to her hive. It was a miracle she came at all. At first they thought it remnant loyalty to her old school. But then, after she filled in some details concerning the last of Sophronia's adventure, she demanded the return of her airship. "That dirigible is my responsibility. I should like it back now."

Since it wasn't part of the investigation, the authorities permitted her repossession. She left, with a few sooties paid to help float, but with no more information about Sophronia's survival than anyone else.

At which point, Soap panicked.

The skinny, black-furred loner wolf started weaving back

and forth, a whine he couldn't control keening out. The Staking Constabulary thought he might be mad, and prepared their silver to attack if necessary.

Soap thought he'd know. If Sophronia died, he thought, somehow he would be aware of that fact—feel it in his bones. But there was nothing, no clue, no message she'd left in the wreckage, just a few of her dresses and some bits from her room in a pile. Her scent was on one or two of the prisoners, their bonds were her handiwork, but nothing more.

Dawn was soon to come—Soap could certainly feel *that* in his werewolf bones. There was only one more possibility. So he left.

He was too far gone in beast to care that Dimity and Agatha stood sobbing to one side, clutched together, certain their friend had died. He registered his old enemy, Felix Mersey, crying, the charcoal smell of wet kohl from the lines about his eyes as it ran down his face. What right had he to cry? His father had survived, although both the duke's legs were broken. Soap spared the duke a glance—the man who had killed him once was in the Bureau of Unnatural Registry's custody amid mutterings of high treason. Wolf Soap found it all petty and inconsequential when his Sophronia was missing.

His beast brain could remember but one thing: Regent Square an hour before dawn. And dawn was coming. So Soap ran back into London as fast as supernatural speed could take him.

Sophronia extracted herself from the Brussels sprouts and thought about the time. She wondered what she should do and how she was going to get anywhere to do it. Her plan had finished with the ship. With no other ready options, she headed to Regent Square on the off chance that Soap would remember their meeting place—because really, what else was there to do?

She had to walk, and it was a long walk, because she hadn't any money and no hackney would stop to pick *her* up—a roughed-up boy with two black eyes, a useless arm, and a slight limp. *Perceptions*, thought Sophronia as she hobbled along, *really are everything in this world.*

She didn't quite make it in time. It was about half an hour before dawn when she finally stumbled into Regent's Park. Sophronia had never been so tired, or so thirsty, or so hungry in her life. She tumbled onto a small patch of ground under a thorny bush and lay there, aching. Every bone in her body had something to say about the state of the universe, loudly and likely profanely. Her skin hurt all over, and her mind was pressed down with the weight of the lives she had taken. Like the mechanicals who had gone before her, she simply shut down.

Soap, who was running a pattern about the park, nose forward, found her sleeping. He entirely forgot he was still a wolf and licked her face all over.

Sophronia awoke to slobber and wolf breath.

She couldn't have been happier. She wound her good hand through his thick black fur and rested her chin atop his ruff. Foolish boy, he wriggled about onto his back, tail wagging in an excess of delight. It was almost embarrassing, if it hadn't been so cute.

Then Soap remembered himself—or at least that there was

another half of himself to remember—and transformed. Only now he was naked, crouched on the ground next to her, and that really was embarrassing.

"Soap, what are you—"

And then they were both kneeling, and Sophronia was in his arms. Embarrassment didn't really matter, for he was kissing her fiercely and that was awfully nice, although also embarrassing. Her lip had been split at some point and her face really did ache, but she hadn't the strength to stop it even if she'd wanted to.

Eventually, he paused, tilted her back, and took a good long look at her.

"I thought you were dead."

"Evidently not, or I'm a rather substantial ghost."

Soap kissed her again, because he could, and because she wasn't a ghost, although this time carefully on the uninjured side of her mouth. Sophronia liked that so much, she forgot about her injuries, for a short space of time, and kissed him back.

Finally he drew away. Both of them were out of breath, as if they had been swimming in a cold lake. Though that was not at all how Sophronia felt.

"It won't work, Soap. The dewan. My parents, society, no one will permit—"

Soap put his hand over her mouth. "Enough of that. Think of it as a challenge."

Sophronia cocked her head.

"No, *listen* to me for a change. What you have forgotten is that we are both already outside of society. I don't have to fit into your world, and you are already in mine. We share these shadows. What did you think would happen with your indenture? The dewan knows that you're better in the field. You'd be wasted on marriage to some prince or duke. Why do you think he's kept me secret? He wants us teamed up—intelligencers to the Crown, Geraldine's trained and werewolf strong. I think we'd make a great pair, in more ways than one."

Sophronia really considered what he was saying. And, shockingly, it seemed *almost* possible.

She stuck her tongue through her lips to lick his hand. With a start, he dropped it.

She looked into his eyes. "Marriage would not be possible. No office would provide a license, not to you and me, not for any bribe."

"Did I ask to wed? I was rather hoping we could live happily in sin for a very long time. *Lovers* has a nice ring to it."

Sophronia huffed out a startled laugh. "How very French. No one of any rank would receive me if they knew." But she kind of liked the idea. *I would never have to lose my freedom to a husband. I thought Soap would insist on being honorable, because he is such an honorable person. Silly of me not to remember he can also be sensible.*

"Shadows, my heart. No one need know."

"Endearments, already?"

If he could have, Soap would have blushed. "Too soon? I've said it so often in my head, it slipped out."

Sophronia tried a tentative smile. "I don't mind. It's only, what do I call you?"

Soap's face lit up. He knew she wasn't trying to evade the

conversation, that she liked the idea. "I'm rather partial to *honey-sop piggle-wig.*"

Sophronia raised an eyebrow.

Soap grinned at her. "You'll come up with something, but it has to happen naturally."

"Very well, dear . . . No, that doesn't work."

Soap wrinkled his nose. He had a very nice nose. "Most certainly not. Too stiff."

"I'll give it consideration, honey-sop piggle-wig."

"Please don't. When you think about things, Sophronia, they only get more complicated. This thing between us could be so very easy, if you let it." He spread both his hands over her waist, daring to move them in a circular caress. Sophronia felt warmer than she ought where he touched her.

"If I choose you, Soap, I intend to honor the choice. We will have to determine, together, what that means."

"I don't want to hold you through loyalty, my heart."

Sophronia cocked her head. "Yes, you do. Loyalty is the only moral compass I have. It's our best foundation. And you have earned it."

Soap's face fell. "And what of love?"

Sophronia was uncomfortable with the intimacy of the question, but she also knew that this would be part of their future. One couldn't live in shadows without some clarity. Soap would need to know her heart. Sophronia examined it closely. *Am I strong enough to risk giving it to him?*

"Yes, that, too. We always did belong to each other, didn't we?" With which she finally took on the responsibility of allowing him to love her.

"Took you long enough to accept." He'd heard the vow under her words.

It seemed almost ritually sacred to kiss at that juncture. It was also terrifying and overwhelming.

And because Soap understood her so well, he drew back, giving her time to realign her perspective on the way the world worked.

He changed the subject. "How did you get here?"

"Oh, you know, I happened to be in town. I hear the new muffs are in from France."

Soap started to smile and then wouldn't let himself. "Oh, but really, my heart, what did you do to yourself?" He whispered fingers near her eyes and nose, careful not to apply any pressure.

"It's a very long story."

"*Two* black eyes?"

"And a shoulder out of its socket. Not to mention various other assorted bumps and bruises. I did jump out of an airship, I'll have you know."

"And take on a whole mess of Picklemen and flywaymen, said Mademoiselle Geraldine."

"Oh, good, she made it down safely? And Dimity and Agatha and the sooties?"

"All in far better condition than you, I'll have *you* know. Even the appalling Felix Mersey. Not to mention the dratted Monique." Soap's lip curled on those names.

Sophronia sighed. "I'll have to give her a different moniker. She did, kind of, save my life, in the end."

306

"How awful for you." He stroked her matted hair with one callused hand.

"I know!"

Soap became plaintive. "Do you think you might leave the world to right itself for a while now?"

"I don't know if I can afford to. What's happened since I fell from the sky?"

"I've not been paying the best of attention. I've been looking for you. We thought you died."

Sophronia struggled to sit up on her own. "Dimity and Agatha think I'm dead?"

Soap nodded, nuzzling her neck on her good side. That did feel nice. It was the only part of her not injured.

But this was serious—her friends were in distress. "I can't have that. Poor dears, we must go to them immediately." She was also worried about the oncoming dawn. "And we should get you indoors."

"Mmm. Quite apart from my werewolf condition, the city will be waking up soon. As it stands, we are both likely to be locked up for indecent exposure. The dewan is at the palace with the queen, has been since the mechanicals attacked. He's no use to us."

Sophronia was hesitant. "We could go to my sister's, but I don't think she could cope with my appearance. I'm certain she couldn't cope with yours. I wouldn't want to shock her into early childbirth."

Soap agreed. "You know the nearest discreet location as well as I. Should we chance it?"

Sophronia was skeptical but willing. "At least I can be assured a bath and a nice change of clothes. We'd better go now, before sunrise. His drones won't let us in without his approval."

Soap stood, and Sophronia looked away quickly, as yet not entirely prepared. *A girl can know too much about the man she loves,* Dimity once said.

He bent and scooped her up.

"I can walk."

"I must carry you to disguise my lack of clothing."

"Oh, very well, although I suggest that when you pull the bell rope, you stop trying."

Soap only strode off. Her weight was nothing to him, and he certainly moved a great deal faster than she could at that point.

The vampire himself answered the door, wearing a robe of royal-blue quilted silk with teal embroidered peacock feathers and gold lace trim, clearly near to taking his repose. Despite this, there was a hum of activity to the house behind him that suggested *things were afoot.*

"Kitten! Is that you? *Horrid* eye paint, my pet. You should fire your maid this instant. And here I was *just* about to retire. Yet I'm certain you are full of *delicious* stories and know everything there is to be known about *everything.* It's *too bad* of you. Couldn't you have come a little bit sooner, poppet?"

Sophronia gave a little smile. "Dear Lord Akeldama, I'm afraid I was all tied up. Or do I mean tying up? But please, may we seek refuge for the day? As you can see, I'm not quite the thing."

Lord Akeldama's eyes were hooded. "My dear *girl,* you aren't in serious legal trouble, are you?" The hesitation referred to

Soap. They had not been introduced, so the vampire could not address him directly. Lord Akeldama's reluctance was to be expected. After all, it wasn't normal, even in his long lifetime, to have a naked black man carrying a badly beaten girl turn up on one's doorstep.

Sophronia presented her bribe. "If I told you that the dewan is my patron and Soap here is the reason, would you let me in to hear the story?"

Lord Akeldama threw the door wide. "Do come in—*I insist!*—and your fine young man. Oh, my, is he wearing anything at all? Sophronia, did you bring me a present?"

"No," said Sophronia, cheerfully. "I brought you a werewolf, but he entirely belongs to me."

The vampire pouted at her and didn't look the least surprised. "Selfish girl. *Lucky* but selfish." However, he also stepped back so they could enter. "Welcome—yes, you *are* adorable—welcome."

Soap, who had just walked through London carrying her and wearing nothing, looked embarrassed for the first time that night under the vampire's appreciative gaze.

Still, an invitation from a vampire was never to be treated lightly. Soap knew enough to say, "Thank you kindly, my lord."

"My very great pleasure." Lord Akeldama closed the door behind them. "Of course I knew the dewan had a new pup."

Soap started at that.

"Don't worry, my beauty. Your secret is safe in my household. But the fact that my little *kitten* here was involved, *that* I did not know."

Sophronia was ready to fulfill her part of the bargain. "Few do. Soap was injured badly, shot by a Pickleman. I leveraged my indenture to convince the dewan to bite Soap outside of claviger status."

Lord Akeldama evaluated Soap again, with something more than appreciation. "And he survived? *Remarkable.* And quite romantic. You two make for an unusual pairing."

Soap began to bristle at the implied criticism, his arms tightening around Sophronia.

"Now, now, little wolf, I *like* unusual pairings." The vampire smiled without showing fang.

Soap relaxed slightly.

"Just back there, my *sweethearts*, into the drawing room. And now, much as I would *delight* in hearing *positively everything else* that has happened to you lately, I'm afraid I am about to drop dead. Bed awaits. Pilpo will look after you." Without further ado, Lord Akeldama whisked up the stairs, seeking his private chamber.

Soap said, "I'm going to need to sleep soon, too. Sun isn't as difficult for me as for vampires, but I'm young and it's challenging. My heart, please don't tell anyone *else* about me? The dewan wants it secret. Not only do I have to obey him, but it's better for us this way."

"I wouldn't worry." Sophronia made her voice as calm and reassuring as possible. "Lord Akeldama is *like* that. And he won't talk. He never talks about important things."

Pilpo appeared at that juncture. Sophronia had met him before. A lifetime ago, it felt like. He was dark skinned like Soap and dressed impeccably, as was always the case with Lord Akeldama's drones. As if by magic, he offered up a beautiful brocade robe for Soap. Relieved, the werewolf put Sophronia down long enough to pull it on.

Pilpo let them into a large drawing room that was gorgeously—if not comfortably—furnished. This was clearly the hub of Lord Akeldama's household, although empty at present.

"Where is everyone?" Sophronia asked as she and Soap made their way over to a small sofa.

They sank down on it gratefully.

"My lord has us all out hunting." Pilpo flashed a beautiful white smile. "Except me, of course. A lot happened last night, and he expects to know everything there is to know by sunset today. I suspect you two will be most helpful in this matter."

"No wonder he invited us in." Soap settled himself on the couch. Then, because he had no manners, he curled up with his head in Sophronia's lap.

She let him. Her lap didn't hurt. And this way she could play with his hair.

Pilpo manfully ignored Soap's feet on the furniture. "But first, what do you need, my dear? Food? Tea? Something stronger?"

Sophronia sighed with pleasure. The very idea that she was safe and could rely on this capable gentleman to see to her immediate needs was a pure joy. "Tea would be lovely. And, unfortunately, I should see a physician, if you have one you trust. Also, my friends think I'm dead. Could you send a message stating the contrary to Miss Agatha Woosmoss? I believe Lord Akeldama is familiar with the young lady and should have her address. She can tell the appropriate authorities that any rumors as to my demise are grossly exaggerated."

Pilpo nodded. "It shall all be done exactly as you wish." And went to fetch the tea.

By the time he returned, Sophronia was also asleep, leaning precariously sideways on the sofa, her good hand on Soap's head where it nestled in her lap. They both looked very young.

Pilpo covered Soap with a blanket and placed a pillow so Sophronia would not awaken with a crick, and then went about putting as much as he could to rights before luncheon.

Sophronia awoke at noon, ravenous, and alone—but for a sleeping Soap—in Lord Akeldama's blindingly golden drawing room. She managed to extract herself from her lover's heavy head without waking him. This required no real skill, for he, like most supernaturals, slept like the dead during daylight. She found a little gold bell next to her elbow that tinkled sweetly when she rang it.

Pilpo appeared. "You're awake? Good. Feel better? What would you like first?"

"I'll take that tea I missed before, if you would be so kind? And some breakfast, please, if it's not too late? And then, more than anything else in the world, I want a bath."

Pilpo laughed. "Of course, my dear."

Other drones were home now, and one of them appeared with a piping-hot pot of some gorgeous tea, a mound of bacon and eggs, a fried kipper, buttered toast, and a scone with raspberry jam. Sophronia ate it all. After that, Pilpo helped her up—she was quite stiff—and showed her to the bathing chamber.

Sophronia spent longer than she should soaking in the fabulous hot water, though it hurt at first and all her wound dressings had to be removed. Pilpo checked on her twice, to make certain she hadn't fallen back asleep. The third time he appeared, eyes averted, and deposited a beautiful day dress on a marble statue nearby. He said not to bother doing up the bodice, as the doctor had arrived and would want to look at her shoulder. There were assorted filmy white underthings, but no corset, which was good, as Sophronia couldn't have possibly done it up herself.

She struggled out of the tub and dressed with care. It seemed to take a very long time. The dress was dark teal silk, with black lace trim and a skirt of three tiers. It had a jacket with tiered sleeves that closed up the front, but even so, Sophronia wished for a lady's maid. It had been chosen with care as easy to put on, but everything was a challenge with only one arm. Nevertheless, Sophronia was on her own, for Lord Akeldama didn't keep female staff. She wondered where the dress came from.

The doctor waited for her in the dressing room. He was a genial elderly gentleman with an air of discretion, very little hair, and sad eyes. He did not ask how she had acquired her injuries, merely treated them with care and concern as to her resulting appearance.

"Such a pretty girl must, perforce, be left without scars."

Certainly, he was exactly the kind of doctor Lord Akeldama would keep on retainer for his drones.

He left her with a cataplasm for her eyes, a sling for her arm—"Keep it *on* this time, young lady!"—and bandages for everything else. He then fastened her bodice for her, in the manner of a man proficient in fashion, because with her arm back in a sling she couldn't do it herself.

Sophronia returned to the drawing room to find Pilpo in his element, entertaining a chattering gathering that included Lady Linette, Sister Mattie, Pillover, Agatha, several sooties, Smokey Bones, and, best of all, Dimity. Soap was still there as well. He was also still asleep.

Dimity ran to Sophronia, looking as if she very much wanted to hug her, but settling for cheek kisses and cooing noises. Despite her bath and visit with the doctor, Sophronia knew she still looked awful. From the thinly disguised horror in Dimity's eyes, she suspected it was worse than even she could imagine.

"Oh, Sophronia, what you must have been through!"

Agatha followed, no less pleased, but not so effusive about it. She clasped Sophronia's good hand briefly with her old shy smile. "Welcome the returning hero."

"Oh, stop," said Sophronia, charmed.

Pillover mooched after the two girls. He was grinning, of all absurd things, a wide genuine smile. Sophronia would never have believed it if she hadn't seen with her own eyes.

Agatha seemed pleased with life. "Pillover is a hero, too, did you know?"

Dimity recovered her composure at that, enough to say, under her breath, "Oh, really. He's no better than a mangel-wurzel."

Sister Mattie, however, agreed with Agatha. "Indeed he is. Helped us to escape, he did. Bunson's was in league with the Picklemen, as we suspected. Well, if not in league, at least complicit. Anyway, Agatha's young man here helped to free Lady Linette and me."

This worried Sophronia. "Oh, dear Pill, will it detrimentally affect your school standing?"

Pillover shook his head. "No, increase it. Bunson's doesn't hold traitorousness against a fellow. After this, I'll have moved up to Reprobate Genius. One step closer to true Evil."

"Where's Vieve?" Sophronia asked, assuming that the little inventor would have been involved in any Bunson's escapades.

Pillover shrugged. "Said she didn't want to see large-scale destruction of her beloved technology. Said she knew it'd be necessary, that you'd probably see to it, but she'd rather not know the details."

Sophronia wondered if Vieve had been thinking of the Picklemen's mechanicals or if she was smart enough to have realized all along that the airship was the target. It hardly mattered, and even if Sophronia asked, Vieve wouldn't tell her. Sophronia respected her all the more for that.

"I left Bumbersnoot with her to be fixed." Dimity's tone was questioning.

"Good decision." Sophronia approved, especially as London was likely rife with anti-mechanical sentiment right about now. "So why'd you do it, Pill? I thought you didn't enjoy adventure."

"Did I say I enjoyed myself?"

Sophronia did not point out that he was grinning, nor did she say anything about the fact that he kept casting little sideways glances at Agatha.

"Happy to have you here, Pill." Sophronia hid her own smile.

"Well," groused Pillover, resuming his normal dour expression, "so you should be."

Dimity tutted. "Heaven forfend you enjoy yourself, you wombat."

Agatha said nothing, although she did look a tiny bit smug.

Dimity inched close to Sophronia and clasped her good hand fervently. "What happened after Monique left you? Please don't keep us in suspense any longer. We were so worried."

She led Sophronia over to a cluster of chairs around a tea table, some distance from the sleeping Soap. Sophronia chose a seat that allowed her to keep an eye on her werewolf. She wasn't ready to let him out of her sight again. The bath had taken long enough.

Still full from her breakfast, Sophronia figured there was always room for more tea, and allowed Dimity to pour her a cup. Sipping gratefully, she leaned back and told them the story of the death of the airship.

"I do apologize, Lady Linette. There seemed no other way."

Her former teacher shook her head, blonde curls bouncing. "We knew it was coming to an end soon, my dear. Geraldine's girls, I'm afraid, are creatures of the past. Admissions have declined steadily over the years. No one wants their daughter to be an intelligencer anymore."

"You won't be starting it back up again?" Sophronia was saddened by this.

Lady Linette and Sister Mattie exchanged looks.

"Not as such," Lady Linette explained. "Mademoiselle Geraldine now has a bee in her bonnet about starting a school for underprivileged boys, training them up to be physicians of all things. Professor Lefoux is intent on returning to France—she says England has gotten too complicated. Sister Mattie was muttering something about Cornwall, weren't you, dear? I don't know what I'll do. Fortunately, I'm trained for pretty much anything." She waggled her eyebrows, and for the first time, Sophronia noted that she wasn't wearing her usual heavy face paint. "I am a mite exhausted by the work. I've been at this for three decades now." She gave a delicate little shudder.

Agatha looked sober. "Thirty years is a lot of Sophronias to deal with."

"My point exactly," said Lady Linette with feeling.

A bell at the door drew Pilpo away, which was when Sophronia noticed how many drones had gathered to hear her story. It was a mark of how discombobulated she was that her guard was so far down. Some were entertaining the sooties at cards. It was hard to tell who would do better out of that deal. Smokey Bones had taken possession of a hassock near the coal scuttle, which was probably why he liked that particular spot. The drones no doubt approved of an animal so innately well dressed. They had brushed the little black-and-white cat to a glossy shine heretofore unheard of, and popped a tiny cravat about his neck. They cooed over him in a manner the sooties took as approval of not simply their cat, but themselves as well. It was lending an air of conviviality to the gathering, only improved upon by the fact that unlimited tea, scones, and sardines were on offer. Neither Smokey Bones nor the sooties had ever had it so good.

Sophronia supposed she should have been more discreet when telling her story, but Lord Akeldama probably knew most of it and could guess the rest, even asleep. Sophronia aspired to be like that herself one day. And the sooties deserved to learn what they had been party to. They'd suffered the whip for it, after all, scones or no scones.

Pilpo returned, trailed by Monique de Pelouse.

"I thought I should find you here," she said.

"You're better at your job than I suspected," replied Sophronia.

"Nice to see you haven't suffered too many ill effects, Miss Temminnick. I brought you the morning paper. You might be interested in the headline." Monique flipped it open and read out: "'Secret Society of Picklemen Exposed.'" Then she stopped and paraphrased. "Apparently, the popular press received irrefutable evidence of a secret society of elites engaged in treason and misconduct. Evidence came straight to them, notes in the leader's own hand. My queen is a little upset that I missed getting hold of the Chutney's notes and the intelligencer records."

Sophronia gave her an arch look. "You can't have it all, Monique."

"Lord Akeldama may feel similarly." Pilpo was looking at Agatha, who blushed faintly.

"Ah. You gave them to Dimity, then, I take it?" Monique was no fool.

Sophronia inclined her head.

Monique sighed. "Well, the repercussions are good so far as my countess is concerned. What with that and the rebellion last night, not to mention two reputed deaths, there is widescale public outcry against mechanical technology. Mobs have dug up the tracks all over London. People are ripping them out of their houses and piling them in the streets. There's scrap metal to be collected on every corner. It's a pity we couldn't control it, but the Picklemen are shamed and disbanding, and that's all my queen really cares about."

She tossed the paper at Dimity, who caught it easily.

"Beautifully done, Miss Plumleigh-Teignmott."

Dimity saluted her with the paper.

There was a long awkward silence. Monique stood, poised. She showed no repercussions from the previous evening's activities. Her skin was flawless. She even looked well rested. It was revolting.

Sophronia reached for her nose, wincing at the touch.

Monique stayed, expectant, her attention on Lady Linette. Monique's posture was perfect, not a hair out of place. Her visiting dress was an expensive French design of printed blue muslin that looked almost like the pattern on Sophronia's mother's fine china. Her sleeves were wide and fringed. Perhaps the gown was a little too spring, but Sophronia realized with a jolt, they were headed into spring anyway. New Year's was over.

A silent battle of wills occurred between Lady Linette and Monique.

The teacher nodded. "Very well. I pronounce you finished, Monique de Pelouse."

The lovely blonde relaxed at that, as if she had been waiting a long time. Perhaps she had. Then, without another word, she strode from the room.

Lady Linette sighed. "Not that it matters anymore."

Dimity said, bravely, "What about us, Lady Linette? Surely Sophronia deserves recognition, at the very least?"

Lady Linette gave a half smile. "She's already finished, which I believe she knows."

Sophronia nodded.

"And you and Miss Woosmoss as well, my dear. It was a brave rescue and a daring charge across the countryside on wolf-back. I could not have devised a more taxing exam." Sister Mattie took pleasure in the pronouncement.

Lady Linette added, "Not to mention the initiative needed to seek help of a hive. Particularly after they once kidnapped you, Miss Plumleigh-Teignmott."

Agatha smiled. "We're finished?"

Dimity looked like she wanted to cry. "We're really finished? Mummy will be so proud."

Lady Linette patted Sophronia on the knee. "We shall overlook that you destroyed my entire school, shall we? Just this once, my dear. Try not to do it again to any other school, all right?"

Sophronia took the recommendation to heart. "I'll certainly try, Lady Linette, but I'm not making any promises."

That night was remembered in infamy as the Great Pickleman Revolt of 1854 and among the untutored masses as the Mechanicals' Uprising. No household in England ever again employed mechanized staff. Most mechanicals were willingly destroyed in the space of six months. The government hunted down the rest. Bumbersnoot, the only mechanimal to survive eradication, was gifted to Queen Victoria in a secret ceremony. He was specially exempt from destruction. Due to Vieve's modifications, he became the Royal Alarm Dog, in case mechanicals rose up again. Queen Victoria grew terribly fond of the little chap, and through him, dogs in general. As a result, the royal household kept a number of canines through the years, a passion that persists to this day. Rumor is that Bumbersnoot still rattles about, well loved and carefully tended, shedding small ash piles in Buckingham Palace—the old family retainer, just in case.

Poor Vieve never forgave England for the technological destruction. She stayed long enough to graduate with distinction from Bunson's and then left in pursuit of further education at L'École des Arts et Métiers in France—still disguised as a boy. She eventually set up shop with her aunt in Paris, producing a respected line of domestic women's gadgets, all of them highly functional and quite deadly. Sophronia, Agatha, and Dimity visited her establishment for all their needs—after all, ladies of quality always shop in Paris.

The school was demolished for scrap. There was no sign of Professor Braithwope, and no one ever saw him again. This was, perhaps, a good thing. If he survived, with so many kills under his cravat, even the most militant of hives would have called for his execution—he was no longer civilized. If, on occasion, Professor Lefoux returned from Paris, and took a long train ride, and then a long carriage drive far out into the wilds of Dartmoor, it was thought mere sentimentality for a life she had lost. If Swiffle-on-Exe heard rumors of a very odd hermit, no one connected the two. If, on the occasional evening, stories of that hermit wearing a top hat and waltzing with the rabbits percolated through the town, scaring schoolboys, he was thought no more than the local drunk. And then the local bogeyman. And then mere myth. For no one thought to wonder that their dancing hermit had lived a very long time, whot?

Mademoiselle Geraldine formally adopted Handle and saw him through medical training. Together, they immigrated to America—fewer vampires—where he wrote a popular, well-respected book in his later years entitled *Plain Home Talk*

Embracing Medical Common Sense, directed at young ladies of quality. It went into multiple editions and allowed him to retire a wealthy man.

Sister Mattie settled into life in a small seaside resort, where she grew prizewinning foxgloves and had a thriving business in medicinal herbs, common pest poisons, and fancy soaps.

Lady Linette opened an acting school in London and produced a bevy of successful female dramatists who all had a habit of treading the boards for more years than was natural, marrying above their station, and ending it badly—for the husband. She numbered the well-known stage siren Miss Mabel Dair among her graduates. Although Sophronia saw her old teacher occasionally, she never did find out Lady Linette's true age. Nor how she had become a lady. Nor where she was born, accent notwithstanding. By then Sophronia had learned to accept that there were limits to even her abilities. So Lady Linette kept her secrets—or possibly other people's.

It took a year, but in 1855 the dewan finally saw his Clandestine Information Act voted into law. All mechanicals were declared a threat to the commonwealth. However, antisupernatural members of parliament were able to include a line naming supernatural creatures enemy intelligencers. In order to prevent vampires and werewolves from accessing mechanical and mechanimal technology, they were forbidden to see the patents. The dewan was livid, but Sophronia, who suspected that control over the technology had been Countess Nadasdy's—and possibly Lord Akeldama's—end game all along, was happy to see mechanicals outside of *everyone's* control.

"I understand a certain mysterious butler was integral to the signing. Will you ever tell me about him?" Sophronia asked the dewan, sipping a small sherry after dinner one evening.

Soap smiled and looked up from his snifter of brandy. "I told you she wouldn't forget."

The dewan huffed in pleased exasperation. "Of course not. How did you find out he was at the CIA signing, little miss?"

"You indentured me for my discretion, sir."

"Mmm. Only with my own secrets."

Silence met that.

He snorted and let the matter drop. "Funny you should ask about him. He's your first assignment. Somewhat."

Sophronia straightened. Since moving in, he'd given her the odd task around town, but nothing that stretched her training. She was getting bored, and the butler character was intriguing.

"He's the guardian of the child who inherited the mechanical patents. I've had to guarantee his signature and his silence over an Egyptian affair by agreeing to protect his ward."

"Egypt?"

"No, I'm not sending you abroad. The child lives here in London. Certain unsavory Italians are interested in the toddler and *steps must be taken* to protect her. You are to be those steps."

Sophronia grimaced. It sounded excessively dull. "You want me to watchdog an infant?"

"Worse. For the sake of propriety, I'm installing you as nanny. There is a ball tomorrow night that the mother will be attending. She's frivolous. You are to become friends, and then a family connection will be miraculously discovered. You will be invited to stay for an indefinite time."

Sophronia nodded. Right now she was supposedly traveling abroad with Agatha, as her parents would not approve of her living with the dewan under *any* circumstances but marriage. Installing her as a semipermanent companion with a respectable family was the single best way for her mother to utterly forget about her.

She reached across the table and took Soap's hand.

His dark eyes were pleased. "You won't be here, but you'll be living close."

"Pup's not trained yet," said the dewan.

"I take it the plan is to set us into motion as field agents as soon as he is?" Sophronia was hopeful.

The dewan nodded. "Between the two of you, there are few infiltration gaps. What parts of society you can't get into, he can. You'll be a good team, so long as you are circumspect." He was glaring at their entwined fingers.

Sophronia did not move her hand from Soap's. "I am *always* circumspect."

The dewan sighed. "Children, if you persist in this you'll be stuck living in shadows all your lives."

Sophronia lifted Soap's hand to her lips and kissed it. "We like the shadows. That's where all the power is."

Soap looked to his Alpha. "We'll spend many happy years together in sinful incognito, interfering with the world for the greater good."

Sophronia added, "Once Soap's safely loaner status, and I've served out my indenture to you, we shall run around having adventures overseas and contribute to Her Majesty's cause in an entirely unnoticed way. It will be delightful."

Soap lifted and kissed her hand in turn. "It will, won't it?"

The dewan sniffed. They were prone to shocking the old wolf. "Young people these days. Incorrigible." He stood and left the dining table in pursuit of less modern sensibilities.

Sophronia and Soap turned their chairs to face one another. Sophronia put both her hands on Soap's thighs, warm and hard under her palms. She leaned forward to kiss him. She liked it so much, and got to do it so often, she was becoming quite brazen about taking advantage of his proximity. No wonder the dewan was shocked.

"I've been thinking about endearments." Sophronia looked serious. "I have settled on *popsey*."

Soap was surprised into laughter. He scooped her up and settled her into his lap. "Oh, have you, indeed?"

"Yes, and you shall endure it manfully."

"If that's the worst I have to suffer from you, my heart, I'm grateful for it." Soap nuzzled her gently.

Sophronia quite agreed. But then Soap was sensible like that.

The End

It's one thing to learn to curtsy properly.
It's quite another to learn to curtsy and throw
a knife at the same time.

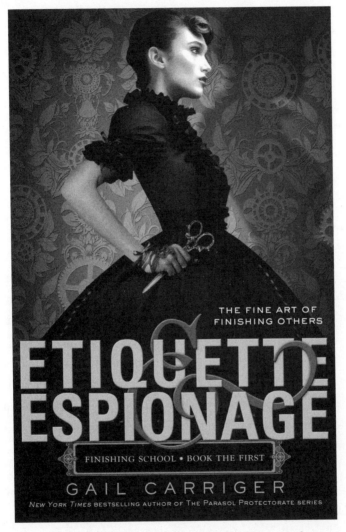

THE FINE ART OF
FINISHING OTHERS

ETIQUETTE
ESPIONAGE

FINISHING SCHOOL • BOOK THE FIRST

GAIL CARRIGER

New York Times BESTSELLING AUTHOR OF THE *Parasol Protectorate* SERIES

See where the story began in Sophronia's first
Finishing School adventure.

TURN THE PAGE FOR A PREVIEW!

The coachman finally regained his senses, realizing this was not some nightmare. There really was a fourteen-year-old girl with mousy hair and a serious expression driving his carriage. He yanked the reins away from Sophronia and pulled the horses up short. They hung their heads, sides heaving.

"Well, then," said Sophronia to the coachman, sticking her nose in the air. She jumped down. A series of cries and wails emanated from inside the carriage. She opened the door to find Pillover sitting and reading his book, while his sister lay in a crumpled heap on the floor.

The boy gestured with his chin at Dimity. "She was shot." He sounded remarkably unconcerned for a brother with any degree of affection for his sibling.

"Good lord!" Sophronia climbed in to see to her new friend's health. The bullet had grazed Dimity's shoulder. It had ripped her dress and left a partly burned gash behind, but didn't look all that bad.

Sophronia checked to make certain Dimity had no other injuries. Then she sat back on her heels. "Is that all? I've had worse scrapes from drinking tea. Why has she come over all crumpled?"

Pillover rolled his eyes. "Faints at the sight of blood, our Dimity. Always has. Weak nerves, Father says. It doesn't even have to be *her* blood."

Sophronia snorted.

"Exactly. And the smelling salts were in her suitcase. Which is now some distance behind us. Leave her be. She'll come 'round eventually."

Sophronia turned her attention to the source of the wails. "What's wrong with her, then?" *Is Mademoiselle Geraldine also injured?* The headmistress was curled into a ball, hands covering her face, whimpering.

Pillover was as disgusted with the headmistress as he was with his sister. "She's been like that ever since we pulled her inside. Nothing damaged except her brain, so far as I can determine."

Sophronia looked closer and caught the headmistress watching them slyly from behind her hands. She was shamming. But why? *So she doesn't have to explain anything? Such a peculiar woman.*

It was then that Sophronia noticed that Pillover was looking unwell behind his sneer.

She turned her full attention on the boy. "And are *you* quite all right, Mr. Pillover?"

"I'm not a very good traveler at the best of times, Miss Sophronia. You might have taken that last half mile a little smoother."

Sophronia tried to hide a smile. "I might. But what pleasure would there be in that?"

"Oh, wonderful," said Pillover. "You're one of *those* kinds of girls."

Sophronia narrowed her eyes. "You could ride on the box next to the coachman. Fresh air would do you a world of good."

Pillover looked most offended. "Outside, like a peasant? I think not."

Sophronia shrugged. "Suited me."

Pillover gave her a look that suggested that her valiant rescue was no excuse and that she was, in fact, now quite low-class in his eyes.

Sophronia returned her attention to the whimpering headmistress. "What are we going to do about her?" And then, more directly, "You're not fooling anyone, you realize?"

Pillover evidently had been fooled. "She's shamming? Well, there's nothing we can do about her. The coachman knows where to go. He can get us to Bunson's. Someone there will know what to do."

Sophronia nodded and stuck her head out the carriage window. "Coachman?"

"Yes, little miss?" The man looked generally upset with life.

"You can drive us on to this Bunson's locale, can't you?"

"Yes, little miss. I know the school. But I'm not convinced I intend to continue on, now. Never been held up by flywaymen afore."

Blast it. How would Mumsy handle this? Sophronia looked the coachman full in the face and straightened her spine as stiff as she could. "You will if you wish to be paid. Keep a decent pace and an eye to the sky and it shouldn't happen again." The moment she said it, Sophronia became completely shocked by her own daring. She was also mildly impressed by how imperious she sounded.

So was the coachman, apparently, because he resumed his post without another word and set the horses a sedate trot.

Pillover glanced over the top of his glasses. "You do that rather well, don't you?"

"What?"

"Order other people around. I've not yet got the way of it myself."

Sophronia thought Pillover was, regardless, doing pretty well at snobbery, for a grubby boy. She was about to say something of the kind when Mademoiselle Geraldine's whimpering escalated.

"Oh, do stop it and explain yourself," Sophronia ordered, feeling she was on an autocratic streak.

Much to her surprise, the headmistress listened, transforming her simulated whimpering into outright ire, directed at Sophronia. "I didn't attend for this, you understand. Easy assignment, they said." Sophronia noted with interest that Mademoiselle Geraldine had lost her French accent. "Nothing to it but improvisational theatrics. Some on-point assessment of new candidates. Simply act older. Put on a bit of an accent and a pretty dress. Such an easy finishing. Others should be so lucky. You're certain to make it through. But no. Oh, no. I had to have a combination retrieval and recruitment undertaking with an unexpected attack from unknown counterintelligencer elements, and no second. How dare they send me on without a second? Me! I mean, did I ask for this? I didn't ask for this. Who needs active status? I don't need active status. This is ridiculous!" She seemed to be progressively building herself up to sublime self-righteousness.

Sophronia felt that there was something else undercutting the flood of words. "Headmistress, is there nothing we can do for you? You seem upset."

"Upset? Of course I'm upset! And don't call me headmistress. *Headmistress*, my ruddy arse."

Sophronia gasped at the shocking word. *Now, that's taking matters too far!*

Mademoiselle Geraldine sat up straight and glared, as though Sophronia were responsible for everything bad in the world. "My face hurts, my dress is in tatters, and I have no slippers!" This last and deepest offense was uttered in a positive wail.

"Then you're not our headmistress?"

"How could I be? I'm only seventeen years old. You can't possibly think I'm the headmistress of a finishing school. You're not that naive."

"But isn't that what we were meant to think?"

"I didn't think about you at all," muttered Pillover, returning to his book.

"Who *are* you, then?" asked Sophronia.

"I'm Miss Monique de Pelouse!" She paused, as though expecting the name to produce some sign of recognition.

Sophronia merely gave her a blank look. "So this begs the question: where is the *real* Mademoiselle Geraldine?"

"Oh"—Monique waved a hand in the air and sniffed—"she never leaves much anymore, and she's useless when she does. They always send impersonators."

"They do?"

"Of course they do. It's easier, and it's a good way to finish."

"And who is *they*?"

"Why, the teachers, of course. But we were talking about me and my problems."

Sophronia looked Monique up and down gravely. "I don't think we're going to solve those in the space of one carriage ride."

Pillover *tut-tut*ted at her from behind his book—but there was clear amusement in the reprimand.

Monique sneered. "Who do you think you are? *Covert recruit.* You're not that special. You're not that good. Proud of yourself and your little carriage rescue, are you? Well, I didn't need your help! I'm a top-level student, on my finishing assignment. Ordered to retrieve three useless *children.*"

Pillover's voice emanated from behind his tome. "I hardly think that was all."

"Of course it wasn't *all*," Monique snapped. "I had the prototype to collect as well, now didn't I?"

Pillover took interest at last. "The one the flywaymen were after?"

Sophronia asked, "What's it a prototype *of?*"

"Don't be daft. I don't know *that*."

"Do you think you might at some point tell me what *finishing* actually means?" Sophronia was getting more and more curious about the particulars of this finishing school. It seemed Mumsy might have been misled as to the nature of the establishment.

"No." Monique gave her a decidedly nasty glare and then turned her attention out the carriage window.

Sophronia wasn't certain what she'd done to incur such loathing. *Should have left her with the flywaymen.* She looked at Pillover, who ignored her. So she sighed and sat back, frustrated. After a moment's consideration, she switched to the spot next to Pillover and attempted to read over his shoulder, ignoring his faintly goaty smell. All boys smelled of goat. So they passed the rest of the ride, until the carriage pulled into the sleepy little town of Swiffle-on-Exe.

As they ratted to a halt, Dimity blinked awake. "Ow. What? Did I fall asleep?"

"No, you fainted. Blood," explained her brother tersely.

"Oh, did I? Pardon." Dimity glanced down at her wounded shoulder. "Oh!" Her eyes began to roll back into her head.

Sophronia quickly leaned forward and clapped her hand over the injury. "None of that, now!"

Dimity refocused on her. "Ouch. Uh, perhaps we could tie something over it?"

"Good plan. Close your eyes." Sophronia worked the long hair ribbon loose from the grip rail inside the carriage door and wrapped it around Dimity's shoulder.

"Oh, I do wish I were more like Mummy. She's terribly fearsome. Wish I looked more like her, as well. That would help with everything." Dimity sat up.

"Why? What does she look like?"

"More like Pillover than me."

Sophronia, who had seen very little of Pillover's appearance, outside of his massive outer garments, could only say, "Oh?"

"You know, *dark* and *brooding*. I should dearly love to be *dark* and *brooding*. It's so romantic and fortune-teller-like. I couldn't brood if my life depended on it."

"Well, the ribbon around your shoulder makes for a certain fortune-telling appeal."

"Oh, does it? Splendid. You know, Sophronia, *you* could probably do it if you put your mind to it."

"Do what?"

"Be *dark* and *brooding*."

Sophronia, with middling brown hair and moderately green eyes set in a freckled face, would hardly have described herself as brooding. Or dark, for that matter.

Dimity's attention, lightning fast, shifted to a new topic. "Where are we?"

"Bunson's, finally," said Pillover, snapping his book shut. He made a show of organizing for arrival. Given that he no longer had any luggage, this was rather like the action of a mechanical without instructions, trundling idly in circles until he ran out of steam.

The carriage door was opened by a stiff domestic mechanical of some advanced outdoor nature.

"What is that?" gasped Sophronia. She'd never seen anything to equal the monstrosity. It was taller than Frowbritcher and conically shaped, with a wheelbarrow attached to its back. Where a face facsimile should be was a confusion of gears and cogs, like the back of a clock.

"Porter mechanical." Pillover stood, clutching his literary tome, and jumped down. "You two coming?" he asked, without turning to see.

"Where is your luggage, young sir?" asked the mechanical. Its voice was louder and brassier than Frowbritcher's. It wore a gray cap, backward, and a brass octopus pin on a cloth cravat around its neck. *That's too bizarre.* Sophronia had never seen a mechanical wear clothing before.

Pillover answered. "Oh, about ten miles back in the middle of the road."

"Sir?" The porter rocked side to side in confusion. It was riding on a set of rails, like a very small train.

Sophronia climbed out of the carriage to get a closer look, wondering if she could take the porter apart.

Dimity followed.

The mechanical's attention instantly shifted to them.

"No females, young sir." It made a whirring, hissing noise and ejected a puff of steam from below its cravat. The material fluttered up against its clockwork face and then flopped back down.

Pillover turned back. "What?"

"No females allowed, young sir." The porter puffed again. *Flap, flap,* went the cravat.

"Oh, those aren't females. They're only girls. They're slated for the finishing academy."

"They read as females, young sir."

"Oh, I say. Don't be difficult."

Sophronia took the diplomatic route. "We need to speak with an authority. Our carriage was attacked and our guardian is overset."

"No females!" The porter mechanical was quite firm on this. Its chest panel moved aside to reveal some kind of weapon, too large to be a gun.

As Sophronia stood, transfixed, it sparked and then *whooshed* to life, hurling blue flames that got close enough to singe Dimity's hair.

The girls dove back inside the cab, and the coachman, who was not having any more tomfoolery on his watch, drove the carriage away at once. The flame-throwing porter did not follow them.

The carriage halted outside the school grounds. Sophronia pressed her nose against the glass above the cab door and looked out. Bunson's was massive, but oddly hodgepodge—not like a respectable educational facility at all. A few of its towers were square, but others were round; some were old, others new; and some were positively *foreign* looking. There were wires stretching between the towers, and sticks jutting outward with netting dangling off their ends. An orange glow lit up various windows, here and there puffs of steam emanated forth, and one large smokestack belched plumes of black smoke up into the sky.

Sophronia looked at Dimity. "What now?"

"Well, my brother's no good. He'll have forgotten about us the moment he got inside."

"It's starting to get dark." Sophronia turned to their erstwhile headmistress. "She's simply going to have to do her job."

Dimity took a deep breath, sat down on the bench next to Monique, and shook the older girl's arm.

"What do *you* want?"

"We don't know the academy's location, and neither does the driver."

Monique de Pelouse said nothing.

Sophronia crossed her arms and glared at the older girl. Dimity looked back and forth between the two for a moment, then crossed her arms and glared as well. Though perhaps not quite so fiercely.

Finally, Monique relented. "Oh, very *well!*" She banged on the roof with her parasol handle. The cab door opened and the coachman stuck his head in.

Monique said, "Take Shrubbery Lane to the Nib and Crinkle Pub, turn left, and follow the goat path behind the hedge. After an hour, the path ends in a thicket of trees. Go around to the right and then I shall issue further instructions. And hurry. We must beat the sunset or we'll never spot it."

"But madam, that's straight out onto the moor."

"Of course it is. What could possibly have made you think we'd stop at the edge?"

"There are stories about Dartmoor. People get lost in the mist and never return. Or are eaten by werewolves. Or are taken by vampires. Or are murdered by flywaymen."

At which juncture Monique proved she could do "commanding" far better than Sophronia. "Stop arguing, my man. You heard what I said about the sun."

Looking very uncomfortable, the put-upon coachman resumed his place. The tired horses started up once more.

At first, everything seemed ordinary, but a few minutes up the goat path the carriage started to sway, buffeted by the most intense gusts of wind Sophronia had ever felt. She pressed her face against the window. Endless rolling grassland stretched around them, brown after a summer's heat, waving in the wind. The moor was mist-shrouded in the distance. Here and there a coppice of trees or a small winding spring disturbed the monotony with a bright splash of green.

"Is this all?" Sophronia was dubious.

Dimity shrugged. "Windy."

"Don't let it fool you," Monique said with an unkind smile. "This is the *only* nice bit. Soon enough the rocks will sprout up like broken bones, and the mist rises so fast you can't see where you're going or where you've been."

Sophronia was not spooked. "You think you can scare me with doomy talk? I've older sisters, I'll have you know."

Monique gave her a dirty look before rapping on the carriage roof again and issuing a new set of directions.

The carriage turned, this time following some invisible path out onto the heath. The mist began closing in around them, or they were moving into it—hard to tell which.

Sophronia actually began to feel a tiny bit of dread in the pit of her stomach. *What if there really are werewolves roaming the moor?*

And then, there it was. The mist broke. The last rays of the sun cast a long shadow out of the carriage and lit up Mademoiselle Geraldine's Finishing Academy for Young Ladies of Quality. And no, the school wasn't dashing around the moor on hundreds of tiny little legs. It was bobbing above it in chubby floating majesty.